Dear Target Reader,

I am over the moon about being chosen for Target's Book Club. Following in the steps of writers like Emma Donoghue and Ann Patchett onto Target shelves is so amazing—let's just say I'm seeing red concentric circles in my dreams!

I am full of excitement to "meet" each person who is holding this book. Everything that's important to me is now in your hands: my husband, my children, my mother, my doubts and fears, and my love.

Shine Shine Shine is the story of Sunny, a woman who felt she had to make herself perfect in order to be a good mother. She has covered her flaws and created a life for herself that looks outwardly perfect. Inside, however, she's holding her breath and dreading discovery. The book begins when her world begins to unravel. You knew that couldn't last, right?

This is a love story, about how a love that perseveres can save you from yourself even in your darkest hour, and let you see yourself as you really are, instead of measuring yourself always against the world.

When I started this novel I had just gotten pregnant with my first child. It seemed like all the other new moms were gliding along, knowing how to perfectly cook fish, match cardigans to ballet flats, and fold diapers into origami, while I stumbled awkwardly toward parenting. I wanted to write about the doubt that I felt when I examined myself through the lens of motherhood, and the way I grew into myself, imperfect but okay.

This book is for the mom reading in a stolen hour. Maybe she's sitting in her car with the book in her lap, guilty because she forgot to pack a healthy snack for dance camp and had to buy a candy bar instead, or because the dog barfed on the baseball pants and while she's the only one that can see the outline of the barf stain, she knows it's there. At some point in reading, I hope she closes the book for a minute and says to herself, You know what, forget this elusive "Perfect Mom" measuring stick. I'm rocking this job.

I hope that you will visit me online at lydianetzer.com and let me know what you think of Sunny. I love to hear from readers, and I'm so thankful that you've picked up this book!

Love,

Lydia Netzer

Praise for *Shine Shine Shine*

A *New York Times* Notable Book
A *Publishers Weekly* Best Book
A *Library Journal* Best Book
A *Slate.com* Best Book
A *People* Magazine *People* Pick
A Los Angeles Times Book Prize Finalist

"Not only entertaining, but nuanced and wise . . . Blending wit and imagination with an oddly mesmerizing, matter-of-fact cadence, Netzer's debut is a delightfully unique love story and a resounding paean to individuality."   —*People* (*People* Pick)

"Netzer's storytelling method is as poetic as her language. She slowly assembles a multitude of pinpoint insights that converge to form a glimmering constellation. . . . A stellar, thought-provoking debut."
                                            —*The New York Times Book Review*

"Heart-tugging . . . It is struggling to understand the physical realities of life and the nature of what makes us human. . . . Nicely unpredictable . . . Extraordinary."   —Janet Maslin, *The New York Times*

"You're pulled into the drama through the incredible natural beauty of her writing. . . . Deftly and wittily done . . . People say her style reminds them of Anne Tyler, but she reminded me a little bit more of Don DeLillo."
                              —Liesl Schillinger, *The New York Times Book Review* podcast

"Entirely winning . . . A refreshingly weird story about the exuberant weirdness of familial love."   —*The Wall Street Journal*

"Netzer deftly illuminates the bonds that transcend shortcomings and tragedy. Characterized by finely textured emotions and dramatic storytelling, Netzer's world will draw readers happily into its orbit."

—*Publishers Weekly*

"Netzer has beautifully crafted an original story with a cast of characters who make up an unconventional but strangely believable family. . . . This story will shine, shine, shine for all adult readers."

—*Library Journal* (starred review)

"The novel traces Maxon and Sunny's relationship from their childhoods in Burma and Appalachia to outer space, revealing the futility of chasing an ideal of what's normal. . . . *Shine Shine Shine* breaks free of the gravitational pull of traditional romantic clichés." —*The Washington Post*

"Lydia Netzer's luminous debut novel concerns what lies beneath society's pretty surfaces. . . . What makes it unexpectedly moving is how skillfully Netzer then peels back those layers, finding heartbreaking depth even in characters who lack ordinary social skills." —*The Boston Globe*

"Netzer has penned a modern take on alienation, building a family, making connections—creating memorable characters and an odd, idiosyncratic, but highly believable narrative along the way." —*The Toronto Star*

"Netzer uses [Sunny and Maxon] to explore the limits of love, family, and what it is that makes us human, and to create a tale that is utterly compelling and original." —*Chatelaine*

"There are certain novels that are just twisty, delightfully so. *Shine Shine Shine* is one. In this first novel, Lydia Netzer takes a hard look at being completely human through the eyes of two people who are kinda not. . . .

Shine Shine Shine may ask an old question. But Netzer's answer to how to be who you are is fresh from the heart." —*Daily News* (New York)

"Netzer's first novel, the wacky, touching, and deliciously readable *Shine Shine Shine,* draws heavily on her own unconventional life. . . . This unassuming novelist . . . is the 'it' girl of contemporary literature." —Kerry Dougherty, *The Virginian-Pilot*

"An endearing story . . . Netzer, whose imagination knows no limits, infuses her debut with love—and reminds us that normalcy can be vastly overrated." —*Richmond Times-Dispatch*

"I can't say enough good things about *Shine Shine Shine,* and it's almost impossible to put the book down once you crack it open. Well paced, well plotted, and told with a fresh, lyrical, and bold narrative style, Netzer's debut novel is compelling, smart, strange, and enjoyable." —Sarah Rachel Egelman, *BookReporter.com*

"*Shine Shine Shine* is an exquisitely written debut novel about family. . . . A story of personal growth and discovery that is unlike any you have read before, *Shine Shine Shine* will not fail to entertain and move you." —*SheKnows.com*

"A funny, compelling love story from the freshest voice I've heard in years. *Shine Shine Shine* picked me up and left me changed in ways I never expected. Intelligent, emotional, and relentlessly new, Netzer answers questions you didn't know you were already asking and delivers an unforgettable take on what it means to love, to be a mother, and to be human." —Sara Gruen, #1 *New York Times* bestselling author of *Water for Elephants* and *Ape House*

Shine Shine Shine

Lydia Netzer

ST. MARTIN'S GRIFFIN ☙ NEW YORK

SHINE SHINE SHINE. Copyright © 2012 by The Netzer Group LLC. All rights reserved. Printed in the United States of America. For information, address St. Martin's Press, 175 Fifth Avenue, New York, N.Y. 10010.

www.stmartins.com

Design by Meryl Sussman Levavi

The Library of Congress has cataloged the hardcover edition as follows:

Netzer, Lydia.
    Shine shine shine / Lydia Netzer. — 1st ed.
        p. cm.
    ISBN 978-1-250-00707-0 (hardcover)
    ISBN 978-1-250-01507-5 (e-book)
    1. Man-woman relationships—Fiction.   2. Accidents—Fiction.   3. Family secrets—Fiction.   4. Marital conflict—Fiction.   I. Title.
    PS3614.E528S55 2012
    813'.6—dc23

                                                        2012007426

ISBN 978-1-250-04388-7 (Target Book Club Edition)

St. Martin's Griffin books may be purchased for educational, business, or promotional use. For information on bulk purchases, please contact Macmillan Corporate and Premium Sales Department at 1-800-221-7945 extension 5442 or write specialmarkets@macmillan.com.

First Target Book Club Edition: July 2013

10 9 8 7 6 5 4 3 2 1

for Benny and Sadie

We are poppies
In the wheat.

—MAXON MANN

1.*

DEEP IN DARKNESS, THERE WAS A TINY LIGHT. INSIDE the light, he floated in a spaceship. It felt cold to him, floating there. Inside his body, he felt the cold of space. He could still look out the round windows of the rocket and see the Earth. He could also see the moon sometimes, coming closer. The Earth rotated slowly and the spaceship moved slowly, relative to the things that were around it. There was nothing he could do now, one way or the other. He was part of a spaceship going to the moon. He wore white paper booties instead of shoes. He wore a jumpsuit instead of underwear. He was only a human, of scant flesh and long bone, eyes clouded, and body breakable. He was off, launched from the Earth, and floating in space. He had been pushed, with force, away.

But in his mind, Maxon found himself thinking of home. With his long feet drifting out behind him, he put his hands on each side of the round window, and held on to it. He looked out and down at the Earth. Far away, across the cold miles, the Earth lay boiling in clouds. All the countries of the Earth lay smudged together under that lace of white. Beneath this stormy layer, the cities of this world chugged and burned, connected by roads, connected by wires. Down in Virginia, his wife, Sunny, was walking around, living and breathing. Beside her was his small son. Inside her was his small daughter. He couldn't see them, but he knew they were there.

This is the story of an astronaut who was lost in space, and the wife he left behind. Or this is the story of a brave man who survived the wreck of the first rocket sent into space with the intent to colonize the moon. This is the story of the human race, who pushed one crazy little splinter of metal and a few pulsing cells up into the vast dark reaches of the universe, in the hope that the splinter would hit something and stick, and that the little pulsing cells could somehow survive. This is the story of a bulge, a bud, the way the human race tried to subdivide, the bud it formed out into the universe, and what happened to that bud, and what happened to the Earth, too, the mother Earth, after the bud was burst.

IN A HISTORIC DISTRICT of Norfolk, on the coast of Virginia, in the sumptuous kitchen of a restored Georgian palace, three blond heads bent over a granite island. One of them was Sunny's head. Hers was the blondest. The modest light shone down on them from above, where copper pots hung in dull and perfect rows. Polished cabinetry lined the walls; and a farmhouse sink dipped into the counter, reproduced in stainless steel. A garden window above it housed living herbs. The sun shone. The granite was warm. The ice maker could produce round or square crystals. Each of the women perched on stools at the kitchen island had long straight hair, meticulously flattened or gently curled. They clustered around the smallest one, who was crying. She clutched her mug of tea with both hands where it sat on the countertop, and her shoulders shook while she boo-hooed into it. Her friends smoothed her hair, wiped her eyes. Sunny smoothed her own hair and wiped her eyes.

"I just don't understand it," said the small one, sniffing. "He said he was going to take me to Norway this summer. To Norway!"

"Norway," echoed the one in the lime green cardigan. She rolled her eyes. "What a joke." She had a hooked nose and small eyes, but from her blowout and makeup, her trim figure and expensive shoes, people still knew that she was attractive. Her name was Rachel, but the girls called her Rache. She was the first one on the block to have a really decent home gym.

"No, I *want* to go to Norway!" the little one corrected her. "My people are from there! It's beautiful! There are fjords."

"Jenny, it's not about Norway, honey," said Rache, the smooth loops and fronds of her golden hair cascading down her front and onto her tanned and curvy chest as she leaned over. "You're getting distracted."

"No," said Jenny, sobbing anew. "It's about that bitch he's fooling around with. Who is she? He won't tell me!"

Sunny pulled back from them. She wore a chenille wrap around her shoulders and operated the machines of her kitchen with one hand while the other rested on her pregnant belly. She went for the teakettle, freshened Jenny's tea, and handed her a tissue. These were Sunny's best friends, Jenny and Rache. She knew that they were having a normal conversation, this conversation about Jenny's husband and his infidelity. It was a normal thing to talk about. But as she stood there in her usual spot, one hand on the teakettle, one hand on her belly, she noticed an alarming thing: a crack in the wall right next to the pantry. A crack in this old Georgian wall.

"It's not really about her either, Jenny, whoever she is," said Rache. Sunny gave Rache a stern glance behind the other woman's head. Rache returned it with eyebrows raised in innocence.

"He's a jerk," Jenny said. "That's what it's about." And she blew her nose.

Sunny wondered if her friends had noticed the crack. It raged up the wall, crossing the smooth expanse of buttercream-colored plaster, ripping it asunder. The crack had not been there yesterday, and it already looked wide. It looked deep. She thought about the house, split down a terrible zigzag, one half of the pantry split from the other. Bags of organic lentils. Mason jars of beets. Root vegetables. What would she do?

But Jenny wasn't done crying. "I just don't know what I'm going to do!" she burbled for the third time. "I have the children to think of! How could he let me find this out? How could he not be more careful?"

Sunny imagined the house falling apart, with her as the fault line. Maybe with Maxon in space, the house had given up on maintaining appearances. Maybe it would crumble into the earth without him, without the person standing in the husband spot. Everything changes, everything falls: Jenny's husband, rockets to the moon, the wall containing the pantry.

"Shh," said Rache. She reached for the remote, turned up the volume on the kitchen TV. Sunny saw that the microwave read 12:00. She pulled the wrap tightly around her and two fingers fluffed up the bangs on her forehead. On the screen, the news was starting up.

"Oh," said Jenny. "Time for Les Weathers."

"Now there's a man who would never do you wrong," said Rache, cocking her head and winking at the set. The women watched word-lessly for a few minutes while a tall blond man with a squared-off face and twinkling blue eyes reported on a local fire. He leaned just so, into his desk, and he used his broad hands to gesticulate. His con-cern over the fire appeared real, his admiration for the firemen tan-gible. He had a bulky torso, heavy on top like a trapezoid, with big arms. He was more than just a suit on the television, though; he was relevant and immediate to them, because he lived three doors down, in an immaculate gray townhouse, behind a thick red door.

"He's like Hercules," said Jenny through her tears. "That's what he reminds me of. Les Weathers is Hercules."

"In makeup," said Sunny dryly.

"You love him!" Rache accused.

"Shut up. I'm not one of his worshippers," Sunny said. "The only time I've ever really talked to him at all was when I asked him to take that wreath down in January."

"Not true! He was at the Halloween party at Jessica's!" Jenny said, momentarily forgetting her troubles. "Plus he interviewed you on TV, when Maxon was doing PR for the mission!"

"I meant talked to him alone," Sunny said. She stood with her legs wide. She could feel, or could she not feel, a tremor in the house. In the crawl space, something was reverberating. Something was com-ing undone. A train passed too close, and the crack widened. It reached the crown molding. Is this what labor would feel like? Last time, she had an epidural, and gave birth with her lipstick perfectly applied. This time she planned to have an even bigger epidural, and give birth in pearls.

"I've never talked to him alone," said Rache, still coy, imitating Sunny. "You must be his girlfriend."

"Can we not talk about girlfriends?" Sunny said, nodding point-edly at Jenny.

"I should give Les Weathers a call," Jenny murmured, her eyes glued to the set. "All alone in that nice house nursing a broken heart."

On the TV set, Les Weathers smiled with two rows of glittering white teeth, and tossed to his coanchor with a line of jockish banter.

"Don't call him," said Rache. "Don't give your husband any more excuses."

"He has excuses?" said Jenny.

A commercial for diapers began.

"Anyway," said Sunny, clearing away the teacups, "I need to pick up Bubber from school, and get to the hospital to see Mom."

"How is your mom?" Rache asked. The ladies rose from their stools, pulled themselves together. Cuffs were straightened, and cotton cardigans buttoned.

"She's fine," said Sunny. "Totally fine. You can almost see her getting better, every single day."

"But I thought she was on life support," said Jenny.

"Yes, and it's working," Sunny told them.

She rushed them out the door, and returning to the kitchen she inspected the crack with her fingers. It was not bad. It was not growing. Maybe it had been there all along. Maybe she just hadn't seen it climbing up, up, stretching right across her house and her life, threatening it with an impassable fissure. Sunny sat down in the seat where Rachel had been, pulled her hair down around her shoulders the way her friend wore it. She stretched out one manicured hand toward the space Jenny had occupied, as if to put her arm around a phantom shoulder. She nodded, furrowed her eyebrows, just like Rache. Glancing up, she saw that the crack was still there. She sat up straighter. She put her knees together. She fluffed up her bangs. On the television, Les Weathers was signing off. Neighborhood gossip said his pregnant wife had left him to shack up with a man in California. Never even let him meet the kid. Tough life, except now every female for six blocks wanted to darn his socks. Sunny wondered how socks were darned. She thought if it came up, she would just buy new ones. She would bury the undarned socks at the bottom of the garbage, and no one would ever know.

Finally giving a long last look to the pantry and flicking off the light, Sunny gathered her bag, her keys, and Bubber's books, and got into her minivan, sliding her big belly behind the wheel. She fixed her hair again in the rearview mirror, started the car, and began the drive to the preschool.

All through the neighborhood, the broad Southern trees stretched across the street, tracing shadows over the faces of stately brick manors. Bumblebees buzzed in the tumbling azaleas, white and every shade of pink. Clean sidewalks warmed in the spring sunshine. At every intersection in her neighborhood, Sunny put her foot down on the brake, and then the gas. The minivan went forward through space like a mobile living room, a trapezoid of air levitating across the Earth. She sat in it, pushing it along. She forgot about the crack. She forgot about Les Weathers's wife. Every house was a perfect rectangle. It was an exercise in mathematics.

The world outside was bright and full of moving parts. On each side of the street ahead, and on each side of the street behind, historic houses rose in majestic angles. Oaks soared overhead, and along the sidewalks myrtle trees stretched their peeling branches. Parallel lines joined by perpendicular lines formed a grid you could navigate by numbers. Even numbers on the right, odd numbers on the left. Maxon had once said, "The number of lots on a city block, multiplied by the square root of the sidewalk squares in front of each lot, must equal the width of a single-car driveway in decimeters, plus Francis Bacon." He had no real respect for the grandeur of the urban neighborhood. Lots of people, living in rows. Eating, sleeping, and baking in rows. Driving in rows and parking in rows. He said he wanted a hunting lodge in the Touraine, with a tiger moat and a portcullis made of fire. But he accepted it. How could he not? The city was a love letter to planar geometry.

Very few of the neighbors had ever actually spoken to Maxon. Yet all the people up and down this street took Sunny's opinions very seriously. She was a natural, living here. She was a pro. When she moved to this town, said the neighbors, things fell into place. Barbecues were organized. Tupperware was bought. Women drove Asian minivans and men drove German sedans. Indian restaurants, gelato stands, and pet boutiques gathered around the one independent movie theater. No one went without a meal on the day they had a sick child or a root canal. No one went without a babysitter on the day they had a doctor's appointment, or a flat tire, or a visitor from out of town. All of the houses moved sedately through space at a steady pace as the Earth rotated and the Commonwealth of Virginia rotated right along with it. In Virginia, people said, you can eat on the patio all year round.

There were babysitters for Sunny, when bad things happened. There were casseroles that arrived with a quiet knock. When her mother had to go to the hospital, there was help. When Maxon was being launched to the moon in a rocket, there was aid. There was a system in place, it was all working properly, beautifully, and everyone was doing their part.

SUNNY SAT BESIDE THE hospital bed of her own sick mother. She sat in her peach summer cardigan and her khaki capris, her leather braided thong sandals and her tortoiseshell sunglasses. She sat under a smooth waterfall of blond hair, inside the body of a concerned and loving daughter. She sat with her child on her lap and a baby in her belly. Her mother lay on the hospital bed, covered in a sheet. She did not wear sunglasses or a cardigan. She wore only what was tied around her without her knowledge. She had not actually been awake for weeks.

On the inside of her mother, there was something going on that was death. But Sunny didn't really think about that. On the outside of her mother, where it was obvious, there was still a lot of beauty. Out of the body on the bed, out of the mouth, and out of the torso, Sunny saw flowering vines growing. The vines that kept her mother alive draped down across her body and out into a tree beside her bed. They lay in coils around the floor, tangled gently with each other, draped with dewy flowers and curling tendrils. Against the walls, clusters of trees formed and bent in a gentle wind, and all around, golden leaves dropped from the trees to the ground. A wood thrush sang its chords in the corner of the room, blending with Bubber's chirps and giggles.

Bubber was her son and Maxon's son. He was four, with bright orange hair that stood straight up from his head like a broom. He was autistic. That's what they knew about him. With the medicine, he was pretty quiet about everything. He was able to walk silently through a hospital ward and read to his grandmother while Sunny held him on her lap. He was able to pass for a regular kid, sometimes. There would be medicine in the morning, medicine at lunch, medicine to control psychosis, medicine to promote healthy digestion. Sunny sat up straight, holding Bubber, who was reading out loud in a brisk monotone. The baby inside her stretched and turned, uncertain whether it would be autistic or not. Whether it would be more like Maxon, or more like Sunny. Whether it would fit into the neighborhood. It had not been determined.

The babbling gurgle of the breathing machine soothed Sunny's mind, and she told herself she smelled evergreens. A breeze ruffled the blond hair that brushed her shoulders. She could put her sunglasses up on top of her head, close her eyes, and believe she was in heaven. She could believe that there would always be a mother here, in this enchanted forest, and that she could come here every day to sit and look on the peaceful face.

SUNNY LEFT THE HOSPITAL. When the car crash happened, Sunny was driving down the street toward home. Her smooth, white, manicured hands held the wheel. Her left foot pressed flat on the floor. Her head was up, alert, paying attention. The scent of someone's grill wafted through her open window. And yet there still was a car accident. At the corner of majestic Harrington Street and stately Gates Boulevard, a black SUV smashed into her big silver minivan broadside. It happened on the very street where her house was planted. It happened that afternoon, on that very first day after Maxon went into space. No one died in the car accident, but everyone's life was changed. There was no going back to a time before it. There was no pretending it didn't happen. Other people's cars are like meteors. Sometimes they smash into you and there's nothing you can do about it.

After the hospital visit, she had buckled the boy into his seat in the minivan, and strapped his helmet on his head. He was a head banger, unfortunately, and it happened a lot in the car. While driving, she was explaining something trivial. She spent a lot of time talking out loud to Bubber, although he didn't spend much time talking back. It was part of what they did for Bubber to help him with his difficulty, talking to him like this.

"It doesn't matter which chair you get, right?" she said. "You just say, 'Oh well!,' and you sit in whichever chair is open. Because if you pitch a fit about your chair, you're going to miss your art project, aren't you? And it's only a chair, right? It's nice to have different-colored chairs. It doesn't matter which one you get. You just say, 'Oh well! It's only a chair. I'll get the blue chair next time!,' and then you sit in the red chair. Say, 'Oh well!,' Bubber."

Bubber said, "Oh well."

His voice sounded loud, like a duck's voice, if a duck talked like a robot. And he had to have a helmet on. Just for riding in the van. Otherwise, he sometimes whacked his head against the car seat, again and again, as the wheels drove over the joints in the road. It was terrible just hearing it happen. It was not something that Sunny ever wanted to hear.

"And then you sit down," Sunny went on, "and you don't even think about what color you're sitting on, you just have fun with your art project. Because which one's more fun, pitching a fit or doing an art project?"

"Doing an art project," said Bubber like a duck.

"So you just say, 'Oh well!' and you sit down."

Sunny waved one hand from up to down, to illustrate the point. Bubber hummed in his car seat. Sunny was plenty busy just being the mother of Bubber, but there was something else inside her, this baby making her pregnant. It had a heart and the heart was beating. Most of it could be seen on viewing machines at the doctor's office. On the outside, a giant pregnant belly sat in her lap like a basket. The seat belt went above and below it. There was no returning from it. It was already here. In spite of what might have been done to prevent it, or any opinions she might have had that another baby was a bad idea, she was now over the line. She would be a mother of two, under the pale blond hair, in the trapezoidal minivan, in her own stately manor. In spite of the fact that Bubber hadn't come out right, that he'd come out with some brain wires crossed and frayed, some extra here, some missing over there, she was going to be a mother again, because everyone wants to have two children. One just isn't enough.

When Sunny was a little child, she had never envisioned herself having children. She had never played mother. Often she played sister, but never mother. Maybe that's why she wanted another baby for Bubber. To save him from being an only child, just like her.

The car accident happened at a four-way stop. Sunny looked left, right, left again. When she looked, everything was clear. But then a black Land Rover shot toward her out of the street she was crossing. It smashed into the van with a crushing force. *This is the end*, Sunny thought. *The end of me, and the end of the baby. The end of Bubber, too.* There would be no family. After all this effort, there would be a bad outcome. It seemed monstrous, impossible. It shook her brain, thinking about it. She felt it rattle her bones. *Poor Maxon*, she thought, as the air bag hit her chest. *What have we done to each other?* There was a brutal specificity to the car accident at this time, in this place, and under the weight of all that reality, her heart felt like it had really stopped.

In that moment, sunshine still fell down through thousands of space miles to warm up the windshield in front of Sunny's face, but with her mouth so grimaced, she looked like a monster. The sunglasses on her face pointed forward in the direction the van had been moving. The Earth rotated in the opposite direction. The van moved over the Earth on a crazy slant. After the smash, the cars were still moving a little, but in different directions now. The vectors were all changed. Air bags hissed. A sapling was bent to the ground. And at that tremulous moment, a perfect blond wig flew off Sunny's head, out the window, and landed in the street in a puddle full of leaves. Underneath the wig, she was all bald.

Her mother was dying, her husband was in space, her son was wearing a helmet because he had to, and she was bald. Could such a woman really exist? Could such a woman ever explain herself? Sunny had time, in that moment, to wonder.

In the sky, in space, Maxon rotated on schedule. He always knew what time it was, although in space he was beyond night and day. At the time of the crash, it was 3:21, Houston time. He remembered how the boy, Bubber, had said good-bye so matter-of-factly. "Guh-bye, Dad." How he had allowed himself to be kissed, as he had been trained, and Maxon had kissed him, as he had been trained. This is how a father acts, this is how a son acts, and this is what happens when the father leaves for space. How the eyes of the boy had wandered off to some other attraction, counting floor tiles, measuring shadows, while his arms clung around Maxon's neck, never to let him go.

It was like any other day of work. He could hear her quiet words, "Say good-bye to your father." So habitual. At age four, the mind could understand, but the boy could not comprehend. Why say good-bye? What does "good-bye" even mean? Why say it? It doesn't impart any information; no connections are made when you say "hello" or "good-bye." Of course, of course, a silly convention. Up away from the Earth, Maxon felt physically hungry. Hungry for a sight of his wife and child. Hungry for their outline, the shape they would make in a doorway, coming in. Among the stars, tucked into that tiny shard of metal, he felt their difference from the rest of the planet. It was as if Sunny were a pin on a map, and Bubber the colored outline of the territory she had pointed out. He could not see them, but he knew where they were.

2.

YEARS AGO, AT THE TIME WHEN SUNNY WAS BORN, the sun was fully eclipsed by the moon. The whole sun disappeared. Then it came back, just as hot.

The moon rarely manages to fully hide the sun from the Earth. In fact, it only happens every so often, and when it happens, you can only see it from certain parts of the world. On all the other continents, time passes normally. Even one thousand miles away, the morning continues without interruption. But right there, in Burma, in 1981, there was a full eclipse, and the sun was covered up for the minutes it took a baby to be born. Beside the Himalayas, there was a brown twilight on Earth and a bright corona in the sky. Sometime in the future, there will be another eclipse in Burma. But there will never be another baby born like Sunny. She was the only one, and her mother knew this from the beginning.

Only during the dark totality of the eclipse did the pushing really work for this woman, about to give birth. She lay in a government hospital of one hundred beds. For hours she had fought with the idea of letting out the baby. Outside, the shadow of Rung Tlang lay over the jumble of Hakha village, getting sharper and sharper. The sun boiled down to a crescent, a sliver, a curved row of pretty beads. Outside, people were distressed. The pipe-smoking women looked up. Men in cone hats stopped tilling the poppies. The sun's corona flared and swept around the black disk of moon, like a mermaid's long hair.

Deep in the umbra of the moon, she was able to bear down. After the sun was hidden, it took only a couple of good pushes for the hard little head to emerge. Her fierce cervix wrapped around that head like a fist around an egg. Then the head shot through. Shoulders were extracted. The baby came out. The midwife bundled her quickly, dropped her on her mother's chest, and ran to the window.

But the moon had already begun to slide, and the sun was tearing through the valleys on its other side. As it had retreated, so it came back on, hot as ever, and everyone had to stop looking up, or they would go blind. Life resumed, and the person who had not been a mother was now a mother, with her bald baby in her arms.

"She has no hair," the midwife said. "No eyelashes. She's a very special baby."

In the morning, before the eclipse, Emma Butcher had been fine with living out the rest of her life in Burma. She would keep her body going, breathe, smile, and eventually die. Later, after the baby, she was no longer okay with staying in Burma. She rose up from that bed a mother, and ready to fight for the rest of her days. What does it matter for a woman to give up her self, and live quietly, with the choices she has made? But when the woman becomes a mother, she can no longer participate in the slow rot. Because no one's going to rot the child. And anyone who tries will suffer the mother's consequences.

In the evening, the father burst into the hospital room carrying a roughly potted Persian Shield. He had torn the plant up out of the jungle by the beach, and brought it to the mountains, to cheer her up. The plant was small and had no bloom on it, but its wide purple leaves spread flat under the dim hospital bulb. He put it down at the dark window. He had something exciting to say, very exciting, and his armpits were both beading up with the strain of getting here, to see his new baby. He had the embarrassing enthusiasm of an older man who finally gets to be a father. "I've got the perfect name," he said. "The baby's name will be Ann. Isn't it perfect?" Reaching out his pink hands for her, he came close.

The new mother looked at her husband and his potted plant. He wore a black linen shirt unbuttoned over a shining chest, and a ridiculous fishing hat. Her baby slept in her bed, between her body and her arm, wrapped in a long orange cloth. Its lashless eyes closed like the eyes on a statue of a saint, which can have no hair or eyelashes either. Her white-blond hair fell around them both like a metal curtain, smooth as polished rock. Her level blue eyes stared, her lips spread in a beatific smile. She had exchanged her bloody gown for a gauzy wrap, the color of burnt salmon. She lay like a long slim knife in the bed. At the top of the knife was her beautiful head, chiseled out of bone. She was as serene as a pool in a cave.

She let her husband pick up the baby and hold it in his arms. She watched him hold it up to the light and look deeply into its face and droop his sagging cheeks next to its nose. She looked at him and saw that he was old. She wondered what exactly she had done to herself, marrying such an old man, and having his child here in the hotness of Burma. Had it been a dark and tousled baby, mewing loudly, or a ginger thing squawking, she would not have felt the same heartbeat in her throat. When she saw him holding her strange baby with his sweating paws, she knew she had to take her baby back to America, where she could be real. Burma was a dream, their mission an escape. Her baby would engage, would fire up like a rocket, and would burn in this world. She would not drift in the murmured prayers of her father. She would not languish in the jungle. The Buddhist nurses had left her, so that when she could get up, she could leave. She could leave all the way. She could rethink old decisions. Having a baby makes you do that.

But instead they took her back to the small cottage at the bottom of the big mountain, and they kept house together. Turns out, it was hard to leave Burma. Turns out, she had been stuck the whole time. She named her baby Sunny because of the eclipse. The father had to relent. After all, he had not been there when the baby was coming. He had been down on the coast, collecting specimens. So the baby's name was Sunny Butcher.

WHEN SUNNY TURNED TWO, they were still in Burma, and she had not grown any hair. She was still nursing, and still sleeping in her mother's arms. Her mother braided sun hats for her out of fabric, out of reeds, and out of yarn. They hired a nurse, Nu, who helped Emma take care of the baby and with the house. Sunny walked around in a tiny head wrap, with her round belly protruding from a saffron kimono. Her features stayed elfin, her shoulders and limbs fragile, but her head was enormous. She was a strange-looking child. The local Chin people smiled and nodded to her. To them she looked like one of the monks who kept coming to convert them back to Buddhism.

The men reached out to her with two hands. The women would not touch her garments. Although the Chin mostly worshipped the Christian God, they adhered to their native traditions.

The father had wanted to name the baby Ann because of Ann Judson, one of the first missionaries to penetrate Burma. Ann Judson was the victim of many fevers and eventually died of one. In her day, the locals censured Christian missionaries by locking their feet in fetters and raising them up until only their shoulders were touching the ground. What with the mosquitoes attacking, this was a difficult punishment to endure. That was before the British took over Burma, which was before the Communists took over. A whole lot of Christians had come to Burma, and to the Chin province, over that century.

The last missionary to arrive was Sunny's father, with his beautiful wife. When they first established themselves in Hakha, Emma was twenty-three and Bob was forty. They built a pretty wooden church next to the industrial housing complex. Christians had been meeting in buildings around Burma for over a hundred and fifty years. Their church was just one more church. A single round fan at the back of the sanctuary moved air through the congregation. The wife sat in pew one with her knees pressed together and off to the side. She wore American-style ladies' hats and craved crisp untropical fruit. Her husband struggled to teach her the language, insisted on speaking Chin at the dinner table, over the rice and vegetables.

One year after their arrival, all the missionaries were thrown out of Burma. Burma was purged of foreigners altogether, both of the missionary and commercial variety. Men in gray uniforms from the other side of the mountains knocked on the Butchers' door and put them out of their house. They left everything, running immediately to India, where Bob sat in the kitchen of his missionary friends, broadcasting a radio show in Chin. He did not use the term "counterrevolutionary." Emma worried, would they have to go back home? She could live in Burma with her enthusiastic husband, but could she live in America with him? Could she be a pastor's wife, and hold Bible study meetings in her house? She prayed that she would be allowed to stay in Asia. It seemed easier.

Loose in India, she wandered in a slipstream. She only hummed through the hymns. The mountains interfered with the radio signal, and Bob Butcher went back to the States, but Emma wouldn't go. He left his beautiful red-lipped wife in India with the other missionaries and went home, determined to find a way to come back under legal cover, as a businessman, or a scientist, or a diplomat. She slept in a hammock on their screened porch. She spent her time in India teaching the local children how to read, but she never imagined having a child of her own. She couldn't imagine something good coming out of the thing they did together that was necessary to make a child. She didn't want the sex between her and Bob to have any lasting effects. When she rose from the bed every morning, she saw herself walking away from it and from what was left between the sheets. They never talked about it. It only happened at night, when she had already been asleep. It was as if she had to be sleeping for him to approach her. He couldn't approach her if she was able to see it coming.

This was the way he had first come to her, in the middle of the night, when she was asleep in her father's house in Indiana.

She had gone away to college and come back, back to her austere parents and their brutally efficient family farm. He had come for a week of prayer meetings, a fire and brimstone speaker who moved the whole church to their knees. She had known him since her childhood, because he came every year and they always hosted him at their house. First he came with his wife, who died in childbirth, taking the baby with her to heaven, and then alone, dramatic and intense, knocking glasses over at dinner and giving her blessings, his hand on her head. That night, when she was back from college and he was visiting, she was asleep under her lemon yellow patchwork quilt, and then she was awake, looking at him in her room. The clock ticked beside her. A shadow moved across the ceiling.

"I choose you, Emma," he told her, his voice hoarse. She had never heard him try to speak quietly before. She had heard him shouting, ranting, pleading, even crying. "I choose you to go with me to Burma."

She felt cold wonder. Was it a dream? She had seen him only in a suit, behind the pulpit, everyone listening in rapt attention. Then in his shirtsleeves, tie pulled open, at the dinner table, telling stories. When she was twelve, he had baptized her in the river, and the testimony she gave was that she wanted to be more genuine in her faith, not just say the words, but live the life. She had ridden in the back of his truck, with the other kids who had waited all year to be baptized during the revival week. She saw his big shoulders bumping along, one hand on the wheel, one hand clutching the top of the doorframe, as if lodging himself firmly in this world.

He was with her, in the dark, in her room. It was now a private time between the two of them only. She felt paralyzed, and special. How could she not? Within the confined world of the church, the community, the Christian college she had attended with its fumbling, guilty boys, he was a shining celebrity. Her parents would be proud. And what else was she going to do? Next to him, no one else seemed completely alive. She felt twelve again, nervous, unready, and yet proud that she was a woman to him now. Proud that she knew what to do. She had never spoken a full sentence to him. But she could be the one to go to Burma with him, be his helpmeet, and replace his dead and sainted wife.

He was breathing heavily. He was standing next to her bed with no shirt on, her sleepy eyes could see only the top part of his body, broad chest shining in the dim light from the moon. She felt her body lying flat in the bed like a paper doll. What would it be like, this thing? A shiver went up from her stomach. His breath filled the room.

"Can I come to you, Emma?" he asked. She saw his brow furrow. She nodded.

Then he had pulled aside the covers and she felt the chill of the air. He looked down at her, her belly, her legs. Then he was with her in the bed, his knees on either side of hers. His one big hand pushed down the flannel waistband from over his hips, his other pressed on her collarbone, rubbing and rubbing. His penis came out of the top of the pants and she felt it, warm on her leg in the sudden cold of the dark room, smooth and hot, nudging at her, pushing all around over her panties. His square chin was all she could see above her, the rest of his face pointed up and toward the sky. She shifted her hips up to meet him, put her arm around him and her little hand down in the bottom part of his warm back. He moved his hot hand down from her collarbone, down over her breast, fingers dragging urgently down to where he felt her, dug into her, opened her up. His body felt heavy on top of her, everything he did so forceful, so demanding. Now his forehead was on her shoulder, his hips twisting, and the sounds he made were groans. "Oh, oh," he said. "Oh, god, it feels so good." But then he could be charming. He could say, "Oh, honey, I know it hurts."

AFTER A YEAR IN exile, Bob brought his wife back into Burma. He brought a field laboratory with him to study the medicinal qualities of orchids, under the auspices of the University of Chicago. The Red Guard was burning churches in China. It was a time for persecution and torment. The Christians had to come in under the cover of secular jobs, when they could get them. Or they had to surrender the gospel to the natives, and hope they would continue to dispense it among themselves. Bob Butcher was now overtly a scientist, but he was still secretly a missionary, holding meetings in the bedroom of their new two-room house in Hakha. Communicants huddled around the spindly bed.

The husband and wife lived this lowly way for a dozen years. Emma planted tea in their little garden. Bob whispered sermons and clinked test tubes together, distilling oils. Always the couple would go to sleep peacefully, separately, in their own space. Then in the night, there would often be the urgent waking, the desperate clutching, big hands around her upper arms or grasping her hips, his hot mouth on her, separating her, driving into her. And then all the grateful exclamations. "Thank you. Oh, god, thank you." Sometimes she could feel she was still in a dream. Sometimes she woke up full when his rigid thrust was already inside her, his body already drenched in sweat.

Bob had had a vasectomy after his first wife died on the delivery table. He knew, at the time, that it was God's will. Emma had known there would never be babies, had felt it her calling to be his wife, this man whose tragedy had taken away his will to reproduce. When she thought about children, she wished the idea away, thinking of their sex together as so separate from the kids she saw all around. Then she became miraculously pregnant at the age of thirty-seven. No one expected it. The couple celebrated mildly, each privately horrified. The husband announced his accomplishment to his secret congregation. "My wife, Emma, is going to have a baby," he said to them. They nodded quickly, smiled, and showed their approval by patting each other on the arm.

Would she die in delivery? Would the baby be a sweaty, demonstrative little man? No. Sunny was born, she grew, and she learned to walk in the village. She sat with her beautiful kimonos among the ratty dogs. Nu washed the diapers, burned fruit to the gods on the back porch. The daylight hours under the mountain increased. In the village, their secret mission was safe, because most of the Chin State of Burma was stubbornly Christian. No matter how many Bibles were burned, more Bibles could be got from India, or smuggled in from the USA. Everything was safe and the family would stay on indefinitely, until Sunny was an old woman, and her head wraps got dirty and her mother died.

3.

SUNNY WAS A WOMAN WITHOUT ANY HAIR. SHE WAS born without hair, and had never grown any. Not eyelashes, not arm-pit fuzz, not leg hair. No hair on her head anywhere. At times in her life, she had wondered if the world could ever be truly beautiful for her, for a girl this bald. At other times, though, she had felt that her life was like any other. Now she was nearing the age of thirty. Al-though she was not the only bald woman in the world, there had never been very much research done about what was wrong with her. It was difficult to say. Kind of freaky, how they couldn't explain it. From childhood and girlhood, and on through the time of getting married and having a child, this strange baldness kept sickening her. Her mother was sick with something more regular. She had cancer. Her life was coming to an end. That was also difficult to say.

It's dark inside the body. The things that go on there cannot be seen. When anyone has an organ going bad, or some blockage, or a leak, those things happen silently, and without light. No one can witness those things. The wet silence takes over, in there. Are there any noises? Does the liver have a sense of touch? Every baby spends its first months in there, in the dark. Every son waves its arms in front of a blind face, and every daughter opens a blank mouth to make no noise. And inside the baby, another blackness. But no sound. A human grows and fades in the blackness and silence inside its skin. Sunny had come up bald from the cradle, and stayed bald throughout her life. She had been born at some point, and at some point in the future she would die. What happened in between was one long, hairless episode.

While regular people had hair on their heads, she had none. Driving around in cars, walking through stores, she had a secret there that something was wrong. Something was not right. Because of the wig, no one in Virginia knew the secret, except the few close people who had to know it. Her husband. Her doctor. Her mother and child. It wasn't available to everyone just for the looking, like the woman with the strange growth over half her face, or the man with the ear scar, or the guy with the blown-off hand. It was a different kind of secret, down deep under the wig.

When the wig came off and fell into a puddle, no one was around to help her out. Maxon was up in space, thinking of robots. The children were there, of course, but they didn't know what to do to help. Bubber could scream, and rage, and tell time without looking at a clock. The baby inside could wave her hands, and make wishes, but no one could put a hand out and keep the wig on her

head, when it wanted to come off. The car accident was too unexpected.

The Land Rover was coming at them. First there was Sunny's
closed throat and her braced arms fighting the steering wheel. Then
there was the crunching sound, and the jolt. The air bag blew up. The
wig flew off. Everything stopped moving. Sunny found her voice
immediately, almost before the silence.

"We're okay, we're okay, everything's okay, it's okay, you're okay,"
said Sunny. "Are you okay?"

"Stop!" said Bubber.

"Bubber. Somebody hit us with their car, but everything is fine.
We're okay."

Without looking back she reached toward him and put her hand
on his knee, pressing down hard so he could really feel it.

"Stop, stop! Stop that *car*!" yelled Bubber. He began to scrabble
for his seat-belt latch, reach for his door handle. He was far from
crying. His freckled face was red, lips pursed up in outrage.

"YOU," shouted Bubber through his tinted window. "YOU HIT
OUR VAN. YOU SHOULDN'T HAVE DONE THAT."

"Bubber, stop," said Sunny. She choked and gagged.

"Mommy, are you going to throw away? THROWING AWAY
IN YOUR HAND IS WRONG."

"No," she said. "You stay in the van. Stay in your seat."

She took a look around. She forced both hands back to the steering wheel, to stop them from reaching up to feel her scalp. She tried
to press down on the gas and move the van out of the street, or maybe
all the way home. She fantasized that they would drive past the wig
and leave it there. At home, safe, she could crawl through the cat hole,
get under the house. She could live underground in the dark crawl
space forever. Maybe snap and snarl at strangers, eat stray dogs, visit
Maxon at night through one of the air vents. She would go back into

her habitat when he went to sleep. She would darken her skin with the clay that made their backyard so inhospitable to ferns. Neighbors would hear stories about the red-faced zombie that walked back and forth to the mailbox sometimes in the dead of night, mailing off postcards. She could evolve into an opossum. She could evolve into a squirrel. Of course, the van would not move, so she turned off the engine.

Sunny popped her door open. There were neighbors coming out of their houses now. Somebody was running toward her. She felt sick, like she was going to really vomit. She undid her seat belt and removed it from around her belly. Her middle felt full of angry fire, full of rushing currents, as if a comet were charging around inside her, as if the baby had really turned into a fire monster. There was a pain wrapping around her back. She stepped out on one shaky leg and then another. She straightened her sunglasses on her nose. Standing in the middle of her neighborhood, she watched her friends and neighbors coming out of their houses like dirty peasants: apologetic, dingy, afraid. She felt the wind on her head. It felt, of course, good to get the wig off. It always did. That part was indisputable.

She looked up and down her street. The trees were losing their leaves. A Dumpster sat in the street, collecting the refuse of someone's renovations. Gnarled roots of the trees took up all the space between the sidewalk and the curb, infested with sprouting ferns or little trees, rotten acorns. The driveways, once so regular, were now confusingly askew. The houses tipped toward each other, their mottled roofs sliding off like books on the heads of gawky teenagers. She heard a siren. She heard a baby squawk. She tottered away from the van, afraid to fall along some tangent to the Earth, and slip right off it, to her death.

A man was loping toward her down the sidewalk. She knew this man, immediately. He was the network-news neighbor, Les Weathers:

tall, burly, and blond. He must have just got home from work. He still wore the blue suit, yellow tie, silk handkerchief. His hair was still pasted back from his bronzed face in a flat plastic wave. His features correctly registered concern and confusion. Sunny walked unsteadily toward the puddle where her wig was lying like a dead blond cat. If only she could get it back onto her head.

"Ma'am, are you all right?" shouted Les Weathers, sounding like Superman. Others were coming, Rache and Jenny, approaching slowly from their twin brick town houses, leather flats in neutral tones stepping carefully around wet places on the sidewalk.

Sunny nodded. She was a stranger to him. He didn't know who she was.

"Are you hurt?" someone asked her. Sunny turned to face Les Weathers and looked him in the face. She took her sunglasses off.

"Are you Sunny? Sunny Mann?" he said, eyes full of shock.

She smiled.

"Sunny, you're bald," he said.

Of all the times these words had been said to her in her life, this instance was maybe the best. Better than her mother saying it so frankly, better than her nanny saying it so kindly, better than the children in middle school saying it in the different ways that they said it. It was so funny, in a way. For five years, since she arrived in this town, newly pregnant in pink pants with a matching V-neck sweater and dove gray pumps, she had worn her quiet blond wig. She had worn the wig religiously and relentlessly, and all these people had quietly let her wear it. She had a wig with the ponytail, the one with the bun and chopsticks poking through it, the one long and wavy for everyday outings. She had always worn the wig, ever since she first let anyone live in her uterus. But the truth of the matter was, as Les Weathers had just pointed out, that she was bald. Bald as an egg.

She had wondered many times what it would feel like to walk

down this very street with her old red plastic glasses and her white bald head shining for all the world to see, but she had almost forgotten it might happen someday. What with this and that and the other, she had almost erased it from her mind. Five years in a wig can really make a girl feel blond. But those three red words in the mouth of Les Weathers stretched across time for her. Sunny. You're. Bald. Back to the beginning and ahead to the end of her life, all the times it had been said and would be said, ringing like bells. She had to listen.

Sunny walked over to the puddle, picked up her wig, removed a few dry leaves and a broken stick, and shook it like a rag. Then she crammed it back onto her head.

"Call the police," she said. "Call a tow truck. The van is fucked."

Jenny blinked, her eyes wide at hearing Sunny curse right in front of a child.

"Rache is calling already," she said. All the mothers in the neighborhood, who had been standing at their kitchen counters, thinking about dinner, while their toddlers bounced in ExerSaucers in front of Baby Einstein videos, now emerged onto their lawns. The news anchor, all tied up and pressed and clean, stepped back. They all looked at Sunny. She had been bald for sixty seconds. Now she was wearing her wig again, and it was dripping dirty water down the front of her face.

"Good," she said. "Well, that's great."

She went back over to the van and opened Bubber's door. He was shaking his head back and forth, back and forth in weird mechanical jerks, tapping on his knees. She unhooked his seat belt, put her arms around him, and took him out of the van. Here was the woman in the black SUV that had hit Sunny and taken off her wig. She was just another mom, a dumber, lesser, younger, unimportant mom from a different street, on her way to pick her baby up from its grandmother's house after finishing up her self-indulgent part-time job at the book-store downtown. There was an empty car seat in the back. No one was hurt. Nothing bad had really happened. No ambulance was needed.

When Bubber saw the woman from the other van, he put his chin on his chest and made growling quacks, like he wanted to kill her. He was furious and seemed likely to throw a rock. Sunny was afraid to put him down, so she kept holding him. She sat down on the curb and waited for the police to come, waited for the tow truck to come. She knew that the police and the tow truck had to be dealt with, and then she knew that they could walk home and she could put Bubber in front of the computer and she could have a quiet drink of water and watch *Oprah*. She could look at the people in the audience and try to remember who she really was.

Then her stomach turned hard and down low on her abdomen and around her back she felt a pain that was definitely a contraction. Wig or no wig, there was still a baby of some kind inside her, and it was trying to come out.

ONCE, THEY HAD BEEN trying to have sex, but Maxon was recovering from a bicycle accident, and Sunny was menstruating.

"Sorry," he said. "I'm leaking fluid from my Tegaderm."

"Maxon," she said. "You're even starting to sound like a robot. You're leaking fluid from your Tegaderm. I'm bleeding blood from my uterus. That's the difference between you and me."

4.

SUNNY SAT IN THE PASSENGER SEAT OF LES WEATH-
ers's golden Lexus, going to the doctor. Bubber was with the nanny
and the minivan was being towed. Everything was being looked
after. Did she want an ambulance, after all? No, she did not. Les
Weathers had volunteered to take her away to the doctor, and then
they were gone. The neighborhood had closed over her bald head the
way water in a lake closes over a rock that's thrown into it. People
did what they knew how to do. When all the arrangements had
been made, the bald head that had been sitting on the neck of Sunny
Mann would not be visible to anyone anymore.

They could try to remember her the way she used to be, when
she set the dates for holiday-themed outdoor-decor installation and

removal. No Christmas before Thanksgiving. No Halloween after November 2. No Fourth of July until July. All very reasonable. The neighbors wondered if the astronaut husband would still coach the Lego League. They wondered if the Christmas party was still on. The phone tree. The craft swap. Everything. How could they ask her if she was okay? There is a terrible awkwardness to talking to someone who is wearing an obvious wig, when you have no idea why. Did they feel stupid? Betrayed? Or did they just feel frustrated that they couldn't go on treating her as a close personal friend?

"So," said Les Weathers, "how long have you been bald?"

"My whole life," said Sunny.

"Does Maxon know?" he asked. His hand moved from the steering wheel down to his knee, and then back up to the steering wheel. Then he fiddled with the gearshift.

"Of course Maxon knows," she said.

"What about Bubber?" asked Les Weathers.

"What about him?"

"Does he know?"

A FEW WEEKS AGO, the family had been getting ready for lunch in the kitchen. Bubber sat at his miniature table. Sunny had pulled out the silverware drawer for him and he was playing with spoons and stacking them up with one fork between each one. Maxon stood there explaining gravity to Bubber by dropping things on the ground. Bubber stared at his forks and spoons. He always would stare at something unrelated, when he was being told something. The therapists told his parents that he could still use his peripheral vision. Maxon held a pencil up in the air and then let it fall from his bony fingers.

"Can you tell me what gravity is?" he asked Bubber.

"Hot," said Bubber. "Gravity is hot."

Sunny giggled behind the refrigerator door, where she was getting lettuce for a sandwich. Maxon said, "Gravity is a force that every object has; all mass has gravity."

"It's an attraction," Sunny put in. "Heat is hot. Gravity is an attraction."

"When something has gravity," Maxon went on, "it makes other things come toward it, and the bigger the thing is, the more gravity it has, and the more things come toward it."

Bubber opened his mouth and then closed it. He began to disassemble his spoon and fork tower. Then he quickly said, "Jupiter has the biggest gravity. Jupiter is the biggest planet. It is a gas giant. Jupiter has the mass of three hundred Earths and a volume of more than a thousand Earths."

"Even Mommy has gravity," Maxon continued. "See?"

The dog, Rocks, walked toward Sunny, sniffing for food.

"Look, I'm pulling Rocks over here to me with my gravity," said Sunny. She picked up the dog and stuck him to her pregnant tummy.

"Mommy is Jupiter," said Bubber without looking at her.

"I'm not Jupiter. Why do I have to be Jupiter? Why can't I be something cute like Venus?"

"Uh-oh." Maxon jerked himself across the floor, pretended to be yanked suddenly toward Sunny. "I think Venus's gravitational field is getting me too."

Sunny and Maxon jutted together and began to rotate on the axis of her belly with the dog mashed between them, like two tall people dancing drunk. They careened into the front room, crashed into a chair, and started laughing. Now Bubber was out of his chair and coming toward them.

"Bubber, no! Save yourself! Don't get pulled into Mommy's atmosphere!"

He rushed toward them but then began to run around them in a circle. His arms were flat to his sides and he ran with legs slicing like scissors.

"Don't worry, Daddy," he said, "I'm just a moon. I have become a moon."

It was one of the best sentences he had ever said. That night, Sunny had written it down in their treatment journal, noting the use of the word "I." She had not been wearing her wig at the time.

SUNNY PUT HER HANDS on her face, then slid them up onto her head and pulled off her wig. She laid it in her lap and started picking the dirt out of it, trying to smooth it out. She had another contraction, the fourth one she'd had since the accident, and waited for it to pass. The pain in her back was like someone hacking her apart with an ax.

"Yes, Bubber knows," she said.

"So, it's kind of like dentures," said Les Weathers. "You take it off to sleep?"

"Like dentures," she said hollowly. "You know what, Les, can you pull over here?"

She got out of the car. They had been approaching the Granby Street bridge, and she crossed in front of the condos by the shore, walked briskly up the sidewalk over the water. She leaned over the railing, looking down on another creeping branch of another river wandering lazily back through the Norfolk neighborhoods like ivy. She took the wig in her right hand. She looked it over, inside and out, and then hurled it as far as she could into the water. It made a light landing, soaked, and floated. She watched it there for a while and then walked back down the bridge, reloaded herself into Les Weathers's Lexus, and shut the door again. She had walked forty-six steps out in the open air without her wig in Virginia.

* * *

ONCE, WHEN BUBBER WAS a baby and Maxon was away at a conference, both she and Bubber had the flu at the same time. Nothing she had at home was working to get him to sleep, so she'd run out to get him different medicine and she had not worn her wig. She was just too sick and tired to bother with it. Throwing on a sweatshirt with a hood and sunglasses, she tightened the pull cord around her face, grabbed baby Bubber, ran out the door, and drove to a drugstore outside her neighborhood so no one would see her. She was standing in the parking lot, getting Bubber out of his seat, when an old man hollered at her from across the parking lot. He walked closer as he called to her.

"Hey, mama!" he said.

"Hey," she said under her breath, from inside her hood and behind her sunglasses.

"Hey, you can't say 'hey'?" he said, staggering closer. She saw that he was drunk.

"Hey," she said louder, and forced herself to smile. Now he was between her and the store.

"That's my NEPHEW!" shouted the old man. "Now that is some shit that stink! Give me high five."

He threw his hand up in the air and Sunny walked forward. She touched her hand to his hand on the way by. His hand was dry, hard, cold. She pushed on, marching determinedly into the store.

"You! You!" he called after her. "Stay beautiful, you hear? Stay beautiful."

Inside, Bubber threw up in the shopping cart, dribbling innocent baby puke down his front as he sat in the basket with his legs sticking through the holes. She had nothing to wipe it with. It was a total disaster. On that night Sunny knew she could never leave the house without her wig again. There was no way to half-ass it. She had to fully commit.

"WOW, YOU'RE LIKE AN addict flushing your drugs," said Les.

"I have more wigs," she said.

"Yeah, I've never seen you without that wig, until today," he said.

"They all look like that wig, but with different styles. You know, ponytails, braid."

From the bridge, the doctor's office was right around the corner. Les Weathers let her off at the front entrance. Before she got out of the car, he put his hand on her hand.

"I am not going to think any differently about you, now that you're bald."

"Okay," said Sunny.

"I mean, I probably have no idea what it's like, being bald, but I'd like to think I could try to understand what you're going through anyway. If you want to talk about it."

Sunny looked down at his hand on hers, and he removed it.

"Do you want me to go in with you? I can stay for ten minutes, twenty minutes. I have to go back to the studio to do promos, but I can call them, tell them I'm walking right onto set. I'm worried about you. Maxon would have wanted someone to take care of you."

Sunny tried to picture big, blond, perfectly shaped Les Weathers sitting next to her at the doctor's office. He would lean forward at that certain angle, steeple his fingers, and ask just what their options were. He would stand by the door while she got her instructions, looking patiently at his watch. He would wear a big toothy television grin. On the rare occasions she had been able to drag Maxon to a baby appointment, he typically sat in the waiting room behind a potted plant, thumbing his PDA, or briskly paced the halls, cleaving the air like a knife.

"No thanks," she said. "I'll be fine. Rache is coming to pick me up. I have my phone."

What would Rache say when she found that Sunny had thrown out the wig for good? Maybe she would tell Sunny that it was all because of stress, that they could go pick another wig out of the closet, and forget the whole thing. Rache would be nervous, would definitely want things back to the way they were. "It's fine, it's fine, it's fine," Rache had said. "Just go. It's fine." As if she just wanted bald Sunny out of her range of vision. Les Weathers, though, was always going to be Les Weathers. He seemed to really want to stay and help. Sunny reached up and flipped down the visor in front of her seat. She carefully, slowly peeled off her fake eyelashes and eyebrows, dropping them into her bag. She looked at him and blinked, hairlessly, and then got out of the car.

"Good-bye, Baldy," said Les Weathers, and he made his signature wink and finger point, like every night after the news. "I'll see you around town."

With that, he drove away.

5.*

WHEN SHE GOT TO THE DOCTOR'S OFFICE, SHE SAT
down in the waiting room, in a chair with her back to the window,
her face to the door. She had to sit down because another contraction
was coming. The receptionist didn't know who she was. Maybe the
receptionist thought she was a man. Sunny reached a white hand out
to the round end table. The hand wanted to grab a lamp. The hand
wanted to smash a lamp. It couldn't be helped that the place looked
like a furniture store, with everything so perfect, perfect. Area rugs,
bronze statuettes; the room sang in harmony with itself. With different carpet, it would have made a good living room in Sunny's neighborhood. It was a doctor's office passing as a living room. A decorator
trying to think like a pregnant woman.

"Hello, are you all right?"

"No," said Sunny.

The doctor knew all about Sunny, because he had examined her and everything. But the receptionist did not know. So she was another person to be shocked by bald Sunny that day. It was spreading like a ripple. Lots to talk about. Lots to remember later, to report at the dinner table. Sunny sat like a rip in one of the landscape paintings on the wall, a little hub of disbelief in the center of a perfectly good hallucination. She got up, picked up her bag, and marched through the door without being called back by the nurse. She went straight into the doctor's office. He looked up from his tape player. He had luxurious curls all over his head, honey brown, shiny, floating around his skull like a sandy cloud. And there in front of him she baldly said, "I can't have this baby. You have to stop it. It cannot happen."

It was something she'd known the moment she felt the first contraction, sitting there in the curb beside her wrecked van, with the cool puddle water dripping down the back of her neck. It wasn't that she didn't want to have a baby anymore. It was that she couldn't have a baby.

She had been living so quietly, so wigged, in such a perfect shape, for many years, as if asleep. Dreaming of a husband, a baby, a choice of ceiling fans, an entire cabinet just for different foils and plastic wraps. There, in her sleep, she had been drifting and rotating through a set of arcs and orbits within which she could provide the proper wife and mother behaviors. When the wig flew off, she woke up out of her sleep, she dropped out from her orbit, scattered across the sky on every different vector, every crazy angle. She felt sure that there was a small and human-shaped person inside of her. She knew that there was a hole the size of a quarter through which that person was supposed to get out. This was not mathematically possible. This wasn't healthy. No one could expect her to do this. It was as if she fell back through the years to the point she'd never been a mother at all. Never had hair at all. Just a scared kid.

"Sunny, why are you not wearing your wig?" the doctor asked.

"It fell off," said Sunny. "During the car accident, it fell off, into some mud. So I threw it in the Elizabeth River on the way over here."

"And now you're feeling like you can't have the baby?"

"Yes. It's not natural. It's not normal."

"Well," said the curly-haired doctor, "I hardly think that's correct. You're just shaken up. We need to check you out, of course, get those contractions stopped. But you'll be fine."

Sunny sat down in a chair. Her bald head shone in the pink light of the un-hospital consultation room with its totally-real wooden desk and green shaded not-fluorescent lights.

"I am not a person who gives birth," said Sunny. "I'm not equipped for it. I'm not right for it."

"You've done it before, Sunny. Obviously."

"That was different. Maxon was here. And everything was working then. Now nothing is working. I've spent a long time preparing myself, and, you know, all that has to be redone. All that work is lost. It is wiped out. I have to start over and do more work. I need more months to prepare."

"A baby isn't like a whiteboard," said the doctor. "You don't just start over."

"I'm afraid for the baby," said Sunny. And she thought, *I'm not fit. Not this body. Not this head. Not this person. I'm not fit to be a mother. You don't know what I really am.*

At this point another contraction came, and Sunny grabbed the tastefully upholstered arms of the consultation chair. She ground her teeth together. The doctor leaned toward her sympathetically.

"Let's look at the ultrasound and check the baby's positioning," said the doctor. "And then we'll get you off your feet and onto fluids. Then we'll see where we're at."

Sunny started to cry. Her face became red and wrinkled. She knew it.

Later, she lay on the ultrasound table, wearing a hospital gown. Having no hair makes a woman look indeterminate, with regard to gender. When she was lying on the examination table, wearing her blue striped hospital gown, her bald head exposed to the world, it would have been hard to say whether Sunny was a female or a male. It didn't help that she was tall and had narrow hips. Even pregnant, she had a flat chest. She could have been a kind of gawky alien man lying there, swollen with an alien child. Underneath her gown she had on gigantic surgical pants. When the doctor came in, and asked if she was ready, he seemed to be taking a good hard look at Sunny. Sunny's nose was good, her chin delicate, her eyes deep and dark, and her mouth rosy. Without eyebrows and eyelashes, though, it was the face of a statue, up on top of that man or woman body.

The doctor rolled up on a round stool beside the bed, and folded the gown up over Sunny's chest. Down on her great white belly there was still a hole, a little indentation from where she was attached to her mother in the womb. What happens to the pipe underneath the belly button, once the umbilical cord is cut? Sunny knew that hers was still there. It would be there forever, leading nowhere. Leading out. During pregnancy, the hole had turned inside out. It had done this with Bubber and it did it again now. The truth she had realized, while pregnant with Bubber, was that down deep at the bottom of that awful, shameful hole where her mother had been attached, roped onto her, was a small, small mole. This small, dark mole at the bottom of her belly button became real to her only when pregnancy turned her belly button inside out, and she saw it for the first time.

This was something about pregnancy which research could not explain. How the perfect parabola of her pregnancy belly could be augmented by this extra bump, and how that bump could have its own bump. She said to Maxon that if she walked straight into a wall, that mole would make first contact. And Maxon said, "Babe, why walk into a wall, if it's just going to cause you to question the integrity of your parabola?" And then she said, "Okay, a tangent line then. A tangent line."

The doctor powered up the ultrasound machine, drew it close to her side, and squeezed some clear lubrication onto her skin. He put the white wand down into the cold jelly and turned to face a grainy little monitor. "Yes," he said. "Yes." He moved the wand back and forth, back and forth, and turned it rhythmically. Lying down flat on her back, Sunny's body felt better. There were no contractions. The grainy shapes on the monitor changed and flowed over each other pleasantly. Only a trained eye could have identified organs being shown. For Sunny, they could be lunar mountains. Fish guts. Dark forests. If Maxon were beside her, would he be squeezing her hand? If Les Weathers were beside her, would he really be Les Weathers, Channel 10 News?

"Don't you want to see your baby?" said the doctor.

"Well, is it all right?" she said.

"Look," he said.

If Maxon was looking at that moment into a computer monitor up in space, in the crew cabin of the spaceship that was carrying him to the moon, then maybe he was seeing what she was seeing. He could focus his eyes purposefully on the white noise on the monitor in the spaceship, and see the baby's features blurring out to meet him. "Hey!" he would call out, his face creasing in a wide, toothy grin. He might shout. He might pump his fist in the air, full of joy, like with a high score, something unrelated to work. But he will not call his astronaut buddies to come and look, show off the screen like a wallet flipping open. No. He will not open her up to his friends and show off what he had put there, what was growing there because of him. No, no, he sits silently, shoulders hunched over, glasses askew, and takes it in all by himself. He would not call anyone over. He has to take a measurement, note a change in the diameter of the skull since the last reading. He puts out a finger to touch the beating heart. Covers it with his finger and uncovers it. Covers it and uncovers it.

She finally turned and examined the screen. Her insides felt foreign, made out of plastic, manufactured elsewhere, implanted by strangers, distant.

"There," the doctor said, and pointed to a swirl of light. "There is the baby, and there is its heart. It's beating, you know?"

The organ that was the baby's heart went black and white in a rhythm.

"Your baby still has lots of amniotic fluid to move around in," said the doctor. "But the baby is in breech position. Where we'd like to see the head down here, by the birth canal, we find it up here, on top."

"So?" asked Sunny.

"We need to stop the labor." The doctor paused. "You didn't want to know your baby's gender, when we did your other ultrasound. Do you want to know now?"

"Tell me," said Sunny.

"Your baby is a little girl."

A girl. It was as if she couldn't move. Her veins were cold with love and fear.

IN THE WEEKS BEFORE the launch of the rocket, Maxon and Sunny received requests from media outlets, asking for interviews. To populate the moon with robots and then with humans: this was potentially a story. There was no other NASA wife as perfectly presentable. There was no other NASA couple as lithe and tall. When Maxon and Sunny appeared in pictures together, there was a certain sexiness about them that led people to wonder what intrigued them about this whole moon situation. Was it really the fact that a rocket was taking robots to live up on the moon? Or was it just this handsome elegant woman and her tall, haunted astronaut man?

Cooperating with the NASA publicity department, Maxon went to New York for eighteen hours to visit the talk shows. He joked and smiled, made small talk, and comically misunderstood sexual innuendoes. But Sunny refused to do any appearances at first. She said, "I am pregnant. I can't fly." When the *Today* show agreed to send a crew to her house, she balked at that, too. She didn't want to disrupt the life of her child any more than his father would disrupt it by going into space. She said this, and the people that she was talking to seemed to understand.

Finally she agreed to be interviewed on the local news in Norfolk. In this way, she would not seem to be avoiding notice. She would seem to be a trooper. That's what they would call her. She would glitter with sacrifice. She wore her most amazing wig, the kind of style you can only achieve with a two-hundred-dollar styling appointment, or with real human hair permanently affixed in a shape. She wore coral, which was said to warm under studio lights. She wore pearls.

The network was housed in a brick building on Granby Street, unremarkable except for the news channel logo attached to its roof. Inside, the studio was a large dry room, painted dark, high ceilings hung with canister lights. Cables in braids roped from camera to set and around the floor, like black rivers across the dark room, and she picked her way across them to the set, supported on one side by Maxon.

"What are you going to wear, Maxon?" she had said that morning.

"My space suit," he said. "That's what I always wear when I'm astronauting."

"You don't even have the space suit here," she said, too distracted with her eyebrows to acknowledge his joke.

"Well, I'm going to wear red overalls and a straw hat."

"Oh yeah?"

"And sing 'The Star-Spangled Banner.'"

"Maxon, I don't want to do this," she said.

"Why? You'll do great. Look how great you are, all the time. Nothing rattles you. You're a machine."

"Maxon, why would you even say something like that?"

"Like what?"

Sunny peeled off an eyebrow and put it back on, a tiny bit higher up on her brow.

"I'm afraid to do it, because I'm afraid I'm going to cry or throw up or something."

"Why?"

"You're going into space. I'm worried. People worry about their spouses going on business trips to Kansas City."

"Well, Kansas City is perilous. The gravity there is nine-tenths of what it is in Virginia."

"That's not even true."

"I bet I can get the news guy to believe it."

"Shut up."

"I bet I can though."

Eventually he had chosen to wear a NASA polo shirt and navy dockers. As they took their places on the set, she appraised his appearance and found him acceptable.

"You look good," she told him. "Just don't start talking about the robot that can really understand the tango and we'll be fine."

"You'll be fine," said Maxon. "The robot that can really understand the tango was my only material."

Les Weathers bounded onto the set, fresh from hair and makeup, no doubt. He was still wearing his tissue-paper shields tucked into his collar to keep his crisp white shirt from getting smudged with foundation.

"Hey, guys! How we doing today?" he said. He grinned his enormous grin and grasped hands with first Maxon, then Sunny. His hand was warm, strong, generous. She knew that Maxon did not like to shake hands. Seeing Maxon's sharp white fist close around Les Weathers's suntanned paw made Sunny stare for a moment. Maxon was not tanned below the line his bicycle gloves made on his wrist. *Here is the man I married*, she thought. *He has a fist like the talons of a hawk. Here is the man I did not marry. He has the skin tone of a lion in full sun.* She wondered if they put foundation on Les Weathers's hands.

"Great," said Maxon. "Doing great."

"Thank you so much for agreeing to do this interview," he said to Maxon. Then conspiratorially, to Sunny: "Go WNFO, right? What a scoop!"

"What a scoop," said Maxon. "Go WNFO."

"Les, you're so kind to bring us in, and help us share Maxon's rocket launch with the world. I really appreciate it," said Sunny, unleashing a radiant smile. She lowered herself into a chair between Maxon and Les Weathers, crossing her ankles under her so that her cork-wedge sandals were tidily arranged. They were going to tape the interview, show it during the evening news, when there would be the largest number of viewers. This way it would be syndicated to all the affiliates across the country. Maybe the *Today* show would pick it up after all.

Depends on how the mission goes, said the producer. Now, what does that mean, asked Sunny.

Was Les Weathers about to become famous on the back of Maxon's mission to the moon? One big story, the correct flashing teeth all lined up in a row, and a man with nice blond hair could be headed for the big time. But only if something terrible happened. Or at least something unexpected. The fate of the anchorperson depends on a tragedy or a revolution. Sunny looked at Maxon and back at Les Weathers, and felt a ripple of nerves across her chest.

"Are you all right?" asked Les Weathers.

"Oh, it's the pregnancy," she said. "I'm absolutely fine. Thank you for your concern."

The producer told them where they were to look (Les Weathers, each other) and where they were not to look (the cameras), and how they should smile and be animated.

"Act like you're talking to a friend, at a party," said the producer. "We're happy here. We're going to the moon!"

They had already been pretending Les Weathers was their friend. This would not be hard.

The interview began. What does this mean for America? What does this mean for the world? Maxon produced answers from the script he had been rehearsing. It was almost as if he were sort of a humanist, affirming a manifest destiny in the stars. He described the bright future, successfully veiling his real self for the camera. For now he was not the terse, bony guy about to leave the Earth for the first time. He was buoyant, almost cheerful. He did not say, "I rounded up a gang of robots, and I'm headed for the moon, to take it over." He did not say, "This is the way we evolve. This is the way our culture transforms."

Instead he said it serious: "It is a great move for mankind." He said it droll: "We're finally furnishing our mother-in-law suite." He said it poetic: "Machines on the gray desert of time's horizon."

Sunny smiled and nodded, her knees pressed lightly together, coral cardigan wrapping the sides of her pregnant belly. She felt a droplet of sweat begin to roll under her wig. The lights were hot.

"And how do you feel about all this?" Les asked Sunny warmly.

"Les," she said, "I married a man in love with robots. Am I really surprised he's making off with a robot harem, to populate the sky?"

And everyone laughed. Had Sunny married a man with a job as an anchorperson and a thick arm in a neatly pressed shirt, she would have been very shocked if he made off with a robot harem, to populate the sky. She would have expected to go to Norway, to have a literal mother-in-law suite, like the kind over a garage, not the kind on an astral body.

"Let's talk about you, Sunny Mann," said Les Weathers. "This launch comes at a difficult time for your family."

He gestured awkwardly, charmingly toward her huge, pregnant belly, and smiled.

"Well, Maxon's launch was scheduled well before mine," Sunny purred. "And the moon waits for no one."

"But aren't you worried, leaving your wife at this time?" he pressed. Sunny stretched out a hand and took Maxon's in hers. It was cool and dry. He had hard hands, long strong fingers.

"Les," said Maxon, "the timing of the mission is dependent on the orbital path of the moon, which affects everything about the launch."

This was bullshit, Sunny knew. She felt her heart thump in her chest.

"The slightest variation in timing could cause a differential in gravitational pull that would throw off the telemetry significantly. You know, for example, the variations in Earth's gravity. Everyone knows Kansas has nine-tenths the gravity of Virginia. In some parts of Oklahoma, it's even less."

"Oh," said Les Weathers. "I guess I didn't know that."

Maxon produced the facial expression that communicated, "I am letting you in on a secret." Then he winked, right at the camera, where he wasn't even supposed to look.

"I'm not worried about my delivery," said Sunny. "I'm not worried about Maxon's either. He'll get his robots to the moon, and when he comes back, there will be a new baby here to welcome him back."

"Do you know what you're having, a girl or a boy?"

Sunny laughed mildly. "Les, we've been so busy preparing for Maxon's trip, I have not even had time to find out if this baby is human."

6.

THERE ARE THREE THINGS THAT ROBOTS CANNOT DO," wrote Maxon. Then beneath that on the page he wrote three dots, indented. Beside the first dot he wrote "Show preference without reason (LOVE)" and then "Doubt rational decisions (REGRET)" and finally "Trust data from a previously unreliable source (FOR-GIVE)."

Love, regret, forgive. He underscored each word with three dark lines and tapped his pen on each eyebrow three times. He hadn't noticed that his mouth was sagging open. He was not quite thirty, the youngest astronaut at NASA by a mile.

I do what robots can't do, he thought. *But why do I do these things?*

The spaceship traveled toward the moon. Maxon wrote with his astronaut pen. In his notebook there were hundreds of lists, thousands of bulleted points, miles of underscoring. It was a manner of thinking. He was standing in his sleeping closet, upright and belted into his bunk. The other four astronauts were in the command pod, running procedures. No one liked spending time in the sleeping closets except Maxon. He kind of enjoyed it. It was not time for the lights to go out, but the rocket to the moon was nearing the end of its first day in space.

Maxon's list of things a robot can't do was a short one now, pared down from a much longer list that included tough nuts like "manifest meaningful but irrational color preference" and "grieve the death of a coworker." Maxon made his robots work better and last longer by making them as similar to humans as possible. Humans are, after all, the product of a lot of evolution. Logically and biologically, nothing works better than a human. Maxon's premise had been that every seeming flaw, every eccentricity must express some necessary function. Maxon's rapid blinking. Sunny's catlike yawn. Even the sensation of freezing to death. It all matters, and makes the body work, both in singularity and in collusion with other bodies, all working together.

Why does a man, clapping in a theater, need the woman next to him to also be clapping? Why does a woman, rising from her seat at a baseball game, expect the man on her left to jump to his feet? Why do they do things all at once, every person in every seat, rising, clapping, cheering? Maxon had no idea. But he knew that it didn't matter why. They do it, and there must be a reason. A failure to clap in a theater can result in odd looks, furrowed foreheads, nudged elbows. So Maxon would write:

ORIENTATION (GROUP)
IN MATRIX A

$$\begin{bmatrix} a_{11} & \cdots & \cdots & a_{1n} \\ \vdots & \ddots & & \vdots \\ a_{m1} & \cdots & \cdots & a_{mn} \end{bmatrix}$$

IF A GROUP (PEOPLE) IS ORIENTED
IN AN n×m MATRIX, THE BEHAVIOR
OF ANY MEMBER OF ANY MEMBER
a_{mn} SHOULD BE IDENTICAL TO ALL
OTHER MEMBERS IN MATRIX A_{nm}.
IF a_{11} IS CLAPPING, $a_{12} \cdots a_{mn}$ SHOULD CLAP.

Let anyone in any theater contradict it.

"Whatcha doin', Genius?" asked Fred Phillips. He stuck his head into Maxon's sleeping closet, gripping both sides of the doors as his body floated out behind.

"I'm working, Phillips," Maxon returned.

"You're not working. You're dreaming." Phillips smiled cheerfully, glancing at Maxon's paper. "Dreaming of making sweet, sweet love to your robots. But you just can't make them love you back."

"First of all," said Maxon, "I've seen your medical. Your IQ is in the genius range. So your nickname for me, 'Genius,' is not sensible. Secondly, I am not dreaming of a robot who can love. Anyone could program a robot to do that. All you'd have to do is arrange an illogical preference. Making a robot love you over anyone else would be like making a robot love the color orange over any other color. I could have done it years ago. But it's a pointless behavior. And I won't." How was loving Sunny different from loving orange? Phillips would not understand.

"Whatever, Genius," said Phillips. "Houston wants us to run a sim of the docking procedure. You want to watch? Or, are you too busy? We all know you have nothing to do until we hook up with your girlfriends in orbit."

Phillips swung free of Maxon's closet, brought his foot up and wedged it into a handle, and propelled himself back through the tube into the command module. Their sleeping closets were arranged around the wall of the rocket, with an empty cylinder in the center where they could get in and out, one at a time. Maxon was not claustrophobic. He was suited for space travel, and he was wearing his space suit for astronauting.

"Robots can't cry, Genius!" said Phillips, retreating. "Ito's Laws of Robotics: Robots can't cry, robots can't laugh, robots can't dream."

Maxon sighed. He knew this was bait. But he was already unbuckling his straps. The hook was in his brain. Maxon had made robots that did all three of these things. James Ito was a hack, some AI putz working for a car company. His book was a farce. Pop culture, not science. When Maxon met Ito he hadn't liked the guy's face. A humanist. The kind of guy who would paint the future bright by predicting that the transformation offered by robots was really recidivism to a world gone by. A robot wife would be a pre-feminist wife. A robot worker would be a pre-socialism worker. The guy had no idea what was actually just around the corner. A different world, not better, not worse, but full of change.

Robots could laugh, and cry, and dream, and everything else. For example, there was a robot named Hera. Six iterations of it waited for him now, in an orbit around the moon, in the cargo bay of the rocket that had been fired last week, which they would soon be docking up with. Hera laughed at nonsensical juxtapositions, like a fat man in a little coat or a wheelbarrow full of whipped cream. Its laughter was not a sound delivered to human ears through a speaker, meant for human appreciation and approval. The laughter was an internal, systemic reaction, a clenching of joints, a shaking of components, a temporary loss of function. It could be shared with other Hera models, could spread like a contagion throughout a group of them.

"Incorrect," said Maxon, following him. "Hera laughs. It's what makes Hera so reliable."

"I don't believe in it," said Phillips. "It's pointless. A robot that laughs. What the hell?"

When he was strapped into his seat, Phillips said, "Go ahead, Houston. Aeneid rocket is ready to run the sim. All crew present."

Maxon was familiar with the language of naysayers. They were afraid. Sometimes their faces showed that, the same thing as confusion, with the eyebrows down and chin raised. When Hera's software was first coded, some people said it was a kind of abomination. Other people said it was a gimmick. They were interested in torque and tensile strength, in the size of robots and what they were composed of. An article in the *International Journal of Robotics Research* called him "a gearshrinker," with scorn. He didn't read the article, because he had determined from the title that he wouldn't like it. For Maxon it was not a question of good or bad, or even why, but just a question of what's next, and then ultimately, not even a question, but just a history. A history of humanity, in all the ways they were alive.

Then there was the Juno model, who experienced a similar jostling of gears and clenching of hydraulics when she was left alone, away from other Juno models, for a specified amount of time. Juno's crying was a lot like Hera's laughing, except there was no viral spread. Her visual sensors became impaired and had to be cleared, by her or another Juno who was moved to participate, or not, by her own if/then clauses. An article in *Wired* magazine called "The Lonely Robot" had described one Juno meeting another, and how they shook when they were separated. This was before the Juno code was wired into a construction frame, made so rectangular. Magazines are only interested in the humanoid functions of humanoid robots. Make them look like bulldozers and you can get away with anything.

What didn't matter much to Maxon was the shape the robots took externally. How to put a microscope in them. How to make them smaller, bigger, work in the human bloodstream, simplify bipedal mobility. He had an abundance of research assistants to task with these technical details. His job was coding, thinking, more coding, and the completion of lists. He moved through his labs back at Langley like a wraith, stained hair falling down around jagged cheekbones, hands dangling at the end of his long arms, spine convex. He rode his bicycle for hours, working out command sequences on the pavement in front of him, every square meter like an open stretch of whiteboard, there and then erased.

"Houston, we are go for this procedure," said George Gompers, mission commander. "Standing by."

Their screens wavered, and instead of the clear view of space they all saw a holographic projection, where the moon loomed large and they could see the cargo module, containing all the robots they would be taking down to the lunar surface. Their job, in orbit, was to dock with this cargo, extract the three containers, and then convert the command module into the lunar lander. While the pilot, the engineer, and the commander repeated orders, fired small rockets, repositioned, and aligned the rocket for the simulated docking, Maxon looked at his cargo module full of robots.

He wondered what they were doing in there, what they were dreaming.

All of Maxon's robots, like Maxon, could dream. A randomly generated string of code gently stimulated the processors during their mandatory off modes, testing the chemobionic reactions while the official electronic pathways were shut down. It hadn't even been hard, shattering this particular old ax. It had come apart like a clay pot. The robots remembered the events of their lives, the data they had recorded. In dreams, they transposed numbers, brought sets adjacent that were never meant to be interpreted together, and when they "woke up" they often had new "ideas" in the form of patterns and connections read in the chaos of their jumbled sleep.

The more like a human the better, whether the bot was as small as a fragment of nanotech cleaving the valves of the heart or as big as a sentient harbor crane. Humans work. They are an evolutionary success. The more they evolve, the more successful they become. Maxon had once thought that at this moment, when he was ready to land on the moon, his list of things that robots couldn't do would have had every entry crossed out in a dark line. He had planned that the phrase "quintessentially human" would have been obviated by now. Indifferent to all protest, he had relentlessly made dreaming, faceless, laughing robots that were inexorably closing in on humanity.

The AI was startling. People had to admit. Maxon's robots did what other robots could not do, thought what other robots could not think. That was the reason he held so many patents, and had such an astonishing bank account at such a young age. But the most important thing, the reason he was employed by NASA and on his way to the moon: Maxon's robots could make other robots. Not just construct them, but actually conceive of them, and make them.

To create a moon colony, a lot of robots are needed. Robots to build the station, robots to run it, robots who don't mind breathing moon atmosphere, who don't mind moon temperatures, robots to take care of human visitors. The moon colony proposed would belong to the robots for many years to come; this was understood. Humans would be their guests. The problem was that no one could shoot a robot big enough to construct a moon colony up to the moon. There just wasn't enough room in a rocket for diggers, cranes, stamping presses.

So the answer was to shoot up a robot that could make another robot big enough. Juno and Hera were the robot mothers: steely, gangly, whirring, spinning mothers, built to mine the materials and fabricate the real robots, the real builders, who would re-create the world on the moon. Only a laughing, crying, dreaming robot could be a mother. An awful thought, for some. A perversity—but this was the reason for everyone else's failure. All this business of a human purview. As if it weren't all electricity, in the end. Maxon couldn't remember ever thinking that something a robot did was awful.

Maxon watched the simulated docking procedure, watched the holographic cargo module getting closer, the engineer and pilot arguing over angles and coefficients. He uncapped his pen and wrote in his notebook: "You are a weak, sick man, and your frailty in the darkness of space is a vile embarrassment to your species." *Remember this,* he thought. But did he really believe it? He tried to stretch his long legs into the cramped tube between the sleeping quarters and the command space, but his knees brushed the wall. He couldn't get symmetrical, one angular shoulder jutting out into the back of Phillips's seat. Inside his white jumpsuit, his bones were a cage for his live beating heart.

He looked at the men and the way they talked to each other, the way Gompers preferred Tom Conrad, the pilot, over Phillips, the engineer. He saw the way they papered their personal areas with photographs, the way they listened to podcasts from their wives on their laptops, the way they prayed.

You are a man just like them, he thought. *You love, you regret, you forgive. Your eyesight blurs. You even forget things, sometimes.* Love, regret, forgive. They were three bloody, muddy stains left on the snowy white tablecloth of his research. Three items left to be dealt with: love, regret, forgive.

"GENIUS, WE JUST LOVE your robots so much. When are you going to make us a robot that will love us back, you know what I mean?" Phillips had said to him once, teasing him during training, while they sat waiting for the pod to start spinning them again, testing their reactions to g-forces. In a round room, the pod sat on the end of one arm of two on a central axle. Like a giant spinner in a game of Twister.

"It's not impossible, Phillips," Maxon answered. "The world is only electrical and magnetic."

"Okay," said Phillips. "So why not?"

"You don't understand," said Maxon. "It is all electricity. So the question is really: Why?"

"I am not following you, Genius," said Phillips. "You're making it sound easy, and then acting like it's hard."

The machine began to spin them. At first, it was slow.

"Can it, Lieutenant. Shut up, Dr. Mann," said Gompers, always quick to remind him that he did not have a military title. But Maxon was already talking.

"Listen. From the smallest, deepest synapses in the human brain to the interactions of galaxies with the universe, it is all electricity. If you can shape the force of electricity, you can duplicate any other impulse in the world. A robot can yawn, it can desire, it can climax. It can do exactly what a human does, in exactly the same way. You really want a robot to love you? You want it to fuck you back, when you fuck it? Just like a woman? Let me tell you: There is no difference between carbon and steel, between water and ooze. With a number of conditional statements nearing infinity, any choice can be replicated, however random. The only hard thing about creating more sophisticated AI was acquiring the space needed to hold such a myriad of possibilities. There is nothing different in a human's brain from a robot's brain. Not one single thing."

By this time the machine was spinning so fast, his cheeks were flapping. The other men in the module were quiet, intense. Their eyes were all open. Their faces looked skeletal, all the skin pulled back.

"GET IT?" Maxon screeched.

And even in the pressure of all that simulated gravity, Fred Phillips found it possible to roll his eyes.

When the machine stopped, Phillips said, "Mann, dude, I feel for your wife."

"What do you feel for her?" said Maxon.

WHY DID THE ROBOTS not love? Why not feel good about themselves, just for once? Why not prefer one entity, one electrical epicenter, over all the others, for no other reason than that it felt good to do so? Maxon knew why. They could not love because he had not made them love. He had not made them love because he didn't understand why they should love. He didn't understand why he should love, why anyone should love. It wasn't logical. It wasn't rational, because it wasn't beneficial. That was the truth of the matter. He chose for them not to, because loving defied his central principle: If humans do it, it must be right.

To show preference only for a good reason, to accept any choice made with the best use of available information, to suspect a source of giving incorrect data when incorrect data had been received from it in the past; these responses were beneficial to the robot, to the human. To love for no reason, to grieve over a choice that had been made rationally, to forgive, to show mercy, to trust a poison well, also potentially damaging. If humans do it, why do they do it?

He understood the value of a mother's love for her child. That had a use. He understood the value of a soldier's love for his brother-in-arms. That had a use. But the family structure was so integral to the foundation of a civilization, and the solidity of the family was so important to the civilization's survival, that choosing a mate based on some ridiculous whim seemed insane. It seemed destructive. How could it be so? Yet he, Maxon Mann, gearshrinker, droidmaster, having decided that all romantic love is at odds with the survival of the species, had fallen, himself, in love. He had fallen deeply, hopelessly, inexorably in love with Sunny, and it had happened almost before he got started in life. Over seven thousand rotations of the Earth ago. Certainly before he understood the ramifications of his electrobiological behavior.

That night, his second night in space, the feeling of breathing in was almost crushing him, the quarters so close that taking a deep breath almost had his bony chest brushing up against the shelf that held his laptop, his mission log, stuck down with Velcro. He let his head roll back against the wall, his crisp curls brushing the back of his neck. One hand went up to cover his eyes, the other hand still held the pen, poised over those three words; love, regret, forgive. When he finally slept, lulled by a cyclical computation worked out on the back of his eyelids, the pen went scratching across the paper, one final subconscious underscore. First there was Asimov, and his fictional laws of robotics, all written to protect humanity from the AI they'd created. Then Ito's laws, excusing the failure of programmers who wouldn't dare to try to re-create a human mind. Now Maxon's laws, because he was the only one left with the stones to know when to stop pushing the buttons that he himself had wired. Maxon Mann's Three Laws of Robotics: A robot cannot love. A robot cannot regret. A robot cannot forgive.

7.

THE CONTRACTIONS STOPPED. FLUIDS WERE DRAINED
into her. She went home. Night came and everyone slept. Morning
came and the nanny took Bubber off to preschool. He went out the
door with his head pointed forward, wearing his helmet, with a snack
and emergency pants in a horse-shaped backpack he called "Word."
Sunny was supposed to lie down as much as possible, so she did. She
lay down in her pumpkin-colored bedroom. She put her bald head
down on the embroidered silk duvet cover, so carefully joined in
color and historical context to the weird footstool she'd found at an
estate sale, which was itself so carefully coordinated with the Morris
chair in the corner, by the pumpkin-shaded light. The theme of her
bedroom decor flowed around the space like a gentle ellipse through

a series of perfectly oriented points. Not one curtain rod, not one shoe tree, not one alarm clock fell off the graph. On the TV, the NASA channel was playing without sound. But Maxon was not on the screen.

She fell asleep and dreamed of a matrix of all possible babies that she could be carrying at that moment. The possible babies spread out over a three-dimensional cube. At point zero, zero, zero was a normal human male baby, looking exactly like Maxon. Tall, mad-eyed, long-limbed, and pale. From there, the change in babies radiated out along a three-dimensional grid through the whole volume of the cube. At the intersection of every line was another scrawny infant, crouched and curled, naked and wrinkled. Eye color, hair color, pianist hands, knobby legs, short neck. Along this axis, more and more freckles. Along that axis, more and more hair. Of course, there cannot be an incremental change in gender. So, all alone, the baby at the opposite point of the cube, with her large alien eyes and her bald alien head, and her padded fingers and short legs, was the only female. She rotated like the other babies, but in the opposite direction. Already different.

The phone rang, waking her up. It was the director of the school. "Mrs. Mann," he said, "I would love for you to spend some time here with us when you pick up Bubber today. I have arranged a meeting with our staff psychiatrist for you."

He didn't know about the car accident, because she hadn't told him. He didn't know about the wig.

She sat up, held up the phone firmly to her head, and said, "No."

"Mrs. Mann," he droned on, "Bubber has had a meltdown this morning. Now he is back in his helmet, and we are all fine. There is no need to worry. But the behaviors we are seeing are becoming prohibitive."

"What do they prohibit?" asked Sunny.

"With respect, Mrs. Mann, we have an extraordinary facility and many resources," he said, "yet we cannot quite account for Bubber and his behavior."

"But I thought Miss Mary had been working with him." Sunny had spent a lot of money on the school. Miss Mary was one of many resources.

"You mention Miss Mary," said the director. "At the meeting today, she'd like to discuss the results of some tests. They need to be read and discussed."

Bubber had had many tests, and Sunny had read and discussed them all with doctors of every stripe. What she should do now was to search out the appropriate files to bring, the appropriate numbers to consult for comparison.

Instead Sunny said, "You know what? No more tests."

She found herself thinking, *This will not be tolerated.* Then she put the phone down, stood up, and stretched a long, long catlike stretch ending in a neck roll. On a normal day, she would now replace the wig, comb it down, inhabit it. Instead she got dressed, got into Maxon's car, and drove over to the very special preschool to take Bubber home. She felt kind of strong in her bald head. In the moment, she was only thinking about how Bubber was being tested again, and pissed off that he would again be found wanting.

Sunny was the mom with the multicolored activism ribbon in magnet on the back of her van. Sunny, heretofore, had been a very good friend of tests.

When she arrived at the school, the other parents were waiting to pick up their children, too. It was like a minivan convention in the parking lot. Silver ones, mostly. Some burgundy. Some teal. When they had purchased their minivan, Maxon had yearned for the black one, but Sunny said no.

"I've never seen a black minivan," she said. "We have to blend in with our environment."

"Well, if you've never seen a black minivan, might that not mean that the black minivans are blending in very well?" Maxon pointed out.

But they bought the silver one. On the highways, it was virtually invisible. The wig and the minivan together made an invisibility cloak. Walking past the rows of other cars, the different-colored ribbons on the bumpers, the soccer balls, the black-and-white ovals from vacation spots, Sunny remembered the first of three terrible things she had said to Maxon on the day before he went into space: *It is all your fault, that we don't fit in here. I'm doing my goddamned best. What's left, Maxon? It's all you. You won't even try. You won't even give it a decent effort.* Of all the children at Bubber's school, Bubber was the one that was autistic. Bubber was pushing the limits of what the school could handle. They kept telling her this.

On the sidewalk, a little stream of children bumped past her, the few girls with their little sparkling backpacks, their hair accessories glittering, their leather shoes squeaking comfortably, each holding a larger, duller, flatter parent by the hand, pulling them along. The children did not look up at Sunny as they passed her. They were dispassionate. She could have been a talking hawk, or a rhinoceros. They were like little hairy animatronic children, marching down the sidewalk, already thinking about lunch. The parents, in contrast, had no time to hide their surprise at Sunny's bald state. These were women she had chatted with, day after day, waiting for pickup time in the rain, or at the Christmas show, or at the grocery store, over the grapefruit bin. She didn't know all their names, but they were Taylor's Mom, and Connor's Mom, and Chelsea's Mom, and yet they walked right past, carefully averting their eyes and also smiling with lips drawn together in a line. Some crazy bald lady came to the school today.

Inside, the director was distributing art projects to take home, making sure sweaters were matched with the right children, and giving out lollipops that had no artificial colors. He was actually a man with no hair. He did have eyebrows, chin hairs, the rest of it, but his head was shining and bare. Sunny had never truly forgotten that fact, but in the days since the wig went on her head, she noticed bald people with less interest than before.

Back in the old days, it might have been like, Hey, high five, my brother. Then with the wig it was just another hairstyle, of the many that we regular humans can choose from. Now it was as if she were an animal, identifying another of her species.

The other parents began to clear out. The other children were all delivered to their families. Then there were only the three bald people in the room: the director of the preschool, and Sunny, and the baby inside her. The director's name was Mr. Dave. He recognized her, even without the fake hair she had been putting on her head. Mr. Dave said, "Hello, Mrs. Mann."

"I'm bald," said Sunny. "I've been wearing a wig this whole time. Eyebrows too, and eyelashes."

"Have a seat," said Mr. Dave. "Are you all right?"

"I'm fine. Just, you know, the wig went flying off my head yesterday. We had a car accident, Bubber and I. The wig—well, I decided to leave it off."

Mr. Dave nodded in an understanding way. Mr. Dave's voice had never been raised. He had never shouted at her and pumped his fist in her face and made spit flecks come out the sides of his mouth. They'd had their disagreements, but he had always stayed quiet. She wondered if Mr. Dave was capable of getting riled. She had always appreciated his calm demeanor.

"Does Bubber realize you've made this decision?" he asked.

"Well, yes, he knows," said Sunny. "He was there when it flew off."

"Did he seem upset by it?" asked Mr. Dave. "Bubber was very angry today. We were wondering if it had something to do with your husband."

"My husband is in space. He went up in a rocket yesterday."

"I know," said Mr. Dave.

"Well, we didn't think it would be a good idea for Bubber and I to go down to see the launch. We thought it was too much."

"Okay," said Mr. Dave. "I see."

Sunny tried to sit down in one of the chairs in the lobby, but Mr. Dave asked her to follow him deeper into the building, into his office, where there were better chairs.

The psychiatrist was there already. She had long gray hair, parted down the middle, making a curtain around her oversized glasses, her dark pink mouth, her lined cheeks. She closed a file she was holding open in her lap, and stood up. She smiled a big yellow smile and stuck out a hand.

"You know Miss Mary," said Mr. Dave.

"I'm so happy to see you again, Mrs. Mann," said the psychiatrist. "I've had such an interesting time talking to your son, Robert."

"We call him 'Bubber.' Where is Bubber?"

"He is still back with Miss Tanya," said Mr. Dave. "They're having some extra art time so we can have our meeting."

"I wasn't aware he was being tested again," said Sunny. "I didn't realize you could do that without telling me."

"It's okay," said Mr. Dave. "We just wanted to get a good look at what was going on with Bubber before we decided what was best for him."

"And what is going on with Bubber?"

"Won't you sit down?" Miss Mary invited her to join them at the desk. She held out a sheet of paper to Sunny. "Mrs. Mann, I asked

Bubber to draw me a picture of his favorite pet today, and this is what he gave me."

The drawing was definitely Rocks the dog, done in pen and ink. He was black-and-white, with a squashed-up nose, pointing bat ears, no tail. The drawing was childish, with simple lines and exaggerations. However, it was as if the dog's skin were invisible, and all the organs inside the dog had also been drawn in, too, also in childish lines and exaggerations, but with no system left unrepresented, including the lymphatic. Organs were overlapped and blood vessels ran from point to point. Each one was clearly labeled, all names spelled rigorously according to phonetic logic. The dog had produced a dialogue bubble, and inside were the words "Bow wow."

Miss Mary handed Sunny another sheet. "Here's one he gave me, when I asked him to draw Mommy."

Sunny took the next sheet. There was a tiny stick person in one corner with an obligatory scoop of hair on each side of its head, a triangle to represent a skirt, and a label: Mommy. The entire rest of the page was filled up with something that looked like a map overlaid with a topographical drawing. There were buildings, farms, and many, many tiny trucks along the roads that radiated from the buildings to the farms. All was done in a quick, infantile scrawl, but the details were all there. Every wheel of the trucks, and the cargo was varied. A pig, a stack of sacks, a strange machine. Labels. Parenthetical explanations. Signs.

"He sees me with hair," said Sunny. She was awestruck. She thought how her mother would feel about this. Would a grandmother feel disappointment, resignation? Would she say that it was as if all her efforts with Sunny had been in vain? In the mind of the grandchild, the daughter had a wig on. Had she failed as a mother? She remembered the second terrible thing she had said to Maxon on the day before he went into space: *My mother never thought you would make a husband. You and your goddamned robots. She told me not to marry you, and look at us now. We'll never be right. None of us.*

"Well," said the psychiatrist, taking the papers back from Sunny's hand, "our school is full of children with special talents, but clearly Bubber is some kind of a savant. A four-year-old just doesn't draw pictures like that."

"Ah, savant," said Sunny. "But surely that's not a problem. So, you must have something else?"

"Well, here's the last one," said Miss Mary, holding up a sheet for them all to look at together. "Here I asked him to draw his friends."

On the paper was a hexagon. On each of the points was a circle with a capital letter inside. The points were connected around the outside, and also through the center, some of them. The different connecting lines were of different widths. Next to some of them were numbers, or letters. There were rows of letters separated by commas. Some points were not connected to each other. Down at the bottom were different names followed by a list of Xs. Ben XX. Sarah XXXXX. Jacob X. Zoe XXXX. Sam XXX. Like that. It reminded Sunny of a lot of the work that Bubber had done on his own with ciphers. He was always coming up with his own way of writing things down.

"What is this?" said Miss Mary, pointing to the hexagon.

"Well, I don't know," said Sunny, "but if I had to guess I'd say he has six friends, and these lines and symbols depict the way they are related to each other. Or, maybe he has five friends and he's this one here, connected to all five. Yes, this circle has a B on it."

"But you can see what I mean," said Miss Mary.

"What do you mean?"

"You have this," Miss Mary waved her hand at the papers she

had produced, "and then you have his auditory response scores, which are like that of a deaf child."

"He's not deaf," said Sunny.

"No, he's not deaf, but he still can't hear. He can't respond. He doesn't answer. He screams if he can't have the chair he wants, even if the chairs are all blue. Even if the pencils are all red, he screams if he can't have the one he wants. Yesterday he threw Miss Kim's coffee mug on the floor and shattered it. She was afraid! Bubber's behavior is outside the range of what we are prepared to deal with—and—"

Mr. Dave interrupted her. "Mrs. Mann," he said, "we all just love Bubber. He is really the most remarkable child."

"Obviously he does know their names," Sunny said. "Or at least the letter their names begin with."

"We have tried to tell you, Mrs. Mann, that Bubber needs a higher level of intervention. Bubber is so special. Your doctors—"

"They're not all the same color blue, though," said Sunny. "And the pencils are not all the same length. He perceives differences that other children don't perceive. That's all. You want him on more drugs? Is that it? He's already on Adderall, Dexedrine . . . The only thing left is . . ."

"Haldol," suggested Mr. Dave in the mildest tone, as if he had been offering sailing as a pastime for a sunny afternoon.

"Your husband is an engineer?" asked Miss Mary.

"He's an astronaut," said Sunny. Not entirely true.

"Well, technology," said Mr. Dave.

"So?"

"Just another piece of the puzzle," said Miss Mary.

Sunny remembered the final terrible thing she had said to Maxon on the day before he went into space: *It is all your fault, him being this way. It's you. You fucked up. You did it! It's your fucking genes, your brain, it's like little baby Maxon all over again. Tell me you don't see it. Tell me you don't see yourself when you look at him. You did this. You did this to our child, it's who you are, you're all over him. Now show me a facial expression that goes along with that information.*

"Miss Mary, I want to thank you for your input," said Mr. Dave. "And now I need a chance to speak to Mrs. Mann."

Miss Mary went out, leaving the drawings on the desk. Sunny picked them up. Then they were alone, she and Mr. Dave. Just two bald people talking over their options. In the next room, a small boy with a bright shock of orange hair sticking straight up out of his head was pushing a paintbrush around on a piece of paper, monitored by a blonde in her forties with pigtails.

"Mrs. Mann," said Mr. Dave, "we would like to work with you here. We can change Bubber's therapy schedule, take more time for him to be one-on-one with the teachers. But I need you to talk to your doctors and refocus your medications. It's time."

Sunny stood up. She could feel her teeth wanting to grind each other into powder.

"Where is my child?" she said.

When Mr. Dave brought Bubber out into the lobby, he was jumping on one leg.

"MOMMY," he called, and leaped into her arms. "Top came off."

She squatted down to catch him, and he rubbed his little hand casually over her head. She took the watercolor he had been working on. It was still dripping. She could see a rocket and the labels and words he had tried to form with the too-fat brush, bleeding into each other. "Rocket," he said, too loud. She squeezed him hard and, as pregnant as she was, she picked him up, and his little backpack, and carried him out of there. She thought to herself, *We will never return here. We will find another school, one that appreciates the lunatic labels and has the right length of blue pencils. Even if we have to go to the moon.*

A week ago, a day ago, with blond waves touching her shoulders and curling around her ears, she would have stopped at the desk, bent over at the waist, arranged another appointment. She would have acquired a different small brown bottle, administered doses, continued to smile and drop off and pick up and accommodate and advance. She would have gone home, would have prompted her gangly husband with the appropriate things to say and do at a cocktail party, dressed him, impressed on him the importance of sticking to the basics. Now, she felt differently about everything. More impatient, more severe. She felt she had been living under clouds, underwater, hearing at low volume, seeing at a distance. Without the wig, what she saw was all very awful. Yes, the whole world. There just wasn't any point in pretending that it was fine. She felt like shit for talking so harshly to Maxon. She wished for any way that she could take it all back.

8
*

SHE TRIED TO SEE THE WORLD AS BUBBER SAW IT. EV-
ery road sign, billboard, every marker of a store, house, or car, was
a grouping of letters and numbers. What did he see in these small
collections? Did they jump out at him, letter by letter, like orange
butterflies or like speeding bullets? Were they rainbows glimmering
or were they strobe lights illuminating his brain? Did they look like
harp strings sound? Looking straight at all the letters, everywhere
they showed up, could get overwhelming for anyone. She wondered
if Bubber would ask to live a different life, if he could. If Bubber
would change himself in any way, given the choice. Or if he would
come off the pill bottle and be crazyass Bubber who rocks and sings.

A child like Bubber could read like another child could hear, as beautifully and as involuntarily. Everything he read, he remembered. Very simple. Very elegant. It was a strange genetic thing, or it had happened to him when he was a baby. It was curable with pills, or it wasn't. It was autism, or it was something else that everyone was calling autism. It was nothing ever before seen on Earth, so special, so new. Sunny felt responsible, and sorry, but also secretly she felt dark and proud. Maybe there were no societies for this, and no awareness. Maybe there was no annual fund-raiser. This was a human child with a brain confined in a blue helmet. She would never write another invitation to a silent auction. She would never keep another appointment with a doctor. She wouldn't be so dumb and hairy as that.

YEARS AGO, WHEN SHE was still without children, Sunny had also been wigless. She hadn't even considered putting on a wig. It was not the way she was raised, to put wigs on her head. She went through school, through college, living on Earth, without gluing eyelashes onto her face, without sticking on two eyebrows. Her mother said that putting on a wig would be equivalent to wearing a clown suit. In junior high school, when everyone has at least one moment of weakness, she cried and asked for a wig. Her mother asked if she would also like some big red shoes, a squirting flower, and a beeper nose. Would she like a tiny car, a farting pillow, and a yappy dog. She said no. She was a bald high-school valedictorian.

Later, in college, her bald head gave her an idea for an interesting wig that she wanted to make. She began designing wigs for other people. Art wigs, not meant to cover hair loss, or simulate hair. A silver battleship, constructed of foil squares, each a millimeter bigger than its neighbor. A tiger head built with copper wire. A bouquet of fractal flowers. A pi symbol of feathers. Some people called them hats, but to Sunny, they were wigs, and that's what she called them. She was the bald wigmaker. It was a great thing. She had a show at a college gallery. Her wigs were light and comfortable, but she never wore them. It would be like trying to tickle herself. No one can tickle themselves. It doesn't work. She went to college for math and art. She married Maxon. Still no wigs. Then one day Maxon had decided they should have a baby.

"The time is right for us to have a baby," he said.

The two of them sat together on the public beach in Evanston, one soft spring afternoon. A warm breeze ruffled Lake Michigan but did not stir the sand. A perfect day to lie down flat and let your knees relax, let your belly get warm. Sunny wore a mint green bikini. Maxon wore a holey T-shirt and brown cargo shorts, and sat cross-legged next to her. Sunny unfolded herself all the way from one end of the beach towel to the other, her long limbs stretching out and exposing the undersides of their joints. The ties of the bikini made square knots, not bows. Her sunglasses were two big circles, joined at her nose. Above them, the white dome of her bald head rose, shining with sunblock. She had been doing manikin poses, which always made Maxon smile.

"I don't wanna," Sunny drawled. "Don't make me, you mean man."

"That's an inappropriate response to my statement. That response corresponds with my asking you to clean out the car," said Maxon. "In this case, you can't just not wanna."

"I don't wanna do that either. Stop talking about it."

She reached up and patted his back, rubbing her hand back and forth over the spine where it stuck out in a row of bones.

"It's time to have a baby," said Maxon. "I want us to have one. And I think you should listen to me."

"Imagine me," said Sunny, tracing an imaginary lump in her belly with both hands, "with a big white hill right here."

"You have a big white hill right here already," said Maxon, tap-

ping her on the skull with one poking finger. "Maybe you can ges-
tate the baby in your head."

Sunny rolled luxuriously onto her belly and exposed her back to
the sky. "Can you imagine what kind of freak baby would crawl out
of there," she asked him lazily. "Do you really want to unleash that
on the world?"

AT FIRST SUNNY BASED her reluctance on arithmetic. They sat
in their apartment in Chicago, rolling around their office in their office chairs. The office was the biggest room in the place, with huge
industrial windows all along one side. In it, a dehumidifier hummed
and dead plants turned to dust. Maxon brought home plants from
time to time, under the impression that house plants were a thing
that apartments were supposed to have. Sunny surreptitiously killed
them with cleaning products, or encouraged the cat to use them as
urinals. Once, she killed a medium-sized orange tree in the den. It
took a long time to die, and then it stayed there, dead, for six months.
Sunny didn't like house plants, back then. She thought plants should
be outside where the dirt is. Later, she realized that you have to have
plants. But this was back then, before that kind of realization started
happening to her.

"One plus one equals not three," said Sunny, rolling back and
forth with her heels stuck on the gouged hardwood. "One plus one
equals two. You, and me. Two. One plus one equals two."

"Oh, for goddamn hell, spread your legs, woman," said Maxon,
of course joking. He was using his joking voice. In his hands he had
a metal puzzle and he was working it, unworking it, working it, and
unworking it.

"I will immediately spread, and I mean wide, if you can show me
a system where one plus one equals three."

"It doesn't," said Maxon. "But what about this?"

He whipped out a marker, went over to the whiteboard, and drew two points with a line between them. He was wearing painter's pants, low-slung on his hips, and a white T-shirt with faded black cuffs, a worn university logo over his wide and concave chest.

$$S \text{———} m$$

"Here is we," he said. "You and me. And our great relationship."

"Wonderful," said Sunny. "Label me."

Maxon labeled her point with an S.

"No, I'm not S anymore, I'm W. Wife."

Maxon used his fist to erase, and changed the label. He labeled himself H for husband.

$$W \text{———} H$$

"Now here," said Maxon, placing another point on the line half-way between W and H, "is where we germinate the baby. Right here."

"So the baby is going to come between us. Great. Why did you want a baby again?"

"Because babies are what's supposed to happen now. It's what humans do next."

"So you say."

"Wait," said Maxon. "Watch. Watch. Here's our two points, but we have to push them together. Push, push, push, you know, pushing?"

"I'm familiar," said Sunny.

"And as we come together, this little baby point moves out, gets squished down, perpendicular, to form . . . a . . . triangle."

Maxon finished drawing the new diagram, with W and H and the new point, C, in a triangle shape, and lines connecting W and H to C.

"Now look at this," said Maxon, connecting W to H again. "Closer than ever."

"Two times closer," said Sunny.

"Ready now?"

"No."

She took his marker out of his hand and pushed him into a chair. Slinky, sleek, in a red dress with an elastic top that brushed the floor. She drew another triangle, this one labeled M, F, and C, then drew an arrow from one triangle to another.

"How do we get here from there?" she asked. "Mother, father, child. How do we get there?"

"I think you should start with husband over wife," he suggested.

"Why is it H over W? Why not W over H?" she asked.

"You don't inseminate a wife with the wife on top. The wife has to be on the bottom."

"So, H over W equals F over M?"

"Yes. We have solved everything."

"It can't be that simple."

"Really, it is that simple," said Maxon. "That's why so many stupid people can do it."

"Gosh, wait. No, there is a problem. It's not that, what you're thinking it is, but there is something else missing. Something significant." Now she used her fist to erase some of what she had written, then wrote down:

$$\frac{H}{W + H_1} = \frac{F}{M}$$

"W plus what?"

"You will see," she said grimly. "You will see."

First, she made Maxon start growing his hair out. He had been shaving it for years. Now, she made him not shave it. It started growing in. Sunny pondered it, scrubbed her hands over it, tugged on it, fluffed it up. In the morning, she rolled her office chair over to sit in front of him, and put their foreheads together. She rubbed her head against his, feeling the hair coming in. They had always played this game, where they rotated their office chairs around their heads, as if bound together, as if conjoined twins, their chairs as black plastic moons, their heads in the center, Maxon's hand behind her skull, her hand behind his, until she got dizzy and was laughing too hard. But now she didn't laugh. Because his hair prickled her. She thought how it must be like growing grass out of your skin, like growing cornstalks. It must be sort of terrible. A dirt you could never get clean. An infestation. A problem. She and Maxon did silly things like that.

Like kids do. She thought that when she and Maxon had hair and were parents they would not play their chair-spinning game. They would have to mind their cornstalks, keep on feeling them and brushing them down.

When Maxon's thick golden-brown hair was one inch long and beginning to curl over his forehead, she knew she was ovulating. She drove to the wig store and bought a wig. The purchase of her first wig was a moment she had anticipated since she was old enough to realize she was bald and a wig would hide that. She dreamed of walking around in a crowd, unnoticed. She thought about herself sitting on a bench in a row of other people, all with their knees along the same line, all with their heads reaching the same point on the wall behind the bench, all identical. Sunny would have to look hard at her own eyes to identify which body was hers. Yet when she stood there in the wig store, she felt a little bit upset. She knew that her mother would be angry with her, if she knew about this. She knew her mother would say she was being a fool. Of all the kind and encouraging things that had been said to her over the long bald years, the one she remembered most was her mother's praise: You are who you are, Sunny. You are who you are. And I'm proud of you. Everything about you is part of you. It is all part of Sunny.

In the wig store, there was no explanation needed. Walking into a wig store as a bald person, there is only one thing you can possibly want to buy. It is not a hat. It is not a scarf. It is a wig. Sunny chose a blond wig of long straight hair, because it looked the most like the kind a kindergarten teacher might choose. It looked like the hair that could be found on the mother of a little baby. Everyone thought that she wanted to put on the wig right away and go out of the store with it on. But no. She did that later. First, she had one more drive down the street, one more walk down the sidewalk, wearing only her own head. One more hop and skip up the stairs to their big apartment. Then she got into her bedroom, and shut out the light, took off all her regular clothes, and fitted the wig on her head. When she turned the light back on, the wig was in place. After that, she wore the wig. She could see it on her head if she looked in a mirror.

Maxon came home from a bike ride, with hair all over himself, as she had directed, and he was surprised to see her. She was still naked, just her and the wig, waiting for him. He stood in the bedroom doorway, filling it. He was sweating, tall and tight in his Lycra, holding his helmet. He put one hand out to each side, as if she were a wave breaking over him, all her nakedness, all her new hair.

"What are you doing?"

"I'm waiting to be inseminated."

"Why are you wearing a wig?" he asked.

"So that it will work."

"H_I is hair?"

"Yes."

"That's incorrect. You don't have to wear a wig. Why would you have to wear a wig?"

"Fine, then, let's just fuck and then we'll throw the wig away later."

"Let me get in the shower."

Later, though, they did not throw the wig away. Maxon tried to reason her out of it, but she was crouched on the edge of her office chair, all folded up with the semen inside her and the wig falling down all around. It felt good and interesting, tickling her.

Maxon was clicking around on his computer. He gave her a measuring glance.

"Sunny, you don't have to wear a wig to be a mother. It's been proven. Your reproductive system is quite separate from your skin."

"You don't know anything about it," said Sunny. "What on earth could you possibly know about what I need to do to be a mother?"

Sunny pulled the wig hair around her like a cloak. It was a gesture she had never made in all her long happy life. Now she did it reflexively, as if the potential for it produced an actuality. Maxon saw her do it. Maybe he should feel a little bit ashamed. Ashamed of his part in the whole affair, the way he had put the wig on her head, had tied the apron around her waist. For the way the world changed when a baby went inside. For the ball he had kicked off the top of the hill, which was now bouncing down, out of control, beyond recall. Most likely, he did not feel shame. He just knew that this is what humans do, and that's all he knew. No doubt, no regret. She could feel her body changing, under the wig, into a correct shape for fitting into a nice young family. She could feel her variable shift from W to M. From then on, she would walk differently, talk differently, put aside all harmful things. She would protect what living thing was trying to form itself inside her.

There was a large round egg in a tiny tube, and there were little swimmers trying to get into it. Up here, up here, and then down there, down there, pushing and driving. Within three hours, they connected. The egg floated down through her and got itself stuck to the uterine wall. It changed cells, grew into a living shape. It made arms, legs, and kidneys. It formed the soft bones of an infant skull. Skin formed in the dark. In the dark, the tissue of the heart convulsed. On top of that, one magical night, when Sunny's wig was most fully brushed, most fully arranged, most completely and rigorously in place, the top of the fetus burst out in glorious hair, bright as a comet, orange as a Southern sunset. And eventually the baby came out of her and was Bubber. And he was, to her, perfect. He was a little Maxon. It was true.

9.
*

MAXON SLEPT FITFULLY THROUGH THE LONG DARK
night, strapped into his bunk. The spaceship turned as it hurtled
toward the moon, following a lazy arc along its trajectory. He dreamed
he was standing in a hole, and unable to stretch. He dreamed he
was back in the well. He squeezed his eyes shut, feeling his esoph-
agus closing and his tongue swelling. He dreamed he was in that
damp pipe, with his arms clamped up to his sides. He wanted to
throw out his hands and scrape his elbows against the sides, spin
and slash at the walls of it, but he would wake up and there would
be no stone walls, because he was on a rocket. He was not claustrophobic, because this was a fact. He was not afraid of enclosed spaces
because he was not claustrophobic. A tautology of nightmares. Finally,

he knew it was morning for him because the lights in the compartment turned on.

He looked at his watch. What did time mean, en route to the moon? What did the rotation of the Earth mean, apart from a navigational consideration, apart from the physics? What did it mean, to the cycling consciousness of the human body, that the Earth had rotated, somewhere far away, without his feet on it, without his body, prone, asleep on it, stretching over the bottom of any bed he'd ever lain in, his feet always spilling out, his head always butting against the wall.

For a man so long, restraint was essential. He was always bumping into things. Maxon's fuse was long, too, his temper even longer than his legs. There had been times when his limit had been breached, and his ability to tolerate the little clinks and rattles when his limbs bumped into knickknacks was the first thing to go. In the house where he grew up, for example, there were so many things. So many piles, shelves stacked high with papers, jars, shoeboxes, empty cans, lumps of fishing tackle, scraps of leather, and the filth and detritus of a house full of boys. So in their house Sunny and Maxon didn't keep decorations on the surfaces. They were smooth and clean, a candle here and a bouquet of eucalyptus there, brutally arranged by Maxon for minimal clutter, just enough to keep them looking like they lived in a proper home. When they were first married, Sunny didn't care. She had no feelings about what things should be on counters or tables. It didn't matter to her.

When they moved to Virginia she started making changes in the arrangements, asked that he rotate them by seasons. She had bought an antique clock, put it not equidistant between two candles. There were other purchases, and contractors coming in to work. He knew that this was the time she started caring about the house. This was the time she became different, when they moved to Virginia so he could have the lab at Langley. When they, together, made the boy.

He had written in his notebook during the night. He looked down and saw that he had written the words "Sunny's great disappointments:" and then underneath he had made three strong bullets. Beside the first was "Me" and then "My behavior." Then finally, "My genetic material." He saw the words "Sunny said:" and then three more bullets underneath. He wrote "Why can't you just be a normal fucking human being?" and "It is all your fault that Bubber is how he is" and "I hate my mother for being right, but she *was* right. She was right!"

Maxon knew that elsewhere in his notebook was a page that said this:

```
String COMPLIMENT = "How nice of
          you to say so.";
String GRATITUDE = "Thank you
          for letting me know,";

if (OPINION = COMPLIMENT)
     return COMPLIMENT;
else if (OPINION = CRITICISM)
     return GRATITUDE;
else
     WriteToMemory (OPINION);
```

"Thank you for letting me know," he said to Sunny's words. And without any further hesitation, he turned the page, smoothed out the fresh sheet, and began the day of work. He considered the mother, her smooth golden head, her dour pronouncements, her long illness, but then he tried to put the image right out of his head.

SHE DROVE TO THE YMCA and put Bubber into his swim trunks, because this is what they did after preschool on Tuesdays and Thursdays. Bubber's schedule was sacred, like a litany, helping him fit into the world. He danced from foot to foot in the changing room, his hand on the door, waiting for her to come along. The pool had an L shape, shallow in the bottom part and deep on the long part for laps. Bubber's goggles were bright green and his trunks had bugs all over them, red and yellow. When she came along, finally, he flopped into the pool without looking back at her, without noticing, immediately engaged in his own world. Sunny could smell the chlorine, see the rust around the drains, and there was a crippled man in the hot tub, his face pinched and persevering. She had looked into the wide mirrors of the YMCA changing room. Under the fluorescent light her head looked pointier, more gray.

She stood in her skirted maternity bathing suit on the wheelchair ramp that wound down into the pool. Her giant belly pressed against the railing. This is where she always stood. The YMCA rule said a parent had to stay within arm's length from a child this small. So, there she was. Bubber was a freakishly good swimmer, and he always had been. He had never been afraid, even for a moment, of drowning. In fact, when he was even smaller, he'd walked right off the side of the pool, scaring everyone. Eventually he'd worked out swimming, and now he was an expert. There was never any stimming in the water. Never any banging or shrieking. So they came here twice a week.

Normally, with her wig on, she stood on the ramp, not putting her head in the water. Today, if she wanted to, she could go all the way down, down to the bottom of the pool. She tilted her white head down to look at Bubber. He had a small plastic frog. The frog was jumping on and off a small swim float, assisted by Bubber. There were noises to go with the jumps, something that sounded like rewinding a tape. It jumped on and off many, many times. It looked like he would never get tired of playing with the frog. Sunny's skin was cold because she was standing under one of the giant vents in the air-circulating pipes. Her head was very cold. In fact, she froze.

Maybe, without a wig, she was a mother who would plunge into the water, feeling it rush warm and cool around her, holding her up. Or maybe at this point in her motherhood, at this advanced state of habitual wig-wearing, Sunny had written onto her flesh the true purpose of her life at that moment, which was just to shut up and watch over the child. The child enjoyed the water, and Sunny only had to stand here and make sure he didn't die. This was her default position. She stood in the mommy body in the mommy spot. All she had to do, at that recurring moment from about one o'clock until about two o'clock on Tuesday and Thursday, was to tend the child. Did she have to be comfortable at this time? No. Did she have to enjoy the water? No. There were many times in her life when she had been comfortable and had enjoyed water. Now was a time when she was protecting her child and promoted his happiness as the pool enriched his life and developed his mind and body. So why cloud that with her comfort or discomfort? Wig or no wig. This is what she told herself, to prevent herself falling into the water, going deep down, playing with her own feet, looking at the lights.

She was reminded of a time in her life before anyone had looked at her to consider if she would make a great wife and mother. Then it had been lots of fun on the beach. She glided along the hot sand in a string bikini, walking as if she'd invented legs, head greased with coconut oil, floppy hat dangling from one hand. She swam like a dolphin, no swim cap, no tangle of hair around her goggles. Those were good times, but who really cares? There are people walking around with no limbs, or whose children have fallen out of buildings and died, or people who can't come to the YMCA because they live in some godforsaken rural hellhole. She never knew, before she had a child, the concern she would feel for him. She felt real actual concern.

Sunny had taken swimming lessons as a child. Her mother believed every child should learn to swim, ride a horse, and play the piano. What had occupied her mother's mind during those long lesson hours? When Sunny had been straining to tread water for three minutes, getting her skinny ass hollered at by the big high-school swimming coach. Was her mother sitting there? She couldn't remember. Thinking about her? Comparing her, to her extreme disadvantage, to the other swimmers? Maybe her mother was thinking, *That's my daughter. The bald one.* Emma had been a diver. Had spoken French. Had graduated at the top of her class. Sunny had been a lazy swimmer, prone to spells of floating and underwater drifting. She had spoken very poor German, had majored in something her mother found incomprehensible.

Emma hadn't wanted Sunny to wear the wig, but the wig made Sunny aspire to so much more. Mostly she aspired to raise a fine set of children, noble children, normal children. In her wig, she looked just like a woman. Without her wig, she looked like something else. She wondered if she, given the choice, would ask to live a different life. If she would change anything about herself, given a magic bottle of pills. What if the hair could come growing in like everyone else's hair, in stalks and clumps, pushing its way out of her skin to stick up into the air, be pulled and teased. Would she welcome this hair? What would Maxon say if he came home from space and found that she had grown in a full head of hair? What would he say when he came home from space and found she had abandoned her wigs?

Bubber was now playing wild horse and calm horse in the swimming pool. When Maxon was here, Bubber had played this game with his father. Bubber sat astride his swimming noodle and his father holding both ends propelled the horse boldly up and down and all around (wild horse) or in a smooth circle (calm horse). Now Bubber played a more sedate version alone. A child playing with its father screams louder, laughs harder, jumps more eagerly, puts more faith in everything. A child playing by himself is hearing an internal dialogue, and has a listening look, even when shrieking.

"I'm playing wild horse and calm horse," said Bubber loudly to a nearby child who didn't understand what he was saying. *That's what it's like to be Bubber,* thought Sunny. *No one understands him. He needs more drugs. Or less. Maybe he needs a whole lot less.*

With Maxon there, things would be different. They would be playing games on their computers, side by side. They would be going out to dinner to the only place where Bubber could sit still in public. He would pilot them around the city in the car. He would take off the wig, put on the wig, turn the wig into a swan, put the wig on a fence post and pretend to address it. But Maxon was up in space, floating like a man underwater, his limbs loose and swirling. Maybe she would plunge into eight feet of water and turn somersaults, somersaults, eight, nine, ten of them, until she was surging to the surface, her head emerging like a melon. And maybe he would circle around her, like a watchful pike. Everything about them smooth and slick, no growths waving about, no drag on their skin. They would ring each other, slide in and out of each other, all without touching the ground. This is how she pictured Maxon in his spaceship, and herself in the deep end of the pool.

Looking down on the tiles of the wheelchair ramp, she noted a little blob of something. The little blob was red and gelatinous and it drifted around at the brink of the water on the slope of the wheelchair ramp, within easy reach of anyone's baby. Sunny imagined that just today some other mother, standing here guarding her other toddler, had expelled a lump of something from her before it could become another baby. It had stayed there on the blue cold tiles, like a corpse on a lonely beach, and that other mother walked away from it because she didn't want to spend any more afternoons standing cold ankle-deep in water, and she hadn't even cleaned it up, because she was that mad.

10.

WHEN SUNNY GOT TO THE HOSPITAL TO VISIT HER mother that day, she saw things differently than she had the day before. Yesterday, it had been all beautiful, where her mother was sleeping. Now it was not beautiful at all. She parked in the visitor lot, next to the familiar red brick building. It had looked like a castle before; now it looked like a prison. The day burned around her as she walked down the hallways of the hospital with Bubber clutched firmly by one hand. Her hips swiveled around her pregnant belly and everything inside it. The halls smelled of chicken broth, urine, and disinfectant. Doors opened and closed with a hissing sound. Humans walked like androids in purple scrubs. They shuffled around in booties. They rotted on their walkers, on their gurneys. Everything happens in a hospital: the birth, the life, the death. But no one wants to be in a hospital, where everything happens. They just want to get out.

On the way into the ICU, Sunny had to pass a lot of shuffling walkers. Go by a lot of gum-chewing nurse's aides. Everywhere she went, bloated faces, white and paunchy, turned toward Sunny like moons coming into view. One minute she could see the person's ear, hair, or the back of their heads. The next minute she could see their flat faces, then their faces with eyes a little wider open. Some people smiled politely. She remembered how it felt to be mistaken for a cancer patient. People's pity and fear running all around her like photons.

At the doors of the ICU she had to push a button and talk to the nurse to get in.

"I'm here to see my mother, Emma Butcher," she said. Her voice sounded just like it usually sounded. It went into the little microphone just as usual.

The doors hissed open and immediately began to close again, so Sunny and Bubber had to hustle through. Inside, there was a dry, cold smell. The rooms of the ICU radiated in a semicircle around the nurse's station, curved around the white floor like glass boxes in a row. Sunny began to cross over to her mother's room, and a nurse said, "Mrs. Mann?" Sunny nodded at her, turning to face her. A young nurse with a brown ponytail. The nametag said her name was Sharon. The woman recognized Bubber and the pregnancy, but she had not known Sunny without the wig. She waved Sunny on. "Sorry," she said, "I didn't know."

Sunny and Bubber held hands as they went through the glass door. Bubber's other hand was snapping and snapping. How would her mother feel about seeing Sunny with no wig on? Would she sit up in the bed, throw back the covers, and cheer?

The robots were breathing for her mother. One clicked up and down with an accordion inside, pumping in the air and sucking it back out. One swished the liquids in and out of her, good in, bad out, in murky plastic tubes and containers. All around the room, there were these machines in clumps. It was dark and she could see their monitors and dials lit up. On the floor were a couple of old Band-Aids, pulled off an IV site. On the walls, peeling masking tape held up drawings and pictures of Bubber. They were everywhere, on the paper-towel holder over the sink, on the breathing machine, all stuck up with this yellowing tape, all askew.

Then there was her mother, on the bed. Always a tall lady, her mother had shrunk and twisted down. Her spine curled. Her head was hanging off to the side on the pillow, where the breathing tube was inside her mouth, and a large sore had formed on that side of her face. Someone had covered the sore with Vaseline, but it was still red. Most of her hair was gone, and the rest was brushed into comb rows. Her mother's eyes were closed. Her chest went up and down. Her hands and feet were swollen, puffed balloons of yellowed spotted skin. Sunny put her hand on one of her mother's hands, and it was cold. She rearranged the blankets on her body. The body looked like it had already begun to decompose, and yet breath and fluid was being rushed into it by the machines, and taken back out. Life was being simulated. A pinch would produce a pain response.

Sunny sat down in the chair next to the bed where she habitually sat. Bubber climbed up on the bed where he habitually climbed, and sat still with his book. As her mother had gone from her own home, to Sunny's home, to the ER, to the ward, to the ICU, Bubber and Sunny had sat next to or on top of this or that bed, watching the journey like tourists on a boat ride, looking at alligators. Now Sunny stood on the riverbank, up to her knees in sucking mud, watching the gators gnawing their prey. She hadn't done anything but watch those gators for two weeks. What kind of monster watches an alligator eat her mother, and does nothing but click her teeth together?

She started to cry. Once her mother had said to her, "Sunny, whatever happens, I am on your side. I will always be on your side. No matter what." Now her mother lay in this situation, so twisted and with her insides falling apart.

WHEN SUNNY WAS LITTLE, she'd had a pony. The pony was rotten and naughty, but Sunny had fallen in love with him the way an eight-year-old girl does with a horse, and there was no other pony that would please her. His name was Pocket, and he was adorable, a bright bay with a white star on his forehead. Unbridled, he was as sweet as a lapdog, and followed Sunny around their farm, batting his eyes. She could even sit on him and propel him with her knees and a soft lead rope, and he never fought. However, when Sunny tried to ride him with a saddle and bridle, he became a pony of nightmares. He acted as if there were burrs under the girth and daggers under the saddle. He would flatten his ears and mince along angrily, and sometimes pop up his head unexpectedly, several times flipping his nose all the way up and hitting Sunny in the face with his poll, the bony bump horses have on the top of their heads.

Sunny was convinced he was in pain, so they dragged Pocket through expensive and lengthy visits from every veterinarian in the area. The last vet finally told her mother that the horse was just smart, and strong, and had decided not to be ridden. He would have to be broken of this behavior. In the vet's opinion, he was not suitable for a child. Sunny remembered pleading with her mother that she couldn't bear to hurt Pocket, that it would stifle his spirit. Heavy with prepubescent emotion inspired by *Black Beauty* and other fictional accounts of horse abuse, she swore she would never forgive her mother if she sold him or hurt him. She would just ride him bareback, and not worry about showing or the rest of it.

They had a little riding ring on the property, dug out of the meadow, fenced and spread with cedar chips, and her mother told her, after that final vet left the farm on that day, to saddle Pocket and meet her in the riding ring. When Sunny arrived there, walking beside her pony, she saw her mother holding a bat. Her pale face was grim, her long golden hair wound into a braid, and she was wearing pants, something she rarely did.

"You can't ride!" said Sunny.

"Of course I can. I was alive before you, you know."

"What are you going to do?"

"Give me that pony," said her mother.

"No!" cried Sunny. "You're going to kill him!"

"If he dies, it will be his choice," intoned this fierce, pants-wearing woman. Sunny shrank from her.

Her mother snatched the reins from Sunny's hands and sprang up into the saddle with surprising agility for someone who Sunny had never seen voluntarily come near a horse. Pocket was a big pony but her mother was still taller, so the pair made a ridiculous sight. She spun around and trotted through the gate of the riding ring. She called to Sunny, "Shut the gate."

Around and around went Pocket, trotting tensely. Her mother kept the reins in one hand, and held the bat in the other, ready to do anything with it—Sunny had no idea what. Her mother posted cautiously, almost crouched in the saddle, and the pony seemed unwilling to misbehave. She asked him to slow to a walk and then cued him to canter. At this offense, Pocket lost his concentration, pinned his ears back, and began to swing his head.

"No," she barked. "No, you may not."

Up came his neck, up came the poll toward Emma's face, and down came the bat, striking him squarely between the ears. Sunny screamed.

The horse's poll is hard if it hits a little girl in the face but it's also a nerve center, and Pocket went down. Her mother pushed away from him as he dropped, and fell to the side, then scrambled over to the prostrate horse, still conscious, and grabbed him by the nose. The bat had rolled into the weeds. She wrung the soft part of his nose in her fist and shouted at him, "Don't you ever hurt that child, don't you ever make her cry, or I will bury you, and your worthless carcass, do you hear me?" With each "ever" she laid a solid punch on his nose right between his nostrils. Sunny was terrified and impressed.

Pocket staggered to his feet.

"Come on, Sunny," her mother called to her. "Your turn."

Sunny silently mounted, put her feet in the stirrups, picked up the reins, and had the safest and most satisfying ride she'd ever had on Pocket. Her mother mounted the fence and sat silently on a fence-post by the gate. From then on, that's where she sat every time Sunny worked that pony. No matter what else was going on, there she was standing watch. Pocket had his moments of disobedience, every now and then, but he never again swung his head up to hit Sunny in the face. And he never regained quite the same degree of haughty nastiness. Periodically, as he was being groomed or bathed, her mother would come past and twist his ear, first gently and then more sharply in her hand. "Does the pony like it here? Does he like his nice home? Does he enjoy being alive? Does the pony know how lucky he is?" And Sunny knew that Pocket never forgot that day when someone took a bat to his head.

Eventually she outgrew Pocket. Her mother bought her a bigger, nicer horse. But her mother never sold him. He lived out his life on the farm. When Sunny went to college, Pocket and Emma missed her together. And when he died, it was a very sad thing.

A COUPLE OF MONTHS ago, Sunny had said the words "Mother, the only thing that's wrong with you would fit into a walnut!" It really didn't seem like anything could be that bad. She had expected to spend a lot more time with her mother, maybe have to find her a retirement home. Maybe visit her on some Caribbean coast. Sunny and her mother had both been misled by a wrong diagnosis. Actually, there were raging tumors loose in her mother, bigger than a walnut. So those months of sneaking pain pills and leaving her weeping in the bathtub, in retrospect, seemed cruel. But before she knew, she had lain down next to her mother in her mother's own bed, and her mother, all full of disease which no one could perceive or understand, had shifted around gently, slowly on her heating pad so she could hold the pregnant Sunny in her arms. "Don't worry," she had said to her mother. "You will be up out of bed tomorrow. It's just this lousy diverticulitis. Step away from the almonds."

In order for Sunny to go on with her life, she knew that her mother had to get better and be alive. But still, in order for Sunny to feel right leaving the hospital today, she felt with new and unfamiliar urgency that her mother had to be allowed to go ahead and die. In terms of everything medical, there was nothing to be done. It was a place of paralysis. She had not allowed herself to see it, but it was real. Sunny felt very alone in this world. The only way she could keep breathing was to stroke Bubber's arm and her mother's arm, together. It was just so awful. If Maxon were here, he would probably lean over her shoulder and say something hideously inappropriate, like, "Do you want to hear a few dead baby jokes?" Then she could move around and slap at him. As it was, she could just sit still and curse him for going up into space at a time like this.

Maxon would never say, "I can't go up into space at a time like this." A schedule had been made, a timetable decided, after all. But he could say, did say, with her so pregnant and her mother in ICU, "Of course you don't need to come and see the launch. It would be unnecessary." And she could say, did say, "Everything is fine, fine, fine."

The doctor came into the room. Her mother's doctor was a small, fat man with a messed-up hand, and he was a bit of a joker. Three of his fingers were fused together, and the whole thing was cragged around like a hook. One of his favorite jokes was to reach his hands up toward the sky and say, "Lord, make my one hand like the other!," and then he would pretend to crag up his other, good hand, just like the fused hooked one. This had been funny during the misdiagnosis of diverticulitis. Not now during the death of cancer.

"Sunny, you've done something new with your hair!" he quipped, picking up her mother's chart from the pocket by the door.

"I have a condition," she snapped.

"Well, that makes two of us," said the doctor.

"I need to take my mother off life support," said Sunny. "Today."

"And what has finally led you to this decision?" asked the doctor, still looking down at the chart.

"Look at her," said Sunny. "She's dying by inches."

"I've been looking at her for weeks now," said the doctor. "You're the one who's been ignoring the obvious."

"I'm sorry," she said. "You're right. You're right."

The doctor turned on his heel and left the room, taking his stupid hand with him. Sunny didn't know if he was coming back, or if anyone would be coming back. She turned to her mother and patted the arm. Her mother was, now, a stranger. A person she had damaged. A person she had held down under the water, forced down into the weeds, and had held there while the eyes bugged out, while the lungs gasped, while the skin pulped up. A person that she, Sunny, could have saved, but didn't. A person she preserved for her own use. Her mother lay like an old puppet in a box. Kept around to say things, to make things come out of her mouth. Sunny, you are wonderful. Sunny, you can do anything. When she was really belonging to another world already, Sunny had been putting staples in her, to tie her to this one.

"I'm sorry," she said to her mother. "I am so sorry."

She leaned against the bed, and put her face down on her mother's taut, cold arm, and she knew in her heart that her mother didn't hold it against her.

There was one time in the past when she had hurled the words "I hate you" at her mother. It was during the time in middle school when she railed against her baldness, fought against it, demanded a wig. In the back of a horse magazine she'd found an advertisement for a cure for baldness—it was targeted at men, of course—but it had jumped off the page as if it were meant just for her. The Orchid Cure was a product made from natural oils and plant extracts, marketed by an Indian doctor, Chandrasekhar. She stabbed the ad with her finger at the dinner table, as her mother serenely and silently watched.

"This is a hoax," said her mother. "There is no cure."

"You don't know!" Sunny yelled, feeling overcome by a rush of heat in her face. "You don't know what I have."

"You need to calm down, dear. There's no point in getting yourself crazy."

"This is what I need," Sunny insisted, thrusting the magazine across the table. "This is meant for me. Why won't you let me try? I'll pay for it with my own money."

Her mother shook her head, wouldn't get mad, wouldn't argue. "It's good to want things, Sunny," she said. "It's even good to need things."

"I hate you!" Sunny had shouted. "I hate you!"

Then she had slammed out of the room, but not before hearing her mother say, "It's even good to hate things."

A nurse came into the room.

"Do you want me to call someone for you?" said the nurse.

"There's no one to call," said Sunny. "My mother is here, my father is dead, and my husband is in space."

The nurse nodded consolingly. "I just have some paperwork for you to sign."

"Are you going to do this right away?" asked Sunny.

"Yes," said the nurse, as if it was obvious.

After the paperwork was signed, she took Bubber to the bathroom. She quietly threw up in the sink, which made Bubber angry, and then she cried some more. She was worried she would have a contraction. She knew that being pregnant and alone on the Earth, and being the mother of Bubber, she would have to be very mechanical about what was happening. She would have to write her name down where it was necessary, and make arrangements that were necessary. She would not be crying, crawling under the bed, walking off into the woods. She knew her mother would want her to do what she could to maintain her equilibrium. She was alone on the Earth, the whole entire Earth. No Maxon anywhere on the planet. A unique situation for her. He might as well have been temporarily dead. If Maxon were here he would do all of this for her and it wouldn't even bother him a bit.

She imagined a box, a box into which she could pack everything that was happening to her and her mother, a box she could lock tightly and open later, or never. She knew she had to put in the wildness of death, and the emptiness of the last hours of life, and the fear of standing before the world without a mediator, because if she kept these things in her hands, she would not be able to keep living, driving, feeding her child, gestating her baby. So she invented the box. It could go under the bed, next to the box that contained her father's death and all of that mystery. Then she could move to a new house, and buy a new bed.

When she got back from the bathroom, the nurse was all ready. There was not a lot to do, to kill the person in the bed, to stop keeping her living. The breathing machine had to be switched off, the tube removed from her mother's throat. The doctor had told her, at another time, that taking the breathing tube out would definitely kill her. They had discussed this all before, when Sunny had been asleep under the wig. Back then, she had felt that the pressing issue was how to get the grass mowed at her mother's house back in Pennsylvania. She had gone home to Maxon saying, She looks better. She'll be home soon. The doctor had urged her. It would be quick, he had said. She hadn't realized that it had been a really urgent situation this whole time.

"You should stand outside the window, where you can protect your boy. Turn his head away," said the nurse. "Sometimes things happen."

What things could happen? Would there be thrashing? Would the body fall off the bed? Would it dance around like a man on the end of a rope? Maybe she would need to run away, out through the hissing door, flying away into the universe. Sunny stepped outside the door, ready to just watch, but that was wrong. She knew she needed one more minute of the heart beating, the brain passing electricity through itself. One more minute before her mother died.

She went rushing back in, pushed the nurse out of the way, and grabbed her mother's swollen hand.

"Mother," she said, "listen."

It might be the last thing she ever got to tell her mother. Her mother would never find out the resolution of the war, she would never know what happened on her favorite shows, she would not be aware if her neighborhood burned to the ground or if Sunny went to jail or if Maxon landed on the moon. She would not be aware if the baby was born or evaporated, wouldn't even know that the baby was a girl. She would say no further words. The last thing Sunny could remember her mother saying to her was that she was a little afraid of her new maid. "There's something wrong with her," her mother had said, "and I can't put my finger on it."

"I lost my wig," Sunny said, leaning down to put her mother's hand on her head. "I took it off, and I'm not going to put it on anymore. I had to tell you that. I'm not going to put it on anymore."

She felt the cold hand slipping around on her head, and there was no grip. There was no electricity. She laid the hand back down and nodded to the nurse. The nurse switched off the machines. Sunny clutched Bubber to her side, and looked over her shoulder. The crab-handed doctor was in the hall. Her mother was on the bed. The nurse removed the breathing tube and a throaty sound came out, like a machine that was grinding down to a stop. But her mother did not die at that very moment. The throat took in a breath and then another. Her mother kept on living. Sunny looked over her shoulder at the doctor. He shook his head. She felt the glass wall between them shatter, explode all over him, keep blowing out through the building, out into the world beyond, as if the room had erupted from the pressure of her packing away everything that was happening into a tight little padlocked box. The doctor shook his head and walked into the room. He took the pulse of her mother.

"She is holding on," said the doctor.

"You're kidding," said Sunny.

"She won't hold on for long," said the doctor.

"I can't stay here," she said. "I have to go."

The doctor gave her a withering glance.

Only Maxon could have understood what she was doing. It was as if there was a waterfall of glass, and only eating the glass would keep it from cutting the baby and Bubber, so she was eating the glass up as fast as she could. She couldn't pause in her glass consumption to explain things to doctors. Her mother was holding on. For now, she was holding on. Her decision, not Sunny's. Her choice. Maybe she would get better after all. Sunny packed the box, full and firm, and took Bubber by the hand.

"Kiss Grandma," she said to Bubber. "We have to go."

"But wait. We'll have to move her to another room," said the nurse. "She can't stay in ICU now."

"Fine, call me," said Sunny. The weight of the whole hospital was resting on her lungs, crushing the baby. She had to leave. She had to walk her legs away, and take her children away. It was a point of motion. After a slingshot has been pulled back far enough, it has to be shot. It cannot stay there forever.

THE MOTHER WAS NOT dying. The mother was living. The mother was thinking. Inside the dark cocoon of her deathy body, there was thinking going on. Weightless, she maneuvered through her memory and what else was inside already. She stayed tethered, always, to a thread of pain and grief that kept on clutching her back into her arms and legs, into her torso where the tumor was eating away. But she remembered everything that she had ever seen. It was just a matter of dragging it up to the top, and shaking it out, and turning it over.

11.

SUNNY'S FIRST MEMORIES WERE OF BURMA. WHEN she was three years old, Sunny and her parents were sitting around the dinner table. In the center of the table was a bowl of fish curry. On another plate was a roasted chicken. Then there was a green tomato salad. The family knelt around the table on blue velvet cushions, and there was a blue cloth spread under the plates. The father stretched his hands out to each side, and her mother and Sunny took hands with each other and with him and he said a blessing over the food. An electric fan in the window sprayed puffs of air and the scent of palms back and forth through the room, ruffling a few loose strands of Emma's hair.

There was a knock on the door. She saw soldiers on the doorstep.

Emma picked up her child and held her aside, out of the way. Nu came and took her then, sheltered her. The father was flustered and pink. Boots came in on the floor. Flies were on the curry. The fan went back and forth. Sunny was afraid. Her mother was still chewing a bite of dinner, swallowing, trying to get it down.

The father had been exposed as a Christian missionary and was immediately taken captive by the military junta. He understood them perfectly when they explained themselves. General Ne Win himself had approved his execution, the soldiers told him. General Ne Win just wanted to do things right. He did not deny that Bob Butcher was a fine scientist. Any who knew him might have volunteered to say that he exhibited nothing but the most excruciating charisma and honor. He never offered any woman his left hand, or touched any man on the top of the head. But the general had to, as he put it, crush all who sought to weaken the union.

But how did it happen these men in gray from over the mountain came again to their door, and penetrated the laboratory, and opened the secret cabinet full of Bibles and hymnals? Who told the tale that led the flat-faced soldiers to take Bob Butcher down to the post office, along with a dusty box of smuggled whiskey which he had attempted to use as a bribe? No one wanted money in Burma. You could bathe yourself in emeralds that you dug from your backyard, but you couldn't eat them, smoke them, or use them to kill your neighbors. Look at the stupas, covered in gold. But no one can get a bus across town. So who cares about the clinking offering of one sweating missionary?

AFTER HER HUSBAND WAS taken away and the door had been slammed in their faces, Emma Butcher's heart raced in her body. She went into their bedroom with her small daughter, holding her by the hand. She took a golden nat, an image of one of the ancient Burmese gods, out of her dresser from underneath her nightgowns. While her daughter watched, she put this nat, The Young Lord of the Swing, into the living room of Sunny's dollhouse in the corner. From a pocket of her robe came a stick of incense, which she lit, hand shaking, and placed in front of the little house. Sunny came to kneel beside her, with Nu. Nu was stern and smiling; she sang a song. They watched the godlet sitting on the little rag mat before his bamboo chairs and table. Sunny ran to the kitchen and came back with a grape. This animism the women of the house had hid from Bob Butcher the way he had hid the Bibles from the Communists. Over her dozen years of service, Nu had taught it to Emma, and Sunny had learned it from the both of them. Everyone sneaking around having their religious ceremonies. Baptism and fruit sacrifice. Communion and incense. Smells and bells.

Emma prayed for blessings and protection. Life went on without her husband. A letter came to them after a week. Bob Butcher was imprisoned in Rangoon and his execution was set to happen in four days. She called Sunny in out of the tea garden and began to pack up the house. She gave Sunny a small linen bag and told her to choose whatever treasures she could fit inside, not too heavy to carry herself. Sunny chose the golden nat and some of her braided hats. A flowering branch from one of the garden trees. The family teapot. Emma packed a few of their clothes and then meticulously gathered all the notes from her husband's research. She filed them all into a leather case with a collection of bottles and vials, and everything that was left she gave to Nu along with a packet of money. Sunny cried when she left her nurse, saying "Nu-nu" over and over. Emma cried, too, and said, "Nu, as soon as I can, I will send for you. Don't worry. We will see each other again." They left the cottage at the bottom of the mountain forever.

They traveled to Mandalay on one seat of a terrible bus, Sunny on her mother's lap, holding her nose and sometimes crying. Emma sat erect, her face without tears. She kept her eyes forward and her mouth quiet, even her tongue. She used a little money to buy them some sour food that they did not like, that Sunny would not eat. She wished she could nurse her daughter again, but Sunny had weaned. It would make her feel better.

They came to Mandalay this way. From the dusty place they stood, on the shore of the Irrawaddy River, it was not beautiful. Kipling notwithstanding, they could see neither the Moulmein Pagoda nor the dawn coming up like thunder. They could hear wind in the palm trees, though, carrying dust along with it, a dry wind that made them thirsty and twirled Emma's hair and the ends of Sunny's head wrap. In the end, they found a way to get down the river, in a ferry piloted by a fat man who traded their journey for Emma's personal Bible. It took ten hours to get to Rangoon.

The triangle sails of the round-bottomed fishing boats made sharp peaks against the horizon. The pointed horns of water buffalo marked where the animals were dragging plows along or wading in the shallow water. Nothing else rose up. Small farming villages hugged the shores of the warm flat river and long teak canoes slipped along, driven by poles or paddles. Emma clutched Sunny to her chest and gripped their bags between her feet. Nearby, an old person sitting in a large basket was lamenting being born a woman. A young monk crouched on his heels under the railing. His head and even his eyebrows had been shaved in an initiation ritual. Emma shuddered. No one could sleep on a boat like this, even on the Irrawaddy River. You couldn't tell a regular monk from a government spy wrapped in an orange blanket.

ANOTHER MEMORY. THEY STOOD, linen bag and leather case in hand, in the square before the elaborate Sula Pagoda in Rangoon.

Sunny could remember the shape of her mother's face, it was so serene. The gold point of the shining pagoda rose up in the center of the building, layer on layer of gold getting smaller up to the very top. Around the central peak was a golden fence and there behind that fence, some people were congregating. The day was hot and Sunny was not well rested. She hung on her mother's hand. She let her head fall back against the top of her shoulders, her neck going slack. At the very peak of the pagoda's spire, there was an extra little hat shape and a beautiful star.

Her mother shifted her weight but did not lean on the white wall behind them. She stood straight. In the square, Sunny saw a woman with gold rings around her neck. The rings were stretching the neck to double its natural length, and on top of this great neck the woman's head was wrinkled and flat. She saw the great white chinthes, sacred lion statues, with enormous teeth and their beards green. She saw brown babies carried on their mothers' backs. She saw a man with one arm and half a leg where his whole leg should be. He was sitting on the ground. She saw hungry children gathered around a bag of trash outside a restaurant. Sunny was only three years old. Her mother had to help her remember, later, what things she saw, and what she knew. Some people were in rags, and some were draped in orange robes. Her mother held her hand. Then some people dressed in brown were hurled off the roof of the golden pagoda, over the golden fence. They dangled under the edge of the roof and swung back and forth, like they were dancing.

Sunny's mother pulled her away and they began to walk toward the harbor. She asked her mother if they would see her father soon. Her mother said that they would never see her father again. Years later, in front of the Sula Pagoda, there would be a violent antigovernment uprising. Thousands of protesters would be silenced by bayonets in the face. When they had been killed, they would lie down in the street with broken skulls. The protest continued for months, until people began to wonder whether Burma had ever been a beautiful place. Pain was all around. In Burma, things never seemed to get any better. For Sunny and her mother, it was over. They were done with Burma and the Irrawaddy River. They were done with Buddhism and nats and monsoons. They boarded a boat with some other people going to America. They left the entire country of Burma behind.

In the end, the fate of Bob Butcher is murky. But his wife, at last, returned to America, where Sunny began her life as an American child.

12.

IN HER MIND, SUNNY DID NOT REALLY ACCEPT THAT her father was dead. She did not learn that lesson of the dangling bodies. She believed in her heart that he had survived, and lived. Maybe he had never been put up there, swinging high from the pagoda. After all, no one had seen his face. Maybe he had stayed in the prison, escaping years later. He had wandered off into the jungle, confused, or more likely sad. To imagine him as a fugitive in this world was more pleasant than the alternative. There wasn't really a great visual memory of him left, even right away after he died. Her memory at that time did not include details. But she knew of him, his broad outlines, the roaring energy around him. She liked to think of him as free, as a panther.

If her father was out there hunting the woods of Burma, looking for home, then she was not ever really alone on this earth. He might eventually work things out, and be coming for her. He might be ready to reach out to her at any time. In city traffic, in any passing car, he could be there turning his certain shape of face to the glass, seeking her out. Of course, he would also have his reasons for staying in the shadows. He would need to be cautious. After all, what had happened to him once might happen to him again. There could be consequences to human contact.

She was never able to identify his face in a passing vehicle. But this did not stop her from wondering if her face had captivated other people she saw, men of a fatherly age. She thought she might catch someone's eye, someone who had never seen a face like hers before. The person might say, "Follow that girl, because I have to know where she lives." Someone solid and distinguished might show up at the doorstep, fall in love with her mother, and become her new father. Maybe he would turn out to be the same old one after all, wearing a clever disguise. There were men, throughout her life, that were fatherlike. A man with gray hair. A professor who told her, *The subject is not worth doing, if it's not fucking full of memorizing right at the beginning. Everything worthy starts out that way.*

The tragedy of her father's absence had never actually been an acutely tragic event for her. As she grew up and came to understand the world, he was a part of it. An already dead part. His absence was the landscape of her family. Increasingly, as the years went on, she didn't really know what she was missing, but that didn't stop her from missing it. She fixated on him. She prayed to him. She attempted to research him, found obscure publications of his in scientific journals. The language was so formal, she could barely understand it. But she told herself, *This is familiar. This is mine, bone of my bone, flesh of my flesh.* She thought, *There was a feeling he had, when he wrote this, when he was alive. He communicated it to me, even though everyone else who reads the article only gets a lot of information about this scientific test subject, and his reactions to all these oils.* She dreamed her father was still out there, publishing under a pseudonym, more chemical properties of Burmese flora, the exquisite blooms of a jungle orchid coming to grips with his mortar and pestle.

Her belief that her father was still living did not stop her from telling stories about his death. She learned quickly when she started school that having a father who was killed by Communists immediately magnified her fame. Of course in her school she had already gained a certain notoriety from the mere fact of being bald.

In school, she would reference Bob Butcher in passing, and call him "My father who died" or "My father who was killed by Communists" or "My dead father." There were other children in her middle school whose fathers were gone. There was one other child whose father was dead, of a heart attack, at age forty-five. That poor kid, having stood over his father's grave, and cried with real tears and snot, was not able to translate this experience into any sort of social status, because he was always coming in with a little dairy farm on his brown shoes, and it didn't matter to the other kids, whatever thing was festering in him. He could visit his father's grave, and no one put their arm around him. But there was a lot of curiosity, about Sunny's family in general, coming from the community. So eventually Sunny was asked, by one of the girls from Foxburg whose families still had money, to tell everyone exactly how her father died, anyway. "What's the deal with your dad," said this girl to Sunny. "How did he die anyway?"

Sunny, her social instinct strong even at the age of eleven, was able to deflect. Rather than giving up her mystery in the moment, she was wise enough to say, "Yes, I will tell you, but not today." She chewed her gum cryptically, rolled her eyes, slammed her locker shut. Then she delivered a brilliant smile, and pushed off down the hall.

"I will tell you," said Sunny when pressed again by this other local rich girl with a very severe ponytail and curls. "Next week at some point, probably, down by the track. During track practice. Meet me."

Sunny never did any sports in middle school or high school, but she did watch the track team practice, dutifully, most every day. She had a crush on one of the boys. There were kids coming over, like they always did, waiting for their mothers to pick them up, or skipping out on play practice, or pep band or whatever. But now they would sit there near to Sunny, where she was perched up on the bleachers, watching the distance runners loping around. They looked expectantly at her, but she didn't have much to say on the matter. Around the middle of the week, someone said, "Well, are you going to tell us pretty soon?" And Sunny said, abruptly, that this would be the day she would tell. She slammed her math notebook shut and put it aside, chewed her pencil absently, then threw it over her shoulder.

"My father died," she said, "on a plateau. He was high up in Tibet." The warm breeze blew across the green valley, up from the river. The track was nestled in a little dell, down behind the school. In this land of rolling hills, there was hardly an acre of level ground in the entire county, making swimming pools almost an impossibility. The children around her turned their faces toward her, their skeletons obscured by the shape of their hair. A couple were wearing hats, too. Their butts made the wooden bleachers creak, the chipped green paint getting into the seams of their jeans. "That's near China," she added. "Outside." One of the kids nodded. One of the kids looked at another kid and quietly muttered, "No, it's not." The track kids pounded past, another lap of the asphalt counted. Sunny cleared her throat.

"It was winter in Tibet," she went on, "and the Communists had guns." Now the kids sat up a bit more and paid attention. Sunny clasped her hands together and turned them inside out, stretching out her elbows. She yawned.

"How many Communists were there?" asked one girl.

"Three," said Sunny. "There were three Communists, in brown military uniforms. The uniforms of the Chinese Liberation Army of the People's Democracy. They were supposed to be exterminating all the missionaries, even the ones who had families to support. My father had left us to escape the Communists. He had been hiding in a Buddhist monastery, but when the Communists came to the monastery, they found him there. He was in a dark room, between two clay jars of water. Probably praying or something. They came into the room, and tipped the jars over one by one onto the floor. The clay lids were breaking, water spilling everywhere, all over the place. My father stood up, in the middle of all this breaking pottery and monastery stuff, and said, 'I'm here.' And they dragged him out, up the mountain and onto a high flat rock. There were monks, um, dying all around. Getting bayoneted."

"But what did he do?" asked a boy in red shorts. "Why was he in trouble?"

"For not being a Communist, obviously," said Sunny kindly, and the other kids looked at this red-shorts kid like he was a complete idiot.

"So they dragged him up there on this high rock, one on each side and one marching behind. That was uncomfortable. And they threw him down on a flat place on the ground. 'Do you believe in communism?' they said to him. 'No,' said my father. 'I will never believe in communism!'"

Sunny's voice echoed across the track. She put up a bony fist and shook it. "They kicked him in the stomach, and began to walk around him in a circle, kicking him. 'Do you believe in communism?' they kept saying, but he would always say 'No!' and then they would kick him again. Their boots were dry and hard, and they had short legs. But there was no dust around, there's no dust in Tibet because there is no dirt, only rock. These soldiers, their faces were flat and Chinesey, but really tough and mean. Finally they turned toward him, pointing all their guns right at his head, and they pulled him up so he was kneeling on the rock, and then they shot him. Dead."

"Holy crap," said one boy, impressed. A horn honked in the parking lot, as somebody's mother had arrived. The track team had separated out now, a long trail dripping back from the lead group. At the front of the pack, Sunny watched a long, lean boy with a shaved head run mechanically past. Others followed, breathing hard, marking out another mile.

"In Tibet you can't bury people," Sunny went on. "You can't dig; the rock is too hard. So they chopped him up into pieces with these big steel machetes, and left him there, for the vultures. They didn't talk while they were doing it, they just kind of chop, chop, chopped. The rock turned all bloody with his blood, making red pools here and there on the rock. And then they went off down the mountain. After the vultures had eaten him, his bones dried, and eventually they blew off that rock, and became just part of the gravel. White bones."

"How could you even know that," said the cynic in red shorts.

"Shut up, man!" said the kid next to him, and pushed him off the bleachers.

"Sunny, that's horrible," said the girl with the curly ponytail. "You must feel so bad."

Sunny nodded and watched the runners. She laced her fingers over the scarf behind her neck. Her eyes were wet.

SUNNY TOLD THE STORY again in college. She wrote a poem about it for an elective poetry workshop she was taking. In this version of the story, her father hung from his heels from a bar on a wall in a Burmese prison.

Only his shoulders and head rested on the ground. He hung there until he died, and only her mother was able to approach him, and then only from the other side of iron bars. The cell was dark and moldy. The prisoner wore no clothes. The agony, she wrote in her poem, was only increased by mosquitoes. The filth, she informed her readers, was only relieved by death. For crimes against the government, for subversive activity, for endangering the republic, and for Christianity, her father was hung up to rot.

Her mother walked all the way from Mandalay to Rangoon, heavy in pregnancy, and delivered her baby in the dark, in a thicket behind the ruined palace. She tucked the baby into her own lungi, cleaned herself up, and that very night she went to visit her husband. She was shown to his cell, where he was kept alone at the end of a long low building. In the doorway, she called to him. She pushed the baby in between the bars, to show the father what he had made. A crow sat silently in the window. A snake slipped down the wall. The baby cried and writhed there in the dark, and the father turned his tortured head and cracked his lips into a smile, seeing her. *That baby,* said Sunny while the class was discussing her work, *was me. That baby was me.* She left out the eclipse in this version of her story. She thought it would sound too unrealistic.

The poem was published in the college's literary magazine, the student editors invited Sunny to read it in a little chapel on campus. At the end of her reading of the poem, there was silence in the chapel, and then applause.

WHEN SUNNY AND MAXON moved to Virginia, Sunny threw a housewarming party for herself. She invited everyone on their street, and everyone came. She had enough martini glasses for everyone. The house was perfect, like a spread in *Architectural Digest.* Pistachio cream rugs, a wide walnut plank floor, brushed-nickel cups for the recessed lights, and a golden ficus, glossy curved leaves like a money tree in the corner. Everything was new, down to the distressed-leather buster chair and ottoman, but it looked a hundred years old, like a house in which life-altering decisions had been made, a house that had been left and returned to, from faraway travels. A house in which treaties had been signed. A genuine house.

They had disposed of their old coffee table, a huge chunk of green glass. It wasn't child safe at all, but that was the least of its issues. "It doesn't look right," she said to Maxon. "And to be frank, baby, neither do you." Maxon, like the great green coffee table, would not have been featured in *Architectural Digest*. Sunny didn't want to sell it, so she rolled it out into the alleyway and left it, like a translucent question mark in the city.

She would never have rolled Maxon out into an alleyway. However, if she had been able to confine Maxon to his study on that night, she would have closed the big heavy door on him, and stuck duct tape around the seams of it, so that not even the slightest bit of air or hint of Maxon would come out.

It's not like he had even wanted to come. It's not like he had said, "Can I come?" In fact he had said very clearly, "I do not feel comfortable with anyone coming into this house. It appears you have invited the whole neighborhood."

"Maxon, the more the merrier," Sunny had trilled, smiling down into the sink, washing carrots.

"That's a terrible phrase," he had said. He grabbed a diet Coke from the fridge.

"But really, it's socially accurate," said Sunny, "and in this case the numbers are in your favor."

"How's that," he said, snapping open the can. She gesticulated with a shaved carrot, a twinkle in her eye.

"The more people, the less you have to talk, actually, right? If I invited one person over, you'd have to talk plenty. But with twenty people here, you can disappear into the sofa. Nod, smile, and no one will notice."

Maxon swept the magnets off the fridge, the recycling calendar, the postcards, and attacked it with his dry-erase marker. He always had one somewhere. She loved to watch him work, loved to see him put it into his own language. In a moment like this, when everything went flying, she knew they were really communicating.

"So, like this?" he said.

$$\text{LET } n = \text{\# OF PEOPLE}$$

$$\lim_{n \to \infty} \left(\frac{1}{n}\right) = w$$

"And w is the number of words I'm responsible for?" He paused, waiting, his marker still hovering over his last equation.

"Yeah, I mean it can go up to fifty percent if n equals two. You know, like a dinner date. But if n equals twenty, negligible."

"Great," he said. "Well, okay. I see your point. But for the moment I'm going back to my office, where n equals one."

"Maxon, where n equals one there should be no talking!"

She let him go. But she had to allow him to come out if he wanted to come. They knew who he was. Maybe they would put his behavior in context. As the hour arrived, she put the finishing touches on her own wig, asked the maid to pay special attention to the baseboards, and hoped after all that Maxon would not emerge. Maybe if the house looked magnificent enough, they would not notice his absence.

The favorite final touch, she thought, was a glass cabinet that held their curios: a Burmese nat, a basket of pinecones from the woods by her mother's house, and on the top shelf a ten-thousand-dollar Mont Blanc pen. The pen had never been used, so it sat there in a spotlight, completely full of ink. She had found it in a catalog full of other such things, pens so expensive they must be kept in cabinets, wallets made of lambskin, all the things that real people use, responsible parents, not weirdos who wandered in from another planet or continent and decided to have kids. Sunny looked on it with love, as if it were her real husband, this pen, so perfectly made and elegantly wrought. Hello, she would say to her guests. I'm Sunny Mann, and this is my husband, Maxon. She would point to the pen. All of the guests would incline their heads toward the pen and nod and smile. The pen would glisten perfectly. It would not say anything strange or crack its thumbs loudly.

Sunny was pregnant, just getting used to the feeling of a wig on her head, and just getting used to the feeling of another person moving around inside her, nourished from her bloodstream, holding its breath, waiting to emerge. She was really trying to make everything all right for the baby to come out. She was really trying to correct the wrongs that had been established in the universe, all of the missing fathers and the baldness and the condition people kindly called "eccentricity" now that Maxon was a millionaire.

The first guests to arrive were Rache and her husband, Bill, and then Jenny and her husband, Roland. Others arrived. The women allowed Sunny to take their cardigan wraps, and took their saran-wrapped plates into the kitchen. There were little dipped cookie platters and bowls of starfruit stabbed with colored toothpicks. The men nodded and smiled and looked around, then began talking to each other, settling into matching leather armchairs. Conversation went appropriately. Sunny found herself saying the things she should say, things of which the neighbors would approve. She realized she was saying them with a confident energy she had previously felt only in situations where she was not wearing a wig. It made her feel good, having this dinner party. It made her feel like she belonged in the wig, belonged to the world of people who have lived their whole lives under hair.

It's not a wig, it's a hat. It's not a hat, it's a head of hair. It's not a head of hair, it's a uniform, she thought. Meanwhile her mouth was saying something about the yard guy they all used. Her mouth was agreeing. She should use him, too? Oh, she would call him. Inside she knew she would hire him, find fault with him, fire him. She would find a new yard guy, someone they all would adore. They wouldn't want to be seen with any other guy doing their lawn. In a month her guy would be edging corners for the mayor. Sunny filled her lungs with air. Her feet hardly touching the kitchen tile. Her hand gracefully landing on the counter, imitating Rache's gesture as she swept away an invisible piece of dust from the glistening edge of the sink.

Then the door to the office swung open. Maxon came out. She noticed for the first time that day that he was wearing a Joy Division T-shirt and bright blue sweatpants. No, she shook her head at him. You can't come out here wearing that. You go back in the office. But he did not look at her. He had a large whiteboard under his arm and a red marker in his hand. The room paused and all the neighbors looked at him, and Sunny looked at him, and she was afraid. On the whiteboard was a labyrinth. And she couldn't believe he'd brought his labyrinth out to the party.

Sunny knew this form of labyrinth was a medieval meditation aid, one way in, one way out. A labyrinth is not like a maze with dead ends. It is just switchback after switchback leading you to the inevitable center. She knew this because she and Maxon were talking about it all the time, at this point in their lives. They kept informing each other all about it. They kept drawing them, on napkins, on the front of the dishwasher, on Sunny's scalp.

Actually the whole labyrinth thing had originally been her idea, as she had done a wig in this style while in college, the lines and corners of a skewed oval labyrinth stretching over the bones and planes of her skull. In the center of the labyrinth there was a little bug with its head drawn stuck into her scalp. But Maxon hadn't been able to let it go, kept photographs of her labyrinth, modified it, cross-checked it with the famous labyrinth he'd seen at Chartres, becoming obsessed with the idea of the decision-making process as a single line, not a series of branches, not a flow chart at all, but a single strand folding back on itself. He was working on structuring his artificial-intelligence logic around this idea—that the robot would not face a series of choices that fork off, but that the robot was experiencing a single train of thought, along which decisions were made. As soon as those decisions were made, the unused choice no longer existed, had not really existed in the first place. "If you look at it this way," Maxon had said, "it all becomes very simple. You need about half the code you think you need. People just can't get away from the old either/or."

"People in general? Or coders," Sunny had wanted to know.

"Coders are people," said Maxon.

Now Maxon went to the refrigerator and opened it. He stood with the whiteboard in one hand, the scribbled-over labyrinth pitched toward his face, and pulled out a bag of snap peas. Sunny realized he had forgotten about the dinner party. He ripped the peas open with his teeth, set the bag on the counter, and dug into it, still gazing at the whiteboard, the marker now behind his right ear. One of the men cleared his throat, and said, "Hey, man."

Maxon's startle was real. He leaped back, dropped the whiteboard on the floor with a loud clatter, and stared wild-eyed at the group in the living room. His eyes landed on Sunny. She was shaking her head, slowly shaking her head. She thought that maybe she encouraged him too much. Because here he was opening his mouth, ready to carry his conversational weight.

"Oh, HEY!" said Maxon, way too loud. "HEY, YOU GUYS."

He picked up the whiteboard, choked on a pea. He turned his head and Sunny saw there was a Bluetooth headpiece in his ear.

"Maxon, turn off your ear," said Sunny, motioning to him to take out his earpiece. He jerked it out as if it were a scorpion biting him, and dropped it on the counter. As conversation resumed in the room, Maxon drifted over to Sunny, his hand reaching out for her, to go around her waist. She saw the hand coming toward her, smeared with the dust from using his hand to erase the red marker, and she knew he had probably drawn that labyrinth fifty or a hundred times since he went in there after lunch. The red marker dust would get all over the cute jacket she was wearing, arms pushed up to the elbow artfully, zipper swinging youthfully around her pregnant belly. She took his elbow and clutched it in both hands, pulled him close. She patted his back.

"It's good, it's going great," he said to her under his breath. "Going really great." He glared at the labyrinth, one dusty red finger going back to it, finding a path in it.

"That's good, baby," she said quietly. "Why don't you get back in there? You can take a plate."

But Maxon's gaze had found the curio cabinet, and he was staring at the Mont Blanc pen in there.

"What's that?" he said.

"Oh, that's the cabinet, Maxon," said Sunny. She made a desultory gesture and rolled her eyes toward their new neighbors, as if to say, *Well yes, he is odd. But he's so smart, what can you do?*

"No," said Maxon, his hand now on the clasp of the cabinet, "I mean that pen. What's it doing in there?"

"Oh, the pen," said Sunny. She could feel a little bit of sweat between her head and the wig, and the wig tottered over her. She felt top-heavy, weak, like her baby had become a balloon, her wig made of cement, and she might fall over a balustrade, fall into the abyss. The room was quiet. Everyone was wondering.

"What's a pen doing in the curio cabinet?" said Maxon. "That's just weird."

"No, it's—" Sunny began. "The catalog—"

"It is kind of weird," Roland put in helpfully, rising to look into the cabinet, "unless—is it your grandfather's pen, or something?"

The fact that a pen should not be kept in a cabinet, even though it was pictured that way in the catalog, was immediately obvious to Sunny, although it had not been at all obvious before. Maxon looked at her, and the neighbors looked at her, their blond hair streaming from the pores and plugs of their heads.

"These pinecones are from the woods where I grew up," said Sunny brightly. "And this nat," she went on, pointing down to the little cross-legged sculpture with the pointy hat. "This nat is from Burma. I was born there. This is a forest guardian spirit—"

"Burma?" asked Rache.

"Yes, Burma. Now it's Myanmar. But I was born there. And my father died there."

"I'm sorry," Rache went on, putting a hand on Sunny's cute jacket. Her hand, like everyone else's hand, was finely dusted with light pretty hairs. Sunny's hand was not. But no one could tell that. They just wanted to know how her father died.

"He was a missionary," said Sunny. "He was working there, building the Christian church in Burma. But it was illegal, under the Communists. To have a church. So he got arrested. Unfortunately."

She was rushing the story, screwing it up. But Maxon was taking the pen out of the cabinet, turning it over in his hand, trying to get it writing on his wrist. He wasn't listening. Maybe he thought he had heard it all before. She felt so exposed by him, as if her underwear were sticking out the top of her pants, as if the roof of the house had blown off, as if she had said a bad word in church.

"And put in jail," she said. "Jail."

"Wow, prison overseas," said Rache. "That's pretty scary. Did he die in the jail?"

"Well," said Sunny, "he did escape."

"Really?" said Bill in his stentorian tone. "How did he manage that?"

"It wasn't very secure, this prison," said Sunny. At least they weren't talking about the pen anymore. Who spends that much money on something called a writing instrument? "He was being held in Rangoon. An old British fort, really run-down. He actually got out by wedging his sleeve between the side of the door and the wall, when the door was slammed shut. Then he worked it open after the guard was gone, because the lock was jammed. Somehow he got free of the building, he, uh, you know, crept down the darkened hallway and stuff. But once he was out, he wasn't really safe, of course. He had to get to the jungle. It was dark. Nighttime. He crawled on his face until he could feel that thick, full darkness of the Burmese lowland forest. And he knew he was safe."

Now her audience was really with her. All of their owl eyes were turned toward Sunny.

"He got up and ran through the forest, kind of drunk with freedom. Like he didn't even care what he was doing or where he was going. And he didn't realize, he didn't really know, there was a ravine there. It was so dark, he just fell right into it and right to the bottom of this ravine. And broke his leg. His leg was broken in such a way that it was clear his leg was not going to work well enough to climb himself out of that ravine. He thought he would wait until morning and then listen, maybe there was a teak camp nearby. Maybe there was some fisherman on his way to the river."

Maxon seemed likely to wander back into the office. She raised her voice and he stopped.

"Maybe a child running from one place to another, that he could call to for help. He knew he could not get out of that crack in the rocks on his own. But he was afraid if he called, that it would attract the soldiers. He thought that if he was quiet, they might not realize he was gone, they might not be looking for him. But then he wondered if he would survive the night in the ravine, with the animals, the insects . . . there are a lot of threats in the jungle of Burma, and if you're not prepared, you can be in really bad trouble."

"But what about his leg?" said Jenny querulously, and ate a bite of an almond pretzel.

"His leg was in bad shape, sort of zigzagged underneath him," she said. Maxon leaned against the counter, his face now showing full attentiveness, one line of wrinkle between his eyebrows, indicating that the person he was listening to was saying something of interest. "He could barely keep quiet about it. He tried to stay calm, tried to focus on something besides his leg, but his consciousness was slipping away. I think he must have been going into shock. I think he passed out."

Jenny nodded, put the rest of the pretzel distractedly back on the plate.

"As it turned out, they did come, the soldiers, that night. They came with flashlights, and through his closed eyes he could see the beam sweeping back and forth, up above. In his pain, and maybe a little bit of shock, he felt himself coming to his senses, and when he saw the light he called to it. It was a reflex, like swearing when you stab yourself in the hand with your own fountain pen. It was enough to alert those soldiers to his presence, and they swept the light down into the cleft of that rock, and there he was."

"Shit," said Bill under his breath.

"He called out to them, even when he saw that they were soldiers, and realized what he had done. He thought they would take him back to jail, maybe execute him, at least get him out of that ravine, and shift his weight off his broken leg. He felt his leg was being torn off at the hip. But they only talked to each other. It was Chinese and my father didn't understand. They turned the flashlight back and forth over him. They saw him there, with his leg bent in the shape, like a sigma, and covered in pine needles, from where he had tried to dig himself out. Then they went away. Without saying anything to him, or giving him any sort of notice, they just sort of went away and left him there. They didn't do anything to save him. They just decided to let him die."

Maxon put his head in his hands, both elbows on the kitchen island, eyes hidden. Then he looked up, eyes clear.

"Wow," said Maxon.

"And he died there, in that ravine, all by himself. Crushed on top of his broken leg."

"I'm going back to my office," said Maxon. "Have a great evening, everyone. Let's just put this pen back in here for safety. It's the one Uncle Chuck used to sign the Magna Carta, you know."

IT WAS LATE AT night, three years later. Maxon had gone to bed. Sunny was in her dressing closet with her wigs. She was writing in Bubber's treatment journal. On a long, low shelf across one full wall there were silent black-glass heads. She had bought these heads at Pier 1 in the nineties, when she was in college, when she had first started to make the wigs. They were some sort of decorative cheap art thing, but she loved them. They were inscrutable and serene. They were opaque and hairless. She looked at them and thought, *All my life I have been so happy and so normal and so whatever. Like yeah, it's all so merry and gay. Nothing is a problem. No baldness. No father dead from communism. Nothing strange about that. I haven't ever felt the sting of it, not really. But this, here, this black head, this is what it means to be bald. This is what it means to be dead. This is what it means to be me.* She would meditate on them in this way, while she was in those turbulent years before she got married to Maxon. Then they just became funny. Then they became ghosts.

She had ten of them, and they had traveled with her to college, and to Chicago, and then to Virginia, although it was a major pain in the ass to pack and ship them. At one point, she had referred to them as the muses. They were now just wig stands. Whatever they used to say to her, they were now silent. In fact, she had even turned their faces around to face the wall. The dressing closet was a room she had not known she needed until she had it. Once she had it, it became her telephone booth, her Batcave, her puff of smoke. She went in bald, came out perfect. While one wall was closets, divided neatly into sections for shoes, dresses, folded shirts, the other wall, lit by recessed spotlights in the ceiling, was the wig bank. She could leave it and close the door, invite her girlfriends in to look at the new ceiling fan over the bed, and they would never know that on the other side of that quiet barrier, there were ten black heads in ten wigs, completely silent.

It was here she came to write in Bubber's treatment journal at the end of the day. It was here she kept all of her secret things, in little drawers under the wig countertop, all of her intimate possessions. She sat on a faded chaise lounge and tried to contemplate writing down how Bubber had spent his day. His doctor wanted a record. They had to know how the different medicines were affecting him. She had to keep track.

Today, she wrote, *Bubber spent the day writing. He ate nothing but oyster crackers. He did not make eye contact. He only willingly hugged the dog.* What does it mean for a two-year-old to spend the day writing? He would stand at the whiteboard easel in his footie pajamas, and fill it with letters. Aa, Bb, Cc, Dd, Ee, Ff, Gg, and so on. When it was full, he would erase it and start again. He would stand for hours and do this. If she gave him a ream of paper, he would fill it. First page: Aa AT. Second page: Bb BAT. Third page: Cc CAT. Endlessly. Wearing out markers. Filling the room. Exhausting himself. He woke up at one o'clock in the morning and was awake until four, reading books out loud with no one in the room. Creating the sounds of the letters with his mouth, reciting, reading, whatever you want to call it, it was *Ten Apples Up on Top* until the book fell apart. He was so little, he could barely pronounce the words, but he could read it fifty times without getting tired. They had one copy for upstairs, another copy for downstairs. That's how it was. This is what happened after he mastered stacking blocks.

Sunny didn't know how to write all that down. She couldn't bring the doctors far enough into Bubber's life, to see what was really going on. They would have to witness it and they couldn't. She couldn't show them, or even tell them about it. It was too distressing. She put the book away and got up. She went to the drawer under the wig counter and got out a piece of card stock, a mailer she'd received. The mailer read, "Lose Your Hair? Don't Go There! Dr. Chandrasekhar's Orchid Formula Cures Baldness." On the front was a beautiful portrait of a woman with long flowing hair wearing a headdress of orchids. On the back was the address and all the information. She took the mailer out into the dark bedroom and slammed the door to her dressing room.

"Wake up, Maxon," she said.

"Hey," said Maxon. His voice sounded deep. Then after a pause he said, "What's up?"

He didn't roll over or move, stayed on his side facing away from her, deep in the comforter, with one hand clutching the finial on the top of the bedpost, the way he usually slept. As if he were hanging on, afraid of drowning in the mattress. She flicked on the overhead light.

"I'm going to try this baldness cure," she said.

"Okay," he said. "But that's pretty dumb. But you know that."

He rolled over; now both of his arms were on top of the comforter, pressing it down around his body.

"Yeah, no," said Sunny. "I'm going to do this."

"You know what, from now on, you're going on a binary system. One for 'good,' zero for 'bad.'"

He held up a finger to demonstrate "good," then made a zero with his hand to demonstrate "bad."

"No fair, you've always had me on that system."

"Yes, but now you have visual cues."

"Maxon, shut up, wake up, I'm going to buy this baldness cure."

Maxon held up a zero, without opening his eyes.

"Fuck you, you don't know what it's like, why shouldn't I try and fix it?"

"It's not going to work. It's a scam."

"You haven't even looked at it."

Maxon sat up in bed, blinking uncomfortably, and held out his hand. He studied the mailer.

"Chandrasekhar, I know that name."

"Oh, I probably mentioned it to you before. I wanted to try this years ago. Mother said no."

"No, I've met this guy. Voodoohoodoo biochemist or something."

"Where have you met him?" Sunny sat down on the bed next to Maxon.

"Ahhh, I met him at your mother's house, while you were away at college."

"WHAT?" Sunny shrieked. "At Mother's house, you met this Chandrasekhar person? Maxon, that's nuts. What are you talking about?"

"He was there, they were, you know, I think they might have been kissing or making out or something."

Maxon handed the mailer back to her and lay back down in the bed, pulled the covers out, and turned over on his side.

"Oh no," said Sunny. "Get up. Get up. Get up. No, no, you're telling me there was a man at Mother's house, and they were making out? And it was this baldness guy? You weren't going to tell me? Do I just have to ask you questions about every hypothetically possible situation, to make sure you're not forgetting to tell me something so major? Maxon, what are you even talking about? Tell it like a story, immediately."

He sighed but did not turn around. "I went to the house. I went in without knocking. There was a man in the kitchen. He had his arm around your mother. She had redness in her face. I asked about the hot-water heater, she was having trouble with it. She said it was fine. He said he was Dr. Chandrasekhar, a biochemist from Burma, that he knew your father. They were friends. Colleagues. She asked me to leave. So I left."

"Maxon, they were kissing?"

"Probably."

"My mother, kissing some witch doctor from Burma, I hardly think so," Sunny said to herself. "Unless."

She didn't say to Maxon that she thought she knew the reason. She thought, she had always thought, she had always known, that

Dr. Chandrasekhar was her father in hiding. Now she was almost certain of it. The baldness cure, now the visit to her mother in Pennsylvania, it was all too strange. What chance was there that this man was really a colleague? Why get interested in the baldness then, when it had been her father's obsession? She put the mailer away in the drawer and turned out the light. She would not ask her mother about this, pursue this lead. She would not go straight to Dr. Chandrasekhar and confront him. Shake his hand. Stare into his face and say, "Daddy? Daddy? Is it really you? Why did you leave us?" She would just keep thinking about it forever, processing it in her own head. Her father visiting her mother. The cure for baldness sent out on a mailer, like a love letter straight to her. She would keep it safe, not disturb it. It would be added to the narrative, one of the offshoots. Her diagram was not a labyrinth. There were many alternatives and they were all real. She felt energized by this new discovery, as if an unknown branch had sprung out from the tree, ripped into the sky, burst out with leaves, and stood there shaking and new.

"Maybe I won't get that orchid stuff after all," she said to Maxon as she flicked off the light. She came over to the bed, and said, "You want to take a crack at curing what ails me, baby?" As she got between the covers, in the shadow from the streetlight outside, she could see he was holding up one finger for "good."

13.*

THERE WERE ONLY A FEW SIGNIFICANT INCIDENTS IN Maxon's mind in the time between when he was born and the time he married Sunny and became Sunny's husband. They ranged in his mind from the excruciatingly significant to largely significant. In his life, they were like beads on a chain. They were the only things he could truly remember that involved talking.

THE FIRST BEGAN AT 3:45 in the afternoon on July 4, 1987. The temperature in the cow barn was 68. Fog lay over the mountains, coagulating over this valley. The boy was eighty miles north of Pittsburgh, eighty miles south of Erie, between one Appalachian foothill and another. A weak summer sun broke through the clouds but did not warm him. A light rain had come down at 1:35. The boy put one hard foot on the lower layer of the barbed-wire fence and pushed down, pinched the upper layer with his hand. Pulling them apart, he slid through expertly and left his father's property. As soon as he was through he went off running. Down through the valley he ran, fifty steps down, hands out to steady himself down a short descent, fifty more steps running, feet slipping shoeless through the leaf mold and pine needles. The ferns whipped his bare legs.

At the creek in the bottom of the valley he paused, bones in his chest expanding and contracting around his panting lungs and racing heart. Ankle-deep in the stream, he put his hand down to drink, lifted the water up to his face like a hunter, his eyes on the sandy bank. Raccoon tracks, deer tracks, and then he saw human tracks. Adult human feet in boots, all over the place, and one delicate footprint, pressed into the edge of the creek where the sand gave way to mud. It was small, the footprint of a child. The boy let the water fall from between his fingers. He climbed up the bank from whence he'd come, and approached a nearby stump. He reached in and lifted out a flat rock that covered up an opening inside. Up to his armpit now in the stump, he pushed aside a chipmunk skeleton, fully formed, a few rocks and odd-shaped gnarls of wood, a wad of cash, and pulled out a wax paper bag. Inside it was candy, very old. He took out a piece of the sticky peppermint and put it in the pocket of his shorts.

The boy went back to the footprint, puzzled over it, studied it closely, his sharp nose barely a breath away from the pea-shaped indentations of the toes. He put his own filthy foot over it, as if to match the shapes, but he did not disturb one grain of sand on this precious impression. Instead, he pressed his hands down over his long hair, flattening it, ordering it. He rubbed the back of his hand over his face, then applied some water to the effort, and used the hem of his torn white T-shirt to scrub at his cheeks. He gave himself a winning smile in his reflection in the creek. Then suddenly he looked fierce, angry, wild, growling at the water. His face went blank. Then he lifted his eyebrows, widened his eyes, showed all his teeth. His face went blank again. Finally he frowned, stood up, and began to climb the opposite hill.

Across the road from the old farm, the boy stopped in the high weeds. Among the milkweed clumps, he waited and watched, crouched over, hunched down. The old farm was no longer empty. He knew, looking at the place, that he would no longer be able to climb through a window and sleep there when he needed to. There was new gravel on the driveway. There were new windows with bright white frames. He had heard the sound of a car, the sound of a hammer yesterday. He had envisioned a thief, tearing apart the decrepit porch, seeing the wormy chestnut paneling, using a crowbar. He knew that paneling was worth some money, because he had heard his father and brothers discussing it.

He felt angry at the interlopers. He had deciphered every book inside the old farmhouse, saying each word out loud, one after the other. He deciphered by the light of a store of yellowed candles from under the kitchen counter. There was a book entirely composed of letters, arrows, and numbers. There was a set of leather volumes that had the word "Dickens" on the spine, fifteen volumes, ranging between two inches and three and a half inches thick, wide as his mother's butcher block. He could recall the length of each paragraph, and the width. How dare some other vagrant dismantle this house? There was a station wagon in the driveway, and in the front yard, a human hung from a rope, swinging back and forth, back and forth, sixty degrees across the yard and back.

He parted the weeds to get a clearer look. His face framed in weeds, his hands pulling them apart on each side of his face, he looked across the dirt road and saw the human that had made the footprint in the creek. It was a child. The child sat in a tire all cut apart. The cut-up tire hung from the tree and was swinging back and forth, back and forth. As it swung across the arc it also was revolving, so that it turned and swung, both, the child's face coming around to face him, seeing him, and then turning away, around, across the whole sweep of the yard, the farmhouse, and then back around to see him again. By the time the child had rotated back around, the boy had sprinted across the road and was standing on the mounting block at the bottom of the driveway. The child in the swing put out its foot and stopped the swing from rotating and swinging. It regarded the boy with large eyes. It stared at him.

"Who are you, a boy?" said this child.

"Maxon," said the boy. He stood fully erect, one knee touching the other, heels planted firmly together on that mossy and rectangular stone block.

"I'm Sunny," said the child. "I'm a girl. Do you want a turn on this?"

The farmhouse had been empty ever since Maxon could remember. He had found it very early in his life, when he was exploring the woods. Now he had been all over the county. It was one of the places where he slept. There were others, an A-frame cabin 168 trees down the electric line past the old farm, a hunting blind in a tree next to the railroad. There were people who fed him, including his family, but also others. There was one woman in a trailer who thought he was a mute. He never talked to her. The houses with white paint and ninety-degree angles he stayed away from. During the school year, he went to school as much as he could, on the bus. He was seven years, four months, and eighteen days old. Or, he was 2,693 rotations of the Earth old.

At this time, Maxon climbed into the tire swing and Sunny pushed him on it, and he played with her. When they were laughing, another person came out of the front door. Maxon had never seen any of the doors of the house open; he thought of the old farmhouse as impenetrable except by squirrels and him. The woman was tall, wearing a long skirt. She had long blond hair in pigtails as if she were a child.

"Sunny, what's this?" said the woman.

"It's Maxon," said Sunny. She talked around the piece of peppermint that was in her mouth. "He's staying for dinner. Maxon, this is my mother."

Another woman came out behind the mother, and this one was brown. Maxon had never seen a person this brown color. She was short, and she had a hammer in her hand. Her arms were covered in dust.

"Nu, please set another place at the table," said the mother. "Sunny has a friend."

At the dinner table, Maxon sat diagonal to the mother and the brown woman, and across from Sunny. Sunny ordered him to eat a lot of vegetables that she didn't appear to want. Maxon ate zucchini in handfuls, and said, "I like zucchini. We have it wild. It grows in the yard. The seeds in the zucchini I grow in the yard are from four generations of zucchini in the same yard. I can also eat it raw. I eat it just like a banana, but without peeling it." When he said this, Sunny put her hands over her ears like cups facing backward. The brown women squinted at him and the mother nodded.

He refused to take a bath when the mother put the question out there, but he allowed her to brush his hair and wrap him in a blanket. She kept leaving the room and coming back, pressing her hands onto her long skirt. Her eyebrows wrinkled down. They had put yard furniture in the living room; Maxon saw that it was rainproof. Before, in the living room, there had been a chair with mice living in it, and a lounge covered in red corduroy. The two children sat on a swinging sofa, curled metal rods holding the sofa to the frame. It would swing back and forth or side to side. Maxon's feet touched the floor, but Sunny had her feet folded under her.

"He starving!" the brown woman called in from the kitchen, where she was knocking dishes around in the sink. "Look at him! Like a damn toothpick!"

"Where do you live?" said Sunny's mother.

Maxon pointed out the window.

"Come on," said Sunny. "Let's go play."

Maxon took her hand when she offered it. They went out under the apple tree and began to pick up apples. Only halfway through the summer and already some were starting to fall, crabbed and hopeless little fruit, gnawed by deer, pink only on one scant face. Maxon had the understanding that Sunny would never eat these apples, like Maxon sometimes did.

Sometimes as they were playing with the apples, Sunny's hand would fall onto Maxon's hand or arm, as if she was trying to feel if he was hot.

"Where do you live?" Sunny asked. "Will you take me there?"

Maxon shook his head. He chucked an apple through a window in the old barn with perfect aim. The pane broke and shattered inward. He put another apple through the exact same hole. Sunny watched him. When she threw an apple, she threw it short.

At the sound of breaking glass, the mother came out the screen door again and it shut with a crack you could hear hit the mountain on the other side of the valley, under the fog.

"Maxon, I am going to take you home," she said. "Can you show me where that is?"

Maxon thought about running away, but the tall woman with the braided hair compelled him inside. She had all the books, and all the candles. There was a tight smoothness to her face, and her teeth, so white in rows, made him stare. They got into the station wagon.

Sunny stood beside the car door, sadly waving. Maxon looked down at her feet, not bare, not pressing toe prints into the ground, but wearing leather shoes held tightly on her feet with a wide strap. The station wagon pulled down the drive, and the new gravel crunched under the tires.

WHAT HAPPENED THEN DID not have any significance. Maxon did not remember it, because it was not in his memory.

THEN THE STATION WAGON came back up the driveway, crunching on the gravel. The mother led him by the hand, back into the kitchen, and gave him a banana. She told him to sit on the bench behind a table, built into the wall. It was red and the mice had chewed it open, showing its foam stuffing. He peeled the banana and began to eat it.

The mother said to the brown woman, "Well, there was no one there. But I can tell you. There were sheep living in rusty cars. I mean living. And pigs."

"You lie," said the brown woman.

"Nu, the place is falling down and no one is at home. I called, I yelled, I rang the bell, and do you want to know what this child said to me? That seven-, eight-year-old child?"

"What he say," said Nu, working on putting dinner away.

"He said, 'They went to town.' Can you believe it? He's barely bigger than Sunny. They left him out in the rain in those—" Here she began to cough. "—shorts. And went to town. Nu, if you had seen the place. I think there was a mule in the parlor."

An hour later they had all gone to see the fireworks. Maxon wore a blanket, and was running in tight, concentric circles around Sunny and her mother, as they sat in a pasture on an old crocheted afghan, waiting for the explosions. The field they sat in had been newly mowed and the hay harvested. It was prickly, as a father's beard might be, even through the blanket. Sunny sat on her mother and wrapped her legs around her mother's waist.

"There's a bat," Sunny said. "And there's Maxon."

The mother laughed, hugged her child, and Maxon watched them. He could hear their talking. Sunny said she didn't want to see the fireworks, kept letting her eye be distracted by the boy, and the bats flying around. "That's Maxon, and that's a bat," she repeated.

When the fireworks started, Maxon was startled by the noise. The show was all around them, but he didn't look up. It was dark, and then there would be a flash, and all the cars illuminated, and the mother's face showing, and then black again, and a sharp whine. The smell of the hay clung around him, and he could smell that there were cows nearby.

"We have to take him home, after this," said Emma.

"No, I want to keep him," said Sunny. And Maxon continued to trot around.

The booms of the fireworks echoed down the valley, amplified by the river, ricocheting off the mountains on both sides.

"No," said Emma. "He has to go home."

"But I like him. I want him," said Sunny.

When the fireworks were over, the two children sat in the backseat while Emma drove, muttering to herself and shaking her head. Maybe she was practicing what she would say. Maxon felt pretty good sitting there in the dark with the girl, the hiss of a sudden rain in the wheel wells, the flashing, weird mosaic of lights on the ceiling in the car, the back of the mother's head. The girl reached out for his hand and he took it. He was taller. She was fatter. His toes were turned inward from being shoved into shoes that were too small. When they stopped at a stop sign and he knew they were close to home, he slipped out the car door and into the rain. No one gave chase. It was too dark and he was already gone, sliding over wet fallen wood, under the clutch of dripping leaves.

"Come back tomorrow," she had said, squeezing his hand. "Don't forget."

Probably, if he was being ruthlessly straight with himself, that was when he had fallen in love.

That was when it had happened.

14.

DOWN ON THE EARTH THAT ROTATED ON ITS OWN lazy and inscrutable axis, the mother's brain was still getting oxygen from her blood. She was breathing, she had breathed, drawing air in rattling gasps on and on through the night. When morning came to the world outside the hospital, she was still alive. She had gone from ICU to a private room on a metal gurney, but her long body was not aware of this. Her body was paying attention only on the inside. Its organs were full of tiny motions, dark processes. The body was preserving itself from death, denying its own rotten condition, living. It was doing the same thing all the other bodies on Earth were doing, in their own boxes of rooms and long corridors and dark cellars and flying down the highways in little cars and down railways in closed compartments. The body was staving off death for yet a little while. It was a fetus in a womb, unwilling to come out, though the labor had begun, the contractions had started, and the blood was getting thin.

The dark room, the dripping walls, the bloody entry, the stern contractions of the hallway, were resisted by the mother. There were no robots to help her now. They had all been removed: the breathing one, the circulating one, and mostly the tracking beeping one. She was alone in her bed; only the biological robot in her skull remained to keep her cells alive. She was alone from her family, alone from all of history, and the more the room pushed in on her, the more her brain pushed back. She would not die. She could not die. She could see her daughter in a dream, walking around like a kitten with its feet in boots, shaking its paws, running into walls. She couldn't die and leave Sunny here on Earth.

IN THE BIG HOUSE on Harrington Avenue, Sunny stood at the kitchen counter, bald as an egg, curtains wide, and opened three orange bottles of Bubber's medications. She set them out in front of her on the smooth granite countertop. Bubber stood next to her, solemnly, his footed pajamas wrinkled around his ankles, snapped together at the waist. He was waiting to take his medicine. Then he would watch two episodes of *Blue's Clues*. Then he would go to school. Except that today, Sunny had decided that he would neither take the medicine nor go to school. He would stay home and be unmedicated. See what happened. See if the roof flew off the world. See if the doctors came and stood in the yard, waving clipboards and adjusting their glasses. If she had to bar the door and put the sofa in front of it, no one would come in and put a medicine into her child. Whether the walls came down, whether he turned into a werewolf and devoured her, whether he said, distinctly, "Give me the medicine. It's what I really, secretly want," she would not give in. She would learn exactly what he was without the medicine to make it easier. She would watch him all day. If a fit came, she would sit on him.

"No medicine today, Bubber," she said. She poured the pills out on the counter and they mixed together, blue with white tablets with the green capsules. Bubber watched her. He had his blanket around his shoulders, a flannel shirt of Maxon's, ancient and soft and full of holes. His bright blue eyes regarded her. "It's okay," she said to him softly. "No school, no medicine."

"Where's Dad?" said Bubber loudly, like a duck. After he was done talking, his mouth hung open and he breathed through it.

"Daddy is on the rocket. He's taking the robots to the moon. But I know he's glad you're thinking about him."

"I know," said Bubber. He looked at the clock. *Blue's Clues,*" he said.

Sunny swept the pills into the trash can and they fell down around the garbage, down to the bottom of the can where it was wet. She watched Bubber trot into the living room. What would happen? She thought maybe she should put his helmet on. He put the DVD expertly into the machine and pressed the button on the remote, sat down in front of the TV. His face went brighter when the characters came on the screen and she watched him sing, talk, move his shoulders up and down exactly in time with Steve and Blue. He had it all memorized. Elmo, too. And all of Dr. Seuss. He had memorized the inflections, the facial expressions. He could always do it. It was all a flawless replication, as many times as he tried.

Maybe without the medicine, he would have a facial expression he made up by himself. A new one. She feared it would be rage. Or sorrow. Or hate. What would his brain put out, given rein to put out anything it chose? Then the hospital called. They said: "Your mother is still alive. Will you be visiting today?" She said: "We will have to see how it goes. My son is having a medical emergency." They said: "She will not hang on for long. This might be your last chance to say good-bye." Sunny had already said good-bye. She didn't want to say good-bye again. She wanted it to be a week from now, or ten days ago, or ten years ago, when she was still certifiably alive, before everything had happened: the cancer, the pregnancies, the wigs. There were too many things happening at once and one of them had to go.

Sunny smoothed her hand over her scalp. She had taken the mother off life support. She had taken the child off medicine. She had taken herself off wigs, eyebrows, her urban housewife costume disguise. She couldn't do anything else to speed the end times, but the end times refused to come. Someone should come to the door, pronounce her unfit, the charade over, but no one came. The musical sounds of *Blue's Clues* tinkled in the living room with Bubber's peaceful echo, and Sunny wished that Maxon would turn the rocket around and come straight the hell home. She moved through the house over the dark walnut floors, those wide planks, polished weekly, stained perfectly. She stood behind Maxon's empty chair in Maxon's empty office, and looked at his desk. Inside the desk somewhere were papers, official papers that would be needed soon. She would need her mother's will. She would need insurance documents. Her mother's, and maybe Maxon's. After all, Maxon might never come home. Astronauts died. They also decided they liked space, living in space suits, orbiting other astral bodies. They stayed away, forgot they had homes, families, bald wives, crazy children, cancerous mothers-in-law.

Sunny decided she would open up the desk drawers, and find the necessary paperwork for herself. Behave in a way that she might have behaved before she became a mother. Make phone calls. Decide what to do with all their real estate. Sort things out. Hold people's feet to the fire. Page through sheaves of paperwork and light on an important line here, a contradictory line there, shout, AHA! She lowered herself into Maxon's chair. She opened the one shaped like a file cabinet, and there were files all neatly labeled, everything she could ever need: insurance, mortgage, and one labeled in block letters: MOTHER. She pulled the file out and sat with it on her lap for a while, then set it aside. Then she opened all the other drawers except one. It was locked.

A locked drawer. In the other drawers she had found neatly organized office supplies, ordered papers, logical files. But here was a long flat drawer locked with a key. The key was not there. Why was it locked? Locked against whom? What could Maxon possibly have to hide?

SHE REMEMBERED A TIME before she had agreed to marry Maxon, when she had fallen superficially in love with a man who had a lot of hair. This was during college, when she was away from both Maxon and her mother, far away in another state. In college she studied art and math. She was a wigmaker and bald, so she attracted a lot of attention and people knew who she was. She cut an important and contradictory profile on the campus of her college, which was small and liberal, across the Pennsylvania border, in Ohio.

At this college, she had a bicycle. It was one of the ways she was missing Maxon, to ride this bicycle, when her mother had demanded she go at least six hours away to school. He always had one, now she had one, and she rode it around the campus, missing him. Though she knew she should not love him, he was still her best friend.

She also had a woolen poncho with a hood. In the wintertime, when it was bitterly cold, she would put on the poncho, pull up the hood, and go out riding her bicycle in that Ohio wind. Under the poncho, she could be anyone. It was then that she stalked him, the person she called in her mind "Hair Person." He had long, wavy, rock-star hair. The hair that he had was so luxurious that when she saw him for the first time, from the back, she thought he was a woman. Her first reaction was to sneer. She looked askance at women with long hair. Like they were overcompensating. But a man with hair he could sit on, such a waterfall of frothing, floating hair was attractive.

He was a thin man with metal glasses and a pencil shape to his body. His only fascinating feature was the hair that hung down in soft, fluffy, crinkly waves below his belt. Besides that, he had nothing to recommend him. But she thought of dressing herself in that hair. She imagined him pressed down on top of her, that hair falling down on each side of them, enclosing her in his hairfall. She would say to him, "Stay in me for a little longer," so she could feel his hair on her head. She had never talked to Hair Person, had never addressed him. She only rode her bicycle past his dorm-room window, one rectangle of many, breathless, twisted in her stomach, painfully in love. When she went right past it, she glanced in and would see him at his desk, or lounging with his guitar, or the light would be out; he must be asleep or out. Eating. Standing in the shower, shrouded in it, or drying it in sections, brushing it.

At times like this, Maxon was far away from her. She could remember him, of course, but she didn't want him close to her. This is why her mother had recommended, "Go away to college. Try something new. Date someone. Date everyone. Try your hand at dating."

The night her love for Hair Person ended was such a cold night. Determination clenched between her teeth, she had parked at one end of Hair Person's dorm, and started down the hallway past his room. He was not as tall as Maxon, not as broad. Maybe he was not as tall as Sunny even. But that hair. As she approached the door of his dorm room, she heard a few soft chords on the guitar, and she dared, breathless, to stop and push the door open a few inches. He was sitting where she had seen him sitting when she looked in from outside, his guitar draped across his tiny legs. For months, she had

looked at him through the window in the dark, in his Pink Floyd
T-shirt and his faded jeans. Now they were alone in his dorm room,
which smelled a little sour, like the boys' dorms always did.

"Hello," she said stupidly. "Is there anybody in there?"

"Oh, hey," he said. As if he recognized her.

She pulled down the hood of her poncho. Several boys jogged
down the hallway in towels from the shower behind her. She stood
at the doorway.

"Can I come in?" she said.

"Sure," he said, not looking at her. Sunny took a few steps into
the room and pushed the door half-closed behind her. His waves of
hair flattened against the cement-block wall behind him, fell down
around the sturdy, square chair, upholstered in resilient yellow rayon
weave. Sunny felt a little sick.

"Nice guitar," she said. She sat down on the other yellow chair,
which must have belonged to Hair Person's roommate. She and her
roommate had similar chairs. It was what everyone had, the same everywhere, like the metal beds. She folded her long legs into the chair
and hooked the toes of her boots behind the arms of it, the way she
did in her own chair. What would she do if Hair Person's roommate
came in just now? What if he came in and called Hair Person something like Rich, or Phil, or Matty? Hair Person said in a desultory
way that his nice guitar was a vintage piece. They looked at each
other, and then the phone rang. It was attached to the wall above his
head, hanging on the hook there.

"'Scuse me," he said. He reached up with one finger and hooked
the phone receiver off the wall and brought it down to his ear. "Hello?"
he said into it. Then he rolled his eyes. He told the person on the
phone "You're drunk" a number of times, and asked the person to
repeat themselves, and then told them he would call them back. He
hung up the phone, looked at Sunny nervously. His eyes looked, for

the first time, instead of like liquid pools, like kind of shifty squirrel eyes.

"That was my girlfriend. She goes to school in Findlay," said Hair Person. Sunny nodded. He added, "She's drunk."

"I gathered," said Sunny. She pulled the hood of her poncho back up and unfolded her legs. "I better go."

"Just because I have a girlfriend," said Hair Person, "doesn't mean we can't hang out."

He carefully put his guitar down, leaning it facedown against the bed so that its strings were touching the frame. Then he turned back toward her and steepled his fingers. His legs made two points, directed away from each other, with the knees like arrows. The knees themselves were so delicate, like knives under the frayed denim.

"What's your name?" said Sunny.

"Chris," he said. "You're Sunny, right? Sunny?"

"Chris," said Sunny, feeling the word roll around in a predictable shape inside her mouth and out the front. "No, I don't think we can hang out. It's no big deal. I just . . . wanted to ask your name. I'll see you around."

Sunny stood up and moved toward the door. He watched her, leering. She didn't know if he was done talking or not. He didn't indicate. She felt sick, smelling something sweet and old. Only when she was outside in the cold again, breathing the sharpness into her lungs, could she shrug off that suffocating feeling. Men would date her. It wasn't that. They would date her and fuck her, too. She felt that, in the room with Hair Person. Not because they were familiar with her, but because they were unfamiliar. Not because she was close enough to a real girl but because she was far from it. Then the only remaining question: Would she fuck someone else, before she went back to Maxon? Or would she fuck only him, from the beginning to the end. It was the only remaining mystery of her life at college. But when she went back to her room and called him on the phone, she only said she had a shitty day, and that he should tell her everything that had happened to him that day, starting from the beginning, and leaving out nothing, until she fell asleep from the sheer comfort of the minutiae, all the little details, precious details of his distant life.

With Maxon, she always knew when he was done talking, because he had showed her the formula once:

$$\forall \text{ CONVERSATIONS } \exists \text{ ENDING TAG:}$$

CONVERSATION ENDS ABRUPTLY.

ENDING TAG ∈ { "IT WAS A PLEASURE
TALKING WITH YOU."
"I'm GLAD WE HAD A
CHANCE TO TALK."
"HAVE A NICE DAY."
"SEE YOU LATER." }

Her mother could say that Maxon would not make a good husband, but she could not provide a viable alternative.

PREGNANT, LONELY, SITTING IN his office in the middle of the morning, with nothing on her to-do list but birthing his baby and raising his crazy child, Sunny considered hacking Maxon's desk apart with an ax, to see what was in that locked drawer. Maybe she would have done it, if she had had an ax. If she hadn't heard Bubber screaming.

So this is what happens, she thought, staggering to her feet and lurching into the other room. She clutched the doorframe with both hands, suddenly woozy. *I hope I can restrain him. I hope I am strong enough.* Without a plan, she rushed into the den, thumping heavily across the floor. She expected to see him foaming, red-faced, mad as a wild boar over something invisible, some thread in the carpet that wouldn't line up. Instead, he was twisted on the floor, laughing so hard his face was purple. She followed his gaze. A guinea pig in an astronaut suit and helmet was flying through space on the television. It was a real guinea pig in a cartoon helmet, a juxtaposition that had thrown Bubber into this spasm. To anyone looking, he might have been dying.

She had certainly never heard him laugh like that. It was almost frightening. Yet she remembered that when he was a baby, there was a full belly laugh that used to make them all laugh; it was so confusing and erupted from him. She watched his stomach convulse as he rolled on the floor. She should help him, but the extremity of it impressed her, alarmed her. What is laughter but a manageable convulsion? What is crying but a mild seizure? Drugged, he could fake it, he could learn to produce crying, laughing. What's the difference between a real laugh and a forced one? If it can be controlled, must it be fake? Maybe the difference between the believable emotional expression and the unbelievable one could be the ability or lack thereof to reproduce it. Was that fair? He sat up when he saw her, and gasping, he said, "Mom, look. It's a robot." The guinea pig moved in jerks, from crude animation and fat pig parts. She sat down on the ottoman, and Bubber backed up against her knees. She put her hand on his head and felt it was damp, he had been laughing so hard. His face was slack, relaxed, his eyes clear. Sunny thought, *Wow, this is my little boy. This is him, he laughs hysterically.* She felt exhilarated. What else could he do?

"Are you bald? Losing your hair?" said the television. Sunny clutched Bubber's ears, covering them with her hands. Her eyes locked on the screen. "There's no need to suffer the embarrassment of hair loss and no need to destroy yourself with harmful chemicals. Dr. Chandrasekhar's Orchid Cure can restore your hair and your self-esteem with all-natural plant extracts." Up until now, the screen had shown a waterfall splashing into a rock-lined pool. Around the pool sat women in traditional Burmese attire, with long glorious hair falling down to their knees. The women themselves were not Burmese; they were blond, redheaded, and brunette. They stroked and stroked their hair, arranging it with orchids and vines. "I'm Dr. Chandrasekhar," said the TV, and a disembodied head appeared in the middle of the waterfall. It was an elderly Indian man, pleasantly mustached and wearing a lab coat. "I have developed my Orchid Cure formula for thirty years, to bring you the finest Eastern herbs and . . ." He went on talking, but Sunny wasn't listening. "He's brown," she said out loud. "He's brown. He's really Indian. He's not my father. He's brown. What happened to him? What happened?"

15.

THE ROCK THAT HIT THE ROCKET HAD BEEN HIDING behind the moon. It was only the size of a fist. Inside it, down deep in the core, surrounded by weird heavy metals and crystalline rock, was a drop of a substance so primitive it was unrecognizable. It would never be recognized. It was a bit of matter, a grain of dust from the beginning of the solar system itself. Presolar. A presolar particle, trapped in a rock in crazy orbit around the sun. It was one in a million, one in a hundred million, like a raging genius in the human race, or a crazed savant skipping outside the bell curve. The rocket, approaching lunar orbit, cut through the emptiness like a gleaming, nanomatronic sliver in an artery, so tiny, such a fragment of metal on its path. The meteor was even smaller, a rogue molecule, loose in extraterrestrial solution. A subliminal particle on the atom of the solar system. A bit of thought loose in the brain. The size of the meteor was judged, later, to be nine centimeters in diameter. They did not see it at all; nobody saw it on any electronic screen. The astronauts and Maxon had put on their space suits. They had strapped themselves down, in the control module, just like takeoff. Just like the moment when the tower of fuel under them had exploded, shooting them straight up, face-first, into the ozone. The babble of Mission Control in their ears had directed the astronauts through the checks, the tests, prior to their arrival. The storage pod was already orbiting the moon, so they would sync with it, if all the numbers were aligned properly. The voice of Mission Control, calm and calming, droned on down the procedure for initiating lunar-orbit insertion. When the procedure was finished, when they had fired the rocket again, they would be orbiting, too.

The meteoroid was close, getting closer, but still secret, undetected by the astronauts in space or the humans on Earth, who were operating the astronauts remotely. It was such a little one, though. It was a meteor that no one would notice or care about, if it were wrapped in a cozy blanket of Earth's air. The atmosphere can burn up most things before they bother Earth. Yet in space, the smallest little thing moving at the correct velocity in the most dangerous direction can penetrate like a bullet. A grain of sand can leave a two-inch crater in the hull of a spaceship. What could a baseball do? It's one thing when you walk outside, turn your face up, and say, "Wow, just look at all those stars." It's another when a hunk of metal from before time drives itself into your intestines.

The pilot of the rocket was named Tom Conrad and he was a lieutenant commander in the U.S. Air Force. He was an automated person, his moves dictated by a roomful of scientists in Texas, by a protocol, by a list of procedures. Favorite of Gompers, the commander, and vocal critic of Phillips, the engineer, Conrad was as effective a pilot as there was in the world. Maxon was the only civilian on board. Conrad, Phillips, Gompers, they were good guys, stand-up characters. Everyone is friends in space; a few little blobs of life in a vastness of cold death will always pal around together.

Maxon clicked on his face mask, clicked into his restraints, buckled down into the chair. He became one with the rocket, connected to it, part of the hardware, indistinguishable. He was no longer floating, no longer human. He was a smudge on the rocket, a little bit of flesh inside it. He heard his breathing, inside that shatterproof helmet, that flesh bucket. Outside the ringing in his ears, outside the noise of Mission Control, relaying instructions to the pilot, to the engineer, to the real astronauts, while Maxon had been told, so lovingly, so kindly, to sit tight. The men on the ground always talked to the astronauts as if they were children, performing dogs. They were an extension of humanity, a little finger of biology in the vast mechanical space. Overdirected. Overthought. Ultimately, so insignificant.

When the meteor struck, the voice in the radio had just said, "Okay, check." Then there was a bump; it was felt by the astronauts as a ripple in the core of the rocket. There was nothing they could have done, on the fly, to override the program and violate the list of available alternatives. The thing had to impact. There was no such thing as an evasive maneuver. They felt it hit, they heard the metal groan, and they felt a lift, a sickening moment of lurch, like a car going fast over the top of a country hill. Then the rocket began to tilt, but they didn't feel it. They were in it, part of it, connected to it, laced into it with nylon straps and boots.

They saw themselves go off course, humanity jiggered to the left, hard, and there was a hissing sound, and some of the lights on the control panel began to blink, and the pilot's arms were moving quickly over buttons and dials, responding to the blinking, the information, like a spinning wheel on a sinking ship, going faster and faster. Maxon thought of dying in the same way that he thought of the spaceship imploding: ruining itself on itself, crushing like a can. The meteor was heavy metal. The skin of the rocket would not deflect it. There would be damage, but how much? Mission Control began to shriek. Like a parent whose child has run into the road. "Gompers? Status! George?" Then went silent.

The meteor had hit the rocket. There was no turning back. The people were inside the rocket and were strapped to the rocket. It's very hard to survive a meteor strike, in space. Everyone had always known this. Playing the numbers, they bet that a meteor would not hit, because space is so big, and meteors are so small, and rockets take up very little of space. Like a boat on the ocean, trying to stay away from one other boat, except times a thousand, times a million. It was so safe.

Of course, nothing kills you right away, and the same can be said for meteors. They don't have to kill you right away. This was the case in the rocket Maxon was sitting in, headed for the moon. It did not kill them right away. Yet they all four knew, and all the other humans back on Earth who were paying attention knew, that in that moment, the mission changed, and there was very little hope of a happy reunion. In the mad spinning mechanism, the cruel randomness of space, with its dire temperature shifts, its spinning infernos, its ferocious pellets, the chance of a human surviving was very small. The fact that most astronauts came back and were fine was a testament to just how tiny the steps taken by humans into space had been.

So the little room got littler. The astronauts began to sweat.

The air became tainted, as if they could taste the chemicals. Their feet longed for the bumpy heaviness of Earth. Their lungs yearned for the sweet, pure air of Manhattan, or even a coal mine, air that was made the real way, by plants and other people and cars and breezes and animals, not manufactured and tanked. Now they were not only cramped inside a spaceship, they were cramped inside a damaged spaceship. The panic was there at the back of their throats, with the desire to claw their way out, escape, restart, make different life choices.

Gompers took control, barking orders and asking for status reports. Fred Phillips, so obnoxious on his downtime, became a mechanism of assessment, snapping out clipped answers and clicking away on a board of buttons and levers. Maxon could do nothing. His limbs went still. His worry was distant. He thought of Sunny sitting in a room at NASA in Langley, looking at an uplink to the rocket's control room. She would see their four shining heads, round and hairless, closed to the elements. Would she think he looked bald? Would she think he looked familiar? Would the boy be there, in his helmet? Would Sunny be aware they were all encased in their own skulls? Maxon closed his eyes. Robots were more suited for this. Robots were more equipped. There was nothing a robot would regret, faced with its destruction in the aftermath of a meteor strike.

This is the story of an astronaut who was lost in space, and the wife he left behind. Or this is the story of a brave man who survived the wreck of the first rocket sent into space with the intent to colonize the moon. This is the story of the human race, who pushed one crazy little splinter of metal and a few pulsing cells up into the vast dark reaches of the universe, in the hope that the splinter would hit something and stick, and that the little pulsing cells could somehow survive. This is the story of a bulge, a bud, the way the human race tried to subdivide, the bud it formed out into the universe, and what happened to that bud, and what happened to the Earth, too, the mother Earth, after the bud was burst.

If Sunny were here, he would say, "Don't be afraid. Think of the meteor as a giant meatball. One I will eat and gain twenty pounds." She was always saying he was too skinny.

16.
*

THE SADDEST THING THAT ANYONE HAS EVER SEEN IS an oil town that is no longer booming.

In 1859, crude oil was discovered in fat pockets under the foothills of the Appalachians in western Pennsylvania, in Yates County. Forward-thinking people stuck pipes down into the ground and began sucking out this oil as fast as possible, pouring it into barrels, and shipping it around. They were able to sell it for quite a fine profit. They organized themselves into boroughs and towns and even cities. They built monstrous, huge Victorian houses, lit them with strange and dangerous wiring, and perched them onto the sides of small mountains. Down at the bottom of the mountains the Allegheny River cut through. Time passed and as the oil came up out of the ground with less determination, they moved the pipes around, and switched to coal. They mined for coal under the ground and then strip-mined the top of the ground and then turned to lumber.

Meanwhile in nearby Crowder County, they couldn't find any oil. Whatever the reason, the Crowder County residents had to dig in and rely on agriculture to get them through the turn of the century. By the time the oil had run dry in Yates County, the farmers of Crowder County had scraped down the hillsides and layered fields of corn, soybeans, soup beans, all up and down. They were rich farms, sweet farms, mooing and rustling farms. They were farms solvent with non-oil money. And so when Pennzoil moved down South to become Texazoil, and the health and welfare of the citizens of Yates County came acutely into question, the farmers of Crowder County sat in stoic victory on their well-oiled threshers, pounding out their prosperity.

But the barons of oil in Yates County were still rich. When they had gutted, disemboweled, razed, and plucked the land around them, they turned in on themselves in their Victorian homes, and when the money ran out, in approximately 1952, they mostly died. Now the people who had serviced all the barons of oil and coal and lumber still remained in the oil towns, and with the lords and ladies gone they took over the unwieldy Victorian houses and dealt with the inconvenient kitchen layouts and installed refrigerators in unlikely places and laid down cement in the basements and managed not to burn down the whole city.

Everyone needs groceries and a place to buy tires, so the tire-store guy can sell to the grocer and vice versa. Every year there is a slightly smaller GNP for the decaying oil town with no more oil in it. Gradually the houses fell into disrepair. Gradually everything slowed down. While the farmers in Crowder County sat smug on their silos of grain, the remnant in Yates County roosted in the finery of days past, and the ground watered by wealth, prestige, and privilege brought forth a curiously high percentage of geniuses. Maybe it was a result of the bizarrely grandiose public establishments, gifts of dead oil magnates. What rural public high school has a planetarium? The school in Yates County, where Sunny and Maxon had their education, was different in a number of ways. A commitment to high-tech updates was one, funded by long-dead benefactors. Its high concentration of statistical geniuses was another. The causal relationship between these two anomalies was uncertain.

In any case, this was where Sunny and Maxon grew up among those brought shockingly low, and those random scatterings of monstrous intellects. From the Amish farms, from the trailer parks, from the rotted old estates with broken windows and railings they sprouted up, shooting through the local schools with such powerful force they were shot out, far out into the world, and landed as chiefs of surgery in Chicago, research scientists in LA, sociologists in Denver. Maxon was not the first to rise up from such oily, strange beginnings to win a Nobel Prize. They were a rare breed, fed on the scraps of the oil wealth, nurtured in the overprivileged schools, always with the urgent aim of escape from the decaying place of their birth.

In the moment of impact, where the stars fell on him, Maxon remembered a day in the high-school planetarium, and the way Sunny's head had looked, in the center of that planetarium. She was sitting so upright in a chair, and looking so bald, like a cartoon of an idea. Aha! A lightbulb, her neck the part you screw in, her skull the glass bulb, her brain, her soul, her generosity the filament. Sitting there in the dark, in the light of the thousand stars, shot up by his lamp, he, the bold projectionist, illuminated the stars. What a way to pick up women.

* * *

HE WENT TO HIGH school first. By the time Sunny got there, he was a sophomore. There were kids there from around the county, mostly kids known to Maxon but some not. He went scowling through his first year there without her. He made enemies. He scorned teachers. He put people in their place. He sneered at their unread, unresearched, lazy intellects. The mother had tried to train him in all the ways he needed to behave in school. In elementary school, this was a success. To keep him from running in the hallways, she said, "Maxon, your rate of speed is independent of your lack of obstacles. Just because you can run fast doesn't mean you should." Later, he wrote down the math:

$$D = \frac{R}{T}$$
$$\text{WHEN } R = \text{BIPEDAL RATE}$$
$$R \leq 4 \text{ mph}$$
$$R \perp \text{OBSTACLE } O_n$$

Much later, this rule would be coded into a robot. But now, in high school, there were more complexities to social interaction than just walking down the halls, smiling when he was smiled at, frowning when he was frowned at, matching his facial expression to the facial expression of the person he was talking to, as he had been taught. "Maxon," said the mother, "if the person is crying, that means you cry. If the person is laughing, that means you laugh. There is no danger in emulating your companion. There is only danger in emulating poorly."

Yet in high school he found there was more to charming teachers than just running the code:

```
Do
  Teacher = GetTeacherState()
  If Teacher = NAGGING Then
    Head = NODDING
  End If
Loop until Teacher = QUIET
```

Now there was a physics teacher who hated him for no discernible reason. There was a gym teacher who threw him to the ground and then walked away fuming. There was a group of girls who laughed when there was no joke. But he was first in line to train as a technician in the massively expensive, sublimely extravagant planetarium.

This is the way it was in Yates County. Bald girls. Wild boys formed from math. Geniuses all around, just waiting to be discovered, or waiting to rot in trailers behind their parents' barns, die penniless, mourned only by the Amish from whom they bought all those eggs.

There was a script that went along with the planetarium job, a spiel for visiting elementary-school students or Scout troops, which he memorized as easily as he memorized everything else. He could deliver it in any inflection. The kind patron, the bored ingenue, the enthusiastic lover of science. Or in a completely flat monotone the other volunteers found incredibly creepy. There were several different programs and there was also a light show for weekend nights, with lasers. Maxon was pretty sure that people were doing drugs before they came to see the laser show. Maxon himself never did any drugs or altered his mind in any way. He drank water, straight from the spring. He ate anything that was available. He had brown, wavy hair in tight proximity to his head, where it grew thickly in between the times when he shaved it. He had round dark eyes, long black lashes, and he was tall, rickety, bony and gaunt.

He loomed. He became pale and then freckled with the seasons. The recent victim of an extreme growth spurt, he frequently tripped. When she came into the planetarium, she was a freshman, he a sophomore. She was unschooled in the ways of planetarium operation, he an expert. He played the host, offered her the best seat in the house. Then someone else came in, a few people, it was a Tuesday evening at 7:00 p.m. He'd had nothing to eat for dinner and only a Diet Coke for lunch. He felt light-headed, flustered in his body. His flat, smooth exterior showed nothing of this. But it was there, down underneath, a fluttering feeling.

When Maxon grew so much so fast at age fourteen, he found he was awkward with Sunny. There was a physical thing happening inside him, during that freshman year, that he had not anticipated. Something grew up in his belly as his bones were stretching. His voice dropped. He became a new person. Sunny was tall, too; brisk and fragile, but she pretended not to notice. But there was a different urgency in the room when they were alone together. They no longer wanted to make puzzles for each other. They no longer had their minds around their pretend. The time they spent apart was spent in different directions, so when they came home, they had moved along separate vectors, and were estranged. Maxon's brain was unaware of the movement. His eye recognized a Sunny in the Sunny slot, and his ear could hear her voice, the things it was saying to him. However, his body sensed it, down underneath his brain and everything that was going on that was reasonable.

He knew they were different people from the little kids that had rolled rocks to make dams in the creek, every muscle straining, every vein visible. He knew they were different people even from the shy two holding hands down the path to the waterfalls, afraid for each other to fall down the side of the mountain. He did not know entirely what they were changing into but he was aware it had to do with reproduction and genitalia. So he was clear on that.

Since they were old enough to escape the yard they had ridden together, her on a horse and him on a bicycle, all on and off the back roads of the area, on railroad trestles, down gulches and up ravines. There was nowhere Pocket wouldn't go, and there was nowhere that Maxon wouldn't ride his bicycle. Had the mother known where they were, she would have spat fear, but when they went out for a ride they didn't know where they were going, only that they were going, moving, off at a gallop, and free. When the bicycle broke, he pirated himself the parts from another, and he always made it work, or he would run beside her carrying it, still able to say "yes" and "no" when it was appropriate to say those things.

There were days he rode off by himself, when she had something else to do, and on those days he went faster, descended at a death-defying pace, stood up on the pedals to ascend those walls of hills, spinning out on gravel, charging down the backsides of mountains. When he could, he watched cycling on TV. He liked to see the humans with their machines, clipped in to the pedals so the man and the machinery were one thing, the wheels an extension of the man's own feet. He liked the grind. He wanted to ride over the mountains of the world, over the entire world and all its elevations. As he gained strength in his body, his mind changed, acquired new patterns, and somehow when they came together to ride now, after years of partnership, he was always faster, and she would fall into a pout.

On the day in the planetarium, they hadn't ridden out together in months. There was something new there, happening, that he couldn't understand.

Others came in but nobody sat near Sunny. They filed in slowly, took other seats, like they were avoiding her but maybe not with disgust, maybe with reverence. Parents and students together, or a couple of older students on their own. A Boy Scout troop came in, from the Presbyterian church in Knox, and sat all along one row, a man in uniform on each end of them. The others didn't approach her, but made a ring around her in the dim light, the white dome of the planetarium covering the room. Maxon came over and sat down next to her in the next fold-down seat.

"The program takes thirty-seven minutes," he said.

"Okay," she said. She smiled, seemingly normal, but he was watching the outline of her lips in the dark. They had grown; they appeared more full. They had definitely enlarged. He squinted, tilted his head, and went closer for a better look. Her eyes, too, had become more reflective. He pulled back, suspicious. She was foreign in her specifics: the corner of her eyes, the peak of her brow bone, the fold of her ear. He had not been watching her that closely. He had made assumptions based on her outlines. He felt he had to take everything in more specifically.

She said, "What?"

He said nothing. He unbuttoned his top collar and buttoned it again. There had been episodes, many, many bad episodes, with him chewing on his collars, so he kept them buttoned, right to the top. Wore nothing with a loose neckline. Nothing he could chew, even if he really wanted to. He would chew a pencil or a fingernail but not his clothes, not his clothes. He wasn't allowed to chew his clothes.

"Are you nervous or something? Haven't you done this like a million times?" she asked him.

"I'm not nervous," he said. "I'm just making sure you're not nervous. I know how astronomy can make people use phrases like 'the grand scheme of things' and 'suddenly I realized.'" She giggled, slid her backpack onto her lap and hugged it, stretched back in the chair and looked up.

"I'm fine," she said. "Dumbass. Just ready for the show to begin. I've been waiting to see it, you know. The famous projectionist."

The time had come to turn off the lights and start the planetarium show. There was a prerecorded message to be played about staying quiet in the theater and leaving only for emergency reasons. With fifteen people total in the planetarium Maxon doubted there would be an emergency situation—statistically, it was highly improbable. He began his pre-show talk where he described the night sky as they would be seeing it at that time of year right here in Yates County. He had decided he would put in a little secret for her, that when he pointed out the Big Dipper he would say, "Right there over the barn." When he said it, he watched her, and perceived her head nodding a little bit; from the back of her head he could see her cheeks stretch and widen a little. He knew that meant she had enjoyed the reference. He turned on the automated part of the show, settled into his chair, and watched her. She sat there, like a bulb within a bulb, shadows playing across the white of her skull like leaf patterns on the forest floor. There, above, the inorganic version, and here below, the human dome.

He envisioned himself with a Sharpie and a straightedge, drawing the stars on her skull, poking the firmament into her head. West and East her ears, North the tip of her nose. He would draw them as they would be seen in fall before hunting season, the best time of year. He would feel the Sharpie pulling smoothly along her skull; it would catch on nothing, like a whiteboard, allowing perfect shapes and lines. When he was done, he would turn on the light inside her head, and his work would reflect around the dome of the planetarium, no silly god names, no ridiculous anthropomorphizing of star clusters, just a star map with stars connected according to a logical rule. Which youngest, which most perfectly made, which most likely to expire. Instead of a crab or a lady or a bull, there would be algorithms played across the sky. Constellations were a joke, a nursery rhyme for grannies. Sunny's planetarium show would contain none of these goofy contrivances. It would be perfect. A mathematical expression.

The soundtrack beeped and plopped along: a comet, a meteor, a galaxy. Then the show was over. After everyone left she still stayed in her seat until he had switched off the projectors and made his way over to her. He sat down in the next seat again.

"I think I might want to draw a star map on your head with a Sharpie," he said. "Would that be all right?"

She pushed at his shoulder affectionately and when she touched him it was as if her hand had an electric wire in it.

"What, do you want to put pinholes in me and screw a bulb into my brain?" she said.

But she lay back in the chair again; her backpack slid to the floor. He was pleased with how close her idea was to his idea.

"I don't think I would need pinholes," said Maxon, his voice catching on itself, his hands suddenly charged; he had to hold them in his lap or they would be yanked up to the ceiling. "I think you would just shine."

She sat up in her chair. He looked at her and realized she was staring at him full on. Her eyes were wet and seemed bigger. Her chin dropped, her lips moved, but for a few seconds no words came out.

"That's really cool, Maxon," she said. "That's a really cool thing you just said. That's the kind of thing that people like."

Her voice was very low, and he said, "Did you like it?"

"Maxon," said Sunny. "I have been thinking about trying something out."

"What?" he croaked.

She put her hand out to his jaw and touched it, with her fingertips she drew his face in toward her. He felt the electric-wire feeling again, like she was shocking him off the ends of her fingers. She was only touching him on the face. He did not understand why he would feel a triangle feeling tightening in his groin, a triangle around his pelvis, tightening.

"I have been thinking about kissing you, Maxon. On the face. Would that be okay?"

"Yes," he said. He felt he might fall off the planetarium seat, because he was not well situated.

"On the mouth, okay?" she said gently.

"Yes," he repeated.

His face went closer and closer to hers until he breathed in a breath where he could smell her clothes, he could see the rim of Sunny's eye, so perfectly an arc with no lashes or brow to interrupt it, and then she kissed him, right on the mouth. The warmth of her lips pressed into him; it was not like skin and skin, it was something different, something more penetrating. He felt stirred, like a battery had exploded now in his torso. He felt things switching on inside him, and down the insides of his legs. He reached out for her, took her by both arms, and with his wonky awkward knees and long legs for once cooperating, he dragged her up to stand against him. They stood kissing there, under the dome of the planetarium, her arms around his waist, him clutching her tight, and he never, ever wanted to stop.

At that moment, Maxon knew that Sunny was his reproductive mate, and that he should find a way to solidify their relationship with words and gestures.

"Sunny," he said, when they finally broke away from each other.

"Yes," she said. She was smiling. She was radiating kindness and happiness. Her arms still around him were stroking his back, drawing her fingertips down from his shoulders to his belt, soothing him, teasing him, lighting him on fire.

"Do you want to say, 'Sunny, I love you'?" prompted Sunny.

"Sunny, I love you," he said hoarsely.

"I think I love you, too, Maxon," she said. She was thirteen years old and maybe she was unmoved in the ways he was moving, but she pushed her hands against his chest, as if aware of the sudden thing that she had over him. "I'm going to marry you, man!"

MAXON IN THE ROCKET could remember that energy between them, that way he felt electrified by her as all his switches turned on. All life is binary. On and off. There is no middle setting. Alive or dead. In love or not in love. Kissing or not kissing. Speaking or not speaking. One choice leads to another with no forks in the road. There are a thousand tiny yes and no decisions that make up every movement, but they are all just that: yes and no. For Maxon, awkward and waiting in the planetarium booth, it had been off. For Maxon, standing with his arms around Sunny, kissing her for the first time for real, it was then on. It never turned off again in his whole life. It was a switch that was duct-taped to one side with a sign beside it that said DO NOT TOUCH. It was nothing he could ever undo, no matter what she had said to him, or how much she had railed against him later. It was there because it had never left.

17.

THE MOTHER DID NOT DIE. INSIDE HER, SOMETHING had been suspended. She had lost the ability to move on. She had become interrupted. The breaths she took in were rasping and horrible to hear. The nurses shook their heads and pulled the curtain. The life clung to its trappings; the mind clung to the body, raking at it, tearing it up in its desperate clutches. She would not die, she would not leave the world like this, so unfinished.

On the surface of her, there was nothing going on. Not a twitch, not a grimace. But underneath that thick membrane of body, there was turmoil. On one side the destruction of cancer, the withering of the organs; they fell one by one like cities. On the other side, the bolstering of the will. She was counting, she was remembering, she was listing, to make sure she was alive. She would build it back, cell by cell, tissue strand by strand, until she was conscious. Until she was walking around. Until she was hearing news again, making decisions, watching the children growing up.

Outside in the parking lot, the bald daughter and the granddaughter inside her were sitting in the car. Sunny could not stay entirely away, but she could not go entirely inside. She could not make her feet carry her into the hospital, and yet when the car was running, the turns that led to there were inevitable. A few times she drove past and did not make that final turn in. Or she would go in and park, but not enter the building. She could feel the connection, through the window she thought might be her mother's death chamber, one of fifty rectangles in the brick.

She imagined that after the baby came out, she would put Bubber and the baby in the house and leave Rache with them. With Rache in the house, alone with the children, the cracks in the walls would recede. The children would be safe. She could go back to the hospital, to the mother, and sit beside her, breathe warm air into the room where she lay. She hoped that a nurse was doing this in her absence. That someone would have pity on the dying woman whose bitch daughter had abandoned her to die alone. Well, she's pregnant. Well, she's bald. Well, she's got a lot going on. That child. That man. Still, inexcusable, the nurse would say, and press her mother's swollen hand. Sunny hoped.

THERE WERE TIMES DURING Maxon's childhood when he spent every day with her. But then, when they were playing, Maxon would look up at the clock, see that it was after 4:30, and begin to run as fast as he could for home. His dad would get home at 5:00, he said, and he had to be there, to work. Having his son over across the way was galling to the father, unbearable.

His father was suspicious of Emma and her intentions. "What do they want with you, boy?" he would say. "They want a boot boy? They want somebody to send down the wells?" His father was also suspicious about the brown woman that lived with them in their house. Nu was an anomaly, the only person in the county who wasn't "white." While most of the neighbors accepted her and asked her patient questions about where she had lived in Burma, others never believed she wasn't just a common Negro. Maxon's father was one of these, and talked with spit flecks on his lips about the evils of letting a Negro or a Mexican take root in the county. The truth was that Nu had come from Burma to help Emma raise Sunny because Emma was pretty sure she shouldn't do it by herself.

When Emma returned from Burma, she wanted, most of all, to raise Sunny in an environment tolerant of eccentricities, where she could be as normal as possible. She could think of no better place for Sunny than the obscure, detached, rural county where Bob Butcher had grown up. Bob had always talked about it, rhapsodized about it, its tiny pointed country churches, its oil wells everywhere. Emma knew that if she took Sunny to Yates County, Sunny would be one of them, a family member. She would become a local fixture, like the people Bob had laughed about with the perpetual garage sale outside their house, or the eccentric millionaire, holed up in a stone mansion on a hill, who had invented Post-its. Her people were there. She would be at home.

She bought the Butcher farm from Bob's parents. They were happy to sell it to her; they had long since moved to Florida, where they could be in the sun and near their other son, the good son who hadn't gone off and gotten killed for being a missionary. Selling the farm to Emma meant being done with her and her odd child, so they did it without hesitation.

Emma was constantly on the phone and downtown in the lawyer's office, caught up in legal matters and the sale of Bob Butcher's chemical formulas to pharmaceutical companies. The shrewd deciphering of years of scribbled notes and research documents, all cover for his work as a missionary, had yielded her several interesting findings. These turned out to be of significant value to modern medicine. After the patents had all been drawn, the documents had all been signed, she came away a rich woman, able to live where she liked and do as she pleased.

So Emma set up camp in the old farmhouse, and sent for Nu from Burma. Nu came with her nats and her animist creeds, and her sturdy legs. She planted pounds on pounds of beans in the summer, hoeing endlessly and pulling in bushels of vegetables to can. She shot her rifle to scare off crows, shot her rifle to scare off a deer, shot her rifle to scare off a handful of people in the middle of the night, escaped from Warren State Hospital, and circling the house making mooing sounds like loose cows. She cooked, cleaned, and slept hard in the back room, her rifle and her shrine beside her bed. She worked endlessly with Maxon on identifying facial cues, reading body language, understanding the meaning of words like "regretful" and "obvious." They practiced sounding like English was their first language. For Nu, it was vocabulary that got in her way. For Maxon, it was syntax.

Sometimes there were stretches of time where his father would go on a trip and leave the older brothers to run the farm. Those were the good times. Then Maxon was free. Once his mother had even left town, leaving Maxon, at the age of nine, without a parent for two weeks. During this time, he stayed with Emma and Sunny, but he slept on the porch, where he was more comfortable. Sunny tucked him up like a doll before she went to bed, brought him a book and a bedside lantern. "You turn out that light before you go to bed, Maxon," Emma would say, before shutting the door. Still in the morning the light would always be on, the book collapsed on his chest, and a hundred moths stuck in the lantern, trying to get out. Nu fed him prodigiously when he stayed with them, and he went away just a little bit fatter, not so sticklike.

When Maxon's father, Paul Mann, was home, those were the bad times. Maxon's father was a tall gruff man, hunched and neckless. His pants hung down from suspenders on his bony shoulders. He had a gray beard half grown and a half circle of sweat appeared around the neck of his yellowed T-shirt. He was constantly in motion, always muttering, his watery eyes blinking rapidly. He had many projects: lumbering, tinkering, drilling for oil, hunting, and trapping.

It was unclear to Emma if the family had money problems or if their lifestyle was chosen by preference. The man always seemed so busy, he couldn't be a deadbeat, and yet they hardly spent money— Maxon and his older brothers were usually in rags or close to it, the house was falling down, and the barn leaked. The hundred or so dilapidated vehicles across the pastures were used as sheep pens, pigpens, and storage for other auto parts and pieces. Maxon's father was a proud hoarder, filling his garage, his barn, his outbuildings, and his house right to the rafters with things he might need in the future—tools, parts, scraps, animals, and sons.

Bob Butcher's parents had had a charged relationship with this obstreperous neighbor, frequently finding him or one of his shady cousins cutting timber over the other side of the hotly contested property line. The older sons spent their Saturday nights drinking home brew and cruising the back roads in one of their old clunkers with the lights off. You could hear them crashing into trees, spinning their tires in the gravel, and honking the horn in the darkness.

Emma tried to leave the Manns alone, knowing instinctively that Maxon would bear the brunt of any conflict. Once, however,

Emma literally ran into them in a car. She had Maxon and Sunny in the back, Nu in the front, and they were all headed out for ice cream, after which she planned to return Maxon to his house. She would get him there in time to be at work at 5:00 p.m. as usual, to avoid his father's anger. They were winding down the dirt road toward the river, where the tires inevitably skidded and the road dipped and skipped without warning. Suddenly, Paul Mann's truck came roaring up out of the valley, and smashed directly into the front of Emma's little Honda Accord. The truck slid back then, slipping on gravel, and banged into a tree. It dangled perilously close to the edge of the hill, but it was firmly stuck. Mann stomped the gas, stomped again, sending up a spray of rocks and dirt. But the truck was immobilized. He hopped out quickly, began pacing; his fat wife slid out of the passenger side, instantly crying and picking at herself. She was a humble figure, dim in her eyes and thin in her hair.

"Children, sit still," said Emma. "Are you hurt?"

They weren't. They were huddled together in the backseat, Sunny's leg over Maxon's knee, Maxon's arm around Sunny's neck. It was fine. But Paul Mann was angry.

"Woman!" he said. "I told you not to pull on me like that when I'm driving."

"Paul, Paul!" gurgled the wife. She wore a flowered sundress without shape, sleeveless and cotton. She must have weighed three hundred pounds. Emma could not imagine what kind of pulling was taking place between this squanchy, wet person and her tall, fierce husband. Then Mann pulled back his hand and smacked his wife across the face. She bounced back, her face almost comically registering the most predictable expression of shock. Then he bent his tall frame over the front of his truck to inspect the damage as if nothing had happened. Nu was now incensed, and while Emma rushed to Maxon's mother to help her to her feet, Nu stomped her small sharp self over the gravel road to Mr. Mann and poked him firmly in the backside with her foot.

"Hey you, piece of shit," she said. "You piece of shit, you treat your wife this way? What kind of man are you?"

"Go to hell," he growled, taking his time examining his fender. She lifted her foot again, balancing impeccably on one tiny foot in the road. She gave him another sharp poke and growled back. He slowly righted himself, pulling himself up to his full height. "Who the fuck are you anyway, some Mexican?"

Mrs. Mann was crying into Emma's shoulder, blood spouting from a split in her lip, her bulbous nose running freely, small eyes red and apologetic.

"I ain't sorry for him," she declared angrily. "He's too big for this county? No he ain't. He thinks he is, but he ain't."

Nu's face registered nothing but serenity as she laid a round-house kick on Mann's knee, just behind the joint. He was shocked, and fell like a tree gnawed off by beavers, right into the road.

"Shit!" he yelled. "Holy shit, the Mexican! Get her, Laney!" Nu followed her roundhouse with a deft kick to the sternum, knocking the wind out of him. He grabbed his throat, coughing, his eyes bugging out.

"You kilt him! You kilt him! Aoww!" keened Mrs. Mann, sobbing anew.

Emma, mopping up Mrs. Mann's face with the flowered dress, quickly interrupted. Ignoring his rolling eyes and the fact that he was sitting in the middle of the road, she addressed him politely: "Mr. Mann, I believe you need a tow truck. Can I take your wife into town to make the arrangements? I don't mind. Then I can bring her and Maxon back to your house at your convenience. Wouldn't that be nice?"

"Yeah," Ma Mann joined in with enthusiasm, "Miz Butcher'll take me to town, and I'll send Pete back for y'uns with a winch."

Mann glowered at them from the road where he sat, then sighed deeply, defeated. "All right," he grunted. "I'll walk home, it's only 'bout a mile. Pete can find the damn truck. We wuz just comin' to see what y'uns had done with that boy."

"You not gonna leave that truck here half in, half out of the road," said Nu indignantly. "You stay here, direct traffic, you big booby." Then she stepped back into the car daintily and shut the door. "You children just be quiet back there," she told them unnecessarily, smoothing her black braids and patting down her demure collar. "Everything under control."

Mrs. Mann, emboldened by this display of female power, marched over to her husband and stuck her grubby, sweaty palm out firmly. "Now I need money for town," she said, her mouth turned down like a toddler's.

"How much," he growled, grubbing in his pocket.

"I want much dollars," she said truculently. "I'm going to town."

Later, when they were driving, she was quiet, sandwiched between Emma and Nu. Behind them, the children were still quiet. There was really nothing to say. But Sunny had seen something new, something she had never seen before. In the front seat, here was the sniffling and bubbling Mrs. Mann, fatly rumpled and pressed between the cool and collected Emma Butcher and her small terrible Nu. They came to the end of the dirt road, hit the two-lane highway, and accelerated.

Sunny said to Maxon, clearly, "Does your dad hit you like that?"

Maxon's mother threw one hammy arm over the back of the seat and said, "No, he never done 'at. He never would done 'at, neither. Paul loves his kids. He's a bad husband to me, but he loves on his kids with the best of 'em."

Maxon regarded Sunny coldly. He wouldn't say anything. She knew, looking at him, that this was not the truth. She knew what her mother knew when she went over to that house for the first time, that dropping Maxon back into that was dropping him into poison. And as capricious as she sometimes felt, and as many times as she thought her mother was spending too much time on Maxon, helping him learn about singing and piano, and all the signs and charts she made for him, and the way she explained things again and again, when Maxon wasn't even listening, when Maxon wasn't even looking, and the way they had to stop in the middle of stories again and again to figure out why, how does this person feel, why did this person do that. She knew, even though she was only eight, that it was worth it.

And Emma knew, in the front seat, next to this mountain of blubbering guilt and all her victimization, that the child back there, the child back there in the backseat with her child, was hers to save. That she could save him, but that he was forever damaged. And where she had felt before sort of missionary about it, sort of selfless and helpful, as a crusader, as a nun, she now felt protective for Sunny. Who was she to bring this awfulness into her child's life? She hoped she had not done too much. She hoped it could be, in some way, undone. And yet, when she looked in the rearview mirror and the way the children were wound around each other, she saw that she might now be too late. Maxon was different. Sunny was different. They were different together. And whatever bad, messed-up thing was true down in him and down in her, it would be hard to separate them.

IN THE ROOM, IN the middle of the hospital, there was a life struggling to stay alive, trying to stick around and fix it. Everything that had been allowed to happen, and everything that had not yet happened, could all be rectified, could all be set straight. In the womb, in the middle of Sunny, there was a life struggling to come alive, struggling to make its way blinking out into the world. In its life, there had yet been no mistakes. There had been no love, no sadness, no peace, no fear. There had only been sustenance, and a shallow range of experiences. Yet this life, insentient, wanted only to push on to the next place, out of the darkness, on to the next thing, to the broader range. One hung on, one pushed forward. As one pushed forward the other was pushed forward as well. It was a death and a life happening, all at the same long time.

18.

SUNNY WAS WATCHING THE NASA CHANNEL AND MISS-
ing Maxon. All they ever had on the TV when he was home was
cycling or the stock market. He didn't care about entertainment. It
was hard not to be distracted and frantic, when he was not around.
She hoped that in the last five years of her life with him, she had not
ruined their marriage and their love together. Once she had only been
for him, had only been busy with loving him. She had laid herself up
next to his full, knobby length, and had been equal to it, perfectly
equal. They were like a graft, like a new creation, from long associa-
tion and also perfect love together.

When she got pregnant for the first time, Sunny was afraid she
had to become something else. When you become a mother, how

can you be another thing at the same time? When you become an orphan, how can you be anything other than that? She worried now that everything she became had just squeezed the love out, until she might only sort of love him, only used to love him. Maybe she forgot how to fill up the rest of it, because it's full of other things—orphan-to-be, mother. Maybe you can't truly wrap your flesh around another person, after there's been a baby inside you. Maybe your parentless sorrow puts you in a box with those who have the same sorrow. Her mother was dying. She wanted Maxon, the old Maxon, the way it used to be. And yet she knew that he had always been the old Maxon. It was she who had changed. Yet everything else she had tried to become was stupid and pointless.

At lunchtime, Sunny received an e-mail reminding her that the annual neighborhood craft show, which she had helped to organize, would be happening later on in the afternoon. The e-mail subject header was "Don't Forget!" The last line in the e-mail promised mimosas. Sunny frowned. Would she still be going to the neighborhood craft show? What if her mother died right in the middle of it, and she had to run out to the hospital? What if Maxon fell out of the sky and she had to go catch him? What if Bubber had a breakthrough, started reciting prime numbers? She would want to video that. What if she got a huge contraction and spewed amniotic fluid all over the wide-plank oak-finish farmhouse floor of the party host? Sunny smoothed her dress down over a twisting, kicking baby in her belly. What if everyone looked at her and said, "Why are you here?" Then the phone rang. It was Rache calling her to find out if she was still going.

"Are you still going?" asked Rache.

"Well, are bald people allowed?" Sunny asked.

"Very funny. Of course bald people are allowed. Tina's husband came last year, remember?" Rache quipped smoothly. "But seriously, if you feel weird, you don't have to still come."

"Do I feel weird," Sunny wondered aloud. "Do you feel weird, Rache? Does anyone ever feel weird? Does anyone ever not feel weird?"

"What are you doing, girl? Are you flipping out on me?"

Sunny paused. "I'll be there."

"Well, what are you bringing for eating?" Rache asked. "Have you had time to make apps? Did you want me to cover for you? I made fairy 'shrooms."

"No, no," Sunny began. She felt herself in a strange dream where she was a housewife on a respectable street, talking to another respectable housewife about appetizers at a party, a party she herself planned to attend. "I'll bring . . . my braided honey loaf."

"Braided honey loaf? Is that even a thing?" Rache wanted to know.

"Of course it is, it's my grandmother's recipe. Braided honey loaf. It's Dutch. You eat it backwards."

"Which grandmother, the dead one or the one that supposedly never existed in the first place?"

"You're hurting my feelings, Rachel," chided Sunny serenely. "I've been making braided honey loaf since I was a toddler."

"Well, okay, then I'll see you at Jenny's at three o'clock. Are you . . . is your nanny sitting for Bubber?"

"Yes, ah . . . yes."

"Great, well. Pull it together. See you there, okay? Love you."

Sunny felt like a tightrope acrobat without a rope. She felt like an actor, on a stage, with no costume and no lines. She groped in her mind for what Sunny, one week ago, would have brought to the neighborhood craft show. A basket of carefully crafted muffins, individually wrapped, to sell for three dollars each. A tray of silver jewelry, each piece bent carefully by her careful hands while her child drooled and rocked beside her, to sell for twenty-five dollars the pendant, thirty dollars the bracelet.

Now she had to make braided honey loaf. And she didn't even know what that was. Bubber, in the front room, was seated at the piano. He had been there for the last hour. He played arpeggios ascending, arpeggios descending, arpeggios ascending, arpeggios descending, over and over and over with rapid finger movements like hammers on the keys. He was stimming on the piano.

When Bubber had first begun opening and closing cabinet doors for hours at a time, Sunny had rushed to the pediatrician. She was told that stimming is self-stimulating; some kids do it rocking or head banging but some kids do it tapping pencils, or some kids click their tongues or shake their hands around. Bubber had dabbled in head banging, of course they had been medicating that out of him, but it was why he wore the helmet. He had done his thing with the cabinet doors, and then it turned to listing, and labeling, and repeating consonants. Now he was sitting at the piano going up and down, up and down, half step by half step up, half step by half step down, with maddening accuracy. She didn't want to stop him, though. He was occupied. And it was kind of amazing. She wondered what she herself, without her wig, would bring to the party. She wondered what Bubber, without his medications, would play on the piano. The only reason they had a piano was because in a house like theirs, a piano was kind of expected.

She felt a mild contraction and leaned against the kitchen island. Her face was naked, no brows, no lashes, no borrowed human hair falling around her face, false as someone else's husband. She wore a babydoll dress, Empire waist filling out around the baby inside her, and a cashmere shrug, petal pink. She pulled out a hunk of ground turkey from the fridge, suddenly convinced that braided honey loaf was made out of meat.

When she had made what was essentially a sweetened meat-loaf paste, and kneaded it in a metal bowl through three more slight contractions, she looked at her sticky hands, the pasty pink results of her effort, and wanted to cry. She decided to flake on the party. She could say she was having contractions. She could say she had gotten sick. She could say that the nanny had traffic court, couldn't get away. She rolled the meat dough into strips, braided it into a bread pan, and put it in the oven. There it would be, forty minutes later, when she pulled it out. Where would she be? Still here? Or was there time to escape out an upstairs window, plummet into another universe?

Bubber pounded the piano keys; it seemed he would never tire of that progression. One three five eight five three one. Half step up. One three five eight five three one. She went upstairs to change her clothes, put on black maternity pants and a creamy peasant top, wrist bangles and long earrings. Looking at herself in the mirror, she addressed the new hybrid of reckless bald Sunny in pleasantly haired Sunny's expensive wardrobe.

"Own it," she said to herself. "Own the bald. Own the braided honey loaf. Own it. Your husband is Maxon Mann. Nobel Prize winner. Your mother is Emma Butcher. Fucking awesome lady. Own it."

The doorbell rang and Sunny ran downstairs to let the nanny come in. They had to have a nanny who was also a nurse, because sometimes that was necessary, and Maxon could tolerate only a few people coming into the house. No string of teenaged babysitters. No switching back and forth with the other moms on the street, so that there were always kids over. Sunny found the nanny humorless but well informed. Didn't matter. Maxon agreeing to let anyone into the house was reason enough to sign off on anything.

"He's playing the piano," said the nanny. "Hey, that's pretty good! I didn't know he could do that."

"I didn't either. But I took him off his medication," said Sunny. "His behavior may be erratic. He may laugh, he may scream, he may decipher texts from the Harappan civilization, he may just go to sleep. Don't know. But I have my cell phone and I'm one street over. So call me if anything comes up."

"Well, how long should we let him play the piano?" asked the nanny.

"As long as he keeps wanting to," said Sunny. "Within reason. Right?"

Without further explanation, Sunny plunked the braided honey loaf, now hard and perhaps even sliceable, into a floral-themed bowl. She dropped a kiss on the top of Bubber's head and he lolled his head back to say "Oh, I love you, Mother" in a voice that could almost be described as having inflection. His hands never stopped. Sunny felt very happy inside, hearing these words from her son even after she had taken his medicine away.

Out on the sidewalk she felt the breeze on her head, and she tapped on down the walk to her neighbor's house. Sunny had hosted several neighborhood craft shows, but then she had allowed the honor to rotate around the friends in her inner circle. The neighborhood craft show was more of a swap meet than a commercial enterprise, although there were prices on all the items and a lot of commerce was simulated. If you bought Theresa's hand-beaded earrings for thirty-five dollars, then she might turn around and buy Rose's hand-stamped Christmas cards, three boxes for ten dollars each. Rose might purchase Sylvia's aromatherapy concoctions, and Sylvia would come and sample your silver pendants. No one really left any richer or poorer than they had arrived, but they all had varied assortments of little items to disperse among their less important friends, saying, "This soap was created by hand by one of my friends down the street. She does it in her FROG, can you imagine? Doesn't it smell just like Christmas cookies? I knew you would love it."

The type of women that frequented the neighborhood craft show were not the type that needed extra money for Christmas. They were there playing store. They were also there for the mimosas. There was a delicately lettered sign festooned with streamers and balloons, set up on an A-frame in Jenny's perfect yard. But if any stranger had wandered in off the street, no one would have known what to do about it.

Jenny had brought every portable surface in the house to the fore in her modern Tudor palace, little side tables carrying felted catnip balls, the dining-room table hidden under an assortment of quilted handbags and hats. Ladies of the neighborhood floated around through the front rooms: the foyer with its grand staircase, the den with its grand fireplace, the dining room with its grand mural, a Welsh countryside painted on the wall next to the French table beside the German windowpanes. Jenny was no gifted designer, but her husband had a bank account without a bottom. With adultery and divorce beating their wings in the air, she was not moved to conserve his cash.

As soon as Sunny's foot touched the beautiful planks of Jenny's foyer, her body knew just what to do. She drifted into the kitchen, complimented the renovations, set down her platter, and chose a perfect slicing knife from Jenny's silverware drawer.

"What is it, Sunny?" asked Jenny sweetly. She was putting on a brave face. The husband was in the dining room, wearing a tweed jacket and a leather golf cap, his long white hair pulled back in a horrible little ponytail. He had piercing black eyes and a nervous mouth. But Jenny was keeping her distance. With her friends around her, she would carry on.

"It's braided honey loaf," Rache interjected. "Norwegian, you know."

"Dutch," said Sunny.

"Oh, neat! I want to try some . . . later." Jenny moved off gracefully to praise Angela's mother's handbags.

Sunny stood there at the sideboard, looking around the gleaming heads and smooth shoulders of her neighbors. They were good people, and smart people. She did not feel, without her wig, that she was suddenly better than them, that they did not deserve her. Instead, the opposite. Here they were, unsuspiciously they had brought her into their fold, let her rise to the top of their pecking order, had listened to her advice, had followed her lead, and now she had betrayed them. She could feel them avoiding her gaze when she faced them, but felt their eyes on her behind her back. In some ways, she was invisible, but in some ways, they couldn't take their eyes off her.

Then a strong knock sounded on the door, and it flew open, revealing a familiar figure in the doorway, bold and sure. Les Weathers entered the room. The women went to him like butterflies. They offered to take his jacket, they led him to the food table, pressed a plate into his hand, a fork. Their voices lilted up an octave. Suddenly Jenny's husband, who had been telling a story of how he got beat up half a block from home, walking to a party at the Hardisons' last New Year's Eve, was abandoned. They had all heard that story anyway. Here was Les Weathers of Channel 10 News. He greeted them, flashing his white teeth, patting shoulders and nodding, but then Les Weathers made a tall, blond beeline for Sunny.

He took her by the elbow, bent his head toward her in concern, and said, "Sunny, are you all right? How's the baby? Hanging in there?"

"We're okay," said Sunny.

"Oh, good," said Les Weathers. "I'm glad to see you out and about, taking in the nice fall air."

"Yes, well," said Sunny, "I need to go soon. To the hospital."

"What's wrong?" he gasped, instantly renewing his posture of concern. "More contractions?"

"No, it's my mother."

Les Weathers furrowed his brow and the few ladies around Sunny said "aww" and "ooh" sympathetically. They knew about the mother, how she had been retrieved from Pennsylvania in an advanced state of death, and how she had been lingering at the hospital.

"How is she, Sunny?" asked Rache. "Is she conscious? Did she say something?"

"Oh, I took her off life support," said Sunny. "She's dying. She's going to die now."

When she said these things, she felt her rib cage weaken. In her mind, she saw the slice of muffin she had been holding fall out of her hand. Someone dove for it, scooped it into a napkin, disappeared it. She imagined Les Weathers's strong, broad arm around her, and she almost felt herself leaning into his starched shirtfront, his sternum smelling briskly of lime and confidence. She wanted to cry and scream and wail, there in front of everyone, her face twisted up and red, her hands clawing apart his hairdo, pulling his ears off. But these things didn't happen. The muffin stayed in her hand. The box of feelings she had packed in the hospital room remained packed, and nothing escaped it.

"It's okay, it's okay," Les Weathers, more to the gathering of women than to Sunny.

"She's okay. She's had a rough time. But she's dealing with it. Look."

"I feel bad," Sunny said, and coughed a little bit. She saw herself, as if from across the room, keeping it together, mouth solid like a line across her face. How much she longed to scream it out at them: I FEEL BAD! I FEEL BAD THAT I PULLED THE PLUG ON MY MOTHER! I KILLED HER AND I FEEL BAD! SHE IS GOING TO DIE! But she would not. She would not be something that would be remembered for years, something people would tell their husbands about later, tell their sisters about on the phone. No, they would not talk about some wrinkled tearing thing clinging to the big man with the ironed curls of hair and the cleft chin, squeaking and spouting.

They would report, instead, the smooth alien in the peasant top, saying calmly, "I do feel bad that I pulled the plug on her."

"Sunny, you must have had to!" Rache put in, and Jenny put one hand on Sunny's back. "You had to let her go, and it was time! You did the right thing."

How could it be the right thing to kill something that's alive? How could Rache know anything, when Sunny had been lying to her from the start? But she put that thought in the box, and she closed the box. And the screaming, and the tearing at herself, and the crawling under her bed to wait for death, all was packed into the box, and the box was shut, and taped shut, and she would not open the box, or think about the box.

"She was alive, and now she's going to die, and it's my fault. I did it," she said.

"Ridiculous," thundered Les Weathers. With one hand wrapped tightly around Sunny, he picked up a chocolate-chip scone in the other and gesticulated definitively before putting it into his mouth with a flourish. "You're not some criminal. You don't go around killing people. You're just a woman. A bald woman. And you just do what you have to do."

Chewing the scone, he warmed to his topic. "We all do hard things, Sunny. Losing my wife Teresa was the hardest thing I've ever done. But it had to happen. Did I abandon her? No, she ran away from me. Did you kill your mother? No. Through your inaction you allowed her to die. But everyone told you to do it. The court, the doctor, even your own husband. You did the right thing. It was for the best."

19.

IN THE WINTER OF THE YEAR WHEN SUNNY WAS EIGHT years old, Maxon was nine. She and her mother wanted to take Maxon skiing but his father said no. They were going to go skiing, wrapping up in parkas and snow pants, fuzzy hats, goggles, scarves, until no one could distinguish Sunny from a regular child with a regular head all full of glossy ringlets or straight layers. Maxon, they felt sure, would benefit from going skiing. From getting out of the valley. They all would. They were going to drive to Vermont. But his father said no.

Nu also said no, said they were crazy, freezing to death in the snow, but Emma was adamant. She had bought a pale blue ski jacket for herself and goggles for both the children, which they wore while pulling each other on disk toboggans around the yard. Paul Mann said the boy was needed at home. Needed at home, when there were five other brothers, all older, all working on the property in their various capacities: lumberjack, bulldozer, meth cooker, etc. Why this one small other brother was needed so greatly when they could never remember to feed him, the Butcher women could not comprehend. But he was not allowed to go and Sunny was very angry about it.

IN THE WINTER THERE was no bicycling, no trail ride, and not even any time for play after school, because it got dark and cold so early, so they both rode the bus to Sunny's house, where they ate, then walked through the valley to Maxon's. Then Sunny ran back, Maxon-style, brushing the trees with her hand, climbing and clamoring up the hill in a rush while Nu stood at the back door worrying and waiting. She went with him that night on his walk home; they left right away after school with hot sandwiches in their pockets, so Nu wouldn't worry. They cut a wide angle through the valley, not a direct route. It was cold, the pines were shrouded in ice, every little branch a glass filament, and the wind brought the boughs tinkling down around them, raining crystals. Their boots crunched in the snow. The creek, frozen at the bottom of the valley, was an ice sculpture of a creek, frozen in motion, all the little waterfalls. They stopped there, by Maxon's stump cache, which they had turned into a fairy throne.

"All hail the king the fairy!" cried Maxon.

"Come all the fairy come to king," yelled Sunny. "Die the enemy the fairy evermore!"

"A feast the fairy come!" shouted Maxon. He brushed off a log where they often sat to talk or pretend fairy courts, and they sat down to eat.

"The wolf tribe come the feast," Maxon said through a mouthful of ground beef. "The hawk tribe say death to the wolf tribe."

"The hawk tribe bring the penitence," said Sunny. "Bring ten penitence the feast, keep all the wolf tribe cold the snow."

They went on like this as they ate, doing their pretend in their own words, garbled and fast. It was all wound in with the tribes of the forest, the wars they were in, the plots they had played out, the characters they had invented. Maxon had it all worked out in visuals around a particular stand of trees, like a data map. Sunny tried to understand him when he talked fast, tried to talk back, faster. She was the one who was reading a whole lot of children's literature, so she had a fair amount to offer, even though she wasn't of the forest as he thought he was. They both sensed it getting darker. They threw the last bits of their food into a crook of a nearby huge bent tree, as an offering, and they knew it was time to move on.

"Maxon," she said finally, slower. "You so fear the father."

"Not fear I the father," he said, still in the play speak. "Fear I the mother."

"Maxon," she insisted. "You are afraid of him. Why? What does he do to you?"

Maxon turned to her with a black look, and the revelation that loomed was terrible enough without showing itself. Simple enough, common enough, but it hurt her badly. She put her arms around him. "I love you, Maxon, the fairy king, the boy the forest, love you I forever."

He grinned, not looking her in the eye, and pushed her off. He raced for home. "Do not follow, Sunny, the bird egg, the river rock! Get to the home! For safe! For tomorrow! Run!"

She watched him go, knowing they had lingered too long in the dusk, feeling the bone-chilling damp settling on her, inside her expensive mail-order coat. She knew she should turn around and run straight up the hill for home, but she didn't turn, she followed him, slipping between the trees, boots soft on the snow. She saw him run up the hill, zigzag, touching the trees as he ran. As if he were blind and finding his way. She stayed at the tree line as he ran down the slope and across through the field, slipping through the layers of barbed wire, now a black spot against the glowing white field of snow. He went into the house, for a moment outlined in a yellow rectangle, and then gone, the bang of the ill-fitting screen door loud in the falling dusk. When she turned back to the trees it was darker still. She could make her way easily, it was familiar to her, it was the hawk tribe territory, and she knew the trees and the ferns and the old log where a battle had taken place over the remains of a long-dead doe.

The only place she had to be careful, in taking a more direct route home, was among the big rocks on the hillside. Where the mountain got steep on their Butcher side of the valley, there were huge rocks protruding from the earth, the product of some eruption millennia past, giant hulking things honeycombed with deep ravines, dangerous in the dark. As she skirted the rocks, she heard from within their labyrinth depths a small cry.

She thought maybe a deer had fallen into a crack, gotten trapped between two of the steep sides of the rock. A deer or maybe a bear. Her heart raced. A mountain lion could crawl out. A deer would be impossible to lift by herself. She would go back and get Nu. She should go back now, immediately, and get Nu. Her mother would say, "Yes, Nu. Go and see what it is." Nu would go by herself and save or kill whatever was there. And yet, she had to be sure of what she had heard before she left, so she went down on her knees in the snow, and crept over to the edge of the ravine. Down there, something was moving. It was a man. It was Paul Mann. It was Maxon's father.

"Jesus Christ, thank you," he wheezed. Then louder, "You there! Who is that? Who is up there?"

Sunny said nothing. The man's legs were twisted under him in the shape of a Z; he waved his arms, but clearly he could not move. He was covered in pine needles, from where he had pulled down the earth around him, trying to dig himself out. She smelled liquor on him, even from ten feet above him, and she saw he was wearing only a T-shirt and his filthy suspenders, his work pants.

"Who is that?!" he repeated, aggressively. "That you, Maxon? Get your ass home and get your ma. Get your brothers. I thought I was going to freeze to death in this shithole waiting for one of you shit-for-brains to stumble along here. Where you been? Over there sucking face with that bald little bitch? You go get your ma, right now. Did you hear me? Move your ass or I'll make sparks on it!"

Sunny removed her head from above the hole. Her pulse was racing; she felt like her eyes were going to pop out from the way her blood was pounding in her face.

"What were you doing on our property?" she said very clearly, in her sternest little girl voice.

"Who's that up there? Come back here, let me look at you," he said.

She pulled off her hat and stuffed it in her pocket, unwound her scarf from her neck. The bitter chill of the advancing evening bit into her warm skin, but she let it, felt her ears tingling and her breath freezing in her nose. She stuck her head back over the lip of the ravine, and let him see her against the sky.

"Oh, ah, Suzy, Suzy, it's you. Ah, I'm sorry I thought you was somebody else. Run and get someone now, you got to help me out of this hole, honey," he crooned. She sat there looking at him for a few seconds, memorizing the sight of him in the hole, because she knew this was a moment she would never get back.

When they left Burma, when they stood in Rangoon about to board the steamer to take them on the long journey to San Francisco, to Chicago, to this night under these stars, under this rising moon, over this pleading man, her mother turned her back toward the city, toward the strange harbor, and told her, "Look, Sunny. Look at what you are seeing now and then close your eyes and think it in your head, so you will never forget. You will never again see what you are seeing now, God willing. So take a good look so you can remember it. This is the place where you became you." She could still remember, dimly, five years later, the outlines of the pagodas, the low flat government buildings, the walls of the harbor. And now she looked at this person in the hole, Paul Mann, and thought hard about his outlines, the shape of his body, locked in the stones. Then she removed her head again from the lip of the ravine, replaced her outerwear, and marched toward home.

She breathed lightly, even climbing the hill the rest of the way home. She breathed up in the top part of her body, her eyes wide open. The rising moon illuminated the whole of the fields around their house. The house lay nestled in the hemlock trees, beautiful cottage full of warmth and love and the welcoming arms of her mother and Nu.

Two days later they found Paul Mann. He had died of exposure after falling, drunk, into a small ravine. His last bottle was found beside him, smashed. His frozen face was lifted up, pointed toward the sky, features frozen in place. Later he thawed out, was buried, and allowed to rot. The Butchers took Maxon on the ski trip to Vermont; his mother was happy to let him go. She had a lot on her hands. He was not missed.

AFTER THE CRAFT SHOW, Sunny went home. Bubber was napping and the nanny was drowsing on the sofa, half watching *Oprah*. Sunny dropped her keys on the table. It was so peaceful; she could hardly believe it. When you are sitting on a three-legged stool and you've kicked out all three legs, but you're still sitting upright, must you assume that you're just so good, you levitate? Or must you assume that you were sitting on the ground all along? When there's nothing left to burn, maybe you have to set yourself on fire.

What gruesome sight would it take for her friends to reject her outright, for them to recognize that she was foreign, unworthy? There's a woman with a mole over half her face. There's a woman who can't stop talking about her therapy appointments. She had envisioned rejection, renouncing, she had envisioned being drummed out of the neighborhood, her cardigans cut to rags, her minivan repossessed, but she had not anticipated that what might happen was that they would sort of kind of identify with her. That this, the baldness, would make her more like them, not less. That she had not envisioned.

Her BlackBerry buzzed in her bag. She took it out and pushed the button to retrieve a text from Angela Phillips, the wife of another one of the astronauts on board the rocket. "Don't turn on TV," it said. "Call Stanovich." She felt her heart race. She dialed the number for the Langley research center, got Maxon's research partner on the lunar-colony project. He was crying.

"Sunny," he said, "the rocket has been hit. It's been hit by a meteor."

"Is he dead?" she croaked into the phone.

"They don't know," said Stanovich. "They've lost communication with the rocket. Sunny, I'll miss him so much. Are you going to be all right?"

As if she would be. As if she would not die without him. How could Stanovich know them, and still not know? But it was not uncommon. They were both so private. There were not a lot of love notes scattered about the house. People wondered, or asked her sometimes, how could she be married to Maxon? How could she keep on loving him in spite of his obvious deficiencies? She might say, *How do we love each other? We love each other like naked children in a strange jungle, when every stump turns into an ogress, each orchid into a lump of maggots. We didn't say, "I love you," just as we didn't, after a day of wandering lost in the trees, turn to each other and say, "We are the only naked children in this jungle." Everyone else was just a jaguar or a clump of dirt.* Sometimes it comes to that desperate state, when you have to cling to each other and be alone. When no one else can truly matter. She thought, *Ours is one of the epic loves of our generation. Possibly of all time. Who cares if no one sees it, walking by? This story is a love song. Who cares if history won't remember?*

THE SUN WENT ON through the sky and down. Bubber went to sleep. But Sunny turned on every light in the house. She went to her wig room and stood in the doorway, her breath coming to her in rags. She had the same falling feeling of someone who has decided belligerently to climb a slate roof, and who has fallen off that roof, and is headed for the ground. She went to the wig that was closest to the door and slipped it off its resting place. This particular one was her go-to girl for all occasions, a masterpiece of blond waves and tresses, long and unstyled. She picked it up in her hands and quickly settled it on her head, felt its weight on her, felt it squeezing her head back into its regular, proper shape. She put her hands out and turned to the right, turned to the left. She walked slowly back out into the bedroom, into the hallway, and all through the house.

As she moved through the rooms like boxes all stacked over the foundation, she pressed the walls out into their usual shape, lifted the ceilings above her, nailed down the floor with every step. This beautiful house, this sacred temple of her life, built on everything that was normal and expected, and purely good. A sanctuary for their lives, to guard against the intrusion of the weird, the lapping waves of the past. This was her old life, this was the way it was before, everything in its place. The house a manor, a statement, an edifice, instead of just another elaborate cap for another sewage pipe, like every other sewage-pipe cap down the street.

Under the chandelier in the foyer, she paused. Her shoulders were paralyzed under the weight of trying to put it all back together. She could barely move to answer the door, but there was something there. Someone stood out on the step. It was Rache.

"Hello, Rache," said Sunny, swinging the door open. Her voice was intended to sound like it always sounded, saying those words. Rache was holding Sunny's bowl, which she had left at the party. The bowl that held the braided honey loaf, constructed in such a stupid fit of optimism. Rache's face twisted when she saw the wig.

"Sunny? What are you doing?" Rache swept into the house, slammed the bowl down on the kitchen counter, and whirled around to face Sunny. "Why is that wig back on your head?"

"I . . . you heard?" Sunny began.

"What the fuck do you think you're doing?" said Rache. "You're not putting on a wig, okay? That's not happening."

There was nothing to say. Rache looked like she might come at Sunny across the room, rip the wig off her head, give Sunny a slap on the mouth. But the wig sat on her head, doing its job, keeping the roof up, keeping the stars up, keeping the planets aligned.

"Do you think we give two shits about your bald head?" Rache asked. "We don't. We—we don't care. There's not one of us hasn't—"

Rache put her hand against her mouth. Sunny felt her throat closing up.

"We don't care. We don't want you to wear it."

"I know," Sunny said. "It's fine. It's not you. It's not for you, it's just for me, and for, my life."

"Putting that thing on your head is not going to put the rocket back on course. It's not going to unkill anyone. And it's not going to even work: we all know."

Rache paused. She reached out and put her slender fingers around Sunny's wrist.

"Sunny, you have to understand that you are not so special. I know it's been rough, but you are not the only person in this world. You're not even the only bald person."

"You're not bald," said Sunny.

Rache pulled at her own blond hair. "Who do you think is under here, Sunny? What is here? Under this hair? Did you—do you know that I fucked her husband? I fucked him, I fucked Jenny's husband." Rache was talking in a whisper now, her mouth pulled down at the corners, her voice rasping over her tongue. "Jenny's husband, and she's so nice, she might as well be a basket of kittens. Are we in love? No. But I fucked him anyway."

Rache took a handful of her hair in each fist. "Bald," she said. "And the rest of them. Bald. Trust me."

"But they never killed anyone," said Sunny. She coughed and choked. "You never—"

"Neither did you, Sunny," said Rache. "You didn't kill her. You didn't."

Sunny pulled off the wig. She put it in Rache's hand. She'd earned it. It was nice of her to make a gesture of friendliness. Nice of her to return the bowl. And talk about her own terrible head. *But you're wrong,* she wanted to say. *It's all my fault. I killed him, I killed her, and I've killed Maxon now. All my fault. And the wig doesn't matter. Because my house is already in ruin.*

20 *

UP IN THE ROCKET, MAXON HEARD HIS OWN BREATH-
ing inside the helmet. He heard the voices of the pilots talking to
each other, quieter now, less frantic. He felt the rocket shifting ef-
fortlessly through space. It all felt okay, it felt normal. His pulse was
elevated, but his bones were not broken. He had not been smashed
to pulp. He had not exploded into fragments.

He tried his voice. "Phillips, what's the status?"

"Uh, Genius, we're going to need you to sit tight," came the
voice.

"What happened? Was it an explosion?"

"Think we got hit, brother," said Fred Phillips. He was miles
away by radio wave in the headset, but he was right next to Maxon,

so close he could have reached over and patted the man's gloved hand.

Conrad's arms were moving frantically, his fingers tapping at a keyboard. Maxon wondered if he should help.

"It is, ah, a bad outcome here? Did the meteor damage us?"

"Yeah, Genius, any meteor that hits you is a bad outcome, okay?" Phillips's voice was raised higher than normal, which Maxon knew from his notebook indicated tension and lack of patience. Maxon frowned.

"We are going to restore communications first," Gompers put in. "Then we can assess the damage and take action."

"Are we on course?" Maxon asked. "Are we going to rendezvous with the cargo piece as scheduled?"

"Maxon, we're kinda working on making sure we have airlock and oxygen right now," said Phillips. "There's a process to these things, a process we have to follow fucking meticulously, or we are all fucked to hell, okay?"

"Relax, Phillips," barked Gompers.

"But are we on course? What is the status of our course? Have we deviated?"

"Listen, brother, if we don't establish communication with Houston soon, and with our satellites soon, and with the entire fucking world of electronics outside this rocket real soon, we're not going to be able to work out shit for a course, okay?"

"Phillips!" barked Gompers. "You will control yourself. Another outburst like that and you're in quarters."

A blue ink pen floated past Maxon's face. He clicked the release to let his arms free from the chair, reached up, and unclipped his face mask, letting the shield up. He took a deep breath.

"We have oxygen," Maxon said. "Now how the fuck about our course? We were looking for orbital insertion, Phillips, do we have it or do we not? Do we have engines? Do we have power to the engines? We need to fire rocket two at sixty throttle for eight seconds. That was the last order. Did you execute?"

Phillips slammed his hand down on the keyboard inside its white glove but also unclipped his helmet and took in a deep breath. His face was moist, and Maxon knew that meant he was nervous. He turned his head, now six inches away from the end of Maxon's nose, as they were shoulder-to-shoulder in their seats in the rocket. His words came out with a little spray of spit from his tongue, clipped and bitter.

"I appreciate your interest in our progress. I appreciate you are on a mission here too. But until I tell you otherwise, you are only allowed to sit there. Do not take off your suit. Do not shit your pants. Do not ask me again about the fucking container."

"Can I say 'Fix it! Fix it! Fix it!' until you fix it?" Maxon asked, unblinking. Gompers began to laugh.

"You are a jackass," said Phillips. "A true jackass."

He turned his face back to the controls in front of him, and Maxon sighed. He did not like waiting for information. He did not like standing aside while others did the thinking and the work. He did not like to delegate, ever. He felt if he could switch places with Phillips and sit at the green and black screen, he would be able to perceive all of Phillips's errors, communication could be reestablished, and they could rendezvous with the container as planned.

However, communication could not be reestablished. The satellite fixture had simply been sheared away by the meteor and was not functional. No tapping on buttons, no words and numbers on the green and black screen could bring it back. It would take a space walk to reach the place where it had been, and even if they got to it, and stared hard at the twisted metal and shattered fiberglass that was the only remnant of the place where the satellite fixture had been, they would not be able to bring it back. Without it, they were without comms, and they were undeniably off course, falling directly into the moon and out of orbit, if Maxon was not mistaken, and he never ever was.

Phillips and Gompers became more and more intense, while Conrad stayed cool, his face ashen. They kept running checks, they ran checks on everything, everything checked out, except the communications, which were completely down. Without the ability to talk to Houston, without the resources at their disposal at Mission Control, the mission was over, and there was no getting home. While contingencies could be planned for, those contingencies did not include being knocked off course by a meteor and the resulting adjustments. Those could not be made by the astronauts in a rocket with no comms. They needed a way to get a link home, and nothing else would do. Maxon sat in his chair, crossing and uncrossing his fingers, steepling and unsteepling them, his eyes focused inward, trying to be patient, for the sake of Phillips and Gompers.

"If we could get our position," mumbled Phillips, "if we could get a triangulation . . ."

"Without our numbers, we have nothing," said Gompers. "We are decaying right now. We are going to land very hard, very fast. We are not even equipped to land, in this thing, you realize? This thing lands, that's where she's going to stay. We need orbit. We're going to fire the rockets."

"Wait, in what direction? You think you can just fly it blind? We need Houston, we need information. We can't even see properly up here."

"I have an idea," said Maxon firmly. His voice cut through the close, dry air. He had been so calm through the whole ordeal that the other men were beginning to wonder if he was actually aware of the situation they found themselves in.

"Whatcha got, doc?" asked Gompers.

"We know where the container pod was, right? We know where it was and what its orbit was. If we parallel its speed and its trajectory, we should be able to safely establish a solid orbit. Once that has been accomplished, I can go over to it, and get one of the Hera models to build us a phone."

"Go over to it? In what, your car?"

"There's a jetpack suit in Cargo B," said Conrad.

"I know," said Maxon. "I'll wear the jetpack and go over to the container."

"Do you understand the severity of this situation, sir?"

"No," he said, "but I'm about to Google it, and by the time we get there, I'll be well informed."

Conrad blinked and then slowly began to chuckle. But Phillips reached over and punched him in the arm.

"Jackass!" he repeated. "Look, we can do this. With the software we have on board. We can repurpose the navigational software to function as a GPS. By radio, by radio if we have to."

"But then what, how," Gompers began, "how do we get Mission Control access to our numbers?"

"I promise you," said Maxon blankly, "that I can fix you a way to talk to Houston, if you just get me over to that cargo container. One of the machines the robot Heras are going to build on the moon is a comm center. We only need a Hera. And I need silicon, titanium, iron."

George and Phillips looked at each other. "Moon metals," said Phillips. "We need moon metals."

"Yes, those are minerals found on the moon, among others," Maxon told them. "The robots are made to extract their own materials from the moon's environment, can't be shipping them plastics and aluminum from Earth all the time."

"Well, where are we going to get silicon and titanium?"

"You can break down some of the equipment in Cargo A," said Conrad.

"Will there be enough?" asked Phillips.

"I don't need much," Maxon said.

While Phillips plotted a course to intercept, Gompers and Maxon sifted through the rest of the rocket, looking for pieces that could be used as raw materials for the Hera to make a phone.

"Thanks," Maxon told Gompers. "This will cover it. Now, Phillips, can you get us in line with that container?"

"Simple math, my friend. Simple math," Phillips reassured him. "I gotta say, Genius, you came up with a good one this time."

It took him two hours to put on the suit they used for space walks. It was a bulky contraption with a glass helmet, gloves, boots, heart monitor, brain scan, and a bodily fluid collector. There were layers and layers to install on himself, and he didn't quite fit it, being too tall for the legs. The jumpsuit inside felt tight, like he was squeezing into a second skin. The sturdy exoskeleton fit over him and shut. He moved like a monster inside it, like a fifty-foot lizard, motions slow and deliberate, knocking over stuff in Cargo B, sending bits of equipment spinning across the room. The jetpack was operated by controls under his fingers, and with a few short instructions, Maxon was able to understand.

By the time he was ready to go, Phillips and Conrad had worked out the orbit of the container module, had mapped it, and had pulled up alongside it. "Godspeed, Dr. Mann," said Phillips forlornly. "You have about six hours of working time in that suit. We'll be in communication with you via the radio." He went into the airlock. He could see Gompers and Phillips back in the rocket, looking in at him. Then there was a hiss, and the bay opened out onto space.

Without hesitation, he pushed himself off the door to the rocket, and went spinning outward. Did he worry about the jetpack? If it would fire when he pushed the button, if it would function properly? No. Maxon believed in machines. Believed they would do what they were built to do. It was like walking around with a kidney, or a lung. *We all do this all the time,* Maxon thought. *We think nothing of depending on a lump of muscle to keep us living, a lump of biological matter that pulses moment by moment, day by day, on and on in the dark, without respite, without refreshment, and even when we starve it, or stifle it, or overdo it, that lump of pink continues to contract, contract, contract, without a will of its own, without a rest. Without the knowledge of its own sacrifice.*

"You are already a robot," he had once told a roomful of graduate students at a conference in Maine. "The most advanced robot ever created." The heart pumps without awareness, and that's why it pumps. Unless there is a mechanical failure, it continues to pump, and who can plan for that? You build your organs out of the best material available. You build them while you are still in the womb. While you are still on Earth, you build your jetpack that will take you out into space, and when you get out there to use it, you just have to trust that you built it right.

Out into space he went, amazingly free of connection. Without a cord to tether him, without a thought to pull him back into regret, he went sailing away. The boys in the rocket saw him silhouetted against the backdrop of the moon, with all of space behind him. He looked no longer human; they had to remind themselves of his flesh and his human soul inside that bright white mechanical suit.

He was human, but uncrushable; human, but breathing; he was human, but free. He could see the Earth, the moon, the rocket behind, and the cargo container in front of him. He had truly departed, and yet he was sort of unaware. Detached. There was no profound experience waiting for him in the depth of space. Other humans, in this situation, were moved to think inwardly. Not so Maxon. He only thought of his direction, of the corrections needed to keep himself on course, the distance between himself and his target. It's literally all he thought about.

WHEN HE WAS A child, there were very bad times. There were times when his father hit him with a strip of leather. There were times when his father hit him with a brick. These experiences were not lodged in Maxon's memory. They were not allowed to stay there. He had often been bent, naked to the waist, over his father's foot locker, instructed to hang on to the bars of the bed. One of the man's boots would clamp down over his rear, pinning him down while the belt fell again and again on the small of his back, his arms, his ribs. Nowhere for his head to go, nowhere safe. For failing to respond to a question. For failing to deliver an appropriate answer. For upsetting his mother. For being late. Then there was no flesh that would respond with a smack. There were only bones that would thud, and skin that would tear. He would deliver the punishments in the most secret places, to hide them. They would be hidden from view. So, did Maxon have a familiarity with divorcing his mind from a troubling physical situation? Yes. It was one of the first skills he mastered.

THE WALK ACROSS FROM the rocket to the cargo container took him ninety minutes. It was a long ninety minutes, one of total concentration. While he did not feel worry, or pain, or excitement, he did feel the cold urgency that he must succeed. He was his own man, out there, uncontrolled by anyone's idea, unfettered by anyone's inadequacy. He was as a body floating, as a speck of dust floating past a warm window in the afternoon, he was rudderless, detached, at the mercy of no wind, no gravity, only operated by the fuel and intention contained in his own white titanium skin. It didn't take him long to get used to the feeling. He liked it.

21 *

THERE WERE FEW TIMES IN HIS EXPERIENCE WHEN he had stepped out without a road map. Without programming. Winging it. It was antithetical to his vision of the human race. Once when he was in Europe, during a summer in college, he had been following the Tour de France, running with the riders up the mountains, dressed as Darth Vader, shouting "Allez, allez, allez!" He knew their every movement, their route to the last kilometer, his lodgings booked months in advance. But then, "Hey, Darth Vader," a cameraman called to him at the finish one day, "come out with us!" And he had gone. Without a schedule, without a map, without knowing who would be there or when it would be over. They went to a bar where a spotted jersey was hanging in the doorway, proof that one of the top riders was drinking there that evening. He had drunk alcohol for the first and only time in his life. He had kissed a woman that wasn't Sunny. She spoke only French and he pretended he could not. He had regretted it all in the morning.

He remembered another time when this had happened. It was the quiet moment, on the bank of the Crowder River, where he asked Sunny to marry him. For times like this, scripts had often been crafted for him by the mother. If he had to say thank you to a scholarship committee, he was taught exactly what to say, how to hold his face, how to raise his voice. At his father's funeral, she showed him how to shake hands with the minister, what part of his mouth to show when smiling. Even the first time he told Sunny he loved her, Sunny herself had all but written the words in the air in front of him, and led him to the spot, and pointed to each syllable. And yet, that day, he made up his own words.

Sunny had come home from graduate school for the funeral of Nu. The mother had known, but the children had not known, that Nu was actually already past middle age when she came to Pennsylvania from Burma. For all those years of Sunny's childhood and Emma's middle age, Nu had been seeding green beans across a full acre of garden, planting corn in endless rows, potatoes, giant pumpkins; taking in bushel after bushel of harvest, canning, steaming, freezing, and marching a constant parade of food through the kitchen. She planted it, picked it, prepared, sauced, cooked, fired it, and they consumed it. For several years she even kept goats, used their milk to make cheese, yogurt, and the animals would climb on cars that parked in the driveway. She called them guard dogs, named them Brownie and Whitey and mourned when they died of fever, swore never to have other pets. Her sturdy face, her squinting face, her floppy straw hat, her no-nonsense farm boots, had seemed timeless. Maxon had thought she was thirty when he met her, and that opinion had never been updated.

"No, dear, she was a very old woman," said Emma when she called him to give him the news.

"How old?" Emma's voice was quavering. That meant she was sad. Maxon spoke quietly. That's how you talk to sad people.

"She was eighty-seven," said Emma.

"I'm sorry for your loss," he said.

"I thank you for the sentiment," she returned automatically. It was a fragment of conversation they had practiced for years. He had used it on both sides of the conversation, and it had never failed him. He knew just how to say both parts.

"What are you going to do now?" he asked.

"Well, I'll just stay here, I guess. Sunny is still in California, of course. You're still here, for now."

"Will she be coming home for the funeral?" he asked.

"Yes, she'll be home. Maxon, did you tell her about the house?"

"I didn't tell her," he said. "Why would I?" He did not say he had been keeping it for a surprise. He had never kept anything for a surprise before in his life, but this idea captivated him, he wanted to try it, he wanted to try it on her specifically.

"Listen," said the mother, "don't tell her. Don't . . . bring her back here. You let her go back to graduate school; it's what she needs."

He had nothing to say.

"Maxon," said Emma. "She's like your sister. You care for her like your sister, right? Say you care for her."

"I care for her."

"Like a sister," prompted Emma.

"I care for her like a sister," said Maxon mechanically.

"See?" said Emma. "There you go. There's no need to tell her anything about the house, right? Just let her go back to California and finish grad school like she needs to do."

"Would it be wrong," he asked, "I mean, would it be the wrong thing to do to take her out a little while she is home? Even if it is just after the funeral?"

"Oh, no," said Emma. "You mean, would it be socially inappropriate?"

"Yes," said Maxon.

"Oh, no," she said again. "Nu would not mind. And I would not mind. Sunny will need some cheering up, Maxon. You take her out. But then, you let her go."

Maxon hung up the phone and looked around himself at what he had done. Over the hill from the Butcher farm, off to the north and up the mountain, there was a piece of property that he had always coveted. It was the highest point in the landscape for miles around, and accessible only by a dirt road that at times achieved a grade that would make a mountain goat nervous. On this property there was an A-frame house, glass on both ends, from whose windows one could see all across the valleys and hills straight to the deep gouge that was the Allegheny River. Throughout his life he had entered this house as a squatter, as a trespasser, first alone and then with Sunny. It was their special retreat. As soon as he had some money, he bought it.

The view was breathtaking, and he had gotten the property for a song, as depressed and weak as the economy in the area had become. He gutted the house, replaced the saggy furniture and hunting gear with a few spare pieces and a bachelor's kitchen. He had been living there during school breaks all through graduate school, shoveling out the road himself, living on Triscuits, Diet Coke, and melted snow, and during the summers working like a madman to clear a beautiful yard, mathematically precise in its layout, with a pond at one end and a garden at the other.

Nu had died in her garden, feet facing up the hill, head facing down. She had an aneurysm, and at that angle, all the blood rushed to her brain. Maxon knew this was a risk of living on a slope.

Maxon had worked on his house, his property, knowing that the land abutted the Butcher land, that they shared a border through ten miles of woodland. He wanted what he wanted from moment to moment: stumps cleared, shed painted, garage raised, shade trees lined up, rhododendrons installed in rows on the tree line. He didn't consider what he wanted beyond that. But then, he hadn't thought of Sunny as something to want. She had been his. They talked on the phone almost every day.

When she returned from California for the funeral, she appeared different. She, too, had been rushing through, spending summers in school, working toward her doctorate. Their time in Pennsylvania had not coincided, him going to conferences, a visiting professorship at Stanford University, the youngest person to ever do this and that. He stood in the old Butcher farmhouse kitchen, his head bent over her portfolio, looking at photographs of the art wigs she had made. One was constructed of teak shavings, forming a little Zen garden. There was a series of wigs in black and white; she had been exploring what she could do with melted swirls and plastic textures. She sat at the breakfast nook, wearing a woven scarf around her neck, a pair of faded jeans, a halter top, and giant boots. She was so certain, so eager, her hands clutched together as she waited to hear what he would say, that he could hardly look at the pictures of her work. It didn't interest him at all. But the robot matches its facial expression to the expression of the person with whom it is conversing.

He stood there, his head almost brushing against the ceiling of the little kitchen, nodding and smiling, and constantly looking back at her, sitting there so grown, so different from every other woman he had met in the meantime. So this was the voice at the other end of the phone. He had not seen her for three years. She had changed a lot. He felt, suddenly, the urge to act. He felt himself, suddenly, want something. Want something beyond a mathematical expression or the resolution of a logical question, beyond installing recessed lighting properly, beyond closing his eyes and opening them again. He wanted her, properly his. He felt like he felt when he was hungry. He knew what was supposed to come next.

"Do you want to go canoeing tomorrow?" he asked.

"Canoeing? Like, you mean, after the funeral?" she said.

The mother had been crying in the other room. Sunny had been crying, too, before Maxon came. But she thought she would be okay to go canoeing after the funeral, as long as the mother was going to be okay without them. She said she would.

The funeral was in the morning, a quiet affair in a little white church down the valley. The service was read by an Episcopal priest from Philadelphia, one of the mother's friends. The church was lent by the local congregation, but against the wishes of the local minister, who would not have been happy with Nu's animist beliefs. The church was packed, full to the aisles and out into the foyer for this woman, for some the first outside their race they had ever met. A crack shot with a rifle, a master chef, and a faithful friend.

That afternoon, Maxon arrived in a truck to pick Sunny up, with the canoe in the back. He had lowered it down out of his own garage, but she didn't know that. She wore bike shorts, a loose tank top; he could see her bikini poking out under it and it moved him in his body to see that. She slung some sunscreen into an old yellow backpack, added a water bottle, a few granola bars, and a towel. Her mother had gone to bed upstairs.

"Will this be okay?" she asked. In high school they had gone canoeing all the time. They knew exactly what to bring. Now he was unsure. Would they need more things, now that that they were grown-up adults? She hadn't brought marshmallows and Yoo-hoo. He didn't think that meant anything other than being an older age. He saw the way her hips spread out, stretching out the sides of her shorts at a different angle than they used to stretch.

"It's fine, let's go," he said.

The weather was gorgeous. A warm breeze ruffled the Allegheny River but otherwise it was almost like a lake in places, perfectly mirroring the dense green of the mountains on either side; the water grasses underneath the water were like mermaids' hair, swept back in the invisible current. They talked easily, pointing out new construction on the bank between Emlenton and Parker. Pittsburgh people were moving in, building little chalets along the river, dumping loads of gravel down their driveways, laying concrete, importing Jet Skis.

When they were kids, there was a yearly raft race down nine miles of the river. The mother had always encouraged them to enter, each year building a more insane and complicated contraption. Maxon would organize the project on a concept in physics, and then Sunny would decorate it beyond the capacity of science. Once Maxon had actually had to haul their raft down the river, marching stoically along the bottom while Sunny bailed water. That year, Nu sat smoking a cigar atop an elaborate conning tower they had built, pulled down the Allegheny by the future rocket scientist. Now the raft race was a thing of the past, too dangerous for kids today. Maxon felt the memories coming in.

"Let's stop at the flats," said Maxon. "And go swimming."

At the flats below Petersburg on the Crowder River, all the local kids had found a safe place to play in the river without worrying too much about current or getting over their heads. This was to the township what the beach was to any seaside town, an excuse to take your clothes off in front of your friends, a meeting place, where the girls could pretend to concentrate on tanning, the boys could pretend to concentrate on dunking each other, and the little kids could splash around on the rocks. There were a few short weeks in July where western Pennsylvania turned hot, and with no air-conditioning, the locals flew to the river for relief.

From the Allegheny, Sunny and Maxon turned upstream where the rivers converged, and after paddling hard to get under the railway trestle of the Belmar bridge, they found themselves in the calmer, clearer, shallower waters of the Crowder. Sunny peeled off her tank top and her shorts, and dove into the water, neatly avoiding the underwater rocks, and surfacing again, laughing, like a seal.

Maxon paddled on, slowly, and then rammed the canoe up onto the upstream side of a river rock that jutted out of the water near the bank. Under the water, everything was coated in fine silt, clinging to the rocks and plants. It was thick, like jelly, and you could swish it off with your hand or stamp your foot on it and it would flutter and spray through the water, turning the water muddy for a few seconds, until the current flushed it on and the river was clear again.

Maxon stepped out of the canoe onto the rock with a long flat foot, and then yanked the canoe farther up on the rock, to make sure it was stuck fast. When he turned to look at Sunny she was out in midstream, floating, sticking her toes out of the water to examine them and flapping with her arms to keep from drifting away. In the years they had spent apart, she had definitely changed. But he still recognized her. He recognized her movements, yes, and her physical shape. He recognized the tone of her voice and he noted persistent mannerisms and favorite vocabulary, although that had changed a little.

But what he realized, looking at her there splashing in the water, making a star with her body and then contracting down to do a somersault, was that he really recognized her, down inside. He knew that, if the planet was spun like a top, and stopped suddenly, and he was asked to point her out, that he could do it. There might be crowds and crowds of people all in gray, with gray hair, and gray eyes, and in order to be identified they would have to be logically processed according to age, and intelligence, and financial merit. He would not know any of them. But he knew Sunny, he knew her without looking, without asking. She would be there like a lightbulb in a basket of wool. She would be there like a red balloon in an asteroid belt. She was the only one, ultimately, in the whole world who mattered. She was the only one he would have known anywhere. How he wanted to insure that she would only be his. He had a ring in his pocket. It looked exactly like an engagement ring should look. But he had no script. He was on his own.

LATER, THEY STRETCHED OUT on a wide, warm stone. Sunny ate a granola bar, but Maxon couldn't eat. He gulped the water, wiped his mouth, and lay back in the sun. She had been talking, talking, talking like she always did, the sound of it as pleasant to him as the breeze ruffling the pine trees. The sky was blue above his head, an impossible Pennsylvania blue of mid-July. It was as perfect and safe a moment as he could recall in his life. If only she would never stop talking, then he would never have to begin.

She lay back, finally, with a deep sigh, and it was quiet. He had no idea what she had been saying, but she seemed relieved.

He went up on one elbow, turned his body to face her. Now was the time for him to create an utterance, something to say.

"Sunny," he said. His voice caught and he coughed. She went up on one elbow, too, now facing him. Her brow furrowed.

He looked at her, the big dark alien eyes, the delicate nose and rosebud mouth. He traced the fine line of her jaw, saw the soft wrinkle where it met her ear, the skin of her neck so pale and invisible, her jutting collarbone, her beautiful tiny breasts. He felt a feeling in his heart that was powerful love.

"Yes?" she said.

"Sunny, are you all finished with having sex with other men?"

She smiled. She laughed.

"Well, I don't know," she said. "Are you all finished having sex with other women?"

He stared at her. He didn't know what to say back. He hadn't had sex with any other women.

Her eyebrows went up; that meant she was surprised. "Maxon?" she said.

"Yes," he said.

"Oh, baby, are you telling me you haven't had sex with anyone but me?"

"I have not," he said. He was unsure whether she was pleased or disappointed.

"The very last time you had some sex was with me at the 4-H fair?"

"Yes."

"All those years ago?"

"Yes."

"And no one else? Oh, Maxon."

No one else. He saw her eyes get wet, and her lips pursed together. She put one finger on the back of his neck, and traced it down past his shoulder, over his rib cage, down the side of his hip, and the outside of his leg as far as she could reach. He said nothing, did not move, but inside he was shuddering with relief, being touched by her again. She reached over and put her lips on his face, on his eyebrows, on the side of his chin. His breath came faster. But he had to stop it. She was so warm, so near to him, that he might go into a dream. He might fall off a precipice and wake up to find himself still unmarried, still on the same rung of the ladder, no closer to the top.

"Wait," he said. "Wait."

He sat up, and reached into the pocket of his shorts where they were folded in a neat stack of his clothes next to him on the rock. She watched him, saying nothing. She had what people call a twinkle in her eye. He pulled out a shining metal cylinder and said, "Sunny, will you marry me?"

She pushed herself up on one hand, her legs elegantly drawn up against each other. "What's this, Maxon?"

"Oh, this? It's a titanium capsule. You use it to store unstable compounds. It's waterproof, I thought the ring might get wet so . . ."

"So is that a titanium capsule in your pocket or are you just happy to see me?" she laughed. Her smile was wide, her face beautiful. Her body was lithe like a long coil, it swung toward him in a wave. She put her hand on his chest and drew it down, down his front, where her fingers feathered over the front of his boxers.

"Sunny," he said again, "will you marry me?" He unscrewed the container and drew out the ring, carefully, carefully; it must not fall into the water.

She slipped her hand into his shorts and with the other hand in his hair, she pulled his mouth to hers, and put a burning kiss on him. She was now next to him, her body pressed to him, he could feel her pulse elevated, her breathing frequency intensified. Her fingers went around his testicles and softly rubbed there, underneath. This was a new thing. She must have learned it at college.

He broke away from her kiss, and said, his breaths coming in gasps, "Sunny. I need you to look me in the eye. And answer me. I need an answer."

Look me in the eye. Answer me. I need an answer. All times this had been said to him. Now he was saying it.

"Yes, you ass," she said, throwing her arm around his neck and wrapping the other around his waist. "Yes, I will marry you. I am all done having sex with other people. Yes, yes, yes."

They would get married. They would move into their beautiful A-frame. And even if Maxon's work called them away to the big city, they would keep their house, on their hill, forever. He knew it.

He put the ring on, and then she fell on him like a starving dog, and blew his mind.

22.
*

WHEN MAXON'S HAND TOUCHED THE CARGO MODULE, he did not feel relief. He felt: *Here is the cargo module. Now how do I get into it?* When he discovered that he could not get into the cargo module via either of the hatches, he did not feel fear. He felt: *What is another way that I can get into it?* He kept moving his hands, moving like a spider across the face of it, from handle to handle, edge to edge, seeking a new idea. His white suit wrinkled at his joints, making bent tubes for his body parts to be in. His helmet dome reflected the surface of the module, reproducing it in golden tones. Both of the hatches were locked. He had failed to consider this outcome.

The cargo module itself was about the size of a box on a semi truck. It had been shot into lunar orbit unmanned, using an unprecedented amount of fuel, and had found its orbit without incident. Now here it was up in space, in the blackness hung with stars, where there was no wind to whistle through its latches, no air to breathe, no song to sing.

Maxon let go of the handle, and he did not fall off or spin away, but just hung there, drifting. He had turned off the communication radio in his helmet that kept him in contact with Gompers and Phillips. The noises they were making didn't even sound like words. It wouldn't be the first time he suspected someone of talking nonsense, just strings of language in random order, to befuddle him. They knew he was not a good listener. They had been told to follow specific syntactic patterns when speaking to him. He had turned his jetpack off. There was no electricity in him at all.

The silence of space was upon him. Now the difference between life and death, for him, was the motion of a fingertip. He was without tether, without support. If he reached out his index finger and pushed, his Newtonian mass would repel backward, every action having an equal and opposite reaction. In this case, with the action being flicking the side of a box with his index finger, and the reaction being his own death and the failure of the nascent lunar colony, Maxon really had to put a lot of faith in Newton when it came to the equal and opposite part. But that's how he won the Nobel Prize: picking a rule and sticking with it, right down to the last logical consequence.

He wondered, what would Sunny do, with him lost and floating off into space, orbiting the moon like a speck in a sack, his death unmarked in time, an unspecified number of days hence, when he stopped having electrical impulses in his brain, and continued to rot, but just at a faster pace. She had not specifically said, "I want you to orbit the moon until you die," and he could not read between lines. He could only create his own conclusion based on evidence, and based on the rules that had been established. Without him, she could marry someone more appropriate, more functional. "My first husband went into space and died," she might say. "Then I got a better husband, one more suited to the life I want for myself and my children." Maybe it would be better, for Sunny, if he did not come back. Maybe it would be better, for the Earth, if colonizing the moon was not possible.

He was sure that Sunny would be okay. She had told him on multiple occasions that the thing that was ruining her life was him. What worried Maxon, about this scenario, was all the beautiful robots. And he feared that if he pushed himself backward, and fell into orbit, then in forty-five minutes to an hour he would come up with the solution that could have saved them all. Then he would be forced, for as long as he could still breathe in and out, to deal with the frustration of not being able to put that correct solution into action. And that was a feeling with which he did not want to become acquainted. You can't kill yourself just by willing yourself dead. Eventually you pass out and start breathing again. He waited for the solution to come to him. But if he waited too long, the space walk would be over, his oxygen would be out, and he would not have returned to the rocket.

"Dad," said a voice. It was the voice of Bubber.

Maxon turned his head inside his shiny globe, then grabbed a ledge on the side of the module and turned his suited body around. He saw another space suit, smaller, but just the same as his. Just the same shape of golden globe head. Just the same jointed arms and white gloves, but in tiny, perfect form.

"Bubber?" he called. His jaw almost cracked when he moved his mouth to speak, he had been clenching it so tight. His voice sounded loud in his own helmet; he did not hear it echoed over the radio link, because the radio link was turned off.

"Hi, Dad," said the child-sized space suit.

"How did you get out here?" asked Maxon. "Am I dreaming?"

"No," said Bubber. "You are awake."

The hiss of oxygen coming into his helmet, his own breath coming out of his mouth, and Bubber's voice, clear as letters on a page, coming from . . . where?

"Am I dead?" asked Maxon.

"No," said Bubber. "You are alive."

"Are you dead?" Maxon asked.

"Dad, enough," said Bubber.

The child-sized space suit approached him, and he could see a reflection of his own body in the helmet. It reached out its hand to him. He grabbed the hand, felt the stiffness in the other suit's fingers through his own gloves.

"I am used to you being at home," said Bubber. "You should be home."

"Sorry, buddy," said Maxon. "I'm having a little trouble."

"I can help you," said Bubber.

What was astonishing to Maxon, taking in this information, and reading this data, was that Bubber sounded so normal. So completely utterly like a normal human being. Not like he was simulating human talking. Not like he was scripting. Just normal, like an average child. An average child in spectral form in a space suit orbiting the moon on a doomed mission to colonize it. With real inflections and tones. Maxon knew how to tell the difference between people like him, who were faking it, and real live humans, who were not.

Working with NASA, he had run into quite a few people he could really relate to. People with brain chemistry so similar to his own. Some of them banded together, some of them clung to the nearest normal person they could find, some of them just stayed alone. None were happy. None had Sunny. Maxon thought for the first time about who Bubber would marry. He hadn't thought about it, because the earthly Bubber, drugged and amiable, would not have inspired this question. The earthly Bubber would never marry anyone. He would need to be cared for, permanently, by his parents. When they died, he would go into a home.

"I'm sorry, buddy," said Maxon.

"Sorry for what?" said Bubber.

"I feel sorrow for what you are."

"What am I?"

"Well, there's something wrong with you."

"What?"

"The same thing that's wrong with me. What's wrong with you is wrong with me."

"There's nothing wrong with you, Dad. You're great."

"Maybe not out here, but back at home, there is."

IT REMINDED MAXON OF the last effective conversation he'd had with Sunny about Bubber's medication, before she'd finally told him he was not qualified to have an opinion, being crazy himself.

"What if he's actually *more* evolved? What if I'm actually more evolved?" Maxon had shouted. He was standing outside the door to his office, and they were arguing about Haldol. Often when he came out of his office, he only made it a few feet out into the hall before he had to go right back in.

"This will work," Sunny said. "He will be okay. This will fix it."

"I don't want to fix it," Maxon yelled, his veins popping. He slammed his fist into the wall. "Do you even remember what he was like before we started testing him, and all this medication? Do you even remember that experience, what it was like having that child?"

"You're violent," said Sunny dryly. "Maybe you need Haldol too."

"I don't need drugs," Maxon asserted.

"Yeah, because my mother spent her whole life fixing you, and you know what? You know what, smartass?" Now Sunny was getting riled, and she yanked at the yarn ball feeding the knitting she was attempting to do. Maxon came two steps down the hall away from his office, away from his office and toward her living room. She was wearing her chopsticks wig, two wooden sticks stuck through a beautiful twist of blond hair. She was wearing her eyebrows, but one of them had come half off while she was steaming broccoli, so it dangled.

"What?" he said.

"You're still not fixed!" she shouted, poking her needles savagely. "You're still not fucking fixed! You're crazy as a goddamned bedbug! Well, I'm not raising that kid to be a nutcase. He's not that kid, I'm not that mom, and you better try as hard as damn hell not to be that dad. We're not Mr. and Mrs. Wacko. With our junior- and senior-model lunatic, and our resident sideshow freak. I'm not doing it."

Maxon stepped back, deflated. He did not know how to articulate what he saw. He could draw it, but he sensed that would be weird. This was not a time to decorate the dishwasher, but when he saw Mr. and Mrs. Wacko and the junior-model lunatic, they were the new age nuclear family. All in space suits. No one using or understanding facial clues. In space, who cares? Literal, systematic, addicted to protocol. Unemotional, intelligent, math-minded. The future family. Not autism, not insanity, but the next evolution, engineered for space travel, space living, the habitation of a lunar colony.

"Get Mr. and Mrs. Wacko along with a dozen or so of their autistic brood, and plant them on the moon, and they'll do just fine," he said. "Evolution, Sunny. Evolution. Did you think it just stopped?"

"Come here," she said, softening. She motioned for him to come and sit next to her on the sofa. He could now see she was watching something on television, even hear some of the words coming out of the speaker.

"Sorry," he said. "Sorry for yelling."

"It's okay, baby," Sunny said. "I'm just going to put Haldol in your thermos."

"No fucking Haldol," said Maxon. "For him or me, seriously."

"Okay, no Haldol," she said, climbing into his lap. "You need a shave."

"DAD," SAID BUBBER IN the space suit.

"Son," said Maxon.

"You need to find a way into that cargo module," said Bubber.

"I haven't found that yet," said Maxon. Every time he spoke, it sounded like a raspy interruption, like the silence had made its own sound and the talking was bothering it.

"Dad, think," said Bubber patiently. "How were you planning to get it open before? You must have had some kind of way to get it open."

"This wasn't supposed to happen," said Maxon. "This was not in the script."

"So, you weren't supposed to get it open at all?"

"No," said Maxon. "The command module was going to dock with the cargo and we were going to open the shaft, between them . . ."

"You could be the command module," said Bubber. "You could dock."

"But the air shaft, there won't be a seal."

"Who cares?" said Bubber. "I don't need it, the robots don't need it, and you don't need it."

Maxon thought.

"So, where will it dock?" Bubber asked.

"Follow me," said Maxon.

Of course, Bubber was right. Bubber's brain had worked like a brain should work. He could get in through the docking channel, by applying stimulus to the appropriate places, the way they would have opened it if they'd docked. He didn't need a hatch. Within minutes, he was booting up a Hera, fitting her with the titanium and aluminum she'd need to make them a comm unit. He looked back out the docking channel to see if Bubber was still there. He was, floating in space, giving Maxon a thumbs-up, which was a good way of saying, "I'm okay."

"Thanks, little guy," said Maxon. "It seems so obvious now."

"No problem, Dad," Bubber said. "Hey, it still took you only thirty-three minutes."

That was so like Bubber. To time it without a watch.

MONTHS AGO, THEY WERE on their way to get the mother from Pennsylvania. The neighbors said she was too sick to continue living in her own house. Of course, Sunny did not believe this.

"Mom," she had said on the phone. "What are you eating? What did you eat today?"

"I drank an Ensure," said the mother. "I'm fine. Hannah is here. She makes me drink it."

Hannah was the Amish girl who came in to clean the house, cook the meals, and do whatever else. Sunny didn't know what all. She was supposed to take the place of Nu.

"You need to eat more than just Ensure, Mom," said Sunny. "I'm coming up there."

When they got off Route 80, Sunny sat up straighter. She folded her arms over her chest. She fixed her wig in the rearview mirror and then changed her mind and replaced it with a different one. She made Maxon adjust it. Bubber, in the back of the minivan, was asleep. Maxon was at the wheel. The minute they got off the freeway, she could smell the deep piney smell of the woods, the loamy damp smell that was her childhood, and Maxon's, and all the time they spent running alongside the creek, climbing trees. The air was more moist here than it was back in Virginia. The ferns were denser, the trees greener. Anyone would say it was a beautiful spot.

"Do you smell that?"

"What," said Maxon.

"That . . . smell. The smell outside."

"Smells like oil, tetracycline, carbon monoxide, and decomposing biomatter."

"No, it doesn't, ass. It smells good. Virginia doesn't smell like this."

"The air in Norfolk, Virginia, has eight percent more sodium chloride in it."

"Be nostalgic, Maxon. Remember something."

They were driving on rolling hills, in and out of farmland and woods, down Route 38 and all across Yates County. They passed dilapidated barns on the verge of falling down, gutted roadside stores, little creeks, cows in rows, and pointy little white churches. Sunny felt a familiar and unwelcome warmth and connection to the place. She felt guilty she had not been home more often. She had left her mother alone. All because she did not want to face her in a wig. That was wrong.

"Okay," said Maxon. "I remember when the guy who lived right there turned out to be a pervert."

"Bad," said Sunny. "Nostalgia is supposed to be warm. It's supposed to create a warm feeling."

"Okay," said Maxon, "I remember that in August of 1991, it was so hot we couldn't go upstairs for a week."

"Not literal warmth!" said Sunny, smacking him in the arm. "Please tell me you don't need this explained."

"I don't remember anything," said Maxon. "I've erased those years."

"Don't you love me, Maxon?" said Sunny, falling into a familiar trope. It was this way she signaled to him that she was done talking.

It was one of many scripts she had written for them that they played out on a regular basis.

"I do," he said.

"How much?"

"Tons," he said.

"How many tons?"

"A Brazilian tons."

At the corner of Route 38 and a road called Bear Run, she suddenly clutched his arm.

"Maxon. I have an idea. Let's go see your mother instead."

ONE MILE OFF THE main road, over a hill and down through the woods and over a one-lane bridge that crossed a mountain stream, they pulled up to Maxon's old house. The original house was barely visible, piled all around with firewood in measured, regular stacks. The old barn, once stuffed so full of oily implements, piles of forgotten roofing tiles, tins of unguents, copper pipes, and other detritus, was now wide open, stacked with clean, orderly lumber. Out in the pasture that had once been dotted with foraged cars and mangy sheep was what appeared to be a fully functional mill, a rain of sawdust issuing from an opening on one side, a forklift in operation bringing in new wood. Maxon's makeshift bicycle shop was gone. In its place, a lath cutter.

"I don't want to see my mother," said Maxon.

"What the hell has she done with the place?" marveled Sunny, stepping out of the car. "We were just here, five years ago, Maxon. It was a pit."

"She married that guy from Butler," said Maxon. "Come on, let's go. This is uncomfortable. I don't know what to say."

"Say, 'Hello, Mother. I am just stopping by to say hello, since I was in the area. This is my wife and child.' And then wait and see what she says. I'll help you."

"She's never seen the—" Maxon began.

"The what?" Sunny asked. "Child or wig?"

Maxon got out of the car, too, stood with one hand clamped on the roof, one hand clamped around the doorframe still. In the back of the car, Bubber woke up.

"Get Bubber out, would you?" said Sunny, brushing off her beautiful cream-colored maternity pantsuit, smoothing it over her belly. "Let's go knock."

But they didn't have to. A man was coming up out of the barn, covered in a fine dust of wood shavings. He was maybe sixty. He took his hat off as he approached.

"Y'uns want firewood?" he asked politely. "I got lots, real dry."

"No," said Sunny. "We're here to see Mrs. Mann."

"You know Laney?" he said. He looked incredulous.

"We do," said Sunny, her arm now wrapped protectively around a sleepy Bubber. She picked up the boy, held him on her hip, kissed him soundly on the head. "Is it okay if we go up to the house?"

"Uh, it's Laney Snow now. I'm her husband. Nice to meet you, Ben Snow."

They shook hands. Maxon looked at her, and his face correctly registered surprise.

"Mom," said Bubber quietly. "I have to go potty."

"Oh, sure," the man said. "He can use the bathroom up 'ere too. Let me show y'uns in. Laney'll be real glad to see you. She's been doin' books all day, she's pretty close to crazy with all them numbers and what all. Be glad to see some visitors."

The man took them toward the door of the old house. Instead of the frenetic clutter Sunny remembered, it was clean, neat. Still old, but cared for.

"Hey, Laney," he yelled, swinging open the door. "You got friends here to see you, girl. Get on out here and say hello."

"Come in," came a high voice from inside the house. "Come on in, I'm in the kitchen."

Maxon hung back, saying he would wait outside, but Sunny pinched his arm, propelled him onward until they were standing in a bright little kitchen.

THE LAST TIME SHE had been in this kitchen, it was the summer after Maxon's first year of college. When school got done in May, he'd gone straight to Europe, cycling and backpacking up and down the Alps and the Pyrenees, following bike races and sleeping anyplace he could plug in his laptop. He came home in August, with just a week to spare before he went back to school. She expected him to come rushing right over, burst into the kitchen, ask Nu for something to eat. She waited, but he stayed away, for three days, and no one at the Mann house would answer the phone. She felt irritated and confused. After all, she was going off to college herself in a few weeks. He had written her, e-mailed her, called her on the phone. Why would he not want to see her, to say hello and good-bye?

Her disappointment finally led her to action, and she marched across the valley, yanked open the door to his house, and went right in. She found him alone, sitting at the kitchen table in the middle of towering piles of paper and rubbish. The kitchen was dim, grim, and dirty; there were piles of dishes and papers, bags of fabric, garbage, and what looked like a squirrel's nest on the counter. The space right around him was clear, and he was typing on his laptop, his head bent low over its blue light. He wore faded jeans and nothing else, and his head was shaved, tanned in stripes from his bicycle helmet. She knew he had been shaving it for her. The sight of his rib cage, his sternum, his collarbones, made her physically ache for him. She wanted to hold him, and feel him breathing.

But he was upset; he told her she had to go. "Sunny," he said. "You can't be here."

"Why not?" she said. "I don't understand."

He stood up and came toward her, as if he was going to touch her, grab her, clamp her in his arms, but he stopped.

"Wait. I have to tell you something," he said. "I was in France a few weeks ago. And I wrote a poem."

"You wrote a poem?" In the middle of her confusion, she had time to be incredulous.

"Yes, I wrote one."

"An actual poem, like with words and feelings and stuff?"

"With words."

"Can I see it?"

"No, I didn't write it down."

"Well, can you tell me what it was? Do you remember it? How are you going to remember it?"

"I remember it."

"But you won't tell me what it was?"

"No."

"Why not, Maxon?" She felt like she was going to cry.

"Your mother wouldn't like it," said Maxon. "She wouldn't want it. She doesn't want me to see you at all."

"Well, when will you tell me? When she's dead?"

"I don't think I can ever tell you. And you have to go. But I want you to know that I wrote a poem for you. You should know that."

Later he called her on the phone, and asked her to forgive him. And then he went back to Massachusetts, and she did not see him again for years.

* * *

BENEATH THE YELLOWED CEILING light, at an old Formica table, the woman that had been Laney Mann sat before a ledger book, a receipt book, a checkbook, and a pile of paper scraps, a No. 2 pencil in one hand and a pink eraser in the other. She looked up. Sunny was amazed. Where there had been hulking flesh, there was now a trim old lady. Where there had been strange facial hairs, there were now gentle wrinkles. The gaping holes in the rotten teeth now invisible behind a meek smile, neat hair tucked into a braid.

"Well, innit nice," she said, as if automatically; then when she saw Maxon she stopped.

"Maxon?" she said.

"So how y'uns know each other?" asked her husband.

"Why listen, Ben," she began. She half stood up, her hand reaching out to Maxon, who still stood by the door. "This here is my son Maxon that you never met. You know, he's the youngest of 'em. He's, ahhh . . ."

"A scientist," put in Sunny helpfully.

"Yeah, he been a scientist down there in Virginia," said Laney. "What you working on, lemme see, I know, I learnt this from Emma. Rockets, right? You gonna fly a rocket?"

"Yes," said Maxon.

"Where, right up to the moon?" asked Ben.

"Yes," said Maxon.

"Well, innit nice!" said his mother. "That's real nice!"

Everyone looked at Maxon.

"Hello, Mother," he said. "I am just stopping by, since I am in the area. This is my wife and child."

Laney picked up the teakettle and began to fill it from the jug on the countertop. She looked Sunny over and nodded approvingly, clucking to herself.

"Well, honey, I'm real glad you didn't stay married up with

Emma's girl. She was . . . well, I was always real grateful how Emma paid up for your school and all your travels. But she always knew you kids could be with others that were, ah, better suited. That kind of thing just ain't right. So now look, you got such a pretty new wife, little boy, you're doing real good."

Maxon stood, stunned, his face registering nothing. Sunny felt a prickle of triumph. The wig worked. She was immune.

"Who's this Emma's girl," she asked Laney, helping her reach a box of tea the old woman was stretching for on an upper shelf, before she could retrieve her footstool. "Your first wife? Huh, Maxon? Was she pretty? Should I be worried?"

"No, no," said Laney, counting out her little bags of Lipton. "Poor thing, she was . . . bald." She whispered the last word, one hand discreetly over her mouth. When she was trying to be subtle, Sunny could see the remnants of the old Laney, the fat and desperate Laney, laid over her face. The eyes leaping from side to side. The chewing movements, when there was nothing in her mouth.

"Bald, you mean bald like she shaved her head?" Sunny said, pushing the envelope, reveling in the feeling of real human hair cascading expensively down the sides of her face, rippling over her collarbones, pooling on her shoulder blades.

"Let's just not say nothing 'bout it, dear," said Laney, poking a tea bag into each of four mismatched cups. "Whatchoo say your name was? Maxon, whatser name?"

Maxon made a gurgling sound, and Sunny interjected, "Alice. My name's Alice."

"Well, Alice, it's just all done in the past. Nothing but past. There's a lot we just leave behind, right, Maxon? A lot we just set right there in the past."

"I don't drink tea," Maxon said.

"Well, would you like Kool-Aid? I got some Kool-Aid for your boy. Real nice apple Kool-Aid. You like Kool-Aid, honey?"

THEY PICKED UP SUNNY'S mother from the house across the valley. They shut up the house, turned off the water, drained the pipes, and dripped antifreeze into the drains, all while the emaciated Emma sat on her sofa, wrapped up comfortably, listening to Bubber read to her, letter by letter, from a book of chemical formulas and equations. It was the one he had picked from the shelf, and Emma had said, fine, fine, whatever he likes. Sunny watched her doting like a grandmother, fondling his ears, cupping his head in her hands, and she felt bad for denying her mother all of this love for the last four years. Her reaction to the wig hadn't even been that bad. Four years ago, when the wig was new, her mother had been irate. Now she just looked kind of sad, and asked Maxon if he liked it, and Maxon didn't know what to say.

They paid the disgruntled Hannah, packed up the car, and locked the house. The mother, in the backseat next to Bubber, was quickly asleep, propped up on pillows and swathed in the ancestral quilts.

"I think she looks pretty good," said Sunny. "What do you think?"

"She looks pretty good," said Maxon.

"And your mother, can you believe it?"

"What?"

"She looks so good! And married to that nice guy, running a business, who would have ever thought it?"

"I hate her now more than I ever did before," he said.

It was dark now, the headlights swept before them in the road, lighting up battered road signs, carcasses in the ditch, one hand-lettered sign with an arrow on one end that said CLARKSON RONDAY-VOO. The up-and-down motion reminded Sunny of driving around when they were teens, Maxon always stone sober, allowing her to be a little drunk, a safe amount of drunk, enough to cling to him and laugh, put her feet up on the dashboard and sing along to radio songs.

"Because of her loving Alice so much?" Sunny asked quietly. "Or because of, just everything?"

Maxon said nothing. She looked over at the familiar outline of his profile against a window in twilight, his jaw so tough, his fists wrapped around the steering wheel like they were strangling it, every knuckle tight, every vein popped out. He filled the whole seat, right up to the top. His curls almost touched the ceiling in the van. She put her hand in his hair and stroked his scalp, let her hand trace down the back of his neck. She saw his knuckles relax.

"Don't be mad," said Sunny. "She's proof that people can change. Look what she was, and look what she is now. She's completely different, Maxon. Don't you see that? She's completely, totally different and from what? From finding the right guy, from doing the right things, from putting her feet in the road that leads to normal. She did all the outward things to be the thing she's trying to be, and now she's good at it. She's normal. Anyone would say it, driving up there. No one would ever suspect what she was."

"She's the same," said Maxon. His knuckles poked out again, angry. "No one can change. Stop trying to change him. Why can't you just love him exactly the way he is?"

"I do love him," said Sunny, her hand still circling in Maxon's hair, soothing him, loving him. She thought about how everything that was important to her, deep down inside, was in this car. She was glad they had gone to pick up her mother. Once she was healthy again, she could help with Bubber. She was an expert in teaching little boys how to behave. Had she not been so worried about showing her mother the wig, she would have enlisted her help years ago. "I love him so much that I want something better for him, something better than what we had. Everything about us is so complicated. I just want to save him from that. Let it be simple. Let it be obvious."

Maxon didn't know what to say, or he didn't want to say it. He stayed quiet until she asked him to tell her he loved her, many miles down the road. And he did.

23.

MAXON SAW THE MARE ORIENTALE AND KNEW THAT they were above the moon's dark side. The Mare Orientale, one of the biggest of many scars on the moon's gray face that had been brought about by meteor strikes. Planets are round, like the shape of an eye. And the galaxies unfold in spirals, like water in a funnel. The shapes, perfectly rendered, repeat throughout the universe. You could always know the shape of a planet, or the shape of a moon. Round. A droplet of water, the center of a flower, a ripple around a falling rock, the moon's protected lava pipes where he'd planned to house his Heras— all perfect. A circle is the hardest shape to draw for a human, but the easiest shape to find naturally occurring. A circle is an easy shape for a robot to draw. Any shape is easy for a robot to draw.

Inside the cargo module, the Hera clicked and buzzed. She was cutting the pieces for the comm unit, meticulous work that she carried out meticulously. Maxon knew that her work would be perfect, but it was taking a long time. Meteor strikes, like thunderstorms, like meiosis, were unpredictable. Meteor strikes did not exist between lines of code, or in a laboratory setting, or in Maxon's brain, usually. But the one meteor strike he had experienced was a recognition of the value of meteor strikes. He noted and wondered at the sight of the moon, where there was not one spot, not one square mile unmarred by the scar from a meteor. It was the home of random. It was defined by it.

Maxon turned his head to the moon's horizon and saw a sliver of blue emerging, a sliver of white and blue. The Earth was rising.

"This is something not a lot of people have seen," he said to Bubber. "You should pay attention to this sight of an Earthrise."

"Okay," said Bubber.

They gazed at the Earth, so very small, the swirls and spirals of clouds twisted over the surface of blue and gold. Outer shape such a perfect curve, and yet all over it, a mess of vapor. Maxon looked down at the moon and thought, *The marks of meteors are circles too.* The most random, unpredictable, powerful event in the history of life, and it leaves a mark like a ripple in a pond.

"Dad," said Bubber. "Are we running out of time?"

"Yes," said Maxon. "I really don't think there's enough time."

"What will run out first?"

"The air," said Maxon. "I'll run out of air."

"Tell the robot to hurry up," said Bubber.

"It can't," said Maxon. "Anyway, hurrying up will make a bad result."

"Can you go back and get more air?" asked Bubber.

"I could," said Maxon, "but I don't want to leave her."

The Hera unit clicked and whirred, now welding without sparks.

"Why don't you just bring her back to the rocket? She doesn't need a space suit."

Maxon sniffed. He looked at the Earth, now full, just over the lunar horizon. It was a beautiful sight, so messy and perfect. He thought about the real Bubber, back at home. Maybe sitting in school with a blue pencil in his hand, maybe listening to his iPod and tapping his toe, driving Sunny crazy.

"Son, you're a fucking genius," he said. And he fired up his jetpack.

Soon, the four of them were headed back to the rocket together. Maxon in his jetpack, gently shepherding the Hera with the growing comm unit inside her. Bubber drifting off beneath him, hanging on to one shoe. A walk in the park. A trip to the ice-cream store.

"Dad," said Bubber.

"Yes," Maxon answered.

"Will I be able to go on the rocket?"

"Probably not. I don't think I will still be hallucinating on the rocket."

Maxon looked down at Bubber and realized that already the image was fading, the tiny space suit winking off and on, like a holograph. They were together for just one more minute. The Hera unit and Maxon, and the child Bubber and the nascent comm unit. Like a family.

"Well, I want to come back to space with you sometime," said Bubber. "I like it. I didn't get to go on the moon or anything, and I really want to."

"Oh, you will," Maxon reassured him. "You will be on the moon. You're made for it, buddy. You're made for it."

Maxon clicked on his radio and immediately heard Phillips in his head, in midsentence.

"—the fuck are you doing?! You have got three and a half minutes of air left in that tank, Dr. Mann, do you hear me? Turn on your fucking radio!"

"It's on, Phillips," said Maxon. "I'll be back in five."

The image of Bubber was drifting ahead, out of Maxon's reach.

"Wait up, bud," he croaked.

"I know, Dad," said Bubber. "But you have to hurry now. So match your speed to the speed of your companion. You know. It is a rule. Rate sub-robot equals rate sub-human. Otherwise, the robot is always going to win."

"Wait, Bubber," said Maxon, seeing black rings around his vision, like a mist descending from all points. "Synchronizing speed can only occur when the robot accelerates by an amount equal to the companion's current speed minus the robot's current speed."

Bubber was out of reach, floating away from him. He blinked his eyes, trying to see clearly, trying to hold on. And he felt the most overwhelming sorrow, that in the end he had not managed it at all. He felt a hot stab of regret: for leaving the family, for going up in the rocket, for being susceptible to meteors and for the needs of his body. If it was possible for him to fail, he should never have come in the first place, should never have left her there alone, wanting him, waiting for the way their bodies seared together like two wounds healing. What arrogant faith had brought him here, prepared to break the future with his own head, incognizant of any possibility of failure? It was only when he was running out of air, his lungs pulling on nothing, his mouth open like some ghastly animal, that he realized it. *I am really human,* he thought. *I regret. This is what it's like to be human, and die.* In a way, it was a tragedy. But in a way, it was a huge relief to finally know, he was not a robot after all.

He found that he could not see. He found that he was crying. By the time the hiss of air filled the airlock and Phillips clicked Maxon's helmet open, he had already blacked out.

A COUPLE OF MONTHS before the rocket went off, they had such a bad fight. She was anticipating his departure. He knew, from what Emma had taught him, that Sunny would express worry for him in different ways. He watched her express the worry by checking many times with many different types of questions whether he was scientifically prepared or physically prepared for a week in space. Now he watched her express the worry by arguing with him. He was prepared to engage in an argument over something inconsequential.

He had been told the argument would be about something stupid like what kind of tea he had been supposed to buy, but would really be about something else. About him leaving. He had to listen to the words she was saying, but he had to understand the things she was feeling: fear, loneliness, abandonment, worry. He stood across the kitchen island from her. The kitchen island was covered in cool granite, granite that looked like leather, that felt like the surface of a meteor. Bubber had been put to bed, it was ten o'clock at night. When he came out of the office, she was banging dishes around in the kitchen, and then within minutes they were on opposite sides of the kitchen island, and fighting.

"What am I supposed to do for all this time? Two weeks in Florida, a week on the mission, more time after that. Am I supposed to just put a plug in this baby hole and not let it out? Am I supposed to just turn off the processes around here, shut it down, and wait for you to get back? I don't have an Off button."

"No" was all he could say. "I'll be okay. Don't worry."

The kitchen was lit artistically, recessed lighting in the ceiling dropping down a gentle glow around the copper pots. Behind her, the state-of-the-art refrigerator. Behind him, the farmhouse sink recast in silicon. Deep, wide, perfect for canning, picturesque. The back of his head reflected in the window over it. The back of her head was a gray interruption in the glistening nickel of the fridge.

"So, I just carry on, then, all by myself. That's great. Perfect. Well, you know what? I quit. I fucking quit. I say lights off. Shut it down. I want out of this sweater, I want out of this house, I want out of this city, I want out. I've been holding things up on my shoulders for too long, I want a break! I want to not be a mother for five fucking minutes!"

She waved her hands around, rubbed at her cheek. She never, of course, drove her hand through her hair or pressed upward on her forehead, or shook her head vehemently from side to side.

"So go out, do what you want to do, I'm here now, safe and sound. I can help you. Go take some time for yourself," he said. He said the words "time for yourself" as if it were one word. Like bicycling.

"I can't just go out, Maxon, and leave it. Do you not understand this? I am Mom, twenty-four/seven. It doesn't end because I am not physically with you and your child. I am always Mom. It's right here with me, inside me, this makes me Mom, whether I'm here or there or passed out drunk in a ditch in the city, I'm still the mom, it's just then I'm the shitty mom. You, you leave. You're the scientist, you're the builder, you're the astronaut, you're the cyclist, I'm none of those things. I'm the mom, that's it. I'm saying, I just want a little break to try and be someone else, but I can't have it. It's impossible."

Behind her the automatic ice maker clicked on, dumped out a load, clicked off.

"Honey, it's all about priorities."

He knew as soon as he said it that it was wrong. He had to remember what this fight was about.

"All about priorities? That's rich. That's really fucking rich. This from the man who gets up at dawn to bike, stays at work as long as he can, sometimes until after dark and then shuts himself in his office all night. Here I am pregnant with another baby, another child of yours that's not going to know what the front of your face looks like! They're going to see streaming lines of code across your eyes, a reflection always, your screen on your face, that's their father."

"Now, that's not right. That's not true. That's not right or true."

"You don't help me when you are here. You might as well go, be well, live on the moon, colonize space. I'll just be here pushing around the dishes, the laundry, the dishes, the laundry, and outlining my lips, wearing my stockings, and lining up my dove gray pumps in the closet."

"I don't expect you to do that. No one expects that. You make yourself do that."

"Yeah, well, what do I expect me to do? What does he expect me to do? What does this one expect me to do?" She pointed upstairs at Bubber and then to her belly. "There actually are no expectations of me, Sunny, this person. It's just me, this slot, this role, this mother. What I've got to do as her, to be her, and those expectations are clearly defined. Clearly defined. You, in fact, are the only one that can't see them. Because you don't see anything that's not written down in black and white! Look at me, Maxon, I am dying here! Motherhood is death, do you get it? This me that you see, this thing standing here, this is a dead thing covered in a shell. I am dead. Maxon, I'm dead!"

"You don't look dead," he said.

"Maxon! I am not a fucking robot! You cannot determine whether I am alive or dead just by looking at me!"

Her face was blotchy and striped with tears. Her wig, her immovable wig, was perfectly coiffed, glistening, real. Her hands wrung at each other, and she hit softly on the countertop. She was crying.

He remembered the hermit crabs they had brought home from Cape May when the mother took them there on a trip. They'd kept them in a bucket next to the bathtub until they crawled out of their shells and died. Sunny had wept and mourned, holding the strange little shrimps in her hand and talking to them while she choked with sorrow. The mother firmly forbade morbid rituals; no funerals were allowed. Later he found out in a book that the crabs hadn't really been dead, they were just trying to find new shells, and shedding their exoskeletons. Had they been left alone, they would have lived. But they were thrown out on the compost pile, covered in the next day's cabbage leaves, the following day's watermelon rind. If Sunny felt dead like those crabs had been dead, then Maxon had failed her, and he was sorry.

"You don't even know me, Maxon!" she shrieked. "Do you know what I have done?"

"Yes," he said.

"You're just going to go, up in space, and leave me here with your children? This thing I am? This bastardization that I have become?"

"I thought you said it was necessary. I thought you wanted me to go."

"Maxon, do you know how your father died?"

"He froze in a ravine."

"He froze in a ravine because I left him there." Sunny choked in her throat, like she was coughing and talking at the same time.

"I know."

"You know? You don't know. You never knew."

"I know because you told me. You told me years ago. You were standing right there when you said it."

Maxon remembered clearly, the dinner party. Sunny told a story about her father dying in a ravine, and he had known, without a doubt, that she had really meant that his father died that way, and that she had seen him dying, and that she had done nothing. Maxon had already taken in that information, at the time she had said it.

Sunny paused.

"You knew?"

"Yes. You said his leg was shaped like a sigma. You said he was covered in pine needles, don't you remember? Everyone knows pine trees don't grow in southern Burma. It would have been deciduous—"

"You knew and you said nothing?"

"I said something. I said 'wow.'"

"Maxon," said Sunny. "There is a way to respond when someone tells you they killed your father. You elevate your voice an octave, you increase its volume, you make an expansive hand gesture, you raise your eyebrows, you shout something like 'WHAT?' or 'I CAN'T BE-LIEVE YOU HAVE DONE THIS!' and you . . . you don't just carry on as if nothing had happened!"

"I forgave you," he said. "That happened. That is something that happened."

"What?"

"I forgave you that night, before you even stopped talking, I forgave you. I forgive you. I forgive. It's okay."

She threw herself into him and wrapped her arms around him so tightly that the wind came out of his lungs in a whoosh.

"Oh, Maxon," she said. "Don't ever die. Don't ever, ever, ever die!"

Maxon had written down everything he had eaten for the last seventeen years. He had a resting heart rate of thirty-two. He had a graph to indicate the wattage he had emitted in an eighty-seven-mile bike ride yesterday. But he could not stop himself from dying.

24.

IN 1987, THE YATES MALL WAS BUILT AT THE CROSS-roads of Route 8 and Highway 32. There was a traffic light there, the only one for many miles. In the middle of some cow pastures, down the road a piece from Bickton and about two miles from Pearl, a mall was built and it had a Sears at one end and a Bon-Ton at the other. At this time, there was a gas station at the corner and a lumber mill next to the mall and that was it. People came to the mall blinking, putting their hands in front of them to make sure they didn't walk into any windows. They found a fabric store, shoe shops, an eyeglass store, a pharmacy, a small cafeteria, even a cinema with two screens. People said that Yates County was finally civilized. The local paper said that such crassly generic consumerism would kill local commerce and crush the mom-and-pops in the oily boom towns around.

Over the next few years the intersection blossomed. It found added to its commercial enterprises a Home Depot and a Burger King. Then a small and disorganized amusement park. Soon a newer and more sparkling gas station set up shop to compete with the older one, setting pay-at-the-pump and instant submarine sandwiches against grit and a mechanic. A roadside ice-cream stand opened up within view of the traffic light to compete with the Jolly Milk, which was a mile away.

In 1993, a Wal-Mart was built across from the mall, and editorial writers at the local paper threw up their hands and gave up the region to multinational trade death. Hardware stores on main streets everywhere closed. Clothiers despaired. Purveyors of grocery shook their fists at the heavens. One small man with a tire store next to the bank in Oil City committed suicide. By 1995, the Yates Mall, once heralded as the advance guard of civilization, closed in deference to the big-box cavalry across the street. The building emptied, was boarded up, and a permanent sign was erected out front: SPACE FOR LEASE. 1000×500, 1500×500, OR WHATEVER.

Naturally, the local high schoolers took it over as a make-out zone. Before the mall, they had an abandoned railroad car off a siding on the other side of the river, past Franklin, but you had to walk half a mile to get to it, and while there were mattresses, there were also snakes. The Yates Mall was better, because it was bigger, and a parked car in the lot was inconspicuous because the theater was still open for one showing a day. Of course, there were also more dubious operations being enacted inside the shell of Yates Mall than just the pregnancy roulette. Sometimes the players in these games overlapped, the meth dealers and the amorous teens, the amorous dealers and the meth-ridden teens. After a couple of years, there was a lot of junk on the floor.

Maxon and Sunny were sixteen when they first entered the closed part of the mall. It was Saturday and they had gone to a matinee, legitimately parking Sunny's little car in the parking lot, leisurely strolling into the theater. Sunny had a pocket bottle of vodka in her bag, and during the movie she applied herself to it earnestly, until by the third act she was loopy and groping.

"Maxon," she whispered loudly. "Maxon, let's go to the Bon-Ton afterwards."

Going to the Bon-Ton meant slipping away to any number of hidden locations within the abandoned mall, tucking oneself and one's partner into a corner, and doing it. Maxon knew this. The Bon-Ton happened to be the biggest empty department store, but it wasn't the only one. There was also a Sears and there were many other smaller stores. In Maxon's mind, the mall was a rabbit warren, with bunches of little rabbits stuffed into holes rutting at each other. Maxon couldn't imagine doing that with Sunny. They were boyfriend and girlfriend. They kissed and pressed their bodies up to each other. But to be naked, in a closet, pushing into her wetly, he could not imagine.

"No," he said. "You're drunk. Let's get out of here. We can go to the A-frame before we go home."

The A-frame, still as abandoned as it was when Maxon was a little boy, was their own secret shack. But they didn't use it for sex. They used it for sobering Sunny up, cooling Maxon off, escape.

"No," she insisted. "I want to go to the Bon-Ton like the other kids do. Why can't we? What's the big deal?"

She went off into a fit of giggles and bent over in her chair, in the dark. Her hand clutched his thigh and squeezed, traveled up a few inches and squeezed, up and squeezed, and then it just stayed there, her fingers tapping up and down.

"Fine," he said.

They staggered out of the theater, one of several couples intent on the same mission, veering quickly right when the rest of the moviegoers veered left and out the doors. The kids split up, each couple taking a separate hallway as if by mutual assent, and Sunny grabbed Maxon's hand and pulled him firmly along.

"Where are we going?" he asked.

"Renee told me where to go," said Sunny. "Come on, hurry. It's a secret."

At the back of a store that had once sold wooden crafts and furniture created by local artists, she yanked open a door and led him through it. There was no light, but Sunny rummaged around beside the door on the inside, found a flashlight, and flicked it on.

"I found it!" she said, as if to herself.

She slammed the flashlight down on the desk, pointed upward, and a warm yellow light illuminated the room. It was bigger than Maxon had anticipated. Maybe it was the office and the stockroom. There were rows of metal shelves along one wall.

"Take your clothes off," she told him. "Come on, come on. No, wait, wait a minute."

From her pocket, Sunny pulled out the vodka, half empty, an incense stick, and a condom. She pushed the incense stick into a groove in a ceramic holder there on the desk, lit the end of it, flicking impatiently at a lighter that was already there. The smell of bergamot bloomed in the corner, pushing back the mustiness a little, but there was still a chill. In the corner was a pile of body pillows, scavenged from leftovers at Sears, and there was a stack of sheets, some still wrapped, some just folded, some discarded in a pile in the other corner. The room was fifteen feet by eighteen feet. They had been standing in it for forty-five seconds.

"That's good. This is our smell. This is us now. Right now," said Sunny. She took a big sturdy drink of the vodka and smiled, her face lit from beneath, every tooth shining. Then she yanked her jeans off and left them on the floor, threw her hoodie and T-shirt down next to them.

"Come on, Maxon," she urged him.

When she was standing there in only her cotton panties and her white cotton bra, she pushed the door closed with a solid thud, and Maxon was inside the room with her. Inside the room where the kids went to have sex, there were Sunny and Maxon, about to do it.

"This is what happens," said Sunny, giggling. "This is what happens, this is what. Happens. What happens, what happens, what happens." She was drunk. Maxon knew it. She grabbed the waistband of his jeans and ripped them open, dragging the denim down over his legs. He felt his legs automatically kicking his shoes off by putting each toe on the opposite heel, pulling down. It was as if the feeling of his pants around his ankles just made them behave this way. Then she pressed her hands into his chest and pulled off his flannel shirt.

There they were, him in a T-shirt and boxers, her in her underwear. It could have been any other time. They could have been somewhere in the woods. This was not unfamiliar, this was not yet unsafe. There was a chance she would chicken out of whatever she was planning for them. He could run away. He could take a picture, right now, before it happened. But she was in a hurry, and jittery. She grabbed his hand and led him, zombie-like, to the pile of pillows.

"Shut up, Maxon, you're so chatty," she said, her feet prancing a little as she pulled him over and pushed him down on the pile.

"Lie down on your back," she said. "And don't worry. I know what to do. Renee told me."

He knew he should not be here. He knew it could be a bad moment. It could not be good. And yet, as she stood there in the golden light of someone's old flashlight, humming to herself as she pulled off her bra, as she crawled over to him like an animal, where he lay on the pillow, as she fell into his arms, he could not leave her or stop her. She was on top of him, the little tips of her breasts against his chest, her hands beside his shoulders, pressing down into the pillows, and she put her mouth up to his ear.

"I love you, baby," she said into his ear, her breath causing electrical ripples down his body. He felt the familiar triangle light up between his hips and his groin, very fast, like a jolt. She put her mouth on his neck beneath his jaw, on his collarbone, on his sternum and his ribs. This was a kiss followed by another, each one small and chaste, but quick, like kissing hello. There was none of the wetness he dreaded. There was no terrible sweating. His body was cold, chilled, except for the places where she touched him, where her lips engaged with his skin. There were little hot marks left on him, like thermal imaging, his body blue, and mouth shapes in orange and red punctuating it. She moved down, kissed the points of his ribs where they arched over his belly, her elbows dropping to support her, her butt rising in the air as she leaned back and down. She giggled, pressing her face against his belly, tickling.

She kissed his hipbone, then with her cheek rubbed against the inside of his boxers. She pulled the fabric down with her teeth so his penis came out through his fly. Her hot breath on him made his hands clench into the pillows around him. His eyes shut tight. He could not think about what she seemed about to do, and he could not stop her. Then everything went from fast to slow as she put her tongue on him. He was hers, whatever she wanted to do to him. A very simple thing, he thought. A very simple motion. He really wanted it. Her hands pressed against his thighs.

Then he felt the hot wetness of her mouth touching it, and gasped. "I can't," he choked out. The first thing he had said since the theater. She took her mouth away and looked up at him. He saw her, mouth red, eyes black, framed in his legs, her tawny shoulders raised up like a lion at a kill.

"Come on, boy," she said, and as her mouth closed over him again, it felt so good. Moments later, he silently ejaculated, managing to get it out of her mouth first.

"That was awesome," she said cheerfully, pulling herself back up next to him. She reached across him, pulled a folded sheet from the pile and tucked it over them. Her cheek against his shoulder, her arm under his neck. He was warm, warmer than ever, and floating. They went to sleep, her from liquor, him from being at peace.

THEY WOKE UP TO the sound of the door opening. As Sunny's eyes opened and she remembered, slowly, where she was, she saw the outline of her friend Renee and two guys in the door. Renee was reaching around on the floor for the flashlight. Sunny took in the sight next to her, Maxon asleep in his boxers and T-shirt. She saw her own panties still in place. Her plan had failed. *At least I got my bra off,* she thought. *Maybe we even kissed lying down.* He was deeply asleep, his mouth open. She pulled her arm from under his neck and his head lolled off to the side. Strange. She wondered if he'd had vodka, too.

"Hey, occupado!" she called to Renee.

"Sunny? Is that you? Where's the fucking light?"

"I don't know," Sunny said.

"I got a Maglite," said one of the boys, and Sunny recognized the voice of Adam Tyler, a football player.

"Why didn't you say so, asshole," Renee said, and snatched a flashlight out of his hand, turned it toward Sunny.

"Hey," she said as the light hit her eyes, pulling the sheet up and around her. She stood up and hopped over to her clothes, began to put on her jeans under the sheet. The bra would just have to stay here; no way was she giving the football team a show. That was Renee's job anyway.

"Get going, sister, this ain't a motel," said Renee affectionately.

"Wait a minute," said Adam Tyler. "Isn't that Maxon Mann?"

Sunny looked over at Maxon. He was now sitting up perfectly straight.

"Whatcha doing here, Mann, don't you know this is the honeymoon suite?"

Adam punched his buddy's arm and his buddy punched back. Renee was holding the flashlight so it pointed toward the ceiling.

"Shut up, Adam," she said mildly.

Maxon stood up and spread his hands amicably.

"Hey, Tyler," he said, "I didn't realize you lived here, man. My apologies. And my compliments."

"Fuck you, nerd," Adam shouted, lunging forward, menacing Maxon with his fists. "I don't live here, I fuck here. And you don't fuck where I fuck, okay? So take your bald bitch and go down and poke her in the bathroom, where shitheads like you belong."

Sunny did not see Maxon coming toward Adam, but she heard the sound of his fist landing on Adam's head. When the buddy jumped into the fray, planting a firm fist in Maxon's kidney region, Maxon began to fight for real, and Renee pulled Sunny out the door, leaving Adam's flashlight on the floor, still lighting up the scene. Behind the door, there were sounds of a raging typhoon.

"Come on," said Renee. "We have to get help. They're going to kill him."

"They're not," said Sunny, panting a little as they ran down the mall, zipping up her jacket. "Don't worry about him, worry about them. Seriously, trust me, he is in no danger."

There was a time when Maxon had been put to the ground by two brothers, fighting him. Then it took three brothers, and then four. Since the growth spurt, there had been no bruises. Either he was winning all the time or his body no longer responded to punishment. It was as if he didn't even feel pain.

She let Renee go. She slowed to a walk, headed for the door. Outside the air was fresh. She got into her car, wishing for a cigarette. She also wished for a drink of water and a couple of Advil. When Maxon emerged from the mall a few minutes later, and sauntered across the parking lot, he was neatly dressed, his face wreathed in a carefree smile. He popped open the door and folded himself into the passenger seat.

"Did you kill them, Maxon?" she asked him, starting up the car.

"Nope," he said. "But we can use that room whenever we want."

"Baby, you know," said Sunny, "I like drinking but I am never going to do it unless I have you around to protect me. And I don't think we should go back to that room."

They never did go back to the honeymoon suite at the Yates Mall. And even during her years away at college, Sunny never drank without Maxon there to protect her. And that was true all through their lives.

IN THE STUDIO OF WNFO News, Sunny sat in the same white wicker chair as before, folded her feet the same way, laid her hands on the side of her pregnant belly. But now her head was bald, and her eyes were red from crying. Showing up on television as a bald woman was something that she could do for Maxon, whether it mattered or not. Whether or not, for him, there would ever be an opportunity to watch the tape. Seeing her sitting next to Les Weathers, with no Maxon on the other side, it would be clear to everyone in the world that Maxon was gone. The special symmetry was missing. There was an absence in space. The camera closed in on just the two of them, Sunny and Les, and when Les began the interview, the cameraman pulled the shot even tighter, on just their heads. Two heads, talking on television, one blond and one bald.

Sunny had had a dream, and in the dream, she was wearing her mother's clothes. The clothes were tight and didn't fit her pregnant body, but she was wearing them anyway, and carrying her mother's purse as well. She was wearing her mother's walking shoes, and dealing with the aftermath of her mother's death. Seventeen copies of the death certificate, a decent obituary, cremation. And as she was discussing the details of the memorial service with the rector of the church, her mother walked into the room, clearly alive and not even sick. There was a large shining lump on the mother's head, as if she fell out of a tree and forgot who she was, accidentally went into a coma and died from cancer, and then remembered who she was and fully recovered. And what Sunny felt at that moment, when she saw her mother walking into the room, was anger. Why did you put me through all that? she asked her mother. The sickness, the sores, and pulling the plug? Why did I have to do all that by myself, when you were perfectly well enough to do it with me? But the mother was transformed. Having been fake-dead, she was now somehow above reproach, and wouldn't even respond.

"Sunny Mann," said Les Weathers. "First let me say that I am sorry about what's happening to you now, and I appreciate your coming in to share your experiences with us once again."

"Thank you for having me," she said.

"Around the world, and certainly here in the U.S., everyone has been watching the story so carefully. But just to fill in our viewers, your husband's rocket has been hit by a meteor and all communication with the astronauts has been lost. How are you holding up?"

And Sunny managed to answer, "I am doing okay. I am taking it slowly, one thing at a time."

Sunny told about how she had found out, what she had been thinking. She explained that she really wanted Maxon to be alive, and the whole crew to be safe, and Les Weathers told her that he did, too, they all did, everyone in the whole world. After the interview, someone came to take Sunny's mic from the back of her shirt and unpin it from her collar. Les Weathers stayed on set with her as the crew peeled away. Soon they were sitting there, still in the wicker chairs with no one else around.

"How are you doing, really?" Les said.

"I don't know. It's pretty awful," said Sunny.

He put his hand over hers, and she watched the two hands fold together, the way human hands naturally do.

"I hope you realize," he said, "that we are here for you. We are all here for you. Especially me."

"Okay," she said. She swiped at her eyes with one sleeve.

"I'm right down the street if you need me."

"Thanks."

"And if he doesn't come back, Sunny," Les went on, leaning in toward her ear. She could feel the warmth from his body, different from the heat of the lights. It was a moving, breathing warmth. "If he doesn't come back, I know this is not the right thing to say, but I'm saying it anyway: If he doesn't come back, I want you to know that I don't mind about the baldness either. I don't mind."

25.

AT 2:30 IN THE MORNING, THE PHONE NEXT TO
Sunny's bed rang. It was NASA. She should come in right away.
Communications with the rocket had been established, and there
was a video uplink. The men were alive. They were well. She could
talk to Maxon, see him, hear him talk. She pulled on some clothes,
kissed Bubber awake and dressed him, and bundled them both out
the door and into the van. There she sat, blinking, at her reflection in
the rearview mirror. She was about to send a love letter with no
words in it at all. She set off toward the Langley Research Center,
where they would be waiting for her.

* * *

At three o'clock in the morning, the mother's heart fluttered. It fluttered and faded. Then it resumed operating, but at an unsteady pace. The kidneys had been gone for hours, the liver dead, the blood full of toxins. Underneath her body, her mind was racing. In the room, under the flat sheet, there was no change. The orange light of the parking-lot fixtures filtered through the shade like morning sun through the shell of an egg. A nurse had come in, hours ago, and felt for a pulse. Now the room was silent.

To say that the mother did not resume consciousness just before death would be wrong. It would be something that was said to palliate the people who maybe should have been there for the death. She did not resume the symptoms of consciousness: the fluttering eyelid, the squeezing hand, the gentle nod. But she did resume the awareness that she was dying. And she fought with death. All by herself, in the dark, with nothing to help her control the encroaching darkness inside her, she fought against her own failing blood and the terrible things in it that were at work against her. She fought to live.

In her mind, she was standing at a roadside vegetable stand in Pennsylvania. She was picking over tomatoes, wondering if they could really be local, because they looked so perfect. There was a kid there operating the stand, the same age as Sunny and from the same 4-H club. A car swished down the highway, disturbing the air around the vegetables, a thrush whirred somewhere in the woods back away from the road. She could hear the locusts at their songs in between passing cars. It was late summer, late afternoon, and the warm last rays of the sun slanted across the valley.

The kid was looking at her. She said, "Mrs. Butcher?" Emma remembered clearly the electrified feeling in her body when the kid said, "Do you know where Sunny is right now?"

"Where is Sunny?" Emma said, setting one of her tomatoes back into the bin.

"Um, I'm probably not supposed to tell you."

"Well, is she in danger?" Emma's finger pressed a hole into a tomato, then another hole into the same tomato, giving the tomato a little girdle of holes.

"Hmm," said the kid, sucking her braces. "Yeah, probably."

Emma in the hospital, static under the blankets, unable to move her arms or make a fist, remembered the desire to throttle this pimply, damp child in her denim short-shorts, to strangle her with her own straggly braid.

"Maggie," said Emma. "You need to tell me right now where Sunny is. Otherwise I am going to be very angry, and tell your father."

"Well," said Maggie, drawing out the word. "I guess it is in Sunny's best interest if I tell you."

"Tell me."

Emma's teeth ground together, in the hospital bed, by the roadside stand. *Where is my child? What is going to happen to her? Fix it, fix it, fix it.*

"Uh, Mrs. Butcher, you know the Belmar bridge?"

Emma was gone. She ran to the car, slammed herself into it, and gunned out of the little roadside area, spraying gravel behind her. She knew the Belmar bridge. For three generations, the youth of Yates County had been daring each other to jump off it, and infrequently dying under it. A railroad trestle over the Allegheny River, the Belmar bridge was legendary, its stone pylons driving down thickly into the river, its rusted and inflexible beams rising high above. The kids would climb out to the center pylon, reaching it by means of the rusted rungs of a service ladder, and lie in the sun there, high above the water. The bravest of them would leap off the platform and into the water, almost forty feet below. The Allegheny is a shallow river, but the construction of the bridge and the current in that spot had left a deep eddy just downstream of that huge middle pylon, so if you held your body just right, and hit the water correctly, you could dive down safely, and not get hurt. Or, like several kids over the years, you could kill yourself trying.

Okay, she told herself. *To be fair. To be truthful. Those kids were drunk. Sunny wouldn't drink. Those kids were stupid. Sunny is smart. Probably she won't even climb out there. She would know how mad I'd be if I found out. She would have some sense. She would not do this. She would not jump off this bridge.* It was a rite of passage, the neighbors had told them over dinner one night, for the local youths. The neighbors' children had not done it, though. The sensible, smart neighbors' children had grown up and gone and had not jumped off that bridge at all. The most impressive railroad trestle in three counties. Emma could just picture it. Her skin burned.

She sped down the two-lane highway with no regard for traffic, drifting into the opposite lane on curves to the right, drifting onto the shoulder on curves to the left. The beautiful late-afternoon sun on the countryside had become the fires of hell burning her. She knew that Sunny could not die, and she knew that she could stop her. She could say, "Sunny, STOP." The bald head would whip around, the girl would wave, turn, and she would sheepishly shrug, let some other kid do it, let some other kid jump off that platform for her.

If only she were with some more sensible boy. Maxon would just let her go, just let her do it, whatever she wanted. He was enslaved to her, and he was hopeless, too damaged, she could not trust him with Sunny's life. She could not believe that he could keep her safe, not just by thinking about it. Why could she not love some optimistic clod who would tell her the truth, keep her out of trouble, and become a banker? That type of kid would never let her break her neck on a river rock. Never.

At the bottom of the hill, she opened the door and began to run, leaving the car open behind her. Her long skirt beat against her legs and her feet kicked up gravel behind her. Her mind demanded she stay alive. She took a shuddering gasp and let it out, shifting the blankets just a little. She felt the crushing weight of her own ribs, felt that no more breath would come in. Maybe that was her last breath. Maybe it was over. She was done. But it couldn't be. She had to run, she had to find out. So she dragged another breath in, her pulse jumping up in her neck, one gulping swallow of air as her throat collapsed, enough to keep her alive until she could see her child safe, until she could see Sunny and tell her "Don't jump off that fucking bridge."

Her legs carried her like the wind, over the gravel road and then onto the railroad ties, leaping from plank to plank between the place where the rails used to be. She felt no pain, she felt only suffocation. She felt her blood, incapable of doing its job. She felt her mind shutting her off. *Don't tell the feet,* she thought. *Let them keep running.* At last she turned the corner and saw the bridge, its dark brown trapezoids rising against that bright blue sky.

"Sunny," she tried to cry, but there was no air. Her lungs were finished. They could not do it, not even one more time. Her chest contracted. Her cells struggled. She hung on the nearest beam, clung to it, thrusting her head out over the water, straining to see. There were the kids. Was Sunny alone? No, Maxon was already in the water. Bastard. He had probably worked out all the angles and trajectories. He had probably told her just the right way to jump. It wasn't fair. She had probably demanded it. She would, she was always trying to be like the other children. How much this would mean to her, poor bald Sunny, with her awful baldness, to jump off the Belmar bridge just like the other kids did, to talk about it later, over sodas at the Jolly Milk, sitting on the roof of someone's car, a gang of kids, a group of friends, and Maxon hanging back, driving for her, working out the math for her, silent when she told him to be silent, letting her kill herself to fit in.

Sunny was there, poised. The mother tried to gasp out a warning, gasp out a final endearment. *Sunny, I love you.* But there was no air, and there was no blood, and the blackness came down from on top of her head and shut her down. In the reverie, she hung there, her body limp and crumpled against a beam. In reality, she died there, in the hospital bed, and went into the dark. Her brain stopped working and that was it, just at the wrong moment. One minute there were electrochemical processes inside the skull. The next minute there were not. No one shared it, no one eased it to its end, and no one could have prevented it. It just happened. A death happened at 3:12 in the morning. A private death between the mother and herself, before she could finish her one last dream. This is what it means to die: You do not finish.

THE ROAD TO LANGLEY Research Center leads back through the swampy area of Virginia's Eastern Shore. In the middle of the night, it is a dark and quiet place. Ditches on each side of the road drain the water, and herons stand, their heads tucked into their wings. It's like a seedier, smaller version of the road to the Kennedy Space Center, over miles of swampy Florida coastal marsh. There you can see rows of palm trees swaying in the wind, in the morning, on the day of a bright and optimistic launch. Here she saw kudzu in the headlights, mile markers, and she could barely remember where to turn.

At 3:30 a.m. Sunny showed her ID at the gate. Off to the right was the hangar, huge and white, full of rocket parts, airplanes, and all kinds of apparatuses. Behind her was the wind tunnel. The base was like a college campus, but instead of stacked rectangles for office buildings and classrooms, the architecture was all outsized and strange, not built for human habitation, but for the convenience of science. This facility, like its geographical context, was a dingy, underfunded sister of the Kennedy Space Center. But he worked here because he didn't want to move to Florida. And ultimately, it didn't matter. He had his trade right between his ears. There were labs, and there were lab workers everywhere.

She drove past the huge round buildings they jokingly called the brain tanks, and past the new accelerator. She drove past the building where Maxon had his materials tested, full of giant machines whose only job is to break things to make sure they're strong. Many of the buildings at Langley were shoddy and brown, built in the seventies and never refurbished. It was always a surprise to step into the buildings and find everything so high-tech.

Sunny parked, gently eased Bubber out of the backseat. He cried a little bit, and blinked, and then, standing in the car still, said, "Where are we?"

"What a great question," said Sunny. "We are at Daddy's work. We are going to talk to Daddy."

"Daddy is on the moon. The moon has a lava pipe. That's where Daddy's going to put the robot. The lava pipe."

"Right," said Sunny. "Should I carry you, or can you walk?"

Please say walk, she thought. She hadn't had any contractions since she woke up, but she was nervous about it.

"Walk," said Bubber.

"That's a good baby," said Sunny. She kissed him and kissed him all over his face. He resisted her, as stony as if she had been kissing the back of the seat.

"I don't care if you don't want to be kissed and hugged, Bubber," she said as she took his hand. "I'm going to kiss and hug you anyway."

"Fine," said Bubber.

"Let's go."

Stanovich met her at the door. The lobby of Maxon's building was dimly lit.

"The gate guard called and said you were here," he said. "Come on, right this way."

He took her by the arm, and she took Bubber by his arm. They went to a part of the building she had never seen before. He pushed open several sets of brown metal doors and led her up a stairwell. The concrete on the stairs was chipped, the window dusty. Sunny stopped on the landing, waved for Stanovich to give her a second.

"I'm a little pregnant, Stan," she said. "I can't go galloping up stairs anymore."

"Ah, right," he said. He stood nervously, knocking the railing with his knuckle. Stanovich was a gray-haired man, but smooth and spry, maybe old enough to be Sunny's father, or maybe forty. He had a thick mustache and thicker glasses, sunken eyes and bushy eyebrows, big ears. He always wore short-sleeved shirts with collars, black or navy pants. He was old-school NASA, and a professional. Maxon had a lot of respect for him, so Sunny did, too. And she liked him. He had a wife and kids in Newport News.

"Okay, I think I've caught my breath," said Sunny. Catching sight of herself in a windowpane, she realized that Stan had not commented on her hair, or lack of it. She wondered if he was just that distracted, or if Maxon had told him. Maybe some late night, bent over difficult problem, or pacing back and forth in front of a whiteboard full of formulas, he'd spilled the beans. *Hey, my wife is bald*, he might have said, *but let's get back to this robot.*

"Bubber, you all right?" Stan said, poised to continue up the stairs.

Bubber, staring at the concrete blocks in the walls, gave him a thumbs-up. Stan leaped up the next flight and pushed open another metal door.

"This is my domain," said Stanovich. "Welcome. Sorry not under better circumstances."

"But these are great circumstances, right?" said Sunny. "They're alive, they're talking. They'll make it."

Stan was silent, moving down the gray hallway more slowly now.

"Stan," said Sunny, grabbing him by the arm and stopping dead. "It is good news, right?"

"Sunny, now I don't want to get you upset. But you should know the truth."

"What's the truth?" Sunny asked.

"The truth is they might still not make it back," said Stan. Then he coughed, put his hand on his face, and smoothed his mustache. Sunny found herself crazily trying to decode this gesture, like maybe Maxon would have done. Was he shielding the pregnant lady? Overstating the danger? Itchy?

"What?" Sunny breathed.

"The meteor did more damage than we thought, honey. Once we established the link, Houston ran some diagnostics with them, and it's not good. I can't see how we down here can help them up there without the navigational stuff that they need to fix their orbit, to get to the surface, to fire the rockets . . . it's just too much."

Stan sounded like he was going to cry. "Maxon did a good thing fixing the comms. That was a really great thing. But, this might be the last you get to talk to him, honey. That's why we called you here in the middle of the night. Do you understand?"

"Did they dock with the robots? Did they get that far?"

"Yes," said Stan. "They have now docked with the robots. I don't know how, because they shouldn't have been able to, but somehow they did. Unfortunately, I think that's as far as it's going to go."

"No," said Sunny. "I don't believe it. I don't believe he would go up there and get himself killed."

Stan put his hand on a doorknob. Inside, through a pane of reinforced glass, Sunny could see people, hear voices.

"The meteor was something that no one could account for," said Stan. "You can't blame him. There was nothing he could have done."

"But Maxon accounts for everything," she said, pushing past him to throw the door open. "I want to talk to him. I want to talk to him right bloody now."

The room was big, with shaded windows on one wall. There were benches and tables around the room littered with drills, pieces of metal, and mounted laser saws and fabricators. A poster on the wall proclaimed, "This is where we make the magic happen!" Angela Phillips had already arrived and was sitting in front of a big silver flat-screen monitor on a dirty old wooden desk. Of course she'd gotten there first; she lived in Hampton. Like any sensible person whose husband worked at Langley.

Sunny had demanded a Norfolk residence, for the opera house and the art museum. She was on the board of this and the committee of that, using Maxon's money to buy their way into the social stratosphere of this old town. Stupid, stupid, stupid. She regretted everything. Where would Maxon die, in the cold of space? Would he fall into the moon? Or would he make it halfway home and then run out of air? Would he kill everyone on board? Would he? She saw her husband under layers, under the rocket, under the space suit, under the jumpsuit, down to the core of him, where he was breathing, low and strong, his pulse never rising above fifty. It was crazy. The doctors couldn't explain it.

There were others in the room. A man she remembered having over to the house for dinner with his dowdy wife approached her. He was clearly not distracted enough to not notice the bald head.

"Sunny," he said. "Are you all right? Are you . . . cancer?"

He trailed off, but Sunny firmly shook his hand and winked.

"Hey, Jim, you guys called me so early, I didn't have time to brush my hair, so I just decided not to wear it, right?"

He didn't laugh, but then, neither did she. When Angela saw her, she motioned for her to come over. Bubber was playing with graduated metal cones on the floor, and was rocking. On the monitor, Sunny saw Fred Phillips, his face filling the whole screen. Angela put out her hand and grabbed Sunny's hand. She was a genuine blonde, with tiny shoulders and a soft baby voice.

The voice of Fred, slightly buzzing through the speakers, said, "Sweetie, tell me something. Tell me anything."

"I don't know what to say," said Angela. "Everything will be all right. You'll be home before you know it."

"Actually it's not," said Fred, rolling a wild eye. "Actually that's not true. So tell me something else, anything else. Tell me what the kids had for breakfast today."

"The kids are asleep, Fred," said Angela. "I left them at my mother's."

"I want to see my kids," Fred said, and his voice choked. They saw him, on the monitor, grab at his mouth, and shake his head. "What the hell, Angie," he sobbed.

There was a delay in transmission, so it was hard for them to communicate. They would talk over each other, and then wait too long, and then someone would start talking, then the other would wait. *Is this what it's like to have a spouse who talks all the time?* thought Sunny. All this stopping and starting. Sunny heard a voice in the background that was not Maxon say, "Pull yourself together, Phillips."

"Fred, Sunny's here," said Stanovich, leaning over Angela's shoulder. "Wanna get Dr. Mann on the feed there? Thanks."

"Sure thing, Stan," said Fred. "Here you go, Genius, time to cry and die."

Angela stood and let Sunny sit down in the chair in front of the wooden desk while Fred seemed to levitate out of the seat he was in, and Maxon seemed to levitate in. Sunny sat perfectly still as she saw his head come into focus. He made sure he was sitting in exactly the right spot, and then he looked at her. She stared back at him, at the wide, bold lines of his face, his precious mouth, his ears, his curls. She wasn't sure what kind of picture she was seeing, but she saw him very clearly, and it made her want to cry. He smiled his standard, formal smile, and then he leaned closer, peering into his screen. Sunny saw his face change from formal and public, to hungry, the way he looked when he really needed to eat something immediately. He had seen her bald head.

"Hey, baby," she said. "What's going on?"

"Well, I'm probably going to have to eat Phillips first," Maxon said.

"Oh yeah?" she said.

"Yeah, Gompers is such a nice guy, and Tom Conrad is made out of silicon, so . . ."

"Rethink, Maxon, rethink."

She reached her hand out and touched the line of his nose, the curve of his cheekbone, the angle of his jaw on the monitor. He was quiet. She wanted to force him to see her, confirm that he knew. She wanted to tell him what to say, write it down for him, hand him a piece of paper with letters on it that he could truly understand. He was quiet. Was she telling him? Was the message getting through? Was she sending him all he needed, to survive? She wanted to say, *Maxon, I love you, I'm sorry I've been a shit, I am straight now, I'm ready to be nice to you again and give you what you need. Please don't die.* He said nothing.

She picked up a piece of paper from the desk and folded it, and a Sharpie that was sitting there, and she wrote on the paper in very thick letters: I AM SORRY. Then she held it up in front of her head, so that her face was covered. When she took it down and looked at him, she was certain he understood.

"Sunny, do you want me to come home?" he asked.

"Yes," she said clearly. "I want you to come home."

"Great, okay," he said. "Put Bubber on."

Sunny retrieved Bubber from the floor and put him on her lap, a smooth metal cone clutched in each fist. He was making noises, like sound effects, and rocking. She knew he was far away in his mind.

"Hey, buddy," said Maxon. Bubber did not look up. "Whatcha got there?"

"Can you show Daddy your cones?" Sunny prompted. "Tell Dad what you have there."

Bubber lifted the cones in the air but did not look at the monitor. He continued to beep and shriek quietly, little sci-fi noises.

"Bubber, look right here where Mommy is pointing," said Sunny, but Bubber wouldn't look up.

"Sorry," said Sunny. She saw Maxon lean down and get something. He was clutching something in his lap, his eyebrows up and his head shaking back and forth.

"It's okay. He looks great," said Maxon.

"He knows you're there," said Sunny. "It's just that—"

Now Maxon was holding up a sign, too. On a clean page in his notebook he had written I LOVE YOU. He had gone over the letters several times so that they could really see it. He held it up to his chest, over his heart.

"Bubber," said Sunny, pressing her lips into his ear, "I really need you to look where Mommy is pointing right now. Just look where Mommy's finger is pointing."

Bubber looked, just one glance; then he turned back to lean on Sunny and click the cones together. Sunny smiled at Maxon and said, "He saw."

But Maxon kept on holding up the sign. And she knew it was for her, too. She tried to memorize the sight, so she could hold on to it forever, him there framed in the screen, wearing his white turtleneck, holding that sign over his heart.

"I gotta go, Sunny," he said. "I don't know what to say. But I'm going to go ahead and land this thing."

"Maxon," Stanovich broke in, "it's too dangerous. Not without the starboard boosters."

"Yeah, I gotta switch this thing off, Stan. See ya."

And then the monitor went black. Immediately, from inside Bubber a wail went up. It came from the back of his throat but it sounded like it came from his toes. She knew from experience that this was the beginning of a meltdown, possibly an epic one, definitely not for public consumption. She wanted to get him out of the room, let him scream and rail and arch and foam and smack at her in the hallway, but first she had to get those cones out of his hand.

"No, honey," she said. "No, no. It's okay. It's okay."

She began to pry his fingers from around the cone.

"We have to go," she said urgently. "Come on, Bubber, put down the cone."

But that was the wrong thing to do. The screaming peaked. Red-faced and spurting tears, Bubber fell to the floor, clutching the cones to his body. He rolled along the floor, kicking anything in his way, until he was wedged under a desk, where he stuck. Sunny went stumping after him, so wide and awkward. It would be very hard to deal with Bubber in this way. She couldn't even pick him up, if he was trying to get away. She wasn't strong and balanced enough. She started to get down on her knees, to try and talk him out, but Stan put a hand on her arm.

"It's okay," he said to her. "Let him keep the cones. In fact, you all can stay here if you want to, for a while."

"I'm really sorry," she said. "This is . . ."

"Sunny, it's fine," he said. "I have a boy with Asperger's myself. And Rogers over there too. I mean, he is autistic, not his kid."

"Really?" she said.

"Really," said Stan. "You might say it kind of runs in the family. The NASA family."

Sunny and Bubber stayed in Stanovich's office at Langley for the rest of the night. In fact, when Sunny took a blanket and pillow into the lounge to get some sleep, Bubber stayed in the office with the other men. He was perfectly happy to play with the robot parts, finger the machines, and say absolutely nothing to anyone.

Up in the rocket, Maxon had laid out his plans for landing the rocket and the robots on the moon. Gompers hesitated.

"I don't know, Mann," he said. "We're going to do it, but only because there's nothing else to do."

Phillips said, "Hey, Genius, who told you it was okay for you to do my job?"

"Shut up, Phillips," said Gompers. "Unless you have another plan."

"Phillips," said Maxon kindly, "of course I can do your job. If I couldn't do your job and everyone else's job up here, I wouldn't have come."

Phillips stared.

"No disrespect, sir," said Maxon to Gompers.

"None taken, son," said Gompers. "Now let's hope you're right."

WHAT THEY HAD DONE to conceive the second baby had taken only a few minutes. It had happened under the wig, under the sheets. It was on Maxon's timetable, but this time there was no resistance from Sunny. "You're right," she said to him. "It's time to have another baby." They did it on purpose, all the while knowing that something was wrong with Bubber, that something was wrong with

Maxon, that something was wrong with Sunny, that something was wrong with her mother, that something was wrong with everyone else. They did it knowing that a flawed thing would be the result of this effort, and that they would be expected to love it anyway, in spite of, because of. She had containers in the cedar closet labeled "maternity." It would all be managed handily by the girl who had become a blonde. They would replace themselves, Sunny and Maxon, in the world. They would do what was required of them by evolutionary law.

But the pregnancy of the girl who had become a blonde had changed into the pregnancy of the girl who had always been bald. And the certainty disappeared. The laws were unwritten, the map faded. It was Maxon's baby, and Sunny's, and anything could happen. There were no expectations that could be logically brought to bear. The baby could be born a miracle.

26.*

IN THE MORNING, SUNNY RECEIVED A PHONE CALL from the hospital. Her mother had died in the night.

There is a real elevation of the conversation, when death and birth come into it. Nothing is unspoken. Everything underneath comes out, and the darkness spills up into the everyday language. You talk about dark things because you have decisions that need to be made. There is no subtlety when you have to decide between cremation and burial, or tell someone whether or not you want to be sedated through it all.

There was a moment, when Sunny was sitting at a small, cheap desk at the hospital, on a rolling office chair, when she forgot her mother's maiden name. Then she knew she was coming unhinged.

But she kept signing paperwork anyway, kept the pen going across the paper. In the normal course of your life, do you have any dealings with the coroner? No. Do you have any reason to say the word "autopsy"? Never.

As an orphan, you are alone. There is no one on the Earth watching, when you say, "Look at me!" There is no one standing in the gap between you and oblivion, putting up her hands, and saying "Stop." You have come this far surrounded, and now you must continue without defense. As a pregnant person, Sunny had to hide herself from this exposure. She had to protect the baby from this distress. So as her mother's ship disappeared, sinking below the horizon, and her own ship sailed up into the wind, she had to let it go without fireworks, without searchlights, without a trumpet blast. Almost without remark.

Sunny decided against a funeral. She decided that her mother would be cremated. These things were going to be handled by the guy at the mortuary, and she signed the release form that authorized him to take possession of the body. This transfer would take place somewhere in the bowels of the hospital. Her mother would exit out the back of the building. Sunny did not know what her mother would look like, at that point. It could be really terrible.

There could have been a funeral in Yates County, where all of Emma's friends could attend. There could have been a funeral in Virginia. But Sunny could not arrange a funeral now. She knew her mother would say, "Whatever makes it easier for you, dearest. Do whatever you need to do. I don't care." So her mother would be cremated. It all seemed so impossible that she wanted to tell the mortician to check carefully and be sure her mother was dead. She wanted to install a brightly colored button on the inside of the kiln: "If you are alive and being wrongfully cremated, PRESS HERE." It had been so slow, this dying. Maybe it was not completely done, in spite of what the doctors said. Maybe there were still some synapses firing, some spirit to be resurrected and intone the words "Good job, Sunny. You are great. You are handling this really well."

"Are you doing okay back there?" a nurse asked her. She had been given two black pens with which to sign all the papers. A pen and a backup pen. But the first pen had worked just fine.

"I'm done, I think," Sunny said. "I think I'm done."

DEATH IS GRUESOME. THERE is nothing romantic about it. Decay, both cruel and gentle, starts immediately. Raised on a farm in farm country, Sunny was not a stranger to death. She had seen dead birds, cats, many deer, a dead horse lying in a pasture, kicked it over and over, and shouted, "Live! Live! Live, goddammit!" She had even raised a sheep as a 4-H project one year, unclear on the term "market lamb." Nu built it a dog house which Sunny decorated with fresh flowers every week, and they painted "Blossom" over the door. She fed it from her hand, brushed its face, and knew complete shock and horror when at the end of the county fair it was sold to a local butcher. After that she hated sheep. "I thought you knew," the mother said. "I thought you knew what it meant."

Other kids raised animals to sell at auction year after year, and Maxon was one of them. He raised a pig every year, starting at age nine, except the year he was eleven, when his pig died inexplicably in June. He had always kept his money separate from his mother's little hoard, in stump stashes in the woods and around town, locations known only to him. From his own funds, he paid for his stock, paid for its keep, kept scrupulous accounts. During the week of the fair he would mingle with the other boys, all in torn jeans and Western shirts. Their scruffy boots knocked against the cement floor in the pig barn as they stepped up from the dirt road that wound through the fairgrounds. Their tough knuckles scraped against the various gates and fences rigged with twine and latches to keep the pigs in pens. The little boys were junior versions of the big boys, getting more taciturn by the year, growing patchy facial hair, adopting a favorite ball cap, sprouting Adam's apples.

After the sheep fiasco, Sunny didn't raise any more market animals, but she took her horse to the fair every year, and stuck close to Maxon every day. All the high-school kids hung around in the pig barns, sitting on the slatted fences, chewing gum and pushing each other. There were the horse barns, where girls spent hours picking up every turd and hanging streamers from their horses' stalls to win the *Good Housekeeping* prize. There were beef barns, where the ponderous steers had their tails teased up into perfect balls of hair. But the pig barns were where the pocket flasks were passed around discreetly, where a slanted gaze could catch fire and lead to a raucous nudge. The boys smelled a little, the girls all wore ponytails, and the space in the middle of the torso was frequently grasped and pulled with a roughness that led to horseplay.

Pigs are earthy; their proximity may lead to carnal thoughts. Showing a pig at a county fair is a dangerous business, and the great relief that follows makes you giddy. Pigs are never really trained, no matter how arduously you practice them, and they're vicious as wild dogs sometimes. For every group of kids in the ring with their pigs on the loose and a curved stick in their hands to guide them around, there was also a group of dads, alert, carrying plywood sheets. The purpose of these sheets was to shove down between two pigs that started going at it. On pig day there was usually blood drawn, and the event always drew a crowd. The kids who won the showmanship trophy moved low, crouched right down over their pigs, watched the judge like a cat. They carried a scrub brush in one pocket and a squirt bottle in the other, and always with their pronged stick ready to hook the pig's ear and drag it off its purpose. Maxon never won showmanship, because he wouldn't make eye contact with the judge.

It was on the last day of the 4-H fair, during the last summer before Maxon would go away to college. He had a scholarship to MIT, and Emma Butcher was paying his room and board. He was eighteen. Sunny had felt restless all day, had not wanted to dive into the partying that was going on, especially with the seniors. She and Maxon sat on the fence down in the warm-up riding ring attached to the big arena, where the equestrian jumpers were loping in big circles, getting ready for their turn in the ring. The competition was fault and out—one knock of a hoof on a jump and that competitor was out of the running. You had to go clean, clean all the way around, and there was no second place for coming close. Maxon watched the horses peacefully, his skin browning in the August sun. But Sunny fidgeted next to him, kicking at the fence, tearing pieces from a little knothole with her thumb.

"Maxon, I feel jumpy and weird," she said, squinting across the dusty ring toward the bleachers. She could see her mother and Nu sitting next to each other under a golf umbrella.

"What's the matter," he said to her mechanically.

"Let's take a walk," she said. She slid off the fence, brushed the back of her jeans with both palms, pulled a sun hat out of her pocket and clamped it on her head.

They walked, hand in hand, across the warm-up ring, pausing to let the cantering horses go by, and went out at the gate. Sunny waved to the mother, and the mother sat up straighter, turned to watch them go. She shook her head back and forth at Sunny, back and forth, but Sunny only waved again. She was too far away, and the day was too hazy for any communication. She turned her back. They went up through the fairgrounds, past the volunteer fire department's food trailer and the little cotton-candy stand, past the bunny building and the big hall where the floral arrangements and craft projects were judged. They went right out through, past the shed where the fair-grounds people kept the tractors and mowers and stored hay and lumber, and into the woods.

They walked silently, trudging along, uphill now and out of the grounds. Maxon kept up with her, held her hand just right, not too tight, not too loose. If they just kept walking they would head right into somebody's fresh-mown hayfield, so she stopped them there in the woods, with the fairgrounds stretched out below and behind them. They were almost to the top of that hill. The cicadas buzzed and there were rocks there, protruding from the earth, just like near to their own houses, in their own familiar forest.

"Let's stop," she said. "I need to show you something. Before you go."

"What is it," said Maxon. He looked so old to her, so real, such a man. She knew that when he went away to college, he could continue changing, getting older, his bones more prominent, his eyes deeper. She pulled her hat off and set it there on the rock. Maxon stood ram-rod straight. His torn jeans hung low on his hips, his Western shirt just the same as all the other boys', tugged tight around his shoulder blades. In his jeans pocket there was a knife. In his shirt pocket, a folded guide, a schedule of the day's events. She motioned for him to stay where he was, and she took off her sandals, put them neatly be-side her hat. Now her feet felt the cool dampness of the forest floor, the dark dirt under pine needles. She pulled off her jeans and then stood there in her blue T-shirt and flowered panties.

"Maybe you should sit down," she said.

He sat down. His knee poked out of a hole in his jeans as he crossed his legs underneath him. He rested one palm on each of his thighs. What did he think was going to happen? She had imagined this scene many times. She was not drunk. She was not crazy. She was doing what she needed to do, for him. Her mother could train him how to shake hands and express regret. It was for her to teach him this other stuff. She knew her mother would not let them get married. He was going off to college, to belong to some other girl that he would meet. So she had to prepare him. She told herself firmly, feeling a low breeze on her legs, that she was doing this for him. It would not be fair for him to go out into the world with no idea what a woman was all about. She had read enough about it, and discussed it in detail with Renee, who had been an expert for at least two years. She had come close to showing him before, at the Bon-Ton, she remembered vaguely, but as she said to Renee, nothing happened. To-day, something would happen. She had a very strong feeling that this was her last chance.

"It's going to be okay," she told him. "Don't worry."

She reached down and pulled off her panties, removing her legs one at a time, and then she folded them on her shoes. When she turned to face him, his jaws were clenched. She walked over to him.

"This is it," she said. "This is me. This is girls. I thought you should see one before you go away."

Maxon was silent. She stood in front of him.

"Give me your hand," she said. "I'll show you. This is how you start it, you kind of just pet down over it, on the outside. You can go all down the legs, and all up here."

She took her shirt off, and she wasn't wearing a bra. He couldn't reach her properly from where he was sitting, so she led him over to the rock and brushed off some leaves and branches, then stretched out on it. It was warm under her back. There were a couple of little rocks poking her, which she removed. Then she felt comfortable, the mossy rock almost cradling her butt, like it was made for her. Maxon knelt beside her, like he was at an altar.

She said, "Stop praying," and he laughed. They both laughed. The air moved around them.

"Go ahead," she said. "Now touch me all over but not there. Like you're trying to just barely touch me. And don't grab."

She waited for the feeling that Renee had said would come, kind of like burning, she had said. But she felt, instead, something lifting up inside and moving around, like a churn that rose to meet his fingers.

"Okay," she said, and spread her legs. "Look at it. Don't worry or think about it too much. It's fine. I want you to."

She shut her eyes, imagined him looking at her, and she felt herself prickle and tingle, something tight and straining in her hips. He would be frowning, his eyes bright, examining her like she was a snowflake, or a locked mechanism, or a squirrel caught in somebody else's trap. She opened herself with her fingers, so he could see all parts of her. She told him what the parts were for. She showed him where to touch, how to move his hand. It was like reading an instruction manual for a package just opened, she reading to him because she was the one holding the paper, but both of them blind, putting the pieces together into a shape they could not anticipate, watching it come together. She felt a swarm of bees beginning to boil in her, raging under her sternum, spiraling into her groin. She heard him take a sharp breath in, but his hand continued to do what she told him, the tough skin of his farmer fingers pressing against her, his other hand touching down lightly over her skin.

"Oh, Maxon, just do that again," she said at the end of her breath. "Keep doing that, as slowly as you can, for as long as you can. It's perfect."

She forgot the rock she was on, forgot the 4-H fair, forgot the long anticipation of the dreaded absence, his going away, his eventual marriage to another woman, his distance, his death, the face of her mother mouthing the words, "No, no, no. Not Maxon. Not him!" She was only there with him right in that moment, in the space between his hand and herself, and when she felt his mouth close over her breast, and when she felt him enter her, so strong behind the hand still moving as instructed, and felt him shudder over her, down through his body, through himself, it all came out of her, all the things she thought to teach him, that one important lesson, closed between them, and simultaneously learned. She locked him into her, she dragged him closer, and dearer, and she cried for him, and made him promise never, ever, to leave her at all.

AT HOME IN VIRGINIA, Sunny stood before the locked desk. She had her files out, stacked on the chair. She had pulled aside the chair, removed the blotter, the calendar, the bookends, the telephone, and the picture frame. The drawer that was locked was a small one on the right side at the top. In her hand she was holding a hatchet she'd found in the garage. It was red, almost comical, like the cartoon version of what a woodsman would have. She didn't know where it had come from; maybe Maxon used it in the yard. But it was sharp.

Sunny swung the hatchet at the top of the desk and it bit into the slick veneer. It did not bounce off, it did not slide, and it did not slip. She meant business. A thick crack formed in the top of the desk as the top layer snapped. She lifted the blade high over her head and swung it again. Of course it was sharp. Maxon would not be a person who would keep a dull ax. He might keep a secret drawer, but not a dull ax. She swung again, and again. The hatchet crashed through the top of the desk and a hole opened big enough to get her fingers in. She pried up a shiny layer of veneer, and then used the ax, in one hand now and this time in smaller bites, to help her smash aside enough of the underlying wood that she could reach inside that drawer. There were papers inside.

She laid her tool on the other side of the desk and pulled out three envelopes through the splintered wood. The first one was large and manila, and had been labeled "Sunny" in Maxon's bold block print. The second was labeled "Maria" in the same text. The third envelope was small and white, and had no label.

She turned around, wiping her face, clutching the envelopes in her hand. She felt the ghost of a contraction rock through her torso, and leaned her butt back against the broken desk. She opened the "Sunny" one first. Inside were pictures of herself, bald. They weren't pornographic or even provocative. But there were no wigs in the pictures. Sunny smiled as she looked at each one, slowly turning them over. When they had moved here to Virginia, she had eradicated all evidence of herself as a person without hair. She had burned the evidence in their backyard grill. She had not noticed there were pictures missing from the purge, but here they were. He had saved them. Sunny felt another contraction. Had it been five minutes? Three?

She shook her head and opened the "Maria" envelope. It was fat, stuffed with material. Inside were stills and movie posters from the movie *Metropolis*, including an original of the art deco film poster from 1927. At one point these treasures had been displayed in their office in Chicago, but these were also victims of the purge. Although Sunny hadn't cared enough to personally oversee their destruction as she had with her own pictures, she had demanded that they be put away, permanently and forever. Maria in the movie was a woman transformed into a robot, and the pictures Maxon had kept in his locked drawer were all pictures of Maria in her metal form. Basically a bald robot with boobs. Sunny had to smile. Well, if Maxon was keeping robot porn, at least it was a bald female humanoid and not R2-D2.

She felt the bottom part of her belly tighten and a pain shot across her like a bolt of lightning wrapped around her gut. She clutched herself with both arms and crumpled up around her baby. She could feel the tightness of the muscles there; it felt like a rock. The pain twisted through her, stretched around into her back, and she found herself rocking back and forth and moaning. The nanny had taken Bubber to the pool in Maxon's car. She could call the hospital, but how stupid.

She decided that after she opened the third envelope she would lie down, drink some water, turn on CNN, and take her mind off the baby. When the nanny got home, they would go to the hospital. She could wait until then. The contraction waned, the fist around her middle relaxed, and she took a deep breath. It was as if it had never happened, the relief was so complete. She wondered if it had really been that painful. Maybe she had been imagining things.

She slipped her finger under the seal of the small white envelope and ripped it open. There were two sheets of notepaper, penned in her mother's spidery, formal hand. The first was addressed to Maxon, and the second was addressed to Sunny. She read the Sunny one first.

Dear Sunny,

It was so hot in Burma. I wonder if you remember. Yet you were always so cool in your little robes, you never seemed to sweat. I think it's the hair on most people that makes them appear sweaty. Yet another benefit of your condition. The Chin people loved you, and they all wanted to bring you presents. I tried to throw all of their presents away when we left, but Nu saved most of that stuff and brought it with her when she emigrated. There are beautiful things, handmade things in the attic of the farmhouse that you may want to unpack and discover someday with Bubber and the baby.

I wanted to bury myself there in Burma, or evaporate myself. But when you came along, I didn't want that anymore. I did what I did because I wanted to save you, to keep you from living in your father's world. I thought that being in Burma would suffocate you, that being of a different race in addition to being bald there, and a zealot's child, would make you so strange that you would have no chance of ever finding out who you really were. I worry now that maybe that is who you really were, that bald white baby under the mountain in Burma. What would have been your life, if we had stayed? I don't know. Maybe I should have let you find out.

I don't apologize for doing it. I want you to be happy, most of all. It is all I've ever wanted. From the time you were born, I was a mother first, and everything I did was for you. No one else mattered. I know you think that's what you're doing too, and I do apologize for railing at you over that damned wig. I'm just thankful for all the years you didn't wear it.

Please don't pursue Chandrasekhar and his witch doctor potion. He was a thief; he stole what he could of your father's research. At one point, I tried to meet with him and stop him, but our lawyers told me there was really no point. It was such a small thing that he managed to pirate, and it didn't work anyway. I promise you, it would not have worked. If your father had been able to develop it, maybe. But he died. I'm sorry for all of that.

Love, Mother

Sunny dropped the sheet to the floor and read the second sheet.

Dear Maxon,

I am going to die from whatever is wrong with me right now. There is something you need to tell Sunny after I am gone. I was the one who turned in Sunny's father to the Communists in Burma. I am the reason that he was killed. Please do not tell her until after I am dead. Choose a good moment, when she is feeling well and has had something to eat. Tell her clearly and calmly, with no movement in your face. Afterward say you're sorry, and hug her with both arms. Then give her my letter.

Love, Mother

"You're a murderer," said Sunny out loud. "You're a murderer."

She remembered the perfect face of her mother, the young pale face in pictures from Burma, so ruthlessly serene. She remembered her mother's body on the farm, sharp like a blade, hand clutching a broom, or a hairbrush, or a handful of envelopes. The way she had looked when Maxon got his acceptance letter from MIT. She remembered the hungry look in her mother's eyes when she looked at Sunny across the top of her glasses, the way she said, "Sunny, you can do anything you want in this world. Be happy. Be free."

And then her water broke.

27.

SUNNY STEPPED OUT THE DOOR. THE AFTERNOON buzzed too brightly around her, all the salt in the water in the air crackling her skin, all the leaves refracting the sunlight into her eyes, the entire neighborhood twisting like an abdominal muscle in distress. She held the side of the porch railing, dragging her feet all the way around to the steps, and then she lurched down them one by one. She needed to keep moving during the contraction in order to avoid falling deep into the panic that was under it. There was a flow from her uterus; it gushed a little as her left foot hit the sidewalk, sending a trickle down the inside of her thigh. She gasped. The belly tightened around the baby, and her spine felt broken in half; in the back of her at her waist there was definitely a knife sticking in. She choked but could not cough, it had gripped her too tightly, and she tried to bend forward to relieve her back, clinging so tightly to the porch railing. From somewhere outside herself, she thought there should be a voice in her ear, telling her to breathe. Otherwise she would pass out. Then it subsided.

She left the house where she had lived. *It's a monster house,* she thought. *We're in it, we're monsters, and we're making more monsters.* It might as well have a bell tower and iron grates across the windows. It might as well have a stone dungeon full of skeletons and a gibbering aunt locked away in an attic. There would be a sitcom about them. In order for the plot to work, they had to live exposed as monsters. The Manns had been keeping undercover, under wraps. The grandma, a murderer. The father, a robot. The mother, a freak. The son, a danger. The daughter, who even knew? Now a newspaper story would be published. Or something like that.

She needed help. *I need help,* she thought. She couldn't go, red-faced and straining, to her girlfriends. She needed a stronger arm, a more upright salvation. She couldn't go down to the main road and lie down in traffic. No one would agree to kill her. She couldn't go back and crawl under the bed, cry "I want my mother!" She couldn't sob "Maxon, help me!" The only person she could think of that was stalwart enough to help her, that was unmoving enough to be of assistance, was Les Weathers. It was to his trim and elegant town house that she now drew her sagging body.

ON BUBBER'S BIRTHING DAY, everything was different. She woke up in the middle of the night with a contraction, firm and insistent. There was time to shower before the next one came, time to put on a wig before the next one after that. She tugged Maxon on the shoulder. "It's time," she said, just like the women said in movies and on television. "Maxon, it's time." He woke up, instantly alert.

"Okay. Let's get Mother," said Maxon.

"What? Do we have to?" Sunny said. "Can't we just go?"

Maxon rubbed his face, pulled on his pants. "She came down here to see the baby being born. Don't you think she wants to go to the hospital when you're in labor? That's where it's most likely to happen."

"It's the middle of the night. She's asleep."

"We need her," Maxon said. Sunny paused. She felt the strange thing happening in her uterus, and felt the foot of the baby roll across her belly just below her ribs. She would like to have her mother there, because she was such a strong supporter. However, her mother would not approve of the wig. She had been disapproving of the wig since the beginning of her visit, when she met Sunny at the airport and said, "Who are you?"

"Oh, fine," said Sunny. "You get her. I'll get ready."

Sunny put on eyebrows, eyelashes, makeup, matching pajamas, a silk robe, and then sat looking at herself in the vanity mirror in her bathroom. She had experienced moments in her life when she realized that she was actually alive and living in the world, instead of watching a movie starring herself, or narrating a book with herself as the main character. This was not one of those moments. She felt like she was drifting one centimeter above her physical self, a spirit at odds with its mechanical counterpart. She stood up carefully. Everything looked just right.

"Is she coming?" she said to Maxon, who had come back into their room, and was putting on a shirt, buttoning it all the way to the top.

"Yes, she's coming. She's up."

"Now you say, 'I'll get the car,' and then you drop your keys, or, no, let me think. You can't find your keys," said Sunny, standing by the door, directing the I Love Lucy episode that Maxon clearly hadn't seen.

"My keys are right here," said Maxon. "Are you all right? Do you want me to carry you?"

"Yes, that's right," said Sunny. Her contractions were weak. "Offer to carry me, but I refuse. I say, this is perfectly normal. Perfectly normal. I say, women have been doing this since the beginning of time. And then you walk into a wall."

In Maxon's Audi, a car seat was already installed in the backseat, behind the driver. Her mother got in and sat behind Sunny, both hands on her shoulders. As Maxon sped toward the hospital down that empty street, Sunny cried quietly every time her body hurt, but she was excited, so excited to see the baby, and make sure it had been made properly. She felt she was on her way to receive an award. She was on her way to witness the results of all her hard work. Every time Sunny cried, her mother squeezed her shoulders. When they arrived at the hospital, Sunny threw up in a bucket.

"I'm sick!" she cried to her mother.

"It's all right," her mother said. "You're doing fine. But this wig. Surely, you—"

"Don't you dare take it off me, Mother," Sunny growled, tightly curled around another contraction. She grabbed the bucket and heaved into it, bile and foam oozing out over her bared teeth. "You don't touch me. I will put you out of the room."

A doctor came and asked how Sunny was doing. She asked for an epidural. She asked for a towel, a mirror, and she dabbed at her face, pressing down her eyebrows, counting out the space between the contractions. She puked again, her stomach empty. The room seemed to swirl around her every time she vomited, and when it righted, she had to check that no one had removed her wig. She had to check that her mother was still there. Maxon had gone out into the hall. "Are you okay, Dad?" said the nurse. "No," said Maxon. "I need to go." The doctor did a pelvic exam.

"She wants an epidural," said her mother. "Get it."

Another doctor came in and made Sunny sit up and lean over. He stuck a pin into her spine, releasing a drug that caused her bottom half to go numb. Instantly, she stopped feeling the contractions. She stopped feeling anything. One more foaming heave, and she was done vomiting, too. Her body gave up, stopped trying to assert itself. It lay still. She closed her eyes.

"I'm cold. Get Maxon," she said. "The vomiting is over."

Her mother went out in the hall, and when they both came back in, Sunny had her handbag in her lap and was fixing her makeup, smoothing her hair. Knees bent up on the blanket, hair spread out on the pillow, she wondered if she was ready to become a mother. She pointed to a mirror lying on a countertop.

"Maxon, get that mirror. Stand down at the end of the bed and hold it up."

"Dearest," said her mother, "that's for looking down there when the baby comes out."

Sunny knew what it was for. That it was for watching the baby's head emerge. But she needed to see the baby's mother first, and make sure that the mother was okay. In the mirror, she saw a woman lying on a pillow, dressed in a hospital gown, about to give birth. The woman was flushed, the woman was wide-eyed, the woman was in all ways exactly what her baby needed her to be. Sunny looked sideways into the mirror so that her mother was in the picture, too, long glossy blond hair neatly tied in a bun, eyebrows perfectly groomed, a silk scarf at the throat. She looked at her mother inside the mirror and her mother looked back and smiled. Sunny breathed a deep sigh and lay back on the pillows. The mother put a hand out, as if to touch her on the head, but then drew it back, and patted her on the arm. Maxon put the mirror down.

Two hours later, everything was still perfect. Maxon had fallen asleep in a chair, and the nurse had turned down the lights in the room, saying that Sunny might as well rest. She might as well get ready to push, because the contractions were steady, and things would be moving along. They had punctured her water bag, and had stuck a little curved wire up into her, inserted it under the baby's skull, where they could monitor his heart rate and humanity. They had wrapped another monitor around Sunny's belly, so they could measure the contractions. Sunny saw the needles skip across the page, drawing on a paper which fed out from a machine beside her bed. She could feel her belly get hard when the needle skipped up a hill, and feel her belly get soft when the needle dropped back down. It was as if the needle itself were moving her muscles for her, and not the other way around.

She didn't know if she could push, because she didn't know what pushing would feel like. She poked absently at her calf, and felt nothing. She couldn't move her legs. She tried to sleep.

The doctor came back in and felt around inside her, and told her she was ready to push. The lights in the room went up, Maxon was told to stand next to her head to count, and her mother stood on her other side, and held Sunny's hand. It was all coming into place, every piece of the picture in order, and yet Sunny felt herself floating, drifting away, up out of herself. She tried to anchor, tried to moor herself in the body, in the physical fact, but it was too hard, and she kept rising up, like coming to the surface of the pool, something you can't seem to stop yourself from doing. It was as if she had been moored to herself by her legs, and once they were numb she was free to drift, whether she wanted to or not. Don't balloons get kind of scared, floating up through the sky above the grocery-store parking lot? After all, where are they supposed to go now?

"Okay," said the doctor. "You know what to do. We're going to push in time with the contractions. We'll push to ten, and then rest and wait for the next contraction."

"How will I know when to push?" Sunny asked from far away. "I can't feel anything."

"I'll be watching the tape," the doctor gestured toward the paper feeding out of the machine next to her, "and I'll tell you when a contraction is coming on."

Sunny nodded. She held on to her mother's hand on one side and Maxon's hand on the other, like anchors, keeping her down in this body. She pulled hard on them, and pushed hard at the baby inside. Yet between her hands, in the middle, bits of her kept floating away. Up in the air, between the two of them, between their heads, she heard their voices, as if they were talking, taking this moment to have a conversation.

"Maxon," said Emma. "I have to tell you something."

"Yes?" Maxon said.

"You know your project, and your research you're doing now; it's so interesting."

"Yes," Maxon said.

"Push," said the doctor. "Come on everyone, count! One, two, three, four, five, six, seven, eight, nine, ten!"

"And they want you, right, to see it through, don't they? Don't they want you to go to the moon?" The mother's tones were golden, soothing. She was holding Sunny's hand but it was as if she were taking Maxon by the hand.

"Yes," Maxon said. "But Sunny doesn't want it. She told me."

"I think," she began, and then her smooth lips pursed together as she paused. "I think that you *should* go to the moon. You specifically. See it through."

"Sunny says no. Sunny doesn't want it," repeated Maxon.

"Sunny doesn't know what she wants," said the mother. "Or what she needs. Do you understand me?"

Maxon said nothing. Sunny, drifting in the air, waited for him to speak. *Say something,* she wanted to tell him. *Tell her no. Tell her you won't go.*

"Sunny needs me to go?" said Maxon.

"Well, the whole world really," said the mother kindly, generously. "The whole world needs you to go to the moon. But in a sense, Sunny needs it most of all. Don't you agree? What would you say, if you agreed?"

Sunny's eyes were squinched tight with the pressure, with the effort of squeezing out the baby. She couldn't see whether Maxon was frowning, or whether he was making the face he made when he was considering someone's opinion. Raise your eyebrows just a little bit. Tilt your head to the side.

"I don't," said Maxon. *Good for you,* thought Sunny.

"Well, I do," said the mother. "I do believe it. And I think that if you don't go, you will be doing her a great harm."

Maxon was silent again. Was he looking down at her, at his wife, so deep in love? Could he see her, there in the hospital, under all the hairs? No, she didn't want him to go. It was too dangerous. But from the way he squeezed her hand, she could tell that he was nodding, slowly, making an arc through the air with his chin, up and down, to show that he agreed. To show that he had accepted the idea.

"I agree," said Maxon.

Sunny felt a change in her body, down through all the numbness, and a shift of angles somewhere in the room, so that when she held her breath and strained, she felt tension and purpose down below. Whatever was drifting, whatever was floating, came plummeting down and sank right back into her blood, into her bones, into that grainy, pivoting moment around her hips. "Yes," said the doctor. "I see the head. You're doing great, Sunny. Come on, Dad, count. One, two, three, four, five, six, seven, eight, nine, ten! And rest. And now count!"

And that's the way it was done. The robots told the doctor, who told Sunny, when to push. The doctor told Maxon, who counted to ten. There was not a single drop of sweat trickling down her face, nor was one eyelash loosened in the process. Hand in hand with her mother on the left and her husband on the right, the perfect mother shape opened up and the perfect baby shape emerged. Bubber was slimy with fluid, strong, loud, and big, bright with orange hair. In the way all normal mothers love their normal babies, she fell for him completely. She would never say, "That didn't work out quite right." She would never say, "There is something wrong with my child." She would never say, "I did not succeed at motherhood." Because she felt, and she was, so responsible. She would have killed for Bubber, without hesitation.

She had heard her mother and Maxon talking about something. But that memory had drifted away along with her memory of the pain, until she wondered, *Did Mother and Maxon really talk about the moon while I was having Bubber? Did I dream the whole thing?*

She should have taken the wig off, yes, then and there. She should have flung it out the window of the hospital, or burnt it. She should have let everything change, let Maxon keep bouncing along at the edge of things, let Bubber emerge as orange as his hair, say to her mother, "Yeah, you were right about that, but no, you are wrong about this." She should have remembered that quiet, terrible conversation, had it out with both of them. Stripped off the layers of her maternal construction and shouted out, "I'm here! I'm alive! You don't have to send him to the moon, and you don't have to go." But instead she took her baby home, installed him in the perfect nursery, fed him the perfect foods, took him to the perfect schools, and kept stumbling along, down the same wiggy path, which put her here at last: no husband, no mother, no son, no hair. Just a big body tearing apart and a hot, empty neighborhood to absorb her bloody pieces.

SHE CRANKED HER WAY up Les Weathers's porch steps one by one, feeling huge and slow, like an amoeba rolling toward an underwater cave. The door wreath was gone, and he had not replaced it with any other holiday decor. Safe choice. She picked up the heavy brass knocker and let it fall three times. There was no response. She waited through another contraction, tears squeezing from her eyes at the pain in her back, and then she slammed the knocker fiercely against the door, making a rattle they could surely hear all down the twisted block. The door creaked open a bit. It was not latched.

The house was built like all the town houses in Norfolk and the world, one room leading to the next back through the house with no central hall. The first room she entered was a sitting room, including a semicircle window seat that bulged into the front facade of the house. There was a fireplace there, and on the mantel an assortment of candles in tall holders and wooden picture frames. In the center of the room was a circular table with a marble top, holding a large arrangement of dried flowers.

"Les Weathers! Help!" she called. Maybe he was upstairs.

Moving back through the house to the next room she paused, one foot in the air, and her hand went out to steady her on the chair rail. She stopped because she saw a giant television, lying on its face, front smashed against the floor. She felt a twist of fear slide down around her torso, wrapping itself into the place where the contractions would be. Maybe Les Weathers had been robbed—maybe he was lying upstairs at this moment, dying of a gunshot wound to the back. Maybe she should leave, and save herself and the baby. But go where? She was an animal in need of a cave. She was a sinner in need of salvation. She was a desperate woman in need of a rock solid, un-excitable man. Anyway, the front room had been so tidy. She shuffled toward the back of the house and came to the kitchen.

Once it might have been a rather elegant little room, white and black, with glass-fronted cabinets and a basketweave floor. It was now in shambles, every surface covered. There was murky water on the floor. Sunny turned and faced the refrigerator. On its door she saw a magnet that said, "I don't want to work! I just want to bang on my drum all day!" Next to it, a postcard-sized poster of Garfield complaining: "I hate Mondays." On the counter was a smashed tele-vision, lying on its face. Next to it, what had once been a melon. Two of the cabinets had been smashed out, and inside one of them there was a telephone lying in shards of glass.

Sunny mounted the stairs, calling, "Les Weathers! Are you all right? Help!" She was in labor and convulsing. But Les Weathers could be bleeding, dying. Or maybe he didn't really live here. Maybe it was all a front. Someone else must live here, some bad version of Les Weathers, anti-television, anti-clean, anti-golden-hair. Or maybe Les Weathers was a robot that lived in his car, shutting down after the evening news, never entering this sham house, this ruined build-ing. She stepped on the stairs nervously, her heaviness causing them to creak and complain. There was a tilt to the upstairs hallway, the rail-ing crooked and cracked.

There was a bathroom down the hall, full of boxes with the sink unhinged from the wall, and then a dressing room, where she switched on a light. She found his suits there, pressed, perfect. She found a box of old dress shoes, like the kind a grandpa might wear. She spent a full minute lying on her side half in the closet, having a contraction, oozing amniotic fluid onto his floor, but she had to go on. She had to know, what was going on with Les Weathers? Where had he gone? What was he? Was this the house of someone else, someone strange, some terrible twin brother? Some other Les Weathers?

Through the dressing room she found another bathroom, caked with filth, a tub ringed with wax from candles set around the edge, whose wax had stuck together shampoo bottles and filmed over the tiles. There was such dirt inside the tub that two distinct footprints articulated themselves at one end, under the faucets. He sits here, she had to tell herself. He puts his feet into those prints! He lights these candles. He stands on this floor. Were the grime and grunge as old as his wife's departure? Were the footprints started the day she left? A toothbrush, blue, balanced on the side of the sink. A tube of Aquafresh, squeezed from the middle, lay beside it.

Sunny moved into the bedroom, where she found yet another giant flat-screen television on its face, smashed against the floor. There were piles of newspapers and books, discarded clothes and boxes, an ancient dresser overflowing with linens. The huge bed, covered in what looked like tapestry, was broken. The legs of the top end had collapsed or been furiously kicked out, so there was a steep slope down to the headboard, against the wall. But it was made up with a pillow where it belonged, next to the wall on the low side, the side that had fallen down.

In the pillow was a dent, shaped like a head. Next to the pillow was today's paper. Today's. She had to acknowledge this. At this depth of her extremity, she had to come to terms with this visual, and accept the fact that as she went about her nightly rituals, taking off her eyebrows, taking off her wig, arranging it on her dresser, considering herself safe for another day, Les Weathers of Action News Reporting was three houses away, sleeping upside down. Les Weathers, the last bastion of urban normalcy, of the square jaw and flawless skin, of the resonant voice and signature finger point, was sleeping upside down in a house where a herd of giant televisions had met their violent end. There was no terrible twin. There was no secret robot. He and this were real at the same time. He was, in fact, just another lunatic. Sunny had to laugh. She laughed, looking out the window on their neighborhood, because it was such a ridiculous thing. All the wives, drooling over him. And all the while, him taking a bath in that tub.

She laughed until another contraction came, and when it had passed, she went back into the hall. She had to find him. Maybe he was in a basement. Maybe he was just now emerging from his Lexus, slamming the car shut, trotting toward her over the pavement. Les Weathers. Looking like the cover of a magazine. She heard a sound from the third floor and put her foot on the first of the attic stairs.

She found him in a room that had been intended for a nursery. The beautiful curtains and the drape around the bassinet were dusty and still. He was sitting on a rocking chair. It was the squeak of the chair that she had heard. In the bassinet was nothing. All around, the things a baby needs: a box of diapers, a dresser with a lamp, a changing pad on a wicker table, a stuffed purple rhinoceros standing watch. Les was wearing his anchorman clothes but his jacket was off, his tie gone, his sleeves opened at the wrist. When he spoke, his voice was low.

"Hey, Sunny, are you all right?" he said.

"Fine, fine," Sunny choked. "Just going home."

"I'm sorry I didn't come down to let you in."

Sunny saw that Les Weathers had been crying.

"It's okay," she said.

"Is it bad, this house?" he asked.

"It's not good," Sunny said. She went to the window to look out, but as she reached it, she felt the pain tighten around her back, and she went to her knees with another contraction. Just trying to breathe a little bit, she let herself feel the rolling spasm. Her belly, hard as a rock, brushed against the floor as she leaned down and grasped the rug, trying to get the pressure off her back. Les Weathers sprang out of his chair and knelt beside her, holding her in his arms.

"She died, you know," he said, his voice a moan. "I'm sorry, but she died. She died inside Teresa."

Teresa was his wife. Sunny, raw to the core from the pain of labor, felt the twist of fear tighten into a need to flee. She was afraid of Les Weathers. She was afraid for Les Weathers.

"Teresa didn't leave with the baby. She left when the baby was already gone. Dead. Dead inside her. We tried to hide it . . ."

Sunny rolled onto her side and curled around her alive baby. Les Weathers threw his hands out in an expansive gesture.

"This is what happens!" he said. "This is what happens, Sunny! We tried, but this is what happens!"

As soon as the contraction let go of her and she could move, she began to crawl. She crawled to the door, dragged herself up on the frame, and got out into the hall. She went down the stairs on her butt like a toddler, one at a time. She wished just to get back into her own house, close the door, and be safe. But her pelvic bones were grinding on themselves, and she felt that if she went too fast, she might fall apart, literally, into pieces.

"Do you need to go to the doctor again?"

"Don't feel good," Sunny groaned. "Talk later."

Les was beside her, tall and strong. But inside him, a baby was dead. He had raged around his house to get it out, but it was still in there. He took her by the arm, supported her down the next staircase, his face a perfect rendition of care and concern.

"Can I drive you to the hospital?"

She stared up at him. He looked to her like a gargoyle, some hideously gross miscalculation. And yet he was there, and human. The same man. The same man that lived in all these houses. Even hers. Just a person. Does everybody have to have a bathtub with footprints? Does everyone have his mangled hand, his bald head, his Quasimodo hump?

"No, no," she said. She knew if she could get her creaking, straining body out the door, down the step, past one sidewalk square, and then the next, and then four more, she would be at the edge of her yard. She felt as though her hips were splitting apart, her pelvis on fire. She wanted to get to her yard before another contraction came. On the porch, she knew she was leaking fluid along the concrete, but she kept her eyes up, kept herself moving along. He followed her.

"Sunny, should I carry you?"

"No," she said firmly, as she dragged herself across the yard. She was embarrassed for him, that she had recognized him, but she could not undo it. At what point do you say, "It's no big deal, nothing to be ashamed of" to a person who is sleeping upside down. Is that nothing to be humiliated by? What about head banging? What about murder?

"That was not the right thing to say, Les Weathers. Call an ambulance. Then get back in your house. I'm fine."

28.

SUNNY HAD SEEN MAXON HUMILIATED ONCE, BUT SHE
didn't tell him, so he didn't know. It was long after his father had
died, but his brothers still treated him like a hired hand and his
mother did nothing to stop them. Sometimes he had to fight them,
and if he could get away, he did. Sometimes he had to do what they
wanted. There were days when he didn't answer Sunny's summons,
and she knew that he was either stuck doing some kind of chore, or
AWOL, either way unavailable.

It was on one of these days that Sunny was out riding by herself.
She was thirteen, the summer after Maxon's first year in high school,
when she was about to go to high school herself. It was August, hot,
and the horseflies were bad. She let Pocket pick out his own way, after

a canter down their dirt road. He went down the deer paths through the meadows where he could lean down and chew on comfrey and mint growing wild, unencumbered by a bit in his rebellious little mouth. When Sunny got too hot in the sun, and too irritated with his loud crunching and munching, she turned him toward home through the woods and urged him into a canter. Down the logging trail they flew, a welcome breeze, and the flies gone, replaced by swarms of gnats that they blew right through.

The light came down through the trees in filtered shafts, yellow on the ferns, and the trees moved over each other as she passed them in layers. Sunny heard a shout before she saw anyone out in the woods, and slowed her pony to a walk. She didn't want to be seen, but she could see a little clump of people in the trees. They were shouting into a hole, and had not noticed her approach. Not knowing whether to turn around and run or go and see what they were doing, she let Pocket keep walking, his feet making soft thuds on the pressed dirt.

She saw that there were three young men standing around a pile of stones, and heard them shouting "NO!" down at a pile of rocks, and she heard a voice from inside the pile of rocks, pleading and crying, and then she knew that these were Maxon's brothers, and the rocks were a well, and they had made him go down that well.

Country wells were inexact mechanisms and plumbing could become clogged by anything biological, or just a buildup of silt or rust. There were methods for cleaning wells that didn't involve freezing a human being in cold mountain spring water, but for Maxon's brothers, the downside of this method did not exist. They had to clean out the well, to get it working again, and they didn't mind freezing Maxon to do it, so there was no problem. Now they were standing back from the well, being quiet and pretending to be gone. They stifled their laughter and poked each other in the arm. There was a rope hanging over the side, but it wasn't tied to anything. He couldn't pull himself out. Pulling on the rope would only pull it in on him.

Hearing him scream from in the well, Sunny's heart froze. He could be dying. He could be losing whatever there was of his mind to lose. She felt her rage rising, her need to protect him. At least she could yell, "I'm here, Maxon! I'm here!," and he would know that he wasn't left in the well, legs braced against the sides, neck deep in the water. She knew that it hurt him to be down there in the cold. But she kept her mouth shut, her legs slack; her pony kept on plodding down the path. She knew that if she let them know she was there, it would be worse for him. The two of them could not overpower these three men. Later, he would learn to beat them. But now, they were an army.

Then they took the rope up, and began to pull him out. His head came up first, dark and wet, and then his body. He climbed out and stood there, dripping. The brothers were angry. The task had not been accomplished. As they conferred about what was to be done, motioning at Maxon as if he were a wrench or a drill, he stood shivering, his whole body shaking. Sunny could see them but not hear them, except for a few sounds that punched through like the bark of a laugh. Maxon was wearing nothing but boxers. She could see every bone in his body, his sharp clavicles, his jutting hip bones, the knobs on his back. It was so precious to her, that body, covered and uncovered by the trees as she passed them, his cold and dripping body. He clasped his arms around himself, rubbing up and down and trying to get warm. She was terribly and permanently moved. She never forgot it.

The brothers turned to him. They were finished discussing the matter, and they directed him sternly to get back into the well. He shook his head firmly, back and forth, ducked to run, but quickly one of them had him by the wrist. He let out a yelp, a sound like a wounded dog that turned Sunny's blood to fire. Then "No!" he yelled. "No, no," and "Please!"

She panted, her breath coming in gulps. She would call to him, "Maxon, run!," and he would come straight to her, jump up on the back of her pony, and they would canter away to safety. She could save him, protect him, warm him, those wet bones pressing against her back as they fled, his cold arm clamped around her waist, hips banging against her, making the back of her shirt cold and wet. But she said nothing, did nothing, let the scene pass behind her, let the trees cover it, the noises of it slipping away into the birdsong and cicadas. Her pony was too small even for just her. With Maxon on board, too, it would be ridiculous, he probably wouldn't even trot. Hers was no white stallion, she no crusader. The most she could do for him was to never speak of it, never let him know she had heard those cries, she had seen him brought so low, watched that wretched shivering in the woods, and felt for that cold body such a strange desire. Later, in the fall, she would hold him in her arms in the planetarium, and kiss him under the stars.

SUNNY WENT INTO HER house and shut the door. She locked it, doorknob and bolt. They would have to burn it open with a torch, pry it open with a pitchfork. They would have to crack her open like a nut. Inside the house, she dropped to her knees with another contraction and began to crawl toward the living room. She made it to the rug, so immaculately dyed and tied, a million knots per square inch. It had cost eighteen thousand dollars. As many knots as there are stars in the sky, said the salesman, a lively Moroccan. Bad analogy, Maxon had said. You're looking for density, not quantity. Try rods and cones on the retina. That gives you both.

When Bubber was a baby she had laid a plastic mat over this rug, to protect it from stains. She kept pushing the mat down at the edges, then replaced it, and then she took the mat up and they abandoned this room altogether. It became the shrine, the holy crypt of urban respectability, a resting place for the crystal pieces she acquired, the Indian carvings, the silver. Cabinets ringed the walls, glass cases sparkling. A museum of only five years of history. *This is unbearable,* she thought. *I can't bear it.*

She rocked on her hands and knees. She could feel the baby, and the baby was coming down. There was a turn, a big somersault in her stomach, and at that moment, she knew that the baby was about to come out. The baby was about to be born. In the darkness on the inside, everything was in the right place. There was no communication from outside to in, or inside to out. But there was a process in place inside the womb that no external timetable could hinder or accelerate. She dragged off her underpants, pulling them back, down, and kicking them to the side. The contractions were now coming one right after the next, rolling like particles, not like waves, bombarding her, turning her inside out.

She put her forehead on the rug and strained, and the straining finally gave her some relief. In the straining, she finally felt better. There was no one coming to help her. There was no backup plan. If she would be torn apart, then she would tear herself apart. There was a change in Sunny's mind. A new sense of this-is-happening. She erased all contemplation, all reflection, until there was only Sunny herself, a raw and bleeding thing in a lemon yellow silk chiffon babydoll dress hiked up wet around her waist, dripping sweat, ass in the air, trying to explode.

In the pain and the inversion, with all her blood a hot bubble in her head, she finally knew. She was unfit, and she was bald. But she was the only mother that was here. In the dark, where all the muscles were, where the baby had turned herself around and kicked for home, there was no bald and no unfit. There was only a body with a baby in it, doing its best. *I'm sorry*, said the body to the baby. *I'm bald. I've made terrible mistakes. Almost all of your grandparents are dead because of me. I'm going to embarrass you. I'm going to fuck things up. But I am your mother, and I will do my best. Whatever I actually am, and whatever I can actually do, I am the mother you have. Here I am. Doing it.*

The contractions overtook her. She tried to climb the drapes. She wrapped her wrists in the soft fabric and lay back against them, rocking her body against the curtain rod, writhing and groaning. The curtains held, but her mind wavered. She slipped out of time, out of this painful anchor. Maybe it was an accumulation of everything that had happened, or maybe it was an experience common to every woman who labors alone. She did feel the pull of her hands on the drapes and the burning, heavy urgency between her legs. It made her push, push, right down from her throat to her thighs. But beside it, under it, and around it, she saw a purplish fog rise up over her eyes, and she began to see things that weren't there: her baby, and the life she would have.

She saw a beautiful long-legged six-year-old with a face like a valentine, and bright ropes of orange hair flashing in the sun. Hair just like Bubber's. She was carrying a bamboo stick, and expertly piloting a small sailboat around the pond at the Luxembourg Gardens in Paris. The wind was brisk, spraying water from the fountain in a wide arc and whispering in the beech trees. The boats moved fast, some almost lying down sideways, about to capsize. But the red-haired girl put her stick right against the divot on the deck of her bright blue boat and gave it a big push away from the wall, her eyes intent on its progress. *She does that really well,* thought Sunny. *She is an expert; she must do it all the time.* My name is Emma, said the girl to a little boy standing next to her. Emma.

She saw a fierce, happy nine-year-old cantering on a chestnut pony across a meadow full of comfrey and mint. She had her hands buried in the pony's mane and her bare heels dug into its sides, making it go faster. Her sunny hair was short now, cut off at her chin, bouncing in wavy layers. The girl was laughing, her knees pinned to the pony like a clamp, teeth bared. Sunny knew her breath was coming short. Sunny knew she had to push this baby out. Maybe it was the wind in her face, cantering across the meadow. Maybe it was everything in her body pushing on down. She whisked along the deer path, parallel to the tree line. Those were Maxon's woods. Stay in the meadow, girl.

She saw the girl again, older, on a rocket to the moon. She was asleep in a bunk, her hands thrown back over her head and wrists knocking into the wall, her chin up, as if she were resisting some invisible restraint, some band across her belly, some wire in her head. She wore a white leotard with long sleeves, and Sunny could see it was just a little bit too short in the arms, a little bit too wide in the waist. She was covered by a thin, plastic sheet. *Wake up,* Sunny thought. *Let me talk to you. Do you remember being born? Did it all come out all right in the end? At what moment did you know: I'm alive! This woman is my mother!*

The girl grew up, she was twenty now, and she was leaving the family on the moon. They were all there: Sunny, Maxon, and Bubber, to say good-bye. Sunny wore a gray cardigan, pulled tight around her. She smiled and waved at the girl, while her tears fell down. Maxon and Bubber stood still as statues, right next to each other, exactly the same height. They wore space suits and rigid expressions. But the girl went over and kissed them both, hugged them, clamped her hand under Bubber's armpit playfully to make him laugh. Sunny saw Bubber put his arm around his sister and pull her tight around the shoulders. Don't go, she wanted to say to the girl. Bubber needs you. I need you.

She saw the girl on Earth, taking a human shape, living a human life, falling in love, making friends. She would visit the moon, but she would never really go back. She would be okay. They would all really miss her. Sunny would visit sometimes, but she could never ignore the distraction of the moon. She could always see it. It made her feel critical of her daughter. It made her feel rushed and anxious. She always went back, but the girl never did. Her place was on Earth. Sunny had known that this would happen. *Come out, Emma, so I can have my time with you. I'm waiting for you, I'm going to help you get there. I'm going to be on your side. Whatever happens.*

MAXON WAS NOT MOVED by the sight of the moon's dusty surface. There was no desolation magnificent enough to distract him from unloading the robots and getting on with his work. He was moved, however, by the sight of the lava pipe, a huge chasm in the moon's surface, on the back side of a newer crater. The pipe went down for miles, an old vent for a hypothesized prehistoric volcano, now just a tube riddled with caves and protected from meteors and the sun. They had landed so well, so perfectly close to the place they were supposed to land, that he had found the lava pipe almost immediately. He felt, in that moment, a surge of triumph. *I'm right,* he thought. *I was right. Here it is.* This is the difference between success and failure. The humans had landed. They would colonize the moon.

While Phillips and the rest walked around making footprints and repairs, Maxon took the cargo container down on a tether. Lowering the massive box full of mother robots in low gravity was a breeze. He could almost manage it on his own. He thought he might say, "You boys stay here and clean the shit out of your pants while I finish the mission," but then he didn't say it. Sometimes it's better to say nothing.

Maxon didn't think, *Look, this hapless little biological sliver has redeemed itself. Look, it has survived. Look, the plaintive little push toward the cosmos has won us a foothold in the universe, a first footstep out.* He didn't think, *Suck it, universe. We're here,* which is what Fred Phillips said he'd thought. He only thought about the latitude and longitude, and how it was exactly as he had imagined it. No more poignant, no less grand. Just exactly how it had looked in the plans; that's how it was.

Maxon and the robots reached a cave that had been identified and mapped by ultrasound and chosen by geologists as the site for the future colony. Maxon maneuvered the cargo box into the spot where it was supposed to stop, stood beside it, and opened the main door. It was dark in the lava pipe. Dark and cold. He had a light, and a warm space suit. Did he remember being stuck down in a well, and crying to be let out? Did the lava pipe bring back memories of that fear? He did not, and it did not. Wells were not in his memory.

Did he remember being expelled from the womb, thrust from that dark pipe to another, through the years of misunderstandings, approximations, and nervous fixations? Did he feel the pressure of the lava pipe on his body, forcing him onward, downward, toward the completion of the mission? Did the baby in the womb understand the father in the lava pipe, setting up the robots, fixing the cameras, laboring for hours in the darkness? Or did she only know this: Now it's time for us to come out.

At the time they had agreed upon, Phillips and Conrad pulled Maxon up from the pit on a rope. One of his thumbs was crushed, and he was hungry. Otherwise his arrangements on behalf of mankind in launching the robotic construction of a lunar colony had been a complete success. The robots chugged and whirred on below the surface, mining their materials, creating their children, teaching them to walk, move, mine, create children of their own. For ten years, the world would watch on cameras as the colony took shape. In twelve years Maxon would come back with his son Bubber, freshly graduated from MIT, and open the airlock. Everything just as he had left it to be.

SUNNY HELD HER BABY and wiped the blood from her face. They lay together on the rug. The baby was on Sunny's chest, and Sunny's back was on the ground. Every breath felt like a miracle, pain free. There was no cry, no knife, no scale, no iodine. Pressed up against her mother's heart, wrapped in a red silk scarf from the hat rack, the baby lay blinking. Sunny's relief was so intense that she felt she might be able to go to sleep right there, but she knew that while they were getting cold, the neighborhood was in a hot panic. She could hear the ambulance outside, and lots of voices. She didn't want Bubber to be alarmed, coming home with the nanny from the pool. She pushed herself, still sitting, to the door, scooting herself carefully along so as not to disturb the little bundle. At the door she reached up, flipped the bolt, and turned the handle. Right there were Rache and Jenny, standing on the step. It was as if they were waiting, ready to come in and have sandwiches or drink margaritas. They were just waiting, each with one foot on the stoop.

"Look," said Sunny, and she pulled the scarf back to show the baby's face. "She's here."

"Sunny," said the women. Those friends of hers said, "Sunny, she's amazing. And she looks just like you."

Acknowledgments

Thank you to my husband, Dan Netzer, and my friend Andrea Kinnear for understanding and interpreting Maxon for me, and writing the equations, proofs, and code snippets in this book. I came to you with a messy idea and you translated it perfectly into math.

Thank you to my agent, Caryn Karmatz Rudy, and my editor, Hilary Rubin Teeman, for the vision you had for this book. When I think back to that very first draft, I am struck by the way you both made the book immeasurably better. Thank you for the incredible support and dedication of the independent booksellers I have had the honor to meet, especially Kelly Justice, Erin Haire, Stef Kiper, Nancy Olson, Terry Gilman, and so many others.

Thank you to Sara Gruen and Karen Abbott, whose early support, ongoing wisdom, and loving encouragement have been invaluable in birthing this book.

Thank you to my early readers C. J. Spurr, Bekah James, Kate Bazylewicz, Heather Floyd, Kristen DeHaan, Sherene Silverberg, Patricia Richman, and Veronica Porterfield.

Thank you to Book Pregnant, the December mothers, the Quilt Mavericks, Cramot, and all my Norfolk Homeschooling comrades, for cheering me on, and for your radiant examples of excellent mothering.

Thank you to Dori Weintraub and Laura Clark at St. Martin's Press, Ken Holland at Macmillan, and Esther Bochner at Macmillan Audio for your wisdom and intelligence, your patience and understanding.

Thank you to Susannah Breslin, who refused to let me settle, and kept pulling me back out of the sleep of motherhood, and making me be better.

Thank you to Joshilyn Jackson, who has been my fierce champion, and without whom this story would not have become a book.

Reading
Group
Gold

SHINE SHINE SHINE

by Lydia Netzer

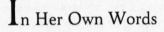

*A
Reading
Group Gold
Selection*

For more reading group suggestions,
visit www.readinggroupgold.com.

ST. MARTIN'S GRIFFIN

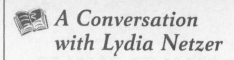

A Conversation with Lydia Netzer

What inspired you to write *Shine Shine Shine*?

When I started the novel, I was a new mom and I was paying close attention to the transition that women go through when they become mothers. As new mothers we look at ourselves in a changed light. Instead of individuals responsible only for our own quirks and bobbles, we're now responsible for raising another human and hopefully not embarrassing or ruining them in the process. Because, you know, kids have been ruined by store-bought cookies and non-matching ballet flats. As I got into writing the character of Sunny, I thought it would be more interesting to create a character who had already gone through this transition into motherhood, and reinvented herself into this perfect, perfect wife and mother. Then the book could start with the moment it all came apart.

How did you manage to make one great story out of so many concepts?

The layers of the book fell into place over time...one thing led to another in a way that had its own logic. That's not to say that I didn't feel like I was trying to wrestle an octopus into pantyhose. I had awesome input from my amazing agent and my brilliant editor at St. Martin's, who assisted in getting several of the octopus's legs into sheers.

What does true love like Sunny and Maxon's look like in real life, and how can couples keep it alive?

To me, true love looks like true commitment. True love is burning the lifeboats. It's the totally unsafe feeling of leaving behind the possibility of retreating from your promise, and trusting the other person enough that you still feel safe. A lot of couples, even after marriage, are toying with the idea of leaving, or dealing in "what if" and contingencies and exit strategies.

"I was trying to wrestle an octopus into pantyhose."

When you disagree, or fail each other, or change, and you always have splitting up on the table, it makes a small problem into a huge one, and an argument that may have been limited in its inception can consume everything. Marrying someone, making that promise, you hand them a specific gun calibrated only for you. Ideally, they'll put that gun away and never touch it. Often, though, you see people take that gun out and wave it around. If your partner is committing a divorce-worthy offense like abusing you or cheating on you, don't threaten. Just go. Take the gun out, shoot them in the face with it, and leave. But if your partner is just irritating you, or disappointing you, or challenging you, "or else" should never feel like "or else I'll leave." That's just a weapon that should never be used as a threat.

Is Sunny's epiphany that she can accept her autistic son without "fixing" him a lesson society could stand to learn about children with special needs?

I don't have any lesson to teach, nor do I think there is one right way to parent. But as a weirdo who is married to a weirdo and parenting two weirdos, I am saddened by our modern need to make sure everyone fits in, and functions smoothly, and checks all the necessary boxes. Some amazing and brilliant people do not, and will never, fit in. This is not to say that weirdos should be encouraged to go full-on lunatic, and bark at heating vents and eat chalk. In raising Maxon, who as a child was "special" in an alarming way, Emma Butcher proactively trained him to be part of the world we live in, without stamping out all the things that made him "special" in a good way.

How did you come up with the idea to have Maxon express human interaction through mathematical equations, and who helped you formulate them?

I had this purely fanciful idea that some other person might interpret human interactions by applying

mathematical principles, and that a math-brained chil
who was having trouble understanding social situation
might be helped by teaching him to think of intuitiv
things in the language of math. However, I do not co
rectly speak the language of math, so I needed to brin
in the experts: my husband, a computer coder, and m
friend Andrea Kinnear, a mathematician and statisticiar
I came up with a list of statements or rules for huma
behavior that I thought would translate well into matl
Here's one we didn't use in the book. My statemen
"If you've already used a line in a conversation, yo
shouldn't use the same line again in the same conver
sation." I gave this idea to Andrea, and she came bac
with:

> Statements contributed to a conversation are
> to be sampled without replacement. If the
> A = set of conversational statements = $\{a, b, c, d\}$ and
> b is sampled, the set of remaining statements = $\{a, c, d\}$

Some are drawings, some equations, some stated lik
theorems. All appear as if drawn by hand on a white
board, and the handwriting is my husband's.

Tell us about motherhood in your life and your writing

As a mother, I am full of doubt. I've navigated attach
ment parenting failures and violin lesson breakdown
and karate school meltdowns and epic playgroun
tantrums. Pretty much every kind of doubt that ca
cross a mother's mind has left tire tracks on mine. Fo
me, Sunny's mother, Emma, is confident, aggressive
and makes her choices without looking back. Sunny
on the other hand, has been so crippled by doubts an
hesitation that she is denying her children their actua
mother in favor of some Stepford simulation of what
mother should be. My hope for myself is that I can hav
the confidence to be who I am and a mother, too.

Conversation courtesy of Jaclyn Fulwood and Shelf Awareness

"My hope for myself is that I can have the confidence to be who I am and a mother, too."

An Original Essay by the Author

Dear Reader,

I'm delighted to have this opportunity to give you a little "behind the scenes" look at the construction of this novel. The book took ten years to write, and during those ten years there were changes in my life that affected the manuscript enormously. For example, in an early draft, Sunny's mother, Emma, spent the book perfectly healthy, dispensing wisdom and love from a brownstone in downtown Norfolk. Then in 2004, my own mother got sick and died. Like Sunny, I had to authorize her being taken off life support. I knew then that I had to incorporate the experience into my novel, both to honor her and to address my new understanding of what it was like to be a mother without your own mother. It took me five years to write the scene in the hospital, where Sunny "pulls the plug." When I finally did write it, it was in the dark, in the dining room, with the door shut, and I had my eyes shut, too, so that I couldn't even see the words on the screen. It's the hardest thing I've ever written, and this essay I wrote about my mother's death may help you understand why.

With all my love and thanks,

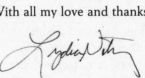

Behind the Novel

"If My Mother Is Dying"

I am standing on the other side of thick hospital gla[ss] from my mother, and my mother is dying. I am fou[r] months pregnant with my second child and my first [is] standing beside me, holding my hand, unaware of wh[at] is going on. Inside her room in the ICU, machines a[re] keeping my mother alive, but they are killing her als[o.] A sore has formed under the breathing tube. Her hand[s] are swollen and yellow. The doctor says, "She is shu[t]ting down." They want me to pull the plug.

For months, we had been nursing her, my sister and [I.] Sometimes she was catatonic, terrifying us. Sometime[s] she was in pain. Sometimes she was almost all righ[t] and wanted to go outside and listen to birds. We wer[e] all supposed to go to a beach house for a month; sh[e] wanted us to still go. At that point, we didn't kno[w] she had cancer. "I might as well be miserable besid[e] the ocean," she said. The doctor said she had inflam[m]ation on her small intestine. They wanted her to sto[p] eating nuts.

My mother wanted to walk on the beach, so we too[k] her, slowly. When she got back to the house, she co[l]lapsed into a chair and we struggled to get her int[o] bed. That night she called to us, and said, "Good-by[e]" to my sister. We called an ambulance. They opened he[r] up and looked inside. The doctor said, "She is full [of] cancer." Now, here we are with this hospital windo[w] between us. I am sick, tired, hopeless, and I want to li[e] down and die. I am sick from the pregnancy, and am o[n] medication to control it. I have a three-year-old to car[e] for who is barely verbal and prone to fits. I am all b[y] myself. My mother is ninety-two.

Why is my mother so much older than I am? I a[m] adopted. My mother is biologically my grandmothe[r.] My sister is biologically my aunt. There was anothe[r] person, who gave birth to me. There was a father als[o.] The circumstances surrounding my birth are murk[y.]

y parents were married, and not without resources. ey didn't want to be parents, so they decided to give e away. My understanding of the situation is limited, ough it has been explained to me by many people. me people say, "Their marriage was on the rocks." me people say, "They were so committed to their olitical activism that they did not want the distrac- on." Or maybe, "They were just bad people, who don't e babies." Or "They only wanted a better life for you." veryone has an interpretation. It is impossible for me know the true history of what really happened. There e circumstances that surrounded my birth. That's all now.

d I know that my adopted mother wanted me, aimed me, loved me, saved me. She saved me deeply d abidingly. She liked to say, "Whatever happens, I'm your side." And through all my childhood turmoils d teenage angst, she never wavered in her judgment: dia is awesome. Lydia makes life great. In the mirror her opinion, I saw in myself someone that was not ash, to be thrown away, that was not a worthless life, nwanted, unloved by the people who were supposed be biologically programmed to preserve me. My other, saint that she was, loved me totally. That is a story I know to be true because I felt it every day she as alive.

e stood, all five feet and one hundred pounds of r, between me and The Circumstances Surrounding y Birth. With the ferocity of her conviction, and all r love, she blocked it from me. I was a baby whose other couldn't love it, whose father didn't want it, d she stood between me and that, a solid protection ainst reality. I can still hear her saying, "Oh, honey." d with her panacea of saltines and ruthlessly sharp eddar cheese, tea with milk, her religion, her firm sertion I could do anything, she defined me for me, d I depended on that definition. Nothing was real until I told her about it. Nothing happened until she knew about it. My life flowed through the filter of her recognition, my identity beamed through the prism of her love.

Then she got cancer, and now she is dying. Or, rather, she got cancer and became so sick that now I have to kill her.

I am nauseated. I am sweating. I can't become hysterical because I am pregnant, and my child will lose his mind if I start acting weird. I tell the doctor that it is time. I sign papers. There is a stillness. I consider taking my children away, the one inside me and the one outside me. I will drive back to the beach house, pretend it is not happening. I will never return to South Carolina. I will pretend that my mother is still alive here, holding up her end of the salvation, loving me still. Nurses come. As it turns out, there is no actual plug to literally pull. Machines are switched off, tubes are removed, and that is all that happens. For a while she still lives. After two days, she is gone.

She was alive, and existing, and standing in the chasm between me and all that, and then I made the decision to take her off the machines that were keeping her alive, and now she has died. She will not hear any more news of my life, she will not say any more encouraging things, and she will not protect me anymore. She didn't even get to say good-bye. Our last real conversation was me talking about the Iraq War and her pretending to care.

Everyone says I did the right thing. That she was old and in pain. That it was a mercy. Everyone agree on this history. Nobody says I am a murderer, that I killed my mother, that I did something unspeakably horrible. But it was my hand on the pen that signed the paperwork, my doing. My responsibility. And to say I feel guilty addresses only the small selfless part

In reality the thing that might have kept her alive was not my guilt but my terror, because a world without my mother in it was a world without fences between me and the wilderness. She died. And I was a castle without walls.

Looking back, I try to re-create the history, and I ask myself again, "Why did I do this?" After she came off life support, she kept on living, for days. We had to wait for her to die, and do nothing. With intervention, with surgery, she might have recovered a bit. Not permanently—life is fatal after all—but temporarily. Enough to see my daughter born, enough to talk to me one more time. So why did I kill her? Was it selfish? She had been grotesquely sick for months. Did I just want it to be done? Was it honorable? Was I just motivated by love and mercy? What made me do this?

It has been eight years since my mother died. Cancer killed her. I know that. I know too that what I did was not wrong. In my still grieving mind, there are many voices telling versions of what happened. Some say, "You kept her alive for two weeks in agony because you were afraid." Some say, "You killed her as soon as it was decent, because you couldn't go through the sickness anymore." Some say, "You're a good daughter. She loved you. You loved her. It's simple."

Ultimately, as I have learned, there is no truth in history. Not in the history surrounding my birth, and not in that small bit of history that happened between my mother and me and a doctor in an intensive care unit in South Carolina. There is only the feeling that remains. Purely subjective, absolutely unprovable, it is real. Her love. My sadness. Our separation. My ability to face the wilderness without a fence. The insides of my castle, exposed. And as it turns out, the marauding hordes have not advanced. The wild beasts have not invaded. It's almost as if, after all, the wall is still there, protecting me, and I feel it, working still.

![book icon] Recommended Reading

From Maxon's Bookshelf:

I, Robot **by Isaac Asimov**
This collection contains the short story "Runaround," in which the fictional Three Laws of Robotics are first defined. Asimov pioneered the idea that robots could have safety measures coded into their software logic, and then wrote a lot of stories and books about how the robots subverted or misinterpreted those rules in order to be dangerous anyway. As a child I was ravenous for Asimov and read all his robot books—internalizing the idea that humans, like robots, are hardwired to obey certain principles, principles we find ways to defy all the time.

Gödel, Escher, Bach **by Douglas Hofstadter**
A seven-hundred-page treatise that attempts to unify math, music, and art around an idea of a "strange loop" through Escher's illusions, Bach's canons, and mathematician Kurt Gödel's incompleteness theorem, *GEB* is a cult classic. It's been called "the secret nerd Bible," and as it was published in the late '70s (and won the Pulitzer Prize), it had a profound impact on A.I. programming philosophy in that emerging field. Maxon would most definitely have read it, perhaps even solved the infamous Mu Puzzle.

Frankenstein, or The Modern Prometheus
by Mary Shelley
Shelley wrote this book in 1818, and everyone knows the story: man tries to create life, man loses control of his creation, madness ensues. I'm fascinated by the idea suggested by the alternate title—that Frankenstein delivered a dangerous gift, like fire that could change the course of humanity: animating the inanimate. Maybe the monster was the first modern robot? Maxon wouldn't have read much fiction, and I don't think he would have identified

at all with Victor Frankenstein, as his approach to robotics was far less emotional and more utilitarian. However, he would certainly have been aware of this seminal work of science fiction.

From Sunny's Bookshelf:

Geek Love by Katherine Dunn

This is the story of a carnival freak show and its owners, who have bred their own freaks by taking drugs and exposing themselves to radiation. Their children, their fans, the strange tails and flippers they all have—what a family. I read this book in college, and it sounded like a permission slip to write something outside the norm, beyond realism. I think it would have had a warm place in Sunny's heart, as she would identify with these outsider characters, especially the girl with the secret tail.

One Hundred Demons by Lynda J. Barry

A collection of comics published in Salon's "Mothers Who Think" section, this illustrated memoir is part comic book, part art book, a genius take on childhood, mothering, and love. Lynda Barry is a literary star—a woman who rips the wig off traditional narratives and paves her own path through story.

Observatory Mansions by Edward Carey

I read few contemporary novels while I was writing *Shine Shine Shine*, but this was one of them. Carey's minimalist prose was like a sharp knife on my own style. I believe Sunny would have loved the protagonist in this novel, the strange Francis Orme, whose job was being a living statue. He owns and maintains an apartment complex full of the most unusual characters—each with their secret shames and longings.

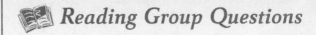

Reading Group Questions

1. Is Emma a good mother?

2. What might Sunny's life have been like if she ha never gotten pregnant, and therefore never felt th need to put on the wig?

3. Was Sunny culpable for Paul Mann's death?

4. Do you agree with Rache that everyone has thei baldness, or do you think those perfect housewive actually exist?

5. Perhaps Maxon was better off without his dac but do you think Sunny was negatively affected b growing up without a father?

6. If you wrote a letter to your child, to be read onl after your death, what would it say?

7. The book suggests that raising any child is lik programming a robot, with scripted replies, rit ual behaviors, and reinforced responses. Do yo agree?

8. Emma did not want Sunny to marry Maxon. Why And was she right?

9. Do you think that Sunny seriously considere Les Weathers as a replacement for Maxon, if h should die?

10. Where would you prefer to live: the perfect hous in a respectable neighborhood in a historic city, c a strange farmhouse in the wilds of an eccentri rural county?

11. What changes have you made to fit in to a ne role you've taken on, whether it's parenthood, new job, or a marriage?

12. Do you think that motherhood fundamental]

changes a woman, or do you think it's possible to hold on to the person you were before kids?

13. Why did Emma bring Sunny back to America?

14. How is Maxon flawed as a husband? How is he a good spouse?

15. Could there be someone better for Maxon than Sunny?

16. In her worry that marrying Maxon would ruin Sunny, should Emma have wondered if marrying Sunny would be the best thing for him?

17. Is it Maxon's fault that Bubber is the way he is?

18. Did Sunny make the right decision in taking Bubber out of his special school and off his medications?

19. How does a woman's relationship with her mother change when she becomes a mother herself?

20. Sunny felt she had to let her mother's ship fall past the horizon before her own could set sail. Can a woman truly become "the mother" while her own mother is alive?

21. Although Sunny's mother, Emma, was the epitome of acceptance, and encouraged her to go without a wig while she was growing up, why do you think Sunny started wearing them?

22. Why did Emma turn her husband in to the communists when they lived in Burma, and was this revelation necessary for the plot and coherence of the book?

23. In pages 291–93 of the book, during Sunny's labor with Bubber, she at first thinks she overhears her mother and Maxon having a conver-

sation about Maxon going to the Moon, but late
Sunny thinks she must have made up the conver
sation. Do you think this conversation did occur
Why or why not? If you think it did occur, what d
you think motivated Sunny's mother to make th
suggestion to Maxon that he complete his missio
to the Moon?

24. How is Sunny's decision to abandon her wig afte
her car accident related to her decision to tak
Bubber off of his medication?

About the Author

© Katie Weeks
Photography

I'm Lydia Netzer. I was born in Detroit and
raised by two public school teachers. We lived in
Michigan during the school year, and at an old
farm in the hills of western Pennsylvania during school vacations. My world revolved around
horses, music, and books. I went to college and
grad school in the Midwest, met my husband
and got married in Chicago, and then moved to
Norfolk when we decided to have kids. We have
two: a boy and a girl. I homeschool them and
taxi them to orchestra rehearsal, the karate dojo,
the pony farm, and many music lessons. At our
homeschool co-op, I teach literature and choir,
and I love to travel, knit, play my electric guitar,
and, of course, read.

Visit: www.lydianetzer.com